Sea of Troubles

D0993735

Sea of Troubles

The Second Nicholas Talbot Adventure

M Stanford-Smith

HONNO MODERN FICTION

First published by Honno
'Ailsa Craig', Heol y Cawl, Dinas Powys,
Wales, CF64 4AH

1 2 3 4 5 6 7 8 9 10

ISBN 978-1-906784-27-0

Published with the financial support of the Welsh Books Council

Cover design: G Preston
Cover image: © Andrew Davidson

Printed in Wales by Gomer

For Oliver, who always thought there was potential, and my family, who proved him right.

My thanks to Bernie for patient help with the electronics and to Bettina Francis, Bob Mason and everyone else who listened and gave helpful advice.

"To take arms against a sea of troubles,
And by opposing, end them"

Hamlet. Act three, scene one

Prologue

London. January 1599

A gaudy playbill flapped and tore in the brisk east wind scouring Willow Street.

THE ROSE

THE AMAZING TRAGEDIE OF JULIUS CAESAR
A MOST MARVELLOUS NEW ENTERTAINMENT BY

MASTER WILLIAM SHAKESPEARE!

!Please one and please all, Be they great or be they small!

Below, in unfortunate juxtaposition on the same post, was a list of those unlucky enough to have come up against her Majesty's rule of law, among them "Master William Shaksper", fined for tax evasion in Bishopsgate.

A mangy dog lifted a leg against the pole and trotted on towards the everlasting sound of hammering. Someone was always building something on the South Bank. Hooves clattered on cobbles. A fine and very angry young gentleman, all in dark green velvet buttoned with emerald and trimmed with lynx, turned out of Cardinal's Cap Alley riding a spectacular grey. The gentleman stopped by the post to read.

"Tuh!" he said. He reached forward and plucked off the indictment, tearing it up and throwing the pieces to the wind. "Miserly cheapskate! Suppose that's why he's moved across near the Clink." He had a good mind not to hand over *Hamlet*, the latest play from Marlowe's pen; it was too good to masquerade under the name of a man who would not pay his dues.

A curly-haired young man stuck his head out of an upstairs window and shouted, "Nick! You're back! About time – wait there—"

Sir Nicholas Talbot, Earl of Rokesby, sighed and sat quietly. He had hoped to go unnoticed.

Chapter One

Nicholas Talbot, knight, second lord of Rokesby, star sign Scorpio, rode steadily on through the rutted lanes, between his fields and barns and homesteads lying in their neat husbandry on either side. In the five years of his absence his steward, Hugh Shawcross, had wrought well and faithfully.

He had also married the woman Nicholas had come home to claim as his bride.

She rode behind Nick at this moment, the child Nick had fathered heavy in her arms. He bore no grudge against Shawcross: the man had done the gentlemanly thing, giving the presumed dead Nicholas Talbot's child a name. Except that Nick Talbot was very much alive. And very far from achieving his object. He had loved Kate Archer from the day she took him into the barn and taught him his business, and forced at fifteen to flee from his usurping uncle he had gone to make a fortune to lay at her feet.

"Romantic fool," he said to himself. "What did you expect…" But she had waited. She had waited and kept from burdening him with knowledge of his child. He was still angry with her for that, she should have known him better. *But you were not here to know,* he thought. In all those years of adventuring, play-acting and

1

intrigue he had come home only twice to reclaim what was his, all other attempts thwarted, and now he was too late. The marriage might be a sham, in name only, but his Kate would honour her vows to Shawcross and Nick was bringing her back to him. He found he was hunched over in his saddle, and straightened his back. He knew his duty. Ignore the pain, take time to know his son, make provision for him and give him his rightful name. What more he could do depended on what he found at Rokesby.

They had passed through the village that lay outside the manor gates now and were trotting up the ridge that sheltered the house from the east winds. A grey raft of cloud covered the late afternoon sun, and a red glow flickered on its underbelly up ahead. Nicholas pulled up and stood in his stirrups. It was not the sunset. He set spurs to Oberon and galloped over the rise.

Rokesby was burning…

The home Nicholas had worked so hard for, that his father had died to give him, was a mass of flames from cloister to dairy, the stone mass of the keep black against the glare.

Shouting to his groom to stay back with the woman and child, he galloped headlong down the hill, his great red deerhound Fearghas streaking beside him. Once past the gates of the keep into the square courtyard, he could see the extent of the fire. The whole of the manor house, built in the current timber-framed style, was blazing: men and women scurrying like black ants to and from well and stream with futile buckets of water that hissed into steam even as they threw it.

Nick grabbed the arm of a man stumbling by. "Where is Captain Shawcross?"

Coughing and red-eyed, the man nodded to a silent heap propped against the wall of the keep.

Nick hurled himself from the saddle and ran. Hugh was unconscious but alive, breath rattling in his chest, overcome by the smoke. Without him the place was masterless. Nick stood up and looked round. Wat the blacksmith was fighting to bring some order into the madness and form the water-carriers into a chain. Nick yelled to him over the roar of the flames.

"Save the old buildings – the dairies! Let the house go!" Wat turned to the voice of authority and recognised him.

"My lord!"

"Is everybody out?"

Bundles of burning thatch were flying up in the heat and threatening the old west wing.

"Get some men on the roof and soak the thatch that end—" he was stripping off his fine cloak and doublet and seizing an axe. "A firebreak…" He was climbing to the saddle between the new structure and the old, intent on saving the stone buildings that were the engine of the house, kitchens, stillrooms, dairies, stables. Wat grasped the idea, found some men, and a degree of organisation began to emerge. The cloisters opposite would stand and the effort was concentrated on the gable-end abutting the fourth side of the quadrangle.

Out of the corner of his eye as he hacked at the thatch, Nick saw Michael his groom and the two beings he valued most in the world canter through the gates. There was someone with them.

Men with buckets soaked the thatch where he was working; others braved the smoke below, stripping panelling and tossing out hangings. He hacked and swore, the skin of arms and face scorching in the heat, his shirt smouldering. The exposed roof beams were already hot. Someone emptied a bucket over his head.

3

It was dark by now, though bright as day in the courtyard, and as so often at that time of the evening, the wind got up, a west wind…

The flames began to blow away from them. Taking fresh heart, the men and women redoubled their efforts and Nick shouted for more water to douse the beams. A sinewy hand grasped the gutter and the lanky form of Tobias Fletcher heaved itself up beside him. Nick had no time to wonder why his friend and associate was here and not halfway to France; he handed him the axe and picked up the pitchfork dropped by a man collapsed on the roof.

The storm clouds that reflected the glow of the fire were massing and moving in the moist wind from the west.

It started to rain. A shout went up, men turned up their faces to the blessed downpour, capering and clapping. Nick yelled, "Come on, we're winning! Now!"

It was enough. The respite gave them time, the firebreak would; serve and the now torrential rain would do the rest. Nick leaned on his pitchfork and turned to Toby.

"Later," said his laconic friend. "When we've tidied up." A bolt of lightning earthed itself down the flagpole of the keep, and Toby grinned. "That's the gods for you – give with one hand and take with t'other. Come on, before we're fried as well as roasted."

It was a long time before they could talk. When Nick climbed down, suddenly dizzy and remembering that he was afraid of heights, he was taken to view a horribly burned body lying under a blanket.

"He set the fire, my lord," said Wat. "Tom here found him. Spoke before he went, seemingly." Tom smeared his sooty face and pulled his forelock.

"Went up with a bang, she did, m'lord. Smelt like cannon – black powder, like."

"You're ex-army?"

"Yes, m'lord, one of Sarn't Ponsonby's mob – served under the commander, sir."

Nick stared at him, trying to see through the soot.

"Tom…Jenkyn, isn't it? You commanded the fourth battery – goddammit, it was your bloody cannon ran over my fingers!"

"Yessir."

Nick held out his hand, and Jenkyn took it.

"My fault, Tom, no hard feelings. So, you think it was an explosion that went wrong for this poor devil?"

"Yessir. Over-egged it, or set a short fuse. Anyroad, he took me for a priest, I reckon, and got it off his chest."

Wat snorted. "I reckon you did a little persuading, my lad."

"What did he say?"

"Paul Talbot paid him."

"On my soul, my uncle…" breathed Nick.

"And something sounding like Mobley."

"Lord Mowbray?"

"Could be." *It could* well *be*, thought Nick. His uncle by marriage, who had dispossessed and ill-treated him as a boy and been dispossessed in his turn when Nick came back grown; and Mowbray, his sworn enemy and nearest neighbour. They deserved each other.

"Tom pulled him out, milord. Not knowing who he was, see," said Wat.

"You deserve a reward, Tom. I'll see you get it."

Tom showed a mouthful of broken teeth.

"Last time I saw you, you was only three foot high, m'lord,

yellin' fit to bust. Thought I were in for a whippin', but Jack Talbot were always fair."

"He believed in learning the hard way. I only go near stage cannon these days. Get your hands seen to. I won't forget."

The smell of burned flesh suddenly nauseated him and he moved away to give orders for the bucket chain to continue in shifts until there was no danger of the fire breaking out again. He shouted for Wat and between them they found the kitchen staff and set those still on their feet to provide hot food. The hay barn would give shelter for what was left of the night. He ordered up beer and cider and went the rounds of his people, talking to them and taking stock. There had been no loss of life save the man who set the explosion, thanks to Hugh Shawcross and his speed in getting everyone out. One or two broken limbs, a concussion and various burns were being dealt with, and one old man, like Shawcross, was in danger from the smoke. Everyone wanted to speak to Nicholas.

It was the early hours and still raining hard when he crossed to the keep. Tobias was waiting for him, his blue eyes vivid in his soot-streaked face, his lint-fair hair dark in the wet.

"All accounted for. Your boy's asleep and – Shawcross, is it? He's being looked to."

"Where's Fearghas?"

"Your blasted hound? Doing his job, guarding little Jack." Nick put his back to the wall and slid down it, suddenly too tired to move, liking the rain on his sore skin. Toby thrust a flask into his hand and sank down on his heels before him.

"Get that inside you and come in out of the rain," he said. "Hot broth and a reckoning. I've news."

Nick drank deep, took a breath and hauled himself up. "So have I," he said.

The ground floor of the keep looked like a field dressing-station. Toby had been busy. The few injured were lying in a neat row on hurdles mattressed with straw, all attended to, women moving among them with water and broth. Kate, her hair coming down and her fine dress filthy, her sleeves rolled up and her skirts kilted, was by the trestle table telling a burly groom to stop being a baby and take the medicine. The man swallowed and Kate turned to see Nick leaning in the doorway. Her hand went to her breast at sight of him.

"Hugh's upstairs, he wants to see you," she said. "I'll come straightway…"

Toby's efficient hand was evident everywhere. Rooms and beds were ready, fires took the chill off the old stone walls, food was on the table. Shawcross was sitting up on a pallet by the fire, a cup of wine in his hand, a blanket round his shoulders.

Cold now, Nick took a seat by the table and waited his turn. Tobias poured them more brandy and went to take the tray from Kate as she climbed the stair. It was very quiet with the door shut, the tick of the fire a tiny thing after the roar of its big brother. Kate came to the table to lay out her bowls and remedies.

Silent tears began to run down her cheeks to drop onto her bodice, black spots on the blue. She avoided his eyes as she attended to his hurts, turning his hands gently to apply the salve, hands with fingers and palms hardened and calloused since childhood from sword and bow, a fighter's hands. Hands that could gentle and caress a horse or a woman.

Nick turned his head away as she carefully lifted the shirt away from his shoulders. He was trembling: she was his first love, his lover, his and not his, married now to Shawcross. He looked across at the man who was his steward and supplanter, a man loyal to

Jack Talbot and wounded in battle at his side. Shawcross had married Kate to safeguard Jack Talbot's heir. Now Nicholas, back from the dead, would claim that heir but not yet his wife.

Tobias was helping Shawcross to a seat at the table. Hugh did not seem a well man these days. He had lost an arm at Beauvais and Nick was beginning to suspect that those old injuries were more extensive than Hugh would admit. He looked grey and exhausted, his eyes rested on Nick with a strange regret. Released from Kate's ministrations, Nick stood up and eased himself into a dry shirt. He thirstily drained the cup of broth offered him. Tobias leaned forward with his elbows on the table to open his budget of news.

"I meant to get here long before this: I might have prevented it," he said. "My horse went lame just outside Banbury and it took an age to find another. Robert Carey's servant overheard Mowbray talking and a message came to the docks as I was leaving. You've a good friend at Court there, Nick, Carey has had Mowbray watched and his messengers followed."

"Master Shawcross, did you know Paul Talbot has been living on Mowbray's estate next door?"

Hugh shook his head.

Toby went on, "Your uncle is Mowbray's creature, Nick. He was summoned to Town and given his orders. I came too late. I'm sorry."

"He found someone else to do the work," said Nick. "I would not wish such a death on any man."

"What do you want me to do, Nick? There are witnesses, Mowbray is exposed…"

"Who went with the escort to Paris in your place?"

"Young Carlyle. He's shaping up well. Nicholas, you can't be thinking of the courier business now, we need to deal with Mowbray."

"I must see to my people here."

At this, Shawcross raised his head. "You will stay?"

"There's a great deal to be done. You are not well. And we must talk, Hugh. Later."

There was a faint cry from upstairs and Kate moved irritably. Nicholas rose.

"His nurse is with him, Nicholas. Rest."

"He is frightened—"

She tightened her lips, rose swiftly and went out. As the door closed behind her, Shawcross spoke. "Nicholas – my lord, I should say – I must—"

"Body of Christ, not now, Hugh! I know Kate's mind. She will not desert you. I beg you, just leave it for now."

"Toby, do as you see fit."

"You have powerful friends in high places these days, Nick. Send to them to tell what's happened and let them deal with Mowbray. I'll be more use to you here."

Nick gave him a grateful smile. "True enough." He got to his feet. "I must make sure all is well."

"I'll come with you." The two young men were at the door when Kate came down, a heavy-eyed Jack at her side.

"He had a nightmare. He wants you, Nicholas. Take him back to bed while I make him a posset." Nick held out his arms and the little boy ran into them.

"And something for us, Kate, if you can manage it…"

"Something stronger than a posset for me, mistress," said Toby. "I'm asleep on my feet and this man of yours is still thinking of things to do."

Kate sent him a killing glance and hurried away. Nick was murmuring to Jack and presently picked him up and bore him back up the stone spiral stairs. A neat, spare woman was waiting there, her hair tidily coiffed in white, and Jack held out his arms to her.

"So, my wee man, your father is here. We can sleep sound. Mistress Melville, my lord, at your service." She was tucking the child with firm hands into a comforting bundle. "Have you a moment to sit?" She made room for Nicholas to sit on the bed and take his son's hand. He sat and spoke to him quietly, telling how the fire had been tamed and made to go away, until Jack's thumb stole into his mouth and his eyes closed. Nick looked round.

"Mistress Melville...?"

"Master Shawcross sent for me sir, for the child's birthing. I stayed for the boy's sake."

"You are kin to me?"

"Daughter to your mother's cousin. A Melville of Linlithgow. You have a strong healthy boy, my lord, he will do you credit."

"I can see that. I have a great deal to learn."

"If you can find time, my lord, with all you have to do."

"I will make time."

In the room below the two men sat on, Toby cursing his tactless tongue.

"You were right there, Master Fletcher," muttered Hugh in the sudden quiet. "That is the man for her."

"Let me help you to your bed, sir. There will be time enough, and work enough, when you're rested."

10

Tobias saw something his friend had not. The extent of the steward's injuries explained why he and Kate did not live as man and wife. Toby thought he also understood what bound Kate to her husband. He felt Nick's anguish as they worked side by side next day, it was a desperate situation for which there seemed no honourable remedy. Even if Nicholas could overcome his own scruples, he had recently sworn vows of knighthood that Tobias knew he would keep. Toby shook his head: it was a capricious fate that gave and stole back with such fickle fingers.

The sun had come out and steam mingled with the wisps of smoke rising from the ruins. The acrid smell of burning was everywhere, and sad heaps littered the courtyard – rugs, hangings, bedding, all thrown out at haphazard and now soaking wet, a desk, a settle, chairs, a few spoiled books. Nick gave a short laugh as he picked up a sodden scarlet cushion and tossed it onto the pile.

"Fuel for another bonfire."

Betsey the cook snorted as she trotted by.

"Waste not, want not, master Nicholas," she said, fielding the cushion. "My lord, I should say. All this can be dried. The other barn is cleared, m'lord, and the men are waiting."

In the steading behind the dairies, brown and white cows were filing in for evening milking, the homely clatter showed work going on as usual. The stable yard was busy; all the usual husbandry was back in order, albeit with some inspired improvisation. Tobias marvelled at the speed with which Nick had established priorities and a semblance of normality from the directionless crowd of workers they had found milling about that morning. He could only suppose that kept at his father's side as Jack Talbot rose through the ranks to commander, and bereft of his mother at birth, Nick had imbibed the skills of command as mother's milk. Knighted on the field, and killed at Zutphen a month later, Jack Talbot's legacy to Nick had been this now ruined building, erected on the foundations of a priory annexed by Henry Tudor. Never a rich man, nor one for ostentation, Nick's father had built in the reigning style of heavy angled beams and herring-bone brickwork, wood and wattle and thatch, keeping only the flagstone floor of the original building. Which was, of course, why it it had burned so fast and fiercely. Now, still smoking, it lay blackened amidst the ancient stones as if it had never been: the centuries-old keep and cloister standing as they had stood when Jack Talbot first saw them.

Nick was watching his friend.

"Yes," he said. "Another blank canvas. All to do again. It'll take some thinking about."

He had turned a small barn into a mess hall and proposed to use another as dormitories for those whose living space was gone. He went now to oversee the setting-up of trestles in the mess hall. They would form a T-shape like the one at James' court in Scotland, both to please the workers' sense of propriety and emphasise the growing unity between master and man. Nick was back in his working gear of leather tunic and frieze leggings, lifting and carrying, cursing and making jokes. Morale was high. A baby had been born to one of the cottagers last night and Nick had his work cut out to prevent them christening the babe Hellfire Nicholas Wapshott.

"I reckon that's what they'll be calling you," said Tobias. "Did your father have a nickname?"

"Not that I heard," said Nick.

"Handsome Jack," said Tom Jenkyn as he struggled by,

encumbered like an ant with an ear of corn, pushing two heavy trestles. "Fair, like I said."

Grinning, Toby lent a hand and Nick went to organise repairs to the damage underfoot from the rain and the bucket chain. He passed on to look in at the barn where sacks were being filled with chaff for bedding and retired sneezing to the brewhouse. From a window in the keep, Kate watched him. Nicholas did not look up.

He worked like a man possessed – possessed as he was by love and desire for Kate, inaccessible Kate married to another. He worked to exhaust his body, but could not control his mind as he lay awake at the day's end. Grieved by what Toby had told him of Shawcross' wounding, nevertheless he was saved the torture of imagining Kate in Hugh's arms. He kept his distance from her, avoiding so much as the brush of a sleeve, beating out his futile rage and frustration on wood and wattle, striving with the others to clear away the devastation.

A schoolroom was improvised and Oliver Knowles resumed lessons with Hugh's thirteen-year-old son Hal, little Jack at his letters with Mistress Melville. Nicholas went to see Hugh Shawcross. The sick man was much improved, propped up on pillows to help him breathe.

"Glad to see you better, sir. I have much to thank you for."

"I did not think to hear you thank me, my lord."

"Don't 'my lord' me, Hugh, if I may call you so. I owe thanks for your care of my child and my – his mother. I shall make provision."

"It was wrong to keep it from you, Nicholas. She would not be prevailed upon and when we had news of your death, it seemed best."

"Wishful thinking on somebody's part, perhaps. A sorry tangle. I know she must make you happy."

"Happy?" He turned his head restlessly on the pillow. "Listen, Nicholas, for the boy's sake I took on myself the guardianship of his mother. I did two other things. I sent for a kinswoman of yours to nurse him and I asked another to stand godfather – he must have been at sea when you were at court or you would have known. William Talbot, Lord Admiral. He didn't get on with your uncle – I'm sure if he had known how you were treated he would have intervened. He would have helped your father to preferment, but the commander wouldn't have it." He smiled. "An obstinate fellow, your father. Your son is the same."

"Did you not stand godfather – you are his stepfather now, but—"

"My health was uncertain, Nicholas. He had to be safeguarded. Sir William made suitable arrangements, but Kate would not leave here. Your instructions were clear, you left her provided for…"

"Things are different now, I shall see to it."

The sick man was flushed and Nick stooped to pour him water. He was finding this interview increasingly difficult. Like a third person in the room there hovered words neither of them could utter. There could be only one outcome.

"There will be no annulment, Hugh. Obstinacy on both sides, I'm afraid. And she is right not to leave you, you have stood our friend in this. Get better soon, we need you."

A day or two later, Toby came into the main hall of the keep and stopped on seeing Kate at the open window. She had her hands clasped at her mouth, her body rigidly concentrated. He went quietly up behind her until he could see what she was looking at so intently.

Nicholas was working in the courtyard, stripped down to his leggings. He and Wat were wrestling with the great carved-oak lintel that had graced the main doors. It was blocking the access to the hall and ruined staircase and Nick straightened up, easing his back with an oath.

"Give me a lever and a place to stand," he said. "That plank over there, Wat."

Tobias suddenly saw him through Kate's eyes: the way the light caught the sheen of muscle as he bent to his lever, the over-emphasised actor's face and the grace of his body with the shoulders and arms of a swordsman. His russet hair clung close to his head in damp curls. *Yes*, thought Toby. *A painful business*.

"Is he much changed, mistress?" he said.

She turned, flushing, her eyes full of tears. "So much. In so many ways. He was still a boy when he left here. Now…"

"Five years is a long time, Kate, and he has lived every second as if it were his last. Nearly was at times."

"You are his friend, Tobias. He tells me nothing – since Deptford we are never alone. He avoids me…"

Toby took her hand and led her to the settle by the fire. The sun might be warm enough to work half-naked outside, but inside the keep it always struck chill. He poured her a cup of wine and sat opposite, nursing his own. He told her what he knew. Then, "I don't know the whole, lady. In Italy he disappeared for days, weeks at a time on his own affairs – a secret he thinks is best kept to himself. But I know he was drawn into Cecil's network of spies by chance. He was very young and thirsty for adventure – a fit tool for their purposes."

"A spy!"

"No, Kate, he is not made for spying and so they found. He is

15

– was – a courier. No fool, your Nicholas. He saw an opening and took it. The Rokesby courier service is making my fortune. His own has come from service to the Queen and he is rewarded."

"The knighthood…"

"And Mowbray's estates. He spoke often of you and his home here with you. He tried many times to come back and always there was some duty to prevent him."

"We heard he was imprisoned – killed. I would have waited—"

"It was a chivalrous act, Kate, that almost cost him his life in the Tower. It's a mess."

"My husband would set aside the marriage, Tobias. But Nicholas will not ask it."

"No."

"He knows I could not leave Hugh. Not now." They sat for a while in silence, Kate gazing into the fire, Tobias watching her face.

"What will he do?"

"He'll not leave here until the danger is past," said Toby. "Then – I don't know. He can't go back to being a jobbing actor – he's a member of the Court and smiled on by the Queen. Re-building Rokesby is a project…I don't know."

Nicholas did not know either. The future he had planned for himself with Kate as his bride lay in ruins like the house. He supposed Cecil would have work for him and there was the ever-present worry of Kit Marlowe, scribbling away in Verona, waiting for him to come back.

He made up his mind. His plans were wrecked. Word of Mowbray's treachery had been sent to Tom Walsingham, to William Talbot and Thomas Melville, Nick's kinsmen at court, and Sir Robert Cecil. He had written to Kit Marlowe in Verona to explain the delay in his return. As always, he was worrying about Kit.

Get Mowbray out of the way and I'm for Verona, he said to himself. *And what of little Jack?* asked a small voice.

Too late to mend, thought Nick. *It can only be borne if I leave.* He had felt Kate watching him. "Please all the gods, let it be soon."

His small son was besotted. He trotted after Nicholas wherever he went, as much his shadow as the red deerhound Fearghas, Mistress Melville never far away. When he failed to keep up, he never cried but would stand, his knuckles in his eyes, his mouth a silent O of misery. Fearghas would stop, sit down and wait; Nick would notice and come back.

"I had nurses and corporals to keep me out of father's way," he grumbled, hindered yet again.

"If that is your wish, my lord, I will see to it," said Mistress Melville.

He looked into his son's face, with its wide gappy smile and the sparkling green eyes so like his own and gave in. He knew this was storing up trouble but could no more hurt the child than he could kick his beloved hound.

The three of them were working in the smallest barn to make further living quarters: Nicholas, his little shadow wielding a broom twice his size, and the ever-present Mistress Melville. A shadow darkened the doorway and Nick looked up to see Kate silhouetted against the light.

"Leave us, mistress, if you please," she said. "Take Jack for his rest." Mistress Melville quietened Jack's cry of protest with a look and a smile, curtseyed and led him off, making a chasing game of it. Kate looked at Nick where he stood in his shirtsleeves, a pitchfork in his hand and a scarf across his nose against the dust, and smiled.

"Nicholas, there must be more than this."

He set aside the fork and pulled down the scarf.

"More, lady? What more can there be?" He followed this up with an explosive sneeze. And she laughed.

"Do you remember this barn, Nicholas? Our first trysting place. Between ardour and sneezing, you were beside yourself. I taught you well, I think…"

"Too well, perhaps. It has begun to seem like a dream."

"You avoid me."

"What else can I do? It has been so long – the smallest touch burns like ice."

"It need not be so." She came to stand close, her whispering skirts raising small spirals of dust. She raised a hand to his face. "Hugh would understand."

Conscious of a strange frisson of disappointment, he caught her hand and held it. "You are Hugh's wife and mother to my first-born, Kate. That is the end of it."

"You had no such scruples last time you came home."

"You were free then."

"And careless. If I had known you would be so long away…"

"If there is blame, it is mine, Kate, but I do not regret it. Jack is—"

"I did not come to speak of Jack."

"I know why you came. There is work to do, lady, to leave this place fit to live in, so that when I go it will be in the knowledge that you and Jack are part of it, somewhere to think of on my travels. As always."

She stared at him. "You are so changed."

He shrugged.

"I have learned a little governance, is all…"

She waited a moment longer, then turned her back and walked out, leaving him cursing himself for a fool.

There were no more intimate meals *à trois* like those they had shared in Deptford. There, it had been difficult to avoid a touch of the fingers, a meeting of eyes. Tormented by a trembling earring, the creamy curve of her neck, her quickness of wit, he had often left the table early, unsatisfied. Now, the family sat along the top of the T, the workers down the stem in the old way. Guests came from surrounding estates to commiserate and offer help; all joined in vilifying Mowbray and his shortcomings as a neighbour. None had had come forward before, or allowed their wives to visit. Nick was ashamed to think what Kate had endured through his fault. He still did not fully understand her reasoning in not sending to tell him of the child.

He sat now at the head of his table, the object of side-long glances, growing steadily more angry. Had he done all that he had done, achieved all he had achieved, knighthood and a fortune to lay at his lady's feet, to be cheated of the reward? It was not to be borne. He had done all he could – taken steps to give Jack his rightful name and inheritance, made provision for Kate and her husband – what was left for him? She had hinted at other possibilities, but he would not serve Shawcross such a shabby trick. He raised his goblet to answer a toast, unsmiling. Kate had kept his son from him for nearly four years, thought him a boy, too young for responsibility. Responsibility, hah! What else was Kit Marlowe, his own work for Cecil and his Queen but responsibility? Kate knew nothing of these things, nor must she. It was a diabolical situation. Shawcross must feel it too. Thinking of what Hugh was going through calmed him a little.

Someone had picked up a lute and was singing. The wife of one of Nick's near neighbours was pressing his foot under the table. Nick glanced at her and she dropped her eyes demurely.

"You have a fine son, my lord. Mistress Kate is fortunate."

"I hope she is fortunate in her friends, Mistress Waring."

Her hand on his knee, she smiled into his eyes. "I would be a friend to Rokesby, my lord."

Kate kept faith and waited, he thought. Women like this shunned her and still she kept faith.

"Mistress Shawcross will be pleased to hear you say so, my lady."

He turned away and joined his actor's voice to that of the singer. Sitting next to Hugh, Kate leaned across to look at him, begged the lute and began a lively melody. Her voice rose in harmony with Nick's, feet began tapping, and soon there were groups of dancers jigging to the tune.

Oh God, he thought. *This is how it should be. My family. My home. And I must leave.*

Tobias watched him smiling, singing, and clapping in time and wondered how long this could go on. Something had to break – and soon.

Something did. A messenger came from Court with a letter bearing Sir Robert Carey's seal.

To Sir Nicholas Talbot, Lord Rokesby.

I am bound for the Border again, my friend. I hear to my sorrow your suit has not prospered – back-stairs gossip, I fear. I pray you remember my words of wisdom on the subject - like the rest of us poor courtiers, you are subject to her Majesty's whim, in marriage as in all else. Take cold comfort from that. To our muttons. Our mutual acquaintance Mowbray is taken up and is in the Tower awaiting trial. It distresses me to tell you that your uncle was found hanged in the most sordid of circumstances. There were marks of violence on him and it is thought M may be responsible - it is known Paul Talbot was his catspaw. The witnesses to both are under guard.

Your presence is required, friend Nicholas - make all haste. Godspeed, R. Carey, Kt.

You will be pleased to hear I am blessed with another son. I understand you are to be congratulated also. Should the boy need a sponsor, think of me. R.

It was with mixed feelings that Nick took this artless note to Shawcross and Tobias.

"Like I said, friends in high places," said Toby.

The work of reclamation was going ahead cheerfully enough and Nick decided to ride over into Lower Rookham, his new estate that had been Mowbray's territory, to see how the land lay before he left. Mistress Melville had been called to a difficult birth in the village, and explaining carefully to Jack why he could not come, and leaving Fearghas behind to keep him company and stand guard over him and his mother, Nick set off with Toby.

The contrast as they crossed the boundary between his own well-kept lands and what had been Mowbray's was marked. Fields had been allowed to lie fallow and were full of seeded weeds: hog thistle, nettle and ragwort everywhere. The meadows by the river were reedy and sour; they passed neglected barns, one with its roof fallen in, and a row of empty cottages. The mill Nick had long coveted lay silent, the uncut hay in the surrounding fields choking the new growth. Trees lay where they had fallen, roots in the air, no sign of husbandry or livestock.

"Good thing Shawcross isn't with us," said Tobias. "It'd break his heart."

They approached the house where it stood on rising ground with caution, using as cover the overgrown shrubs taking over the courtyard. The buildings were two hundred years old, in the Perpendicular style, towers and turrets and tall thin windows. It seemed deserted. At Toby's insistence, Nick waited in the shadows.

"They don't know me," said Toby. "You, they'd shoot on sight." Presently he came back to report.

"The ship has sunk and the rats have left," he said. "In a hurry, by the look of things. Perhaps they know something we don't."

"Or perhaps they're headed for Rokesby," said Nick, suddenly uneasy.

"That doesn't seem Mowbray's style," said Toby. They turned back, nevertheless, and made for Rokesby at the gallop. There was no sign or sound of fighting as they rode through the gates, but the place was like an upturned beehive.

Jack was lost.

"Where's Fearghas? They'll be together," said Nick, white and shaking.

"We can't find him, my lord."

"The forge? The stillroom?"

Jack's liking for jam and haunting the smithy was well known.

"Nowhere, my lord. We sent after you…" A terrible foreboding was filling Nick's mind.

"He may have followed us, but – Toby, you ride the way we went, I'll try the London road…"

"London – here, take my pistol. Fire if you need me."

Nick vaulted back on Oberon and was gone, hammering through the village and onto the road, sick and furious. He caught sight of a riderless horse in a field up ahead, limping, its reins dangling, and he dug in his spurs. Rounding a bend, he saw a bedraggled heap lying in the dust.

It was Fearghas, dead, a dagger through his breast. Raging and breathless, Nick drew Toby's pistol, primed it, and fired into the air. He knelt by his hound, passing a hand over the warm matted fur. Cradling the head, Nick saw his jaws and teeth were clenched and bloodied, scraps of cloth and flesh between his fangs. Nick dashed away the tears and saw a trail of blood leading away. Icy cold now, he laid aside the pistol, drew his dagger and ran on. The gouts and splashes grew thicker and more frequent: the trail swerved off the road into a spinney of birch. Crouching, Nick skirted the white-boled trees, circling round. The fury had hardened into fierce purpose, and he stole silently on the damp carpet of last year's leaves, listening hard. He heard a whimpering sob, man not child, and he leapt forward, dagger upraised. A figure was huddled by a welter of bramble, a heaving sack at his side. He struggled to his knees as Nick came on, one hand out, the other dangling useless and torn. He was smothered in blood, his face was half-gone and his thigh ripped open to the bone.

Mad with anger and grief, Nick raised his dagger to finish what Fearghas had begun.

"No!" roared Tobias, racing up behind him. "We need him…"
He seized Nick's arm and tried to wrestle it down. Nick fought
him silently, brutally, in the grip of a berserk rage.

"Look to the child," gasped Toby, flung about like a rag doll in
his efforts to hold on to the dagger hand. A cry from the sack
penetrated Nick's fogged ears and he dropped the dagger, to fall
on his knees by the struggling bundle. He managed a few words
to Toby as he pulled away the sacking,

"Get that thing out of my sight—"
Jack had pulled off his gag, his face red and blubbered with
tears. Nick shielded him with his body from what lay on the
ground behind, petting and soothing, holding him close and
telling him he was safe, his own tears running unchecked.

Help arrived, and a terrified Kate. Nick handed over their son,
who was trying hard to be brave, without another word and
walked back to where Fearghas lay, covered by someone's cloak.
He picked him up gently and set off on the long walk back to
Rokesby, a man leading Oberon behind him.

The kidnapper made a statement before he died, witnessed by
Shawcross and Wat the smith. This had been Paul Talbot's last
service for Nick's enemy. Nicholas was not present; he was burying
his friend in the orchard, in a spot where the morning sun would
find him, beside a bank of wild flowers. All the Rokesby people
were there and Nicholas did not attempt to hide his grief as he laid
back the last turf and set a stone. Kate was in the gatehouse with
Mistress Melville, attending to their frightened son. She came out
to him presently, where he sat alone beside Fearghas, fashioning a
garland for him and wondering how all this had come about.

Mowbray. He summoned up what he could remember of the
man: choleric at the Queen's tourney, a great slab of a man, furious

at being beaten by Nicholas, and empurpled with temper at their first meeting. Nick himself had surely done nothing to harm Mowbray save making him look a fool in the eyes of his ladylove.

Nick had fallen wildly in love with the Lady Rosalyne, that night she had granted him still haunted his dreams. Mowbray must have heard about it, the swift withdrawal of the lady from court and the rumours must have reached his ears. Then Mowbray had offended the queen, in what way Nick did not know, and it was unfortunate that his confiscated property had been ceded to Nick.

The reaction was monstrous. Jealousy and pique seemed to have fuelled a disproportionate rage. *Mowbray must be dealt with, once and for all.*

Nick looked up to see Kate coming towards him. Why in God's name had she not been minding their child? All the bitter, useless anger boiled up again and he thought, *Not here. Not now.* He placed his garland on Fearghas' grave and got up and walked away, not trusting himself to speak.

That day, they had their first real quarrel. Unforgiveable things were said, hurtful things, accusations, blame. Unable to listen to any more, he strode across to take her arms and shake her into silence: instead he pulled her to him and kissed her. All the passionate longing of the last five years went into that kiss. And she responded, her hands behind his head, pulling him closer. So for a long spinning moment both of them lost, until she broke away and struck him as hard as she could.

A horrified silence, and then… "I'm truly sorry about your dog," she said quietly, and went. Nick stood gazing after her with unseeing eyes. After a while, he stirred, and left the room to climb to the bedchamber he shared with Tobias. He shovelled his belongings anyhow into his pack and then sat at the table by the window to write to Jack. He embellished the letter with the drawings the little boy liked, sealed it up and wrote another to Sergeant Ponsonby, who provided the trained men to escort the courier service. That done, he went to find Toby. Conveniently enough, he was in the stables.

"I'm going," Nick told him. "I've written to Ponsonby to send an armed guard to patrol the place. You'll say the horse has bolted, but still… Will you stay 'til they get here? I'll meet you at Dover to go over with the next batch. Take Caesar. I'll see Michael home and go on to Scadbury. I must see Tom Walsingham before I go. This is for Jack. Find him a dog of his own."

Tobias looked into the bleak face and nodded. There was nothing to be said.

Chapter Two

Nicholas Talbot rode towards London, his hopes and dreams dust and ashes behind him, the ghost of a great deerhound cantering at his side. He passed a bluebell wood, birch and elm and larch with their feet planted in luminous blue, a stream banked with primroses and kingcups running between. It was painful to him, the coming of spring with all its promise.

His new honours – a knighthood and the earldom of Rokesby, so blithely won – weighed heavy on him and he certainly did not look the part in his well-worn leathers. Only the jewelled sword at his side and the magnificent black Friesian between his legs showed any sign of wealth or rank. He was building, stone by painful stone, the wall that would mark the beginning of a new life, a life without those left behind. There would be no Kate to lie beside him and stroke him smiling into sleep, no gap-toothed little boy to run laughing into his arms, no royal hound to lope at his stirrup. This, for the time, was the only way to bear it.

As he came in sight of the forested masts of the London docks he sat straighter in the saddle. He would look forward. He would not think of Kate, he could not think for the moment of the son he had known only a few weeks. He had promises to keep, duties laid on him, important tasks overshadowed by recent events. He thought of the words emblazoned on his crest: The readiness is all.

Good, he thought, *I am ready. The past must take care of itself. For now. I've a duty to the Queen, and this other thing...* He had neglected his duty to Tom Walsingham, his friend and benefactor, too long. Nicholas was Walsingham's only contact with Christopher Marlowe, his exiled lover, and Tom relied on Nick as the link between them. He would be waiting for news.

And the plays, Christopher Marlowe's great plays. There would be more to bring back for Master Shakespeare to claim as his own, as well as those he still carried in his satchel. Nick cursed the day he had conceived that mad idea. Yet it was working. As he had promised Kit, the plays were seen and loved and applauded. The great lie must go on. And no doubt Robert Cecil, spymaster extraordinary, had more work for him.

Few words were spoken on the ride back to Deptford. His man, Michael, married to a woman made dumb by the smallpox, had little to say at the best of times, and he smoothed the journey in his usual quiet way. They stopped only once, at Aylesbury, to rest the horses, riding in late and disturbing a gaggle of sleeping ducks. Through the rest of the night Michael heard his master pacing to and fro, unsleeping.

Coming into London from this direction Nick remembered that first time, jolting in on a cart full of actors, all of them happy to be coming home to their theatre again. He had been stupefied by the crowds and noise and stink, yet within a week he had adjusted and the playhouse became home to him too. *I was happy then*, he thought, *until I got caught in Cecil's net. I might have been a good actor*. His mind, more disciplined now, set aside the might-have-been and instead he decided to detour south through the vinegar-smelling tenting fields alongside the bear-baiting arena and the Rose theatre, avoiding Paris Gardens and Willow Street and possible acquaintance. Only light airs disturbed the spring evening, bringing the roaring of the bears and a trumpet-call and a bang of stage cannon from the Rose. There seemed to be some kind of celebration going on at the Elephant. Past the bloody whiff from Butcher's Row and up Shipwright's Lane they rode, to Crosstrees, the house lent him by Marlowe's lover, Tom Walsingham.

The house stood just as they had left it a month before, standing foursquare and sturdy in its paddocks and orchards. The evening sun cast long shadows across the grass and striped the coats of the two horses trotting to the gate in the inquisitive way of their kind. Rowena and her offspring, now a sprightly two-year-old, poked their noses over and Rowena whinnied her pleasure. For once Nicholas ignored them and walked straight into the house, calling for ale. There was a pile of letters waiting for him on the table and he leafed through them without interest, cursing when he came to one sealed with Lord Cecil's crest, dated some days ago.

"You can wait a while longer, little spider," muttered Nick. He intended to drink himself into oblivion.

The next morning found Nicholas dousing his head under the pump and yelling to Michael to saddle up Rowena to cross the river to Whitehall. Riding between the tall narrow houses that lined the bridge, he had to push his way through packed and heated crowds of people among the stalls and shops that spilled onto the walkway, selling cheese and fish and roasted meats. The noisy crowds did not lessen as he rode through the streets and he saw that new buildings, if you could call them that, were being squeezed in between others wherever a space could be found, their timber and thatch almost meeting overhead so that a man could reach out of a window to climb through into the one opposite. He reined back just in time to avoid the splash of a chamber-pot being emptied without the usual warning "'Ware piss!", into the street, the window banging shut over his head. On the way in to London, he had noticed how the outlying villages were being swallowed into the maw of the expanding city – the world and his wife must be coming to town.

The smell of London was its own smell, and in his present disenchanted state he was more than ever aware of it. Not like the perfumed reek of Venice with its underlying hint of watery decay, or the fishy, salty air of Bruges and Amsterdam – London stank of humanity. Heaps of night-soil lay piled at street corners waiting for the carts, the filthy runnel in the middle of the cobbles added a grace-note of urine to a bouquet that stung the nostrils, and the occasional fat rat ran from under Rowena's hooves. Faded red crosses still showed on too many doors from the last outbreak of plague. Once he had to draw aside for a troop of horse clattering by in single file, and an urchin with an old man's face tugged at his stirrup. He tossed a coin and other ragged children appeared from nowhere. Rowena fidgeted and he rode on through, past beggars – more, surely, than before – some obviously back from war, others equally obviously faking it. A drab with the face of a pock-marked angel called to him, and all the bells of the city began to ring at once. It was with some relief that he turned into the wider streets round Whitehall. The scent of lilies and jasmine came to him over a wall and he quickened his pace, trotting under the rotting heads on the Tower Gate and past the sentries into the Palace yard. He was known these days, and a man came running to take his horse.

Walking past the tall windows of the long corridor to Cecil's office, nursing a fearsome headache, he bumped into a man he vaguely recognised coming out, but could not for the moment place him. The man turned his face to the wall as Nick passed, which made him wonder. Once inside Cecil's door, surly and out-of-sorts, Nick got the rough side of his master's tongue. He stood before Robert Cecil in the travel-stained clothes he had worn yesterday, tall and broad-shouldered and smelling of horse. He would not bend the knee or bow his head to this man any more. He had nothing left to lose.

Except my life, except my life, except my life, he thought. Marlowe would make something of all this.

As he had known quite well, one night's solitary drinking had done nothing to ease his pain, and he faced the Queen's spymaster with a murderous scowl.

"My commiserations," said Cecil, urbane as ever. "Work, you will find, is a better cure than the bottle. Now, I have a task for you more suited to your newly-elevated position."

"I am bound for Italy," said Nick.

"Exactly so. I wish to know what our undead friend Kit Marlowe is doing to earn the money I pay him. We have had no communication with him for months. I did not pay good money to save his exquisite hide for this. Tell him, the corpse bearing his name can still rise from the grave to accuse him.

"Incidentally, Lord Stanley, our esteemed ambassador to Venice, is a broken reed. I am recalling him. You shall have the pleasure of telling him so."

Nick frowned. He had rather liked the old man.

Cecil went on, "I must have someone to keep a finger on the pulse – that whole region is in a state of flux. You learned the ropes last year – you can replace Stanley for the time being, and find out why Kit Marlowe is incommunicado. By the way, your friend Gallio is turned pirate. I trust you will not regret having spared him."

"Imphm," said Nick, Scottish side uppermost. *Little bastard always knew everything.*

Cecil leaned back in his chair, his little feet searching for the footstool as usual, his hands laced across his dusty black doublet, his furred robe trailing on the floor. He was smiling. Nick eyed him warily. Cecil waved an expansive hand, a spiteful glint in his eye.

"Come, come, *Sir* Nicholas, a hair of the dog, I think. Don't you? We have come this far together, my dear lord Rokesby, I would drink to your health and continued wealth. Or t'other way about. And that of your loved ones, of course. What does the poet say? The course of true love and so on…"

"Have I failed you, my lord, that you seek to threaten me?"

"Threaten? What are you saying? Pour the wine and sit down with me, I grow tired of looking up at you." He leaned across to hand Nick a goblet of wine. "No, *Sir* Nicholas, I am merely a little irritated that so likely a youngster as you seemed to be has risen so fast in the world that his uses to me are now circumscribed. No matter, you will from now on move in circles a mere *agent* cannot reach. All I ask is that you keep your eyes and ears open and apply what I always suspected, your considerable intelligence. Brains and brawn – a fighting machine." He raised his heavy crystal goblet with a nod. "Do not mistake me, young man. I do not begrudge you your rewards – you earned them of your own merit and so we must move on."

He turned to the notes on the small table by his chair. "Yes. I should tell you that my lord Essex is due back from Ireland very soon. He and Lord Mowbray were very close. Although in the Tower, Mowbray remains your bitter enemy, I fear." He was sorting through his papers. "You have been much occupied of late, Nicholas, and may not be aware of what has been going on with the troublesome Irish. Much of the trouble of our own making, of course. Essex has not helped. Do you still have his ring? Lose it. You are already in disfavour with him, you can hardly make it worse. He considers himself slighted. You disdained his offer of preferment, and an even greater sin, gained the notice of the Queen. Your return to Italy is opportune; he is hoping for permission to fight again in France. We may hope that in so large a cockpit, you will contrive to miss each other."

"I seem to have lost one enemy to find another."

"Know your enemies, young man, that is the trick of it. The faster the rise, the more tripwires come in your way."

Degrees of loneliness… thought Nick. *I would not be in his shoes. I do have loved ones, and it is quite plain what I have to do to keep them safe.*

"Are you clear as to your tasks?" Cecil was asking. "First, find out if the Council of Ten are making use of your excellent work last year. If Venice is to collapse and our trade affected, I wish to know. Second, what is Christopher Marlowe up to."

So he doesn't know quite everything, thought Nick.

"Not only Marlowe, but the Antolini brothers seem to have made themselves invisible – no word from them."

"When I saw them last, they were planning to run for home. Sicily."

"Ah," Cecil made a note. "A pity. A useful pair."

Useful pair of murderers, thought Nick.

"No doubt they can be replaced," he said. "But once matters looked more stable, they may have changed their minds."

"Or their coats. Find out. In a dark room, I like to know the whereabouts of the broken glass." Nick snorted.

"At last. A smile. Do we begin to understand each other, I wonder."

I shall never understand you, thought Nick. *What of your design can I read in your face?* All this flattery and helpful advice was unsettling.

Cecil fished out another sheet of notes.

"Your courier service prospers. Good. It may be useful. Travel with it as befits the Queen's ambassador to Venice, your orders and dispatches will be in the diplomatic bag. Seek out that wretch Marlowe and put a squib under him. He owes us service." He paused and looked up. "You owe me nothing, Nicholas Talbot, but your loyalty to your country. As a loose cannon you could be dangerous, and so I do not scruple to rein you in." He leaned forward, squinting. "You had other plans?"

"No, my lord."

"Actors are good liars, Talbot."

"I seem not to be an actor any more."

"No. A pity. I hear you were quite good. We come to these crossroads in life, young man. We must be sure to choose wisely."

"You offer me a choice, my lord?"

"How old are you now? Twenty-two, is it – a recent birthday? You have achieved much in your short time on earth, Rokesby. Busy, busy. Girdling the earth like that puckish creature in the play…"

He pulled himself up. Nicholas stared at him. Was the man human, after all? Cecil coughed and shuffled his notes.

"Duty and loyalty are hard task-masters, Rokesby," he said in pious tones. "Time and useful work heals all, and so you will find. There is much for you to accomplish still."

"My thanks for the advice."

"Yes, you are sore. Come, my lord, is this not to your taste?" A pause.

"I need employment, sir. This task will do as well as any other."

"So world-weary? You betray your youth, my lord ambassador. So, a new beginning – I will not keep you. My regards to Tom Walsingham. Collect the bag on your way out; funds are deposited with the Medici." He waved a dismissive hand and Nick swallowed his wine and rose to leave.

"Her Majesty will wish to see you before you go. The Mowbray affair and her unwitting part in it has angered her. Be prepared for some fireworks; she would rather I sent you back to Scotland to nursemaid James."

I prefer Robert Cecil unsmiling, thought Nicholas. *He has teeth like a ferret.*

"Of course, what she really wants is for you to decorate the Court; her handsome admirers are scarce these days, what with Essex and Ralegh and Oxford all away. A thousand pities she never married."

"Some horses can never be bridled, my lord."

"True." He sniffed. "I trust you will not present yourself to her smelling of the stable. Off with you."

"My lord."

"Send Faulds in, and go with God."

Cecil's chief spy was kicking his heels in the wide corridor, and greeted Nick with an ironic smile, sweeping off his cap in an elaborate bow.

"Congratulations, my lord Rokesby. Flourishing, I see. A little above my touch these days."

Nick gave his short nod. "Glad to see you well, Ned. Greetings to your fair cousin."

"Meg was asking after you."

"I may visit her. Best not keep my lord waiting."

Faulds passed him with a friendly shrug, and Nick thought, *Why not? How long is it since I lay with a woman – if I can't have Kate… Why in hell not.*

He crossed the Bridge to Bankside and left his mare in a stall at the Elephant; the familiar actions of stabling Rowena here rolled back the years to his first recruitment to Faulds' network. At seventeen he had been so proud to be the owner of this fine horse, so brash and confident. Both eager and apprehensive of what might come, he had trodden through the snow to the Cardinal's Hat, as he now avoided the piles of dung and the puddles left by the early morning rain. He was known at the Hat by now, and was admitted at the side door without question. He ran up the stairs and knocked at the door on the left. The trollop opposite was busy already by the sound of it. Faulds' widowed cousin opened the door, exquisitely point-device as ever, her hair demurely coiled under her head-dress, immaculate pleated lawn filled the neck of her bodice. The room behind her was full of the spring sunshine, clean and sweet-smelling, fresh rushes on the floor, her needlework set aside on the blue cushion of the window seat.

"You offered me a bed once, mistress. Then I had no need of it, but now…"

"Come in, Nicholas. I know something of what has passed. You are welcome." She drew him in, closed the door, slid the bolt and turned to help him with his buttons.

He could not be gentle. She accommodated him willingly, knowledgeable and pliant, pleased to give him what he wanted. The first storm past, he lay with her in his arms, tears he would not openly shed leaking back into his hair and, catching his breath, told her of his boy and of the death of his hound Fearghas. Of Kate he said nothing and Meg did not ask. Presently he tried to make amends, untangling the wreck of her head-dress, stroking her face and seeing the fine lines where the usual artifice had been swept away. Slowly and carefully they did away with the rest of their clothes and made love this time with quiet words and even a little laughter.

Meg had been drawn to him from their first meeting years ago, the tall gawky young man with chestnut hair and long green eyes alight with excitement. She knew him better now, had watched him deal with what life threw at him, grow into his strength. She had kept her feelings to herself, until now. They spent the rest of that day and part of the night together, and Nick had fallen asleep at last, when a quiet footfall and a lift of the latch roused them. There was a double-knock and Meg slid out of bed. She pulled on a robe, whispering, "That will be Ned. Lie quiet, I'll go out to him." She drew the bed-curtain across and Nick heard her draw the bolt and then Faulds' voice, soft and urgent.

"I'm looking for that young devil, Talbot. Has he been here?"

"What do you want with him? Is he in trouble?"

"The Queen is sick and Essex is on his way, passing Maidenhead as we speak. Hah! Our lord and master wants Talbot out of the country, *tout de suite*."

"If I see him I will pass on the message. Is he not at home?"

"Tell him to avoid the river. I'll try the Mermaid. God bless, Meg."

She closed and bolted the door, and came back into the room to light candles and stir up the slumbering fire. "You heard?"

Nick was up and struggling into his clothes. "I must go." She came to help him with points and laces, and stopped him as he fumbled in his pouch.

"I may live in a whorehouse, Nicholas, but I do not lie with men for money. I keep a safe house for my cousin, is all." Nick drew out the jewelled pin he had thought to give Kate and offered it.

"A keepsake, Meg." She shook her head.

"I shall not forget. Hurry, Nicholas, and remember what I told you once before, if you need me I am here."

He kissed her gratefully and left her at her door. He went quietly down and stood in the shadows for a moment, watching to see if Faulds was waiting for him. There were no flies on Master Faulds. The Cardinal's Hat was in its night-time mode of drunken singing and furtive opening and closing of doors, no sign of a watcher. Nick slid past the swaying lantern over the sign and hastened to find Rowena.

He rode back past the docks where the incessant racket of ship-building was silent for a few hours, to Crosstrees where Rowena's colt was sleeping in the field. Rowena whickered and Hotspur woke, untangled his legs and trotted over, his coat silvered by a rising moon. Nick made a fuss of him, unsaddled Rowena and turned her loose, and went silently into the house on legs that seemed to belong to someone else. There was moonlight enough to find candle and tinderbox on the table; the candlelight discovered a covered platter of food, a pitcher of water, his favourite silver goblet and a bottle of aquavit. Too tired to eat, he picked up the jug and drank thirstily. He took the candle and trod up the stairs to find his pack and clothes for the journey to Venice and Kit Marlowe. He found the pack empty, the clothes he needed to take all lovingly furbished and hung neatly in the press: cramoisie and cinnamon silk, emerald brocade and costly black double-velvet embroidered with carnations and trimmed with fur, immaculate. The ride out to Scadbury was of a sudden a ride too far, the task of finding and folding, packing and saddling, too much. He pitched down on the bed, still in his boots, and slept his first dreamless sleep since the fire.

It was far on in the day when he woke. The afternoon sun shone bright between the open hangings, their crimson already beginning to fade. It shone on the tray by the bed, a mug of ale, a trencher of bread and honey, fruit. The scent from the lilac outside the window stole in to mingle with the smell of the fresh bread, and conscious of a feeling of well-being, he fell upon the food and presently went to stand at the window, bread and honey in his hand, to watch Alice at the pump with a bucket and the horses bucking and kicking up their heels in the field. Life was going on as usual. He became aware of his stale clothes and unwashed body. Cramming the last of the bread into his mouth, he peeled off his tunic, toed off his boots and ran downstairs pulling his shirt out of his breeches to chase Alice away and get under the pump himself. Michael came out with soap and towels and pumped with a will. Nick shouted aloud with the pleasure of it, the cold sting of the water, the warm sun on his back.

Dry and enjoying the feel of clean linen, he ate a second breakfast of coddled eggs, beefsteak and spinach, and cherry pie, leafing through the letters pushed aside two days before. Among them was a thick heavy packet brought by hand from Scadbury.

The packet contained a fat script from Verona and two letters. The first was part of a letter from Marlowe.

...without Nicholas Talbot I should have been lost in a sea of dark, he is my star of the morning, light-bringer. Nay, sweet Thomas, no jealousy, as far as I am concerned, he guards himself like a vestal virgin – our love is chaste and the better for it. I send this to you because I fear some trouble has delayed my Mercury and I would have news of him. Write soon, Tom, I am alone and in torment bringing to birth my new thoughts, this piece I send is the last of its kind – a trumpet-call to wake the sleepy English to the barbarian at the gate...

The other was a note from Walsingham.

I pray you, Nicholas, go to him. I fear for him. This Henry Fifth is a splendid piece and will please the crowd and the court, and he had the sense to disguise it, but he took a risk in sending it openly to me. A copy has gone to Master Shakespeare, this is for you to see his mind. He is lonely and may do himself harm in his exile. I enclose his letter.

There is another thing. Away so long you will not know – his beloved name is being dragged in the mire. Those prune-faced Puritans inveigh against him still, even as the last words he penned here in my house are being published. Poor Ned Blount has done his best, but who pays heed to the small voice of a publisher seeking to sell his wares? As to his friends, no-one listens to Nashe these days and, craven as the rest, my hands are tied. I pray with all my heart, that so far from our ken, Kit may be safe from this odium. It would be a second death to him. 'Rumour speaks with many tongues...' travellers will talk, he is famed still - his 'Jew' is still 'packing them in', as you would say, at the Theatre.

It is a cruel thing, cruel, Nicholas, that his greatest works should not be named as his. Yet there is this. You and I know he has much to say still. Can you not make him see that at last he has the freedom of speech he shouted for? Exiled, he may say what he likes, be witty where he will, there is nothing more that can be done to him. In his 'death' there is the liberty he craved. He will say liberty for him only is not enough - let him still cry out for it in singing words as only he can.

His sweet body is missed, others may enjoy it, but his spirit remains and must bear fruit. Stay faithful, Nicholas. Of all your present duties and desires, this must be the greatest. You have my love and heart-felt thanks. TW

Nick sat back in his chair and read it again. The despairing words came straight from the heart of Marlowe's lover and pierced through his own misery. He was back in Verona, listening to Marlowe talking through the night, carried along on the tide of words and ideas. Ideals of a world free of dogma, of men and women literate and free to speak their minds: "Give me leave to speak my mind, and I will through and through cleanse the foul body of th'infected world." *Inspiring stuff.*

"I believed in him then," he said aloud. "It is important – above all important. Cecil and his secrets, back-stage plotting...one day, Kit. A free new world. Speak on."

He took time to send a note and some drawings to Jack, with some questions for him to answer, and to pen a letter to Tom Walsingham of Scadbury, Marlowe's erstwhile lover. He was not ready to write to Kate.

41

My dear Sir

My plans are changed and I am bid with all speed back to Venice. This sits well with the need to see our mutual friend and see what he has ready for us. Master WS is still complaisant, indeed is making his fortune in these borrowed feathers. M should be warned – my master C grows impatient with him. C feels he took much pains and risk (not to mention the expense) to spirit our friend out of the danger in which he stood, for little return. There may be trouble. M would take this better from you, sir, I feel. I would there were some way to contrive a meeting between you, he grows lonely and capricious, missing you sorely and the air of England, but it would not agree with him, I fear. If you have letters for him, send to the White Boar at Dover – I will call for them. Trust in me, Tom, I will not fail you.

In love and duty, N

He sealed the letter with his ring, gave it to Michael to deliver, and went to find his satchel with its precious manuscript. He had kept this one back, it had not seemed sensible four months ago to bombard Master Shakespeare with three plays at once. He saddled up Rowena, and set off for the city. He left her at the Elephant, where he was well known and pushed his way on foot over the crowded bridge with its overhanging shops and stalls cramming the walkway. The Mermaid seemed the best place to start looking for the playwright, and he went a roundabout way through St Paul's Churchyard, through the pimps and beggars and scholars and whores, a wary hand on his purse. He wanted to visit the stationers' to see if there was any new thing to take back for Marlowe. Passing the tall bookshops with their tables piled with books and pamphlets, his attention was caught by a flapping broadsheet on one of the pillars outside Ned Blount's establishment.

HERO AND LEANDER, it proclaimed. **OUR BELOVED POET'S LAST WORK! ENDED AND EMBELLISHED BY OUR SWEET-TONGUED GEORGE CHAPMAN.**

He picked up a thin quarto volume bound in buckram. It was a second edition, published by Linley, and to Nick's surprise, Chapman had written a dedication to Tom Walsingham's wife Audrey. He rummaged further among the books and found Blount's first edition, published earlier that year and dedicated to Tom with a letter invoking Marlowe's corpse, the poem as Marlowe had left it: unfinished. He pushed into the shop with the books hoping to find the publisher but he was away at the printshop. The spotty-faced clerk was little help, except to say with a sigh, "My master seeks to defend Master Marlowe. His name is mud – this may do something to restore it. A wise choice, my lord. A great poem and a sad loss."

Nick paid him and, tucking the books under his arm, went to seek out the gossip at the Mermaid. It was afternoon and most of the players were still of course at their various playhouses acting their boots off. They would be back soon and he was hungry. He turned in through the familiar door and walked straight into Ben Jonson shouldering his way out with his usual band of acolytes. He did not recognise Nicholas and pushed past declaiming words from a play Nick did not know. Nick gazed after him and looked at the innkeeper, who shrugged.

"I wonder he favours us with his custom now he's got his little club set up at the Queen's Head. All puffed up with his new play. Going to put it on for the Queen herself, he says. It'd better not be like the last one or he'll be back in clink before the cat can lick her ear. Your pleasure, sir?" He did not know the young player of five years ago. Nick ordered his meal and turned to survey the room. The man he wanted was there.

Will Shakespeare jumped as Nick came and stood over him and he sidled along the bench, casting a hunted look round. He was well dressed these days, his cloak trimmed with fur and his doublet of cut-velvet. His cuffs were grubby and his fingers stained with ink.

"What do you want?" he muttered.

"Glad to see Master Jonson a free man," said Nick. "Who bailed him out this time?"

"Don't know. He's the rising star of the moment," said Will, with a lift of the lip. "Good, though. This *Everyman* – it's good. I played in the first version, you know. Have you brought me something?"

"Not here. Where are you lodging? You've a fine house in Stratford, they tell me. With ten fireplaces. And granted a motto at last – *Non sans Droight!* What rights are these, may I ask? Are money and fame not enough?"

Shakespeare blinked. "I live in St. Helen's – Bishopsgate. But I'd prefer to meet elsewhere…as to the other—"

"Never mind. Over the river, then. At the bear-baiting." His meal arrived and Shakespeare swallowed his wine and got up.

"It had better be good," he said. "We've some serious competition."

"Eight of the clock," said Nick. "Don't be late."

Before fetching Rowena, he walked along Willow Street and squeezed into the Rose at the back of the gallery. He was in time to see the denouement of the trial scene and Shylock booed and hissed off the stage. As he thought, the boy actor, Orlando, made a fine thing of Portia. He remembered the fine lady gliding over the lagoon in Venice, and smiled to himself. He had been younger then.

Kit would be pleased, he thought as he pushed through the cheering crowd. He felt quite homesick as he walked back to the Elephant – whether for Venice or the playhouse or Rokesby, he could not tell. With time to fill before his meeting with Will Shakespeare, he looked out his dog-eared copy of the *Merchant* to re-read it. As he turned the pages, he noticed faded brown writing that had appeared on the back of one of them, ink that had been invisible until heated on its many journeys in his body-warmth. Marlowe had probably meant to destroy it.

My Niccolo will come soon, like the morning star, walking like a dancer. I watch the clock for his step. His eyes will be sparkling like the sun on the green and changeable sea that darkens when the stormclouds come. My young cock is in fine glossy plumage these days, but I prefer him when he comes to me most often in tunic and leggings, smelling of horse. He is grown so. I shall not have him now, he will not give himself to me, yet I yearn for his touch, so gentle when I was in pain. Fie on it – I am jealous of the women who enjoy his embrace, but when he rejoices I rejoice, when he is sad I must needs comfort him. Niccolo, my lovely boy, you open the door and teach me how to love, and write of love. Vile phrase, vile words, but I am the better for setting them down. Paper burnt with my words can be burned, I shall not dull his ears with my meanderings.

"Oh God," said Nicholas, his face hot. "Kit, what am I to do – I was not meant to see this. I have been away so long… Better make what haste I can." He crumpled the page and struck tinder to burn it, watching his hero's words go up in smoke. The man was lonely; the sooner Nick could reach him the better.

Back at Crosstrees, he went upstairs two at a time to pack the parcel of clothes he would need in Venice. Yesterday's interview with Robin Cecil had been salutary and abrasive, Elizabeth's little spymaster had no truck with sentiment. It was still painfully clear in his mind. He suddenly remembered where he had seen the man coming out of Cecil's office. He had been at that meeting of the School of Night in Cobham. *What was his name... Poley, that was it. One of the three embroiled in Marlowe's fake killing. So he was still in the picture, was he?*

I'll bear it in mind, thought Nick. He saddled up his black Friesian Nero and hastened to keep his appointment with Shakespeare. *Henry Four* – starring the groundlings' favourite, fat Falstaff – safely delivered, he returned in haste to Crosstrees to thank Alice for her care of him, and with the grey, Oberon, as his spare horse, he flung a leg over Nero and turned his face for Italy.

Chapter Three

The first person he saw on the quayside at Dover was Tobias. Tobias, the organising genius who had joined with Nick to create the Rokesby courier service. In partnership with the choleric Sergeant O'Dowd, and with the veteran Ponsonby in charge of training, it was building up nicely. About to hail him, Nick hesitated. Toby was standing with his arms folded across his chest scowling fiercely at the passengers boarding the ship. This was so unlike the habitually cool, nonchalant Toby that Nick squeezed Nero into a trot.

Toby heard the clatter of hooves and looked round. His heart lifted. His friend, last seen grey-faced and desperate, looked almost his old self. His colour was high, and if his demeanour was grave and the long green eyes serious, at least he looked alive. A ray of sunlight broke through the clouds to catch the russet hair under his cap and the strong bones of his actor's face. Full of his own grievances, Toby offered up a short prayer of thankfulness and hastened to meet him.

There was an orderly bustle going on as the passengers assembled for the journey; a gleaming parcel of personable young men in half-armour bearing the hooded falcon of the Talbot crest was in evidence, shepherding the ladies toward an elegant brigantine called the *Mermaid*, bound for Ostend. At the foot of the gangplank stood a startlingly handsome young man, beautifully tailored in the Rokesby livery of black and gold.

"Who's that?" asked Nick.

Toby sniffed. "That'll be the new boy brought in by O'Dowd. Been singing his praises for weeks – thinks the sun shines out of his fundament. Jocelyn Russell by name, paragon and *nonpareil* by nature."

"You don't like him."

"Don't know him. Never met him. Just heartily sick of listening to Lucius O'Dowd."

"Doesn't sound like Lucius…"

"The man's bewitched. Don't mistake me, Nicholas, Master Russell has all the right qualifications and comes highly recommended. He can handle weapons and himself, I gather, but I've never heard our esteemed partner speak of anyone in such terms – not even yourself. Quite the white-headed boy, our Jocelyn."

"Sour grapes, Toby? Why is he in charge and not you?"

"O'Dowd didn't know we were available, did he?" Tobias turned aside and began to pace up and down. "We're expanding too fast for my liking. Over-reaching ourselves."

Nick stared at him. "I did you a disservice, Toby, keeping you with me at Rokesby. You've done all the spadework in this enterprise so far. I don't wonder your nose is out of joint."

Toby stood still. "Look, Nicholas," he said angrily. "It's no such thing. We're equal partners in this venture and O'Dowd's brought this man in over our heads. It's bound to upset the men, seeing preferment given to a complete newcomer. For me, he has to prove himself, that's all."

"If that's all," said Nick reasonably, "let's not cramp his style. He doesn't know us by sight, does he? Why not board as last-minute travellers and see how it goes? Listen, Toby. You say we're expanding. O'Dowd is right, we need to train up new leaders – look how Carlyle was pitched in at the last moment when you came to Rokesby. He's turning out well, but mostly because he can rely on your staff work—"

"You listen. You remember our backer suggesting a two-tier approach – one strictly for traders and one – um – one…"

"Tour *de luxe*?"

"If you like. Well, this is the first of those. We have an uncommon rich convoy here, Nick. They're paying a peck of money and expect money's worth. 'Train up!' This isn't a school outing – we should have experienced men – Lucius should have come himself…"

"Take over then, Tobias, take over. Let him watch and learn as second in command."

"O'Dowd—"

"I'll back you with O'Dowd. Do it now, before it goes any further."

"An argument with the paying customers looking on? I don't reckon that'll fill them with confidence, do you? Christ, Nick, we have wealthy men and their wives and their attendants and all the blasted pets – look at the fortune round that woman's neck!"

"What about our men?"

"Ponsonby's pride and joy. Every one of them officer material… He says."

"He should know. Look, it's too late, they're boarding."

The passengers were climbing the gangplank, costly in velvets and taffetas and furs. As they passed the comely Jocelyn Russell he greeted each by name and title with exactly the right degree of assured deference, his manner pleasing, his smile charming and confident. Assessing this performance with an actor's eye and ear, Nick had to agree with Tobias. Master Jocelyn Russell would bear watching.

Conferring with Toby, he rode off to the White Boar to change his appearance and collect any messages. Michael was there, soaking wet from a sharp shower of rain, with another letter from Scadbury with an enclosure for Kit. Tom simply said, "The world and I eternally grateful." Nick shook his head and stowed the letter for Kit in his pack. He changed his leathers for tawny velvet slashed with saffron and trimmed with red fox and topaz buttons, the gold chains of the Queen's ambassador and the Scottish Order of Merit across his shoulders, the thumb ring he had bought for Kate on his wedding finger. Toby's blue eyes opened wide at sight of him and he pursed his lips in a soundless whistle.

"Tell you later," said Nick. He had decided to take his mother's name and he and Tobias were to join the party as Lord Melville and his brother-in-law, Master William Squire. He accepted with grave dignity the cabin eagerly offered up to them by one of the burgesses, newly rich and anxious to please. Even this piece of comedy failed to amuse Tobias; Nick had never seen him so ruffled. The two friends had seen their horses and baggage taken aboard and were at the foot of the gangplank, preparing to board, the delightful Jocelyn Russell was coming to meet them with a welcoming smile, when a hoarse shout and a clatter of hooves froze him in his tracks. A sweating messenger wearing the Queen's badge was thrashing a lathered horse at a gallop over the muddy cobbles, jinking between scattered bales and piles of rubbish, and shouting

"My Lord Rokesby – hold! Wait, my lord, wait!"

The skipper of the *Mermaid* had come to the head of the gangplank, fidgeting about his tides. Russell opened his mouth.

"A moment if you please, captain," said Nick pleasantly, inwardly seething. "A matter of some importance, it seems." He took the letter handed down to him, broke the seal with his thumb and cast his eye swiftly over it while the messenger lay panting over his horse's neck.

"Tuh," he said and found a coin for the man. "See to your horse, and my thanks."

A cannon boomed from the ramparts above the fort as two fine galleons hove into view, their canvas a towering cumulus against a blue-rinsed sky. The tired horse threw up its head and fly-jumped; the courier, plastered with mud, fell off into Nick's arms and slid down him to the ground.

"Oh my God, oh Jesu," gasped the man gazing up at the draggled fur and gold chains and mud-smeared velvet. "Forgive me."

"See to your horse, I say," said Nicholas quietly. "No harm done." Another coin joined the first. "It was worth your pains." The man gaped up at him and struggled to his feet, pulling off his cap.

"Your servant, my lord." He bowed low and led away his drooping horse. Nick met Toby's laughing eyes. "And was it? Worth it, I mean," said Toby.

"I'd as lief he'd fallen off well before." Nick smiled through gritted teeth at the interested passengers lining the rail and addressed Russell in honeyed tones. "I had hoped to join you unbeknown, Master Russell. Not to observe you but to avoid notice. You will be relieved to hear I shall be leaving you at Calais." He bowed an apology to the restive captain, the gangplank was drawn in, orders were shouted, whistles blew and a slice of oily water appeared between ship and dockside. The deck was suddenly no place to be as the *Mermaid* got under way.

Nicholas, in his shirtsleeves, faced Toby across the tiny table in the cabin given up to them.

"So much for our plan. You are still unknown to this escort. I suggest you continue as Master William Squire until Basel. Don't want Master Russell to feel you breathing down his neck."

"Did you say you were leaving at Calais? Someone gives you orders, Nick?"

"Still low in the pecking order, friend, with plenty to lose. Levers and wheels. Stay William Squire and keep watch – my thumbs prick, there is something… If I can, I will join you before Basel. Take my horses and baggage, I will ride post."

Toby had his maps out and was tracing out the route for him. He looked up.

"Who will watch your back in Calais, Nick? You don't fool me with your thumb-pricking."

Nick laughed and shook his head. "My cover on this trip is in tatters. Lord Rokesby will step ashore and disappear. I'll catch you up, never fear. And if not—" He shrugged.

"I do fear for you, Nicholas. You have your whole life before you and you seem to take no care—"

"For my life? I hold it at a pin's fee. But I plan to live as long as I ought, not as long as I can – who can say more? The best is likely still to come. Come, Toby, one gaudy day at a time – we'll drink to a successful journey, no brigands, no accidents and a fat tip."

He lifted his goblet and Tobias raised his, resigned and a little reassured. Never base metal, his friend had passed through the crucible and emerged stripped down and refined to the true essence. His risks were his own; he was not going to reveal what was in the letter.

Nicholas stood in the prow of the Mermaid, her figurehead dipping below him with her gilded nipples and mermaid hair, her coiled tail reaching for the water, watching Calais come toward him. He had been here before, a child on campaign with his father, getting ready for a march into Flanders. He remembered it as a blowsy, bustling town, full of markets and traders, its sea-basins crammed with shipping – wool from England, silks from the East, wheat and rice and iron ore and tin, wealthy ships, fighting ships, slave ships. He remembered being told about the destruction of the castle, central to the town since Edward the Second's time. In English hands stable for 300 years, in the last 50 it had changed masters three times. And it showed. Now won back again by the French, its walls were battered and pockmarked, in some places tumbled down and only half rebuilt. Of the castle there remained only the tower, riven in two not by man's hand but a recent earthquake.

The crossing had been smooth, untroubled by the pirates usually harassing the harbour – *Drawn off by bigger prey*, thought Nick – and the *Mermaid* sailed calmly up the narrow channel past the squat cylinder of Fort Risban, still being repaired, two lonely cannon peering over the ramparts. The small harbour opened up before them, its canals stretching protective arms to circle the town on either side. The surrounding fields were recovering from their recent drowning, but Nick could still make out the earthworks and channels made by sappers mining towards the town.

"We should never have lost Calais," he said to himself. "Why did they not raise the sluices and flood the plain? I thought that was the idea, stop the guns getting near enough." The English-held town had had competent commanders. The French had brought an overwhelming force of mercenaries, mostly German and Swiss, at an unexpected time of the year, led by the best French troops the brilliant Duc de Guise could bring to bear. Nick shook his head. Calais had fallen. Then had come the Armada and the English fire-ships and after that, only three years ago, capture by the Spanish, eager to loot the wealthy town. That had ended last year in the bloodless paper-battle of the Treaty of Vervains and Calais was French once more. Nick could see the reconstruction work still going on and the walls and towers of the new Citadelle rising to the west. The only thing plaguing Calais these days was the fleet of pirates infesting the shipping lanes and the mouth of the harbour like the mosquitoes in the lagoons of Venice.

He thought about his new orders. Somewhere within those walls lay a man who, if he broke under the question could light the fuse under many an enterprise, Nick's great deception included. George Poley, last glimpsed in the corridors of Whitehall, had been taken prisoner by the French as a spy. Poley, the man concerned in Marlowe's faked murder, and many another plot besides.

"Get him out or stop his mouth," said the order.

Find him first, thought Nick. He was trying to recall what he could of that Flanders campaign with his father. It was strong in his memory: it was the last time he had seen Jack Talbot before being packed off to school to learn to be a gentleman. Hah! He painted the picture in his mind, always a good way to remember dialogue, he found.

…Go along the tented lines to his father's pavilion, larger than the rest as befitted a commander, lit inside, the flap folded back, his standard, black falcon on gold, planted beside it, a man in armour on guard. Creep round and under the canvas at the back, hide under the high campaign bed, his favourite place. Jack Talbot

54

knew he was there and only hauled him out if he had serious matters to discuss. Nick remembered the damp smell of the carpet, kept free of mud and grass, the brass-bound chest that served as desk and table, the embossed leather of the folding chair, the stools and the cot he was sometimes allowed to sleep in, the stack of armour in the corner.

Calais. A snatch of conversation came back to him. Jack Talbot had been entertaining an old comrade and they were re-living old battles.

"We should never have lost Calais," Tom Scarlet was saying. "Too little too late as always. If—"

"Ancient history now," came Jack Talbot's beautiful voice. *He could roar like a rutting stag and coo like a turtledove*, thought Nick. A heritage he had been glad of. "Before my time," Jack had continued. "We might have stepped in when the Armada failed, but the French are well dug in – it's a wealthy town these days. You were only a boy then, Tom, running errands for Lord Grey. What happened to him? And Hastings – he left me to join up with Halsinger's mercenaries. No loss to me, mind you."

"The pesky French took me and Noel Trueblood, Grey's bastard son. Good name for a bastard, hey? Took two years for Grey's ransom to come through. I was lucky. Some poor devils are still waiting after all these years. Be warned, Talbot, you give body and soul for your country and they forget you."

So, thought Nick, back in the present, *there may be English prisoners still in the Citadelle. Her Majesty's ambassador to Venice shall call on his opposite number and enquire. It's a start.*

The *Mermaid* slid smoothly to her mooring and the party disembarked without incident under the graceful supervision of Jocelyn Russell. Nicholas bade farewell to a scowling Tobias, promising a rendezvous before they reached the Rhine. "That or a message," he said. He stood on the dockside and watched the travellers assemble for the start of their long journey. Among them was an elderly gentleman, quiet and dressed in sober brown velvet, well tailored and plain. He was keeping to himself and it bothered Nick that he reminded him of someone and he couldn't think who. Nicholas shook his head and put it to the back of his mind, accosted a member of the *Mermaid*'s crew bound for the nearest tavern and paid him drinking money to bring Nick's baggage to the English embassy. This proved to be a tall thin shabby building in the Place de l'Armes, with a fine and tactless view of the statue of the victorious Duc de Guise in the middle of the marketplace. It was growing late and the stalls were sheeted for the night, men and women tallying their profit and heading for home or the nearest inn. Nicholas paid off the seaman and sent in his name.

The first sight of the English ambassador was not hopeful, an unlikely looking candidate for convivial gossip. Sir Walter Allen was a spare elderly man of medium height, he looked as if he felt the cold. He wore a black felt cap with lappets pulled down over his ears, a furred robe down to his ankles, and mittens. His desk and chair were pulled close to a roaring fire. He stood as Nicholas was announced, pulling off his spectacles.

"Talbot? Nicholas Talbot? I knew a Jack Talbot once—"

"My father, sir."

"Well, I'm blessed. Come where I can see you – yes, you have the look of him, sound like him, too. A sad loss. Come and take a cup of wine with me. Bless my soul, Jack Talbot's boy. And what's all this – ambassador to Venice? You have done well for yourself, he would be proud – and so young, you can't be more than sixteen…"

"Twenty-two last birthday, sir."

"Upon my soul, where does the time go. Still…so young for such a post – another young man in a hustle. You are welcome, my lord Rokesby, what can I do for you?"

Sharper than he looks, thought Nicholas. *A straightforward approach, I think.*

"I am come to enquire for any English prisoners awaiting ransom. Our Queen takes thought for every fallen sparrow and would have news." He caught the ironic glint in Allen's eye and grinned cheerfully. "Of course, no money as yet."

Allen snorted with laughter and caught himself up.

"Yes, money, connections – some unfortunates with neither petition me daily. I do what I can, food, letters and so on. There are three or four left here to rot. If anything can be done, lad, it should be done soon. It's a disgrace. Any hope you can offer will be welcome."

"I can visit them at least. Where are they kept? I saw the old castle was gone. There is much new building since I passed through as a child."

"All prisoners are housed in the new Citadelle, you will have seen it to the south. Let me see, I have their names here – yes, Noel Trueblood, Harry Munro, Captain Hastings, Lord Arthur Seton – all to pot, that family – and poor Johnny Balfour. He won't last much longer, poor fellow. Mind you, one or two have made themselves too comfortable to move. Tch."

I'll be damned, thought Nick. *Hastings and Trueblood. One failed mercenary and the other a bastard. Well, as the man said, "God stand up for bastards." I'll see what I can do.* "Can a visit be arranged? I take it they are not housed with the common criminals."

"Better conditioned, but close. I can see you do not wish to

57

tarry, young man. Your father was always in a hurry. It can be arranged. Will the morning suit?"

"Admirably. But, sir, I pray you will dine with me. You have much to tell me, and…" he smiled down into the shrewd old eyes, "I am new to this business."

"Afore God, you *are* like him. You will stay here, Nicholas Talbot. We dine at seven."

And so it was that Nick had his convivial gossip after all. He learned a great deal about his father that he had not known and heard a firsthand account of his knighting in the field. He felt he had made a new friend. He would have to make sure the task confronting him did not reflect badly on this kindly man.

In the morning, as promised, he presented himself and his credentials at the gates of the Citadelle and was passed through to the Commandant, who was polite and distant and raised no objections. Nicholas visited the sick man first and used his eyes on the way to the infirmary. An iron-barred gate led away to the right, a man-at-arms guarding it. Someone was screaming beyond it, weak monotonous desperate screams, and Nick shivered. There were worse tortures than those he had suffered; for him the mental torment, the fear of losing his hands had been almost worse than the pain. The scars itched under the fine lawn of his wristbands. He hoped they had not begun on Poley; he did not want to have to put him down like a sick dog.

Tears stood in Johnny Balfour's eyes at sight of an Englishman. Nick sat with him and spoke of home and listened to his rambling story until the man grew weary and fell asleep. None of the prisoners were relics of the Siege of Calais, of course; Nick learned they had been taken in other, more recent skirmishes and brought here by their captors. Harry Munro had escaped twice and was now confined alone in a small room with a high barred window. He had a narrow truckle bed, a chair and table all littered with books and paper brought to him by Walter Allen. Nick was taken aback at sight of him: he was not much older than Nick himself.

"I trust I do not disturb you," he said. "Can nothing be done – how long have you been here?"

"Five years." Munro's voice was rusty. "I was fourteen. My father was killed in the Low Countries, and I was wounded. It was my first fight." *He is much younger then,* thought Nick.

"You're a Scot," he said. "Why are you still here – have you no kin?"

Munro shrugged. "The title is an empty one – no lands, no money. Who cares? I wonder they didn't just let me escape. Or shoot me."

"A bad example, perhaps. How did you do it?"

"First time – fooled the guard with a dummy and walked out – an old trick. Then I was down below and started digging. Now I'm up here. What are you doing?"

Nick had dragged the table across and was standing on it to look out of the window.

"I can see the old revêtments from here, over there where they are building. That's where the French sappers tunnelled to lay the mines isn't it? And then they brought the guns up."

Munro clambered up beside him. "Good engineers, the French," he said. "They're using the tunnels to run the new drains. They've left that hole in the wall to cart the stone."

"You've been watching. What time do the sentries come on?"

Munro stepped down and looked up at this large handsome individual in the fine clothes.

"Sundown. You're an ambassador?"

"Almost. Do they keep your door locked as well as the outer one?"

"Yes. And before you ask, the guard who brings my food has both keys. The other three are in together, in the square tower." He was a wiry young man, sandy and freckled; his blue eyes had pale stubbly lashes and a direct gaze.

"Do they let you exercise?"

"Down there. I practise."

Nick looked out of the window again, down at the large courtyard with its bare earth and high walls. He made a note of the relation of the old workings to the wall and the tower, pulled out his good Parisian watch and took a bearing. He climbed down and contemplated the books and papers.

"You have been using your time," he said.

"My father didn't believe in book learning. I've been catching up. Look, what are you doing here?"

"Seeing what can be done. Five years is a long time."

"We've fallen between the cracks. French bureaucracy and the code of chivalry at its worst, passed from one to another. Chivalry – you can keep it. The others have given their parole. Not me."

"You're a Highlander?"

"Ross, in the West. I doubt I've been missed."

Mindful of the way his own Scottish kinfolk had rallied to him when he needed them, Nick was growing angry.

"What were you doing, fighting for the English?"

Munro flushed. "I was born in England. My grandfather swore the oath to King Henry after Fludden. I was going to go back."

"How much is your ransom?"

Munro named what seemed to Nicholas a paltry sum and it seemed to Nick the youngster had nothing to lose. Poley's rescue was going to be difficult, Nick had no idea what state he might be in and he would be glad of someone on the outside if things went wrong. He made up his mind.

"It shall be paid."

Munro laughed. "Who by?"

"Never mind. I shall be waiting at the gates when you are released. You can come to the embassy – I have a proposition in mind." Munro looked at him warily and Nick shook his head, laughing.

"A business proposition. You may be able to help me. Be patient, I must see the others." He offered Munro his hand, knocked to be let out and was taken to see the remaining hostages. The contrast surprised him. The three men had made themselves very comfortable. They were playing cards in a fug of tobacco, wine on the table in a spacious room. Trueblood and Hastings were both elderly, Seton a pale lily of a man with a vacuous smile. According to them, Munro was a troublemaker, their ransoms had been difficult but would surely come soon. It was a short visit. He next asked to see the commandant again, and over a glass of excellent Madeira – courtesy of the routed Spanish – and a quantity of little sweet cakes, congratulated him on the good spirits in which he found his countrymen.

"They have given their parole, Lord Rokesby, and except the young one, are free to move as they will – within the Citadelle."

"A beautiful building. In Italy I became interested in such structures – Venice, of course has its unique problems of drainage and so on. Here I imagine the problem is flooding."

"Ah, my lord, a great deal of the work was done for us during the – er…"

He paused delicately.

"The siege, yes. A sore point. The fortunes of war, commandant."

They bowed politely to each other and the Frenchman went on. "There will be sluices and back-flow channels…" Nick looked puzzled and the man went to a map-chest and pulled out sheaves of drawings, pointing out with the zeal of an enthusiast how the new drainage system would make use of the old tunnels. Nick gave them only a cursory glance and pushed them aside with a courteous nod, letting them roll up. One glance had been enough to confirm his hopes. As an actor this trick of memory had been useful, for an agent of the Queen it was invaluable. He came, obviously a trifle impatient, to what was ostensibly the reason for his visit, Munro's ransom. He dickered amicably over the terms of the Scotsman's release, and promised the other prisoners would not be forgotten. He admired the portrait of the governor's wife and children, exchanged further compliments and left on a wave of politesse. Once outside the gates he hurried to find a merchant bank that would honour his note–of-hand, pledged his Scottish Order of Merit and arranged for the ransom to be paid forthwith.

He returned to the embassy to inform Sir Walter of what he had done. "I shall take Munro with me," he told Allen. "I have work in mind for him, he'll work his passage, never fear." The old man gazed at him narrowly.

"I see I should not seek to know more, Nicholas Talbot. A generous action must not be questioned too closely. Will you bring him here?" Nick shook his head. "We shall leave the town with all due ceremony in the morning, sir, with as much fuss as possible. A joyous occasion. You will excuse me this evening, sir, I have business in the town." This last was accompanied with a scurrilous wink, and the old man sighed.

"What it is to be young. I shall see you off tomorrow."

Nicholas changed his finery for clothes more suitable for trawling the inns of the town, and set off, looking for a tavern near the Citadelle that might be the haunt of other ranks and the common soldiery. He found what he wanted and, unregarded in his worn leather tunic and workaday breeches, his noticeable hair covered with a woollen cap, made himself at home on a bench with a mug of ale in his hand. He had his eye on a man in the uniform of a Citadelle guard, who seemed to be having an argument with the woman on his knee. She flounced and pouted, he stood up and she slid to the floor with an unladylike yell.

"I don't make the bloody roster," he shouted. "I shall be late, get out of my way, you stupid whore." She was struggling up, and was pushed aside as the man strode out, cursing. His mates were laughing and calling lewd advice after him, Nicholas caught her eye and raised his mug, tilting his head in the age-old invitation. She tossed her head and sidled over with a swing of the hips. Nick made room for her and called for more ale.

"Deserted you, has he? Not the way to treat a fine wench like you." His French was tinged with a guttural Flemish accent.

"Oh, he'll be back." Nick made a mock pretence of fear. "What, soon? I must watch out."

"Never fear, you are twice the man he is. Anyway, he's on duty – so he says."

"A soldier, is he? I wouldn't care to cross a man of his temper."

"A soldier? No, he's only a prison guard, spends his time rattling his keys and twiddling his thumbs. Not even guarding the gentlefolk, just those waiting for the drop. Though, mind you…"

63

She shivered. Nick called for brandy. He hoped he wouldn't have to take the wench to bed to get what he wanted.

"Frightens you with his tales, does he? Get that down you, you'll feel better." He slid a comforting arm round her and she snuggled up.

"I don't say he enjoys it exactly, but he were lickin' his lips over what they'll be doing to the new one. Must have done something bad – he's going into Little Ease. Softens 'em up, Carl says. I don't like it," she said, looking up with swimming eyes. "You'd be kind, wouldn't you – come outside with me?" Nick had learned what he needed and not wishing to get the woman into any more trouble, slid her off his lap into the corner and stood up.

"I have a better idea," he said. "I'll find us a room – I like to take my time." She giggled and he found a silver coin in his pouch and slipped it into her bodice with a kiss. "You wait there, pretty, I won't be long. Get us a bottle." He eased past the crowded backs and through the door to the privy. From there it was a short walk through the damp cobbled streets back to the embassy, one hand on his purse and the other on his poniard. He reached his chamber without any trouble, feeling distinctly grubby. "What I do for you, Robert Cecil," he muttered as he shucked off his clothes and washed. *Little Ease*, he thought. *Shouldn't be hard to find – once I'm in. Horses first, tools. Fetch Munro and we'll see how the land lies.*

By the morning he had changed his mind about Munro. The lad did not deserve to risk imprisonment a second time. He would manage on his own, send him home. He dressed with forethought in showy doublet and hose, jewelled and embroidered as befitted the ambassador to Venice, breakfasted with Walter Allen and took his leave to put his plan into action. He hired three good post horses, sent a boy to the chandler's by the dock to supply him with thin rope, a crowbar, mallet and chisel and a sack to put them in.

A dark lantern and a spare tinder-box and stub of candle were to go in as well, together with an extra flask he meant to fill with aquavit. This first reconnaissance might be just that, he could add more once he knew what he was up against.

He was waiting at the gates of the Citadelle with a smart escort from the embassy when Munro was brought out. The young man had nothing but what he stood up in and Nicholas made a great deal of fuss over fetching all his books and belongings and spare clothes. By the time it was all loaded onto the third horse, a small crowd had gathered to cheer them on their way. They rode out of Calais with as much pomp and pother as Nicholas could muster, through the Gate and over the canal to take the road leading north over the flood plain, where the escort left them. Young Harry Munro had uttered hardly a word. Now he drew a deep breath of the salty air and pulled his horse to a halt. A brisk wind was bending the marram grass and with Calais behind them, an eggshell blue sky stretched from horizon to horizon.

"All right," he said. "What is this all about?"

"You are going home. There is a place for you with my escort service if you want it; if not you are a free man."

"Why all the performance? I am nobody."

"It suited me to be seen to be leaving. Take your gear and go. If you want to take up my offer, make for Basel and find Tobias Fletcher. I will send a message and if fate allows I shall see you there. If not, find yourself a boat. Have you money?"

"No... What are you going to do?"

"I have unfinished business in Calais. Here is money. Go."

"You're going to try and get into the Citadelle, aren't you—"

"As far as you are concerned, I left you at Gravelines to join my party to Venice. The sooner you are on your way the better."

"Who paid my ransom – I owe you, don't I?"

"You owe me nothing. Except perhaps obedience. We are wasting time. Go." With a mutinous look, Harry Munro set spurs to his horse and walked slowly on.

"In Basel, then. I shall see you are repaid."

"Get on with you and godspeed."

Nick watched him for a while, the lad waved without looking back, and Nick turned to pick his way back across the marshy ground towards the Citadelle, leading the second horse. He circled round to the beginning of the siegeworks he had noted, dismounted and stood to check his bearings and consider what he meant to do. If he was right, this salient should link up with the new drainage system and lead him into the prison area. It all depended on the state of the tunnel and how far the engineers had got with the work. If Poley was in Little Ease, he should be easy to find – and the woman had implied there was only one guard. If he was wrong – there were a lot of ifs. Nick shrugged, stripped down to hose and boots and pulled on a dark tunic to hide the pale sheen of his body. He tethered the horses in a clump of scrubby trees bent sideways by the wind, unloaded his gear, took a deep breath and a long look at the sky and bent to push through the bushes that had grown up round the entrance to the tunnel. It was dry and sandy underfoot, and he crouched down to light his lantern. Bent double, he picked his way forward.

The sappers had built well, shoring and roofing as they went, but there had been occasional falls that partly blocked the way and Nick was able to ease carefully round them with his heart in his mouth, fearful of bringing down more earth and sand. Animals had been here since the humans, but the smell was not unpleasant, a musty farmyard smell. Once he came upon a skull and a tumbled heap of bones and metal, then others further along. That stopped him for a moment; the tunnel seemed to close in and the weight of earth above bore down on him, he could not breathe. He fought with the fear and presently moved on. After what seemed an endless time of crawling and wriggling, pushing the lantern ahead of him and dragging the sack, he came to what he had been hoping for. At no time had there been a real shortage of air and here was the reason. Work on the new drain had indeed begun, flat stones were laid and revetted, curving overhead, locked and cemented together. A current of air was coming from somewhere. He lay and listened for sounds of masons, but by now work had finished for the day: he saw a pile of tools left clean and ready for the morning. Blessing the skill of the French engineers, he was able to crawl forward and sit up and straighten his legs.

He lifted the lantern and looked around. The drain sloped upward, dry and smooth and ended in a short vertical shaft. The stones of this were laid dry and it would be an easy climb. He emptied out his sack, made a long double loop through the ring of the lantern and tied the ends to his belt. He put back all the tools except the chisel and slung the sack round his neck; the lantern he left on the floor to draw up from above. He drove in the chisel as high as he could reach for the first swing up and found plenty of good handholds. A slab of wood covered the top of the shaft and Nick balanced his foot on the chisel and hung there a moment, listening. There was no sound and he slid the cover gently to one side and hauled himself out. He pulled up his lantern, untied it and paused, orienting himself. There was a foul smell up here, different from the earthy smell in the tunnel. To his right, where he reckoned the cells would be, the stink was stronger. Forced to crouch still, he shuffled along until he came to the first of the garde-robes. This one had been in use, its sides were stained and stinking, the surface dry and crusty. It was just wide enough to take his body. He sank down on his heels a moment to work it out. It was either a guard room or an empty cell. In his experience, cells were seldom given the luxury of a garde-robe: the surface was dry, possibly a guard-room not in use. Worth a risk. He moved over beneath the short shaft, raised his arms and stood up, easing his shoulders through. It was a tight fit and his fingers were within a few inches of the top. He sank down again and thought. His chisel was still in the drain. He needed to be able to get his elbows on the edge. He tied the end of the rope to the back of his belt and moved his poniard round to lie flat down his belly. He took the crowbar and scraped out a toehold in the side of the passage and stepped up to thrust his body through the narrow opening. It was suddenly pitch dark, his body hid the light from the lantern, but his elbows were clear and he could get enough leverage to pull himself up. Grateful for muscles tuned in the jousting arena, he wriggled out. He could see again now, as he straddled the opening. The door of the garde-robe swung open and the glow from below showed an empty room with table and chairs. No sign of regular use. He padded across and opened the door onto a passage lit by a single cresset. To his left was the iron-barred gate he had noted yesterday – was it only yesterday? To the right the passage turned a corner where a lamp was burning. He held his breath and listened hard. He heard someone moaning, and below that the hiss and slap of cards and a low mutter. Two guards, then? Cursing to himself, he eased the door shut and pulled out his poniard. Gripping it in his teeth, he pulled up the lantern and coiled the rope round his waist and, with the long dagger in his fist, crept out and along the passage. At the turn he waited. The light from the lamp cast a single shadow up the wall and as he watched he could make out what the man was doing. He was not dealing, he was laying out a game of solitaire, Nick could hear him breathing and muttering to himself, his back was turned. Nick reversed his poniard, stepped out and hit him hard behind the ear. The man fell forward without a word and a ring of keys spun off the table. Nick caught them before they hit the floor, stuffed them in his tunic and bent to immobilise the guard, taking off the man's belt and pulling his tunic up over both head and arms and binding them with it. He picked up the lamp and went on down the line of cells, looking for a door lower than the rest. This was very different from London's Tower, he thought. There the ancient stones breathed agony of body and spirit, the air foul, the narrow passages dark and low, scored and stained with God knew what, enough to instil fear and dread into the stoutest heart. There had not been time for this building to absorb the suffering of those imprisoned there as yet, although the sounds were familiar enough. He passed muffled sobbing, piteous groans, someone was praying. Steps down and he came to it at last, a small solid door with no grille. He set the lamp down and sorted through the ring of keys. He tried three before the wards turned and the door scraped open outward. Poley's face in the light of the lamp was contorted with fear, his eyes screwed against the light, his breath sobbing in his throat. Little Ease was a cell less than five feet in any direction and the man Nick had come for was shackled to the wall, so that he could neither sit, stand nor lie. His body had begun to jerk with fear.

Nick said quietly, "A friend. We are leaving." Poley made a mewing sound and Nick hastily looked for the key to the shackles. There was only one small key on the ring and Poley fell into his arms with a cry of agony.

"Quietly, if you can," said Nicholas. He pulled him as gently as he could into the passage and re-locked the door. "You know me. Nick Talbot. We are going now. What time does the guard change, do you know? Can you tell me?"

Poley licked his lips, he was crying. "Midnight," he whispered. "Three shifts." Nick found his flask of water and held it to Poley's lips.

"Better delay them a little," he said. He ran on silent feet along the passage to the barred gate, pushed in a key and broke it off. He gave the unconscious guard an extra thump as he passed on his way back, and stooped to pick up the groaning Poley. He hefted him over his shoulder and returned to the guardroom. Here, he locked the door and knelt at Poley's side. The man's cramped limbs were useless and he was grey with pain and fear.

"How long?" asked Nick.

"This morning…" Long enough, thought Nick. He knew very well what this felt like. He himself, in the Tower, had been hung by the wrists, thick chains weighting his shoulders, for much longer and he remembered the dread of not knowing how long it would go on, knowing very well what would come next. He unstoppered the aquavit and poured some between Poley's lips. A little colour came into his face and he muttered, "We'll never get out, no one escapes…" Nick supported his head and gave him more, Poley squinted up at him. "How the devil did you get in?"

Nick tied the rope round the man's narrow chest. "Up the Citadelle's arse, where else. Save your breath. I'm going to lower you down. Try and straighten your legs." But he could not and Nick had to do it for him, giving him the rope-end to bite on. It was done at last and Nick lowered him and followed him down with a rush, coiled up the rope and surveyed him in the light of

70

the lantern. The man looked half-dead, he would have to be carried. Determined to hold on to his tools, Nick made two journeys of it, leaving the lantern to mark the head of the shaft. He knelt on all fours to get Poley on his back and rope him there and crawled on elbows and knees, their combined girth just missing the ceiling. At the shaft he eased Poley off and he lay there groaning. "Oh God, what now…" Nick did not answer, he pushed aside the wooden lid and lowered the lantern on a running loop with the tools, retrieved it and tied it under Poley's arms. He rolled him over and lowered him down, dropped the rope and climbed into the shaft, pulling the slab across. He climbed down carefully, not wishing to land on the man still lying at the bottom. Once down, he paused for a moment to get his breath and think of the next step. He sat, scraped and bleeding and covered in filth, and contemplated Poley lying there moaning, his limbs curled like a poked crab. He had pissed himself at some point in his ordeal and he stank of sweat and stale urine, another part of the humiliating misery Nick remembered only too well. *"Get him out or stop his mouth."* Well, he'd got him this far. Getting him through the salient was another matter. He rested his back against the side of the shaft, took a draught of water and thought. The falls in the tunnel were the problem. If Poley could help himself a little – it might be worth waiting. His way in would puzzle the guards for a while, but after all this effort he did not feel like gambling on it, perhaps coming out to find them ready. "Do you think you can move?" he asked. "Anything broken?" Poley shook his head and moved feebly. Nick gave his short nod and shifted round to examine the mining tools piled in the shaft. There were planks for shoring walls and roof, picks and mattocks and spades. He got to his feet, bending, and went to pull out some of the lengths of

71

timber. He cut off some of his useful rope and tied two of the planks together as a rough litter. "This will not be easy," he said to Poley. "I would ask you to be as still and quiet as you are able." He eased Poley onto the litter and strapped him there, made a harness for himself that left arms and legs free and chose a mattock from the miner's tools. He fastened the harness round his body and took up the burden.

It was punishing work, the tunnel was one long Little Ease. Bent over and laden with lantern, mattock and crowbar, he struggled on, dragging Poley on the makeshift stretcher until he came to the first of the falls. Sweating hard now, he took a brief rest and a drink of water, giving Poley a few drops of the aquavit. To his dismay, little trickles of water had begun to pool in the floor of the tunnel; it must have been raining hard. He used the mattock to scrape gently at the fallen rubble and presently had cleared enough to get Poley through. He took up the strain again, forcing screaming muscles to move faster. The next fall was the larger one, and he shrugged off the harness. As he hacked away with the mattock, he found pieces of broken timber that he used to shore up sides and roof. He towed Poley head first through and clear, his legs dragging and bumping, his boot heels kicking. Nick had picked up the lantern and mattock and turned towards him, preparing to resume the harness, when the worst happened.

His heel caught the edge of a joist behind him and with a soft rumble and roar the tunnel fell in. It flattened Nick with his head next to Poley's, a weight of soil and timber across his back and legs, sand and dust billowing up to clog mouth and eyes and nostrils. In the sudden darkness the rumbling went on and, clear of the fall, Poley started to scream. Half-stunned, Nick lay for a moment, gathering his wits. He shook his head and spat to clear the dust and tried to assess the damage. A sharp edge was cutting into his shoulder blades, one arm was trapped under him, the other, still holding the mattock, had a little movement. No pain as yet from broken bones. He fought down panic and tried to think. It felt like a roof timber slanting across his back, saving him from complete burial. *"To lie in cold obstruction and to rot,"* he thought. *No. Not here, not like this.* He gathered all his strength and heaved upward. The beam was immoveable, but he found space for his arm. It was difficult to think with Poley screaming beside him.

"Quiet, for God's sake," he hissed. "Untie yourself and help…" The screaming went on and Nick turned his head and bit the ear nearest him. A yelp and the screaming stopped. *I can move my legs,* thought Nick. *It can't be a big fall.* He was wriggling his fingers up the shaft of the mattock, until he could grasp the head of it. Poley would need a tool. He found he had movement in his elbow, thanks to the angle of the timber and began to wheedle and scrape the precious mattock until it was level with his ear.

"Roll over," he told Poley. "Put up your left hand and take the handle by my head. Gently does it." There was an agonising wait while Poley fumbled with his lashings and rolled over at last. Noisome breath panted in Nick's face and a trembling hand felt over his hair to grasp the wooden shaft and pull at it weakly.

Nick became aware of water gathering under his chin and along the length of his body. Suppressing the urge to yell at Poley to hurry, he said, "Try and dig above the beam."

Poley was having difficulty holding the handle and Nick, in a cold sweat, found the water was actually helping him, turning the earth beneath him into sludge. He worked his arm free, took back the tool and managed to scrape away enough of a hollow to ease his upper body sideways and free the other arm. The timber groaned and settled a little, Nick held his breath. It stayed, and with both arms free, Nick tried to drag himself forward. The weight on hips and thighs was too much, it was getting hard to breathe, his neck was on fire from the effort of keeping his head out of the water.

"We are going to drown," said Poley in matter-of-fact tones.

Grinding his teeth, Nick said, "Pull those planks nearer, under my arms." Silence, then effortful groans and the edge of the litter nudged Nick's arms. He got them under him and the relief it gave was enormous: he could breathe.

"Dig," he said to Poley. "Or drown." He heard the mattock begin to strike, Poley's breath sobbing with every blow. Nick's body was beginning to sink in the muddy trickle, the earth settling above him, he was losing the feeling in his legs. Poley was taking too long. He grasped the planks, dug in his toes and prepared for a mighty heave. Something touched his ankle and he heard a steady rhythmic noise. Poley had stopped trying to dig. Nick felt a hand on his leg. It squeezed and the rhythmic sound began again. The weight came slowly off his body and he was able to make a convulsive effort and heave himself out from under the beam. He felt for Poley, took back the mattock and began to dig from his side. Soil fell away, a hole opened up and there was light. The freckled face of Harry Munro appeared.

"Rest a bit," he said. "I'm going to make safe. No point in bringing the rest of it down."

Nick let himself slide down to sit in the mud and thank his maker for Scots obstinacy. Poley was shaking at his side.

"They've found us," he muttered. "We are taken…"

"A friend," said Nick curtly. "Get ready to move." He found his faithful rope and harnessed Poley with it. The hole widened, Munro was using broken pieces of timber to shore and roof the opening, a neat workmanlike job. He backed away and Nick crawled through, trawling the rope, forestalling the frantic Poley. Between them the young men hauled him through and helped him up. The water was still rising and they wasted no time, splashing along to the entry and the open air. It had stopped raining, everything smelt wonderful and to Nick's surprise it was still daylight. He seemed to have been underground for days. The horses stood where he had left them, placidly tearing at the coarse grass.

All three collapsed on the turf, scarecrow figures, soaked and plastered with mud, Nick with his hose in tatters and the skin grazed and bleeding. His hands were no better, and his jerkin was torn open, the hair of his chest matted with mud and blood. Poley lay with his eyes closed, wheezing, the marks of the shackles livid on his arms.

"You stubborn bloody Highlander," said Nick. "My thanks. All debts cancelled."

"You would have managed."

Nick shook his head and lay back to look up at the mackerel sky, barred with pink and silver and blue, arrowed by a skein of geese. A curlew called from the marsh. The evening breeze blew chill, cooling his skin to gooseflesh, waking all the aches and pains. Munro nudged him and handed him a flask. Nick took a deep breath, sat up and took it. "We should be moving," he said.

Munro got up and fetched a pack from his horse. "Clothes."

They stripped and cleaned themselves in a stream that burbled along, gradually filling its channel. Nick found his wallet of remedies and attended to his various hurts. Back in his embroidered velvet, he did the same for Poley and helped him dress and mount up. He wanted to put distance between them and Calais before the hunt was up.

Using what cover there was, they rode with all speed west and north, away from the coast. By nightfall, they were thirty miles off and found an empty barn to rest. Nick lifted a fainting Poley from his horse and consulted his inner map. He wanted to get Poley on a ship for home. There were light rations in his pack and he shared them out. He settled his back against the wall and said to Munro

"We'll make for—" He was asleep before he finished the sentence.

Nick woke to find a pile of sacks under his head and a horse-blanket over him. Stiff and sore, he ran a hand over his bristled face and got to his feet to look at Poley. The man was still asleep. He went outside and met Munro coming back with a pan of milk, a capful of pearly, pink-veined mushrooms and a couple of eggs. Nick began to think this young Scot would be wasted on escort duty.

Over breakfast cooked by the resourceful Munro, Nick discovered that Poley had a connection in Zeebrugge that would find him a ship bound for Gravesend. Hot food and a night's sleep had done him good, and Nick saw no reason to nursemaid him further. He took Munro aside.

"Listen," he said, "I had it in mind to offer you a billet with my courier escort, but unless you have other plans, there is something else."

"What other plans could I have?"

"I was gifted land in Scotland, and a tower. I've never even seen it. Would you go there and send me a report? Perhaps take it in hand. You would have letters and a commendation to my kinfolk."

"Kinfolk?"

"Melville. I trust that is not a difficulty."

"No feud with the Melvilles that I know of. I accept." They clasped hands on it, delighted with each other.

"I never asked," said Nick. "How came you in the tunnel?"

"Did you think I would take your money and ride away? I smelt something. Followed you."

"I am heartily glad of it. Now, money and letters you shall have, and, I pray you, do not travel with our friend there."

"Does he have a name?"

"No. His mother may know him, but we do not." Munro made a Scottish noise in his throat and they grinned at each other in complete accord.

They changed the post horses at the nearest town and parted, Poley to Zeebrugge and Munro to Antwerp to take ship for the wilds of Scotland.

With only three days to make up and wounds to lick, Nick decided not to ride immediately after the Rokesby party. Instead he found himself a comfortable inn with an accommodating landlady and took his ease for a day or two. He came up with the travellers a hard-ridden two weeks later, just a day's ride from the Rhine, where they would take to the river at Koblenz. The party was staying at a charming small hostelry, on the Pilgrims' road and off the beaten track, offering plentiful good food and hospitality – Toby's forward planning was superb, thought Nick. His friend was looking decidedly out of temper and was surprised to see him so soon.

"What kept you?" he said.

Nick laughed. "This and that. Is all well?"

Toby's gaze slid to Nick's hands, still scabbed after two weeks. "Been in a fight?"

"No. What's happening?"

Toby told him. It was hard to tell why or how it started to go wrong, he said. Small things: the fresh horses were not there at the arranged time for the changeover, a delay of eighteen hours, and the landlord's food and patience ran out; the next inn had burned down the night before. A lady's baggage was unaccountably left behind and had to be fetched, a pet dog took sick and died. Russell had dealt smoothly with all this, but all the same, muttered Toby, I don't like it.

"You think it's deliberate?" asked Nick.

"I don't know – it's probably coincidence. We'll see."

Nick was as delighted to be re-united with his own horses as they were to see him. He slept soundly and saddled up Nero in the morning in high spirits. They were late starting; a pet monkey was lost and eventually found terrified, unaccountably shut in one of the outhouses with the pig.

"See what I mean?" said Toby.

They set off at last, the sun high in a sky piled with white cumulus over the mountains. On they trotted, admiring the spectacular views, over a pretty little hump-backed bridge, the escort among them chatting and pointing out points of particular interest, Nick ranging ahead. It was a tempting stretch of road with a wide grassy verge and he flashed past a scowling Tobias and gave Nero his head. He passed a chattering stream spilling out of the hillside and rounded a redstone bluff into the shadow of a stand of firs. His eye caught a flash of steel. He pulled Nero up short and slid off to run a hand down his leg, listening hard, and heard the unmistakeable rustle and creak of a body of horsemen.

He remounted and rode slowly back round the outcrop. Once out of sight he dug in his spurs and galloped full speed back towards the party still ambling along.

They paid no attention until Nick drew his sword, stood in his stirrups and waved it round his head. Tobias, whose eyes had been everywhere, spurred towards him, shouting to the escort to form guard. Jocelyn Russell took no notice and rode calmly on, but the party was unsettled by the approaching madman whirling a sword, and lost cohesion, milling about aimlessly. The escort, eight in all, closed in and waited. Russell, trying to mask his anger, turned to urge the travellers to keep calm and continue on.

"There is nothing to fear," he was saying, and the escort, obeying his muttered orders, fanned out at the rear to drive their flock gently forward.

"Back!" yelled Nick. "Over the bridge!"

Tobias wheeled and began giving orders in a voice that brooked no disobedience. The "officer material" woke to the situation as a group of marauding horsemen rounded the bluff at a gallop towards them. Flanking the merchants and their wives, seizing bridles and slapping rumps, they succeeded in turning the party back over the narrow bridge and obeying the shouted orders, took up position on its hump, four bowmen at the rear, sword- and spearmen to the fore. Nick and Toby made their stand either side of the funnelled approach to the bridge, Jocelyn Russell sullen-faced behind Toby. It was unlikely there would be archers among their attackers, and before they got within pistol range, Toby gave the word. A hail of arrows met the oncoming horsemen and the front line broke, spoiling the aim of the rest. Toby could loose fifteen flights a minute, and the other four were not slow.

"Charge!" someone shouted.

"Hold!" yelled Nicholas, and set Nero across the narrow opening, determined to hold their advantage. The constant rain of arrows kept the main body of bandits at a distance, one braver than the rest came on followed by another. It was a long time since the last brush of this kind, but Nick felt the same ice-cold clarity descend on him. He had not been carrying pistols and he sheathed his sword, let the attackers get within range of his throwing knives and then let fly. A man screamed, clutching at the fountain of blood spurting from his neck, and toppled into the path of his companions. Another fell across the neck of his horse without a sound. Nicholas drew his sword, ready to charge, Toby lowered his sightline and downed the man in the vanguard. One more flight of arrows and it was all over; the brigands turned and made off the way they had come, leaving riderless horses and groaning men on the ground behind them.

The women of the party were shrieking and sobbing, the men white-faced and furious. They had paid good money for this not to happen.

"Well done," said Toby quietly. "Bring them back to the village, Russell. I'll go on ahead." The young man bridled, opened his mouth and shut it again at the look in Nick's eye. He joined the men in calming the party and shepherding them back to the inn, while Nick took a couple of men to deal with the wounded. There were three dead and four injured, one dying. Nick's companions were all for dispatching them outright, but he insisted they should be attended to and taken back to the village. He found his water bottle and lifted the dying man to help him drink. He saw to his surprise the man was English; his tunic showed him an outcast from the recent wars. The man sipped a little and coughed, a trickle of blood at the corner of his mouth.

"It was s'posed to be easy," he whispered. "Comin' along all sweet-like…takin' suckets from a babby, he said…"

"Who said?"

The man looked up at him. "Tell my old 'oman…" A rush of blood smothered the words and his head fell forward. Nick laid him gently down and closed the staring eyes. He dug the ground with his heel. It was like iron.

"Lay them in the ditch," he said. "There are stones enough to give them decent burial. Leave a marker." He retrieved his knives, left the others to pick up arrows and himself strapped the wounded to their horses and rode with them to find the rest of the party, thinking hard.

Chapter Four

Arrived back at the inn they had left so gaily a few hours before, Nick found Jocelyn Russell confronting the wealthy burgher who had given up his cabin on the *Mermaid*. Arthur Bullivant was red in the face and shouting. His origins were showing.

"Stow you! Who's running the game here, that's what I want to know! While you were pussyfooting around, we could all have been killed – I didn't sport my bit to be cozened out of it by some rakehelly cove still wet behind the ears—"

"I assure you, Master Bullivant—"

"Assure my arse—"

Toby intervened smoothly, "My colleague and I are here for this very contingency, sir. It was felt a covert extra guard would be less alarming for the ladies."

"This young applesquire were acting contrary—"

Toby trod on Russell's toe to stop him rising to the insult.

"It will not happen again, sir. As you saw, one of us always rides ahead. Master Russell—"

"You'll not cut your teeth on me. Me and mine will be turning back."

The quiet man in the well-cut brown velvet stepped forward and addressed Nicholas.

"My Lord Rokesby, I believe. John Challoner, at your service.

We must thank you and Master Fletcher for your excellent and timely action. Don't you agree, Master Bullivant. Masterly. Such things are to be expected in these times and we were well protected. Why, we even have the two leaders of the Rokesby enterprise to guard us."

"What I'm saying—"

"You were understandably affrighted, sir, as indeed was I, but now we are blooded, as it were, I have the utmost confidence in our safety." This urbane flow with its insinuation of cowardice quite took the bluster out of the angry merchant, and he turned away, muttering.

"He called me a pimp!" said Jocelyn Russell.

"Thieves' cant, Master Russell?" said Toby. Russell turned and stalked off.

Nick turned to Challoner. "Do I take it you have come along to oversee your brother's investment, Master Challoner? I couldn't quite place the likeness," he said, frowning.

"No, sir. When I am carrying what I am carrying I prefer to be unrecognised. As do you, evidently. Nevertheless, so far I at least am satisfied. You took no hurt?"

"Was it necessary to announce our identity, sir?"

"For the good of the enterprise, I think so, yes. If it inconveniences you, I'm sorry."

Nick looked at him. "Enterprise?"

"Why, the courier service, of course. What else?"

That night, when all was quiet, Nick beckoned Toby out into the innyard, where a gibbous moon was highlighting the snow on the distant mountains. They both spoke at once

"How did they know where—"

"They were tipped off."

Toby grunted and drew out his pipe. He carefully tamped down the tobacco and got it drawing to his satisfaction before he spoke.

"Who, d'you reckon?"

"The man who died – he was English. Tipped off, as you say."

Toby hoisted himself up on the wall and sat smoking. "The men aren't given a detailed itinerary," he said presently. "Best if they don't know – makes 'em stay on their toes."

"Been a damn sight too comfortable," said Nick.

"Mm…" Toby blew a smoke ring and another. "What d'you reckon to Russell, now?"

"If you're sure about the men…" Nick leaned his elbows on the wall. "Those other little incidents…"

"Planned, I reckon."

"Someone after two things, perhaps. Sink the enterprise and rob the party before we get to the banks."

"Mowbray's in the Tower."

"This must have been thought of some time ago. What do you mean to do?"

"Speak to the men. Watch Russell." He sat swinging his legs, thinking.

Nick swung himself up to perch on the wall beside him. "Wait and see what comes out of the woodwork," he said. "Whoever it is will know we're on our guard by now."

"Set a watch, d'you reckon?"

" Whom do you trust – apart from Challoner?"

"Ah…" Toby tapped out his pipe, nodding. "Right. We split the guard between we two, and keep an eye on 'em until Koblenz. We should rendezvous with O'Dowd at Basel on his way back and exchange the escort there. How's that?"

"Excellent. Send Russell ahead to arrange it?" Toby burst out laughing and thumped him on the back.

"Two birds with one stone! If he doesn't get there, we'll know for sure, and if he does, we'll at least be rid of him for a while. You're a wily bastard, Nick." Nick grinned and slid down.

"On the other hand, it may be safer to have him where we can see him. Think about it. I'll take first watch. You get to your bed."

Nick patrolled the inn quietly until the last candle was out, and settled himself in a dark corner of the stable yard, among the quiet noises and shifting of the animals, his poniard lying ready by his hand. He had plenty to think about. It seemed to him that attempting to undermine the reputation of the courier service was a flimsy excuse for the violence they had met. Robbery pure and simple was the obvious answer, but the subtlety of the delaying tactics argued against it. Someone in the party was responsible for that. Possibly one of the travellers was the intended target. After consideration, he dismissed the notion that it might be himself; he had been an unexpected latecomer. He recalled Challoner's remark – "when you are carrying what I am…" John Challoner was brother to the goldsmith who was backing them, and Nick assumed it must be diamonds Challoner spoke of, a common enough commodity on this trade route. He shook his head. That led back to the idea of robbery. Suppose it was something other. Challoner had seemed strangely pleased with himself, a man with a mission. *Keep an eye on him,* he thought.

He got to his feet to make another round of the inn, silent in his soft boots, holding his sword close. Nothing stirred except an owl swooping across the moon-white open field to the wood, no sound but the bark of a dog fox. He could have been back in England, at Rokesby. He explored the thought cautiously, as a man probes with his tongue at a sore tooth, waiting for the pain. There was only the remembrance of it. Back in his quiet corner, he made himself comfortable on a half-empty sack of straw, knife out and ready. Below the surface watchfulness, his mind was busy with this new freedom. That little skirmish, after the successful rescue of Poley, had been a catharsis, cleansing, clearing away the fog of melancholy that had been hampering him. This, after all, was his métier: to take action had been his way of life. "Very well," he said to himself. "It was not to be – or not yet. There are those to provide for. Do it. The opportunity is there – seize the day. Away with this green-sickness, I am knight and ambassador to the Queen – something is afoot here. Get on with it."

A rub of boot on stone brought him to his feet and Toby rounded the corner to find a blade at his throat.

"Easy, friend," he said. "I take it you have had quiet guard. Get to your rest, Nick. Oh yes, I've been thinking. I reckon our backer would bear watching."

Nick snorted with laughter. "My thoughts entirely. I could do with a look at his baggage."

"No chance. A watch only, I reckon."

Nick nodded and went to roll himself in his cloak on the straw in Nero's stable and sleep a dreamless sleep.

Tobias left early to go on ahead and it was a subdued party that set off later that morning, Nicholas riding in front, captain of himself and his enterprise once more. The more senior of the escort took the flanks and Jocelyn Russell passed among the party with soothing words, pointing out the efficiency of the action taken the day before. Nick watched the reaction of the escort to this, picking out the men likely to be trusted. John Challoner discreetly oiled the wheels, the travellers gradually regained their spirits and they arrived in Koblenz charmed with the idea of floating up the Rhine.

"Floating", with its implication of effortless leisurely progress, would hardly describe it, Nick thought. The struggle against the seaward currents would require pairs of horses to draw the barge, or barges, depending on what Toby had been able to find, aided by poles and oars and sail. At this time of year the river would be full and fast from snowmelt and extra traffic. All the same, it was as fast a way as any other and safe from outside attack at least.

Tobias was waiting when they jingled into the town. He had done well. A vessel that had once been a royal barge, built in England for an early Tudor, was drawn up near the riverbank, with its attendant wherry. He had sent messages to O'Dowd and acquired a crew. He proposed to ride alongside as far as the horse walk would allow, with three of the escort. Both young men were weary: Tobias had been working hard and Nick had had no-one he trusted to share the nightly vigil. Toby groaned when Nick pointed out the amount of work still to be done to make even this brilliant find suitable for a "tour *de luxe*". "If you think so, my friend, you do it," he said.

They divided the labour: Toby took over the guard and saw the party comfortably settled with two days' entertainment in view while Nick set about restoring the second-hand barge to something of its former magnificence.

Cabins were scoured, garnished and hung with cloth, awnings erected on deck, couches, cushions and carpets brought in and provisions stored. When the party came to take ship, everything smelled of paint, the decks were white and scrubbed, the brightwork sparkled and the stubby masts were gay with bunting. The crew were clean and looked hunted, the skipper white-faced and tensely smiling. In the galley the hired cook chivvied his two helpers and fought the ship's cook for the space. The Rokesby elite service was keeping up standards. Nick was still sweating below decks stowing the livestock and finding room for a second galley to prevent murder being done, when Master Jocelyn Russell, immaculate in apricot velvet, conducted the travellers aboard to some pretty piping from the bosun.

Nick came on deck at last, tired and filthy, to find John Challoner waiting for him, a jug in one hand and two leather tankards in the other.

"Your partner had the better division of labour this time," he said with a smile. "If this venture makes a profit, you'll both have earned it."

"Not until Naples, sir."

"And you leave us in Milan, I understand."

"You will be in safe hands."

Challoner led the way aft, where the noise and clatter from the new galley masked their words, and turned to face him. "I fear I may be the worm in the apple, Nicholas. A particularly juicy one, if I am taken. I think it's time I took you into my confidence." He ducked under a handy awning and settled himself on the deck. Handing Nick a mug of ale, he went on.

"I am here at the bidding of our joint master, Nicholas. If his right hand ever knows what his left hand is doing, it will surely be the undoing of him."

Nick stared at him, unbelieving. The fatuous self-importance of the man was frightening. Surely Cecil could not be relying on a crutch as frail as this for anything – or was he? No mention had been made to him of any other task, but it would be typical of the spymaster to stir a pot and see what came up with the stink.

Challoner looked around and lowered his voice. "I am carrying letters from James' queen to the Pope. Without the King's knowledge, I need hardly tell you. You have met the man. Ann is a naïve creature and expensive, as you most likely know. What you may not know is that she would like to see the country return to the old religion. My brother and I have provided her in the past with jewels and necessaries (for which she has not paid, incidentally,) and she looks on me as a useful friend."

"With Cecil's encouragement, I imagine."

"Quite. He is eager to know what his Holiness will offer."

"Your return journey promises to be equally interesting, sir."

Challoner laughed. "I shall contrive. It is hard to surprise you, Nicholas."

Nick shrugged. Challoner was obviously flattered to death to be invited into these dubious circles. *Ann is not the only naïve one here,* he thought.

"If I can be of help..."

"Go on as you have been," said Challoner, importantly. "Someone would like to see these letters. James is not named successor yet and if his queen is discovered in this he will never be. It could not be ignored, whatever our Queen might wish."

"Why not destroy them?"

"In the last extreme, I will. But Cecil wants the answer from Rome. Our master likes to know how things lie."

"Where the broken glass is," murmured Nick.

"What?"

"No matter. It occurs to me that as the Queen's ambassador I have privileges. They may be of help. But I agree. 'We need to know our enemies...' I quote." Nick drained his tankard and climbed to his feet. "I should like to see you safe home, sir. And the King's succession secure. I liked him," he said reflectively. "In spite of all, he seemed a rational, tolerant man, and God knows we have need of such. Another bloody regime like poor Mary's would be the death of us. May her God forgive her, for I can't."

"A Douglas? A Spaniard? Essex? God help us indeed."

"Essex?"

"Oh yes. The Queen has both spoiled and disappointed him. There are rumours. If her Majesty allows him into France and offers preferment, trouble may be averted, but if his friend Mowbray is put to the question, I fear the outcome."

"Mowbray has been busy."

"An angry and frustrated man, Nicholas, with no love for you. He has connections. Even from the Tower he can do harm. The sooner he comes to trial the better."

"He cannot be behind our troubles here, surely."

"No. Someone at the Scottish court has got wind of the queen's indiscretion – you are right, Nicholas, the link is someone in our party." He got up. " I have kept you too long…"

"Where is this letter?"

Challoner looked at him sharply. "It were best you do not know."

Not displeased with the outcome of his fishing expedition, Nicholas watched Challoner go. It was clear now what had been behind the petty upsets on the way, if not who. Not a professional, he felt sure, the scheme was over elaborate and, so far, ineptly carried out. Someone operating from a distance, perhaps, wishing to stay in the background. At least Challoner emerged as an honest man if a foolish one. *Better warn Toby*.

Fastidious as a cat, Nick was eager to get out of his reeking clothes and went to fetch clean linen from the tiny cabin he was to share with Toby and two of the guard. Most likely he would be sleeping on deck. They were moored some way upriver from the little town, with its red roofs and twin steeples, and he trotted ashore and walked along the bank until he found a secluded spot among some willows, stripped and waded into the river. The sun was high in a piercing blue sky and warm on his shoulders, but the water was icy, cold enough to make him shout. He plunged in and swam and frolicked and kicked and yelled, until a splash by his head brought him to the surface. Tobias was sitting on the grass in his best clothes playing ducks and drakes, a pile of flat stones at his side. He laughed as Nick splashed to the bank.

"That's cut you down to size. Cold, is it?"

Nick kicked a shower of water over him and sat down in the sun beside him to dry off. "Got anything to eat? You usually have."

Toby passed him a sack and Nick opened it eagerly; he was ravenous. There was a loaf, half a cold fowl, cheese, apples and an onion. He banged his friend on the back and set to.

"Who's in charge?" he said with his mouth full.

"The skipper and a couple of men. Did you find out whose side my potential uncle is on?"

"A little breathing space, Toby, for God's sake." He sat chewing and considering his options. Tobias looked at him, found his pipe and tobacco and lay back, quietly smoking. By the time he had finished eating, Nick had decided to take Toby completely into his confidence. Half a tale could put him in danger. He wiped his hands on the grass and took the proffered flask. It was a very good local wine, tasting of flowers.

Tobias lay watching him through a blue haze of smoke. This was a very different man from the untried youth he had first met outside Milan. The spring sunshine made a burnished halo of his drying hair and glinted on the short hairs lying along his arms as he sat elbows on knees, the flask dangling from his hand. The scars showed white against the smooth skin, the hardened sinewy body was relaxed for once. Through Nick he had met the woman he hoped to marry, in some hazy distant future, and made a sizeable amount of money: working alongside him he had grown to esteem their friendship even more. Nick seemed to have put aside his concerns over Kate and his small son, but Toby knew him better than that. The cool composure that had first attracted him and prompted friendship was even more apparent now, but Toby knew what it concealed, harshly reined back. There had been times when the actor in Nick broke free and led to hilarious escapades, and it amused Toby to tease him until he dissolved in helpless laughter, but those days seemed past.

His mind made up, Nick drained the flask and lay back on his elbows. He told his friend all he knew and guessed of the present situation, and Toby nodded.

"Do you think he's right about the Scottish connection?"

"Possibly. I thought of contacting Carey."

Toby found the last apple and bit into it. He shook his head. "Take too long, and the fewer the better, I reckon. Watch from this quarter, find a loose end and pull it. Now we know what we're looking for."

Nick rolled over to look at him. "I had hoped to avoid drawing you into this, Tobias."

"It is happening on my watch. And I would not want a return to the last blood-frenzy any more than you."

He put out a hand and Nick took it with a smile.

"Your good Lord Cecil does not scruple whom he uses," offered Toby. "To involve an old man like Challoner…"

"A puppet-master. A chess-master. Pawns are there to be sacrificed."

"Bastard."

"A cunning bastard. But loyal to England as well as his own self. Just remember not to underestimate him."

A little breeze rattled the leaves and blew chill on Nick's naked body. He got up and began to pull on clean clothes, ready now to step back into the world. He caught Toby's speculative eye and grinned.

"Back to work," he said. He rolled his discarded clothes into a bundle and, dressed now in suitable dark green wool pearled and paned with ivory satin, followed Tobias back to the barge.

The stately progress up the river was unmarred by any incident, unless you counted the fire that broke out in the new galley. "That old adage of the swan comes to mind," said Nick to Toby. "The legs going like buggery underneath..." The weather staying fine, entertainments were devised on deck. One of the escort, Walter Grimaud, could play the lute, Nick's capacious memory provided ballads and poems and stories from plays, Tobias arranged sports and competitions and risky games. One or two of the ladies formed their own little courts under the awnings, mimicking the old Courts of Love, with their tales of chivalry and romance, and if all this dalliance led to more dangerous intrigue, Nick felt that was their own affair. Himself, he avoided any such entanglement and watched Russell's polished performance with grim amusement. Challoner maintained a discreet distance.

At the first opportunity, Nicholas found a quiet place and unwrapped Marlowe's script, which had been burning a hole since Dover. *Henry the Fifth*. As Walsingham said, it was a splendid piece, daringly pre-Tudor but echoing the essence of Elizabeth's famed speech at Tilbury. It was inspirational, funny, heroic and tragic by turns, but Nick sensed the underlying homesickness and the longing for men of his own country. There was a deeper, more sympathetic understanding of those men, of their courage and failings, and somehow their Englishness. And the language! A clarion call indeed – great oratory. Thomas was right, the common people and the darlings of the court would both see themselves in this. Would Elizabeth see herself in the "little touch of Harry in the night"?

"A-babbled of green fields…" thought Nick. Poor Poule, Cecil's agent stranded in Venice, wrote much the same of the shade of English oaks. On the brink of plunging into melancholy himself, he pulled up. He was reading too much into this perhaps. Marlowe saw it as a wake-up call, and so it was. He shook himself and got up, patting the pages together and stowing them away. Her Majesty's Ambassador in Venice must wait a little longer for his relief. A visit to Kit was the first concern.

They entered a deep gorge, its towering sides terraced with vineyards and crowned with firs and reached the end of the new horse walk, still being worked on by the local villagers. The men who had been riding alongside came aboard, the draught-horses were sent back and the crew took to the oars and long poles. When the winds were favourable the sails went up and the journey went on into spectacular country. The mountaintops were still covered with snow, and the passengers exclaimed with delight at the tiny villages, each with its church and bell-tower, and the glimpses of grey turreted fortresses high in their quilt of forest green.

Still no mishap. Nick and Tobias took turns watching over Challoner and hoped very much that O'Dowd would be on time.

The roofs and spires of Basel came in sight, the wind died at the last moment and the crew sweated and strained to bring the vessel neatly to her mooring. A smart body of horsemen in the Rokesby black and gold livery was on the quay, a glittering pennanted island in the bustle and hubbub of busy traders, looking as if they had been waiting a long time. Tobias leapt ashore to greet O'Dowd, leaving Nick to oversee the landing of the horses and Russell to see the passengers disembarked. They would lose some of the party here and take on others. Nicholas would be glad to see the back of Master Bullivant and his various womenfolk, and several of the other merchants were bound for Geneva with some of O'Dowd's men. The new escort had brought fresh horses and litters for the ladies, and lost no time in rounding up the party like elegant sheepdogs and clattering off into the town. Nick had persuaded Toby to keep their suspicions of O'Dowd's ewe-lamb to himself, and he watched his two partners ride off in perfect amity.

He finished his tasks and engaged the shipmaster for transport in the future, paying him off with a handsome bonus. The man had earned it. He turned to survey the bustling little square with its rosy, cosy houses, patterned bricks and fretted white shutters, its housewives neat in close-fitting white caps and starched aprons coming to buy, and tidy servant-girls on their errands with sly smiles for the sailors. The place smelled of mud, baking bread and fish, good plain smells. He looked up at the sky, densely blue still, only a streamer of cloud flying from a distant mountain. *We were lucky with the weather,* he thought. *Hope it holds for the St. Gotthard.* Savouring the pleasure of solitude in the noisy throng of hucksters and townspeople, sailors and beggars, he made his way towards the three cranes silhouetted stork-like at the end of the quay. On his last visit to Basel, he had been crippled by a wound in his thigh, concerned only with getting himself aboard ship. Now, always fascinated by any mechanical device, he wanted to see how the arrangement of cogs and wheels and river water worked. Shouldering his pack, he pushed through the crowd towards the central giant crane that dipped and swayed, swinging a net of barrels up out of a ship's hold, and paused, seeing a familiar figure in sober brown velvet standing beneath it, waiting. He frowned. Why was Challoner here and not with the rest of the party? He must have given Tobias the slip. Challoner turned towards him, and in that moment Nick caught a flash of movement at the notched wheel of the crane. With an eldritch screech of tortured wood, it juddered, rocked and stopped, its load of barrels swinging wildly to crash against its neck. Nick dropped his pack and was already moving as the net tore, spilling its load to split on the cobbles in a silver flood of fish and broken staves. He cannoned into Challoner as the crane tottered and the barrels fell and they sprawled together on the cobbles under a cascade of herring and splintering wood. Challoner was caught a glancing blow and cried out.

"Your pack – it's in your pack…"

Nick looked over his shoulder in time to see a small ragged figure making off with it, eeling through the yelling crowd. Sliding and cursing, Nick went after him, hindered by the crush, but once out of the square his long legs gained rapidly. The thief turned into an alley, shirt-tails flying, and Nick put on a spurt to bring him down in a flying tackle. The thief went down on top of the pack with a shrill cry and Nick rolled him over to see he was no more than a child. Startled, he drew back and with a quick wriggle the boy was up and away, leaving the pack behind. Nick let him go.

Back on the quay it was chaos. The broken-necked crane leaned at a perilous angle over a swarm of yelling townsfolk, Challoner was sitting in a heap of herring irritably swatting away attempts to move him. His right arm hung limp and he was obviously in pain. Other men were lying groaning among the wreck of wood and iron, half-buried in fish. Nick shoved and slithered to come to the old man and knelt at his back to assess the damage. The only harm seemed to be a broken collarbone, and Nick took a deep breath. This kind of injury was a frequent one in the jousting arena and he knew what must be done. It had been done to him. Saying, "Hold still," he grasped the elbow and guided it firmly across Challoner's chest. Challoner cried out as the ends of the bone grated into place and collapsed back, fainting, against Nick's chest. Using his belt, Nick strapped Challoner's arm across his body and looked round the jostling, shouting crowd for help. To his relief he saw Alan Bakewell, of the new escort, pushing through towards him. Bakewell had come to tell him of a change in billet and between them they improvised a litter to carry the injured man.

"That Jocelyn falls on his feet," panted Bakewell, as they pushed through the milling crowd with their burden. "Got the mayor to recommend a better hostelry and we're staying in a by'rlady castle." He spat. " Need a by'rlady cart to get this one up there."

"So be it," said Nick. "Go and find one. At the double." The man straightened up, caught Nick's eye and saluted, off like a jackrabbit into the warren of lanes. Challoner was stirring and Nick knelt beside him. "Rest easy, sir, all is well. The letter is safe. I fear we have further to go than I would have liked; it will not be comfortable."

"I came to warn you," whispered Challoner. "I thought I heard someone last night, I was afraid. I put the letter in your pack… I am not a young man, Nicholas, I am not cut out for this…"

"It is no longer your concern, sir. You will be going home."

Chapter Five

The mayor of Basel had a cousin who had lined his pockets selling arms and equipment to both sides in the recent and recurring wars and built himself a mini-fortress in the hills that flanked the town, a monument to greed and efficiency.

The new-made Count Barger had carried his fantasy to extraordinary lengths. Great heaps of stone could be glimpsed through arrow-slits in towering crenellated walls, showing where building work was still going on. Through a gatehouse complete with fake drawbridge a courtyard fronted an attempt at a gothic castle, round towers still rising at each corner. Iron-studded doors led into a dining hall conceived as a vast solar, with a minstrel's gallery and bedchambers leading off into the towers. Huge fireplaces with heavy soot-stained overmantels stood at each end, craggy with crests and carving. Nick thought of the plain comfortable house his father had built and was faintly amused. He would do things differently when he rebuilt Rokesby. The thought brought him up short. He was beginning to think again of his home and the future.

He established a grey-faced Challoner in bed, looking his full age and, while he waited for a physician to arrive, investigated the room. A lavish hand had curtained solid stone walls and the four-poster with tapestries, but there was no washing-stand, and when he opened the low door in the wall, he found it gave onto a primitive garde-robe, which no doubt accounted for the lingering smell. The physician proved to be the local bone-setter, just come from delivering a sow of awkward piglets. He felt the injury, professed himself satisfied and advised poppy-juice for a good night's sleep and pig-grease for the bruising. Nick paid him and got rid of him as soon as he could, gave orders for a strict guard to be set and found his own chamber two floors above up a winding stair. He and his clothes reeked of herring. No chance of getting a tub of water lugged up those stairs, and he cleaned himself as best he could in the small basin provided and looked in his pack for clean clothes. The wretched letter was there, pushed into the toe of his spare pair of boots. He stuffed it inside his shirt and trotted back down the stair in his second-best suit, wondering whether an oubliette had been included in the mad architect's plans. He found Tobias chafing. Apparently there would be further delay on their way: O'Dowd had arranged for the travellers to rest here awhile before splitting up, in addition to which the count had planned a grand expedition into the mountains to hunt the chamois.

"Though why they need a rest after sitting on their backsides for ten days I don't know, this journey seems to be turning into a holiday," grumbled Tobias.

"Chance for us to do a little investigating, friend. I don't fancy the Gotthard with this hanging over us like an avalanche."

Toby pointed two fingers against the evil eye. "No talk of avalanches, if you please."

Hans Barger was delighted to welcome the titled, rich, and the untitled newly rich English with their smart escort of personable young men. He and his stout wife and daughters set themselves to make an impression, and by the time Nick made his appearance the party was in full swing. The solar-cum-banqueting hall, two storeys high, was groined and beamed and spiked with antlers and stuffed heads of all descriptions: below hung tapestries of hunting scenes lit by flambeaux, smoking, like the fires, into the height above. An enormous black bear (stuffed) snarled in one corner, flanked by suits of armour (empty); huge fires blazed at either end of the room emitting volumes of smoke, and musicians plucked and blew busily in the gallery. It was like stepping back two hundred years, or so he imagined. No civilising influence was apparent in the laying of the table, wooden planchets were set at each place; no finger-bowls or napkins, guests were expected to bring their own knives. Huge haunches of venison, beef and boar sat congealing in their grease, dishes of pigs' feet and platters of saffron-yellow fungi fought for space with tarts and pies and flagons and stands of candles, flickering and spilling their wax in the draught. "Last century German cuisine at its finest," said Toby in his ear. "The man's obsessed. The mushrooms are safe, but sour, I'm told."

The new-made count had other guests. His cousin, the mayor, was there with his wife and three sons, several councillors, a justice, a minister and two minor officials, all with their families and all wearing their best clothes and furs and their favourite scent. Nick's nose gave up the struggle. A token artist scowled in the background and tumblers and jugglers exhibited silent skills under the gallery. A harpist sat with her hands idle in her lap. Nick noticed two new faces among his own party. They must be the additions to the group going on to Milan. He took his seat quietly beside Toby, taking out his knife-case.

"How lovely it is to have money, heigh ho," murmured his friend. "I wonder how many cannon bought this lot... How is the old man?"

"Well enough." Nick was miles away. Like Tobias, he was chafing at the delay. In spite of the happenings on the way they had made good time, and he was anxious above all to know what Marlowe was doing. The sticky webs of Cecil's weaving were hampering him as usual. *Sort out this Challoner thing and get on*, he thought. A steaming platter of roast boar hovered over his shoulder and he came back to himself with a jolt. He raised his goblet to the count's daughter who was smiling at him and got on with the task in hand, making manful inroads into the beef and wishing for an English sallet.

O'Dowd was leaving in a few days with Russell and the two of them were at the far end of the table: O'Dowd in fine form, scarlet in the face, toasting their host and telling jokes and tales of past battles. A giant of a man, he looked what he was – a veteran, utterly reliable and the man to have with you in a fight. His work in training up the men of the escort was invaluable. Never the most discreet of men, however, he had not been taken into Nick's confidence regarding the letter, or his suspicions of Jocelyn Russell. It would be enough to have the young man out of the way.

Covered by the din of the banquet, Nick conferred quietly with Toby. The two newcomers to their party were the Marquis de Longhi and his sister, from Paris, making a tour of Italy. De Longhi was a black-haired, sulkily handsome young man and his sister, Diane, a raving beauty, with glossy black hair tired with jewels, violet eyes and a Frenchwoman's poise. Seated next to Jocelyn Russell, she listened to him with cool amusement and gazed down the table at Nick and Tobias. Nick caught her eye and

101

she inclined her head, the myriad tiny ornaments on her headdress trembling and catching the light. She looked like trouble.

She leaned into Russell and murmured something. He rose and bowing, took her hand to lead her round the table to where Nick was seated.

"May I present Sir Nicholas Talbot, Earl of Rokesby, my lady." Nick stood and bowed over her hand.

"I am told great things of you, milor', such brave action…" Her accent was difficult and he ventured to answer in French.

"Our service is to protect, my lady. It will be our delight to see you safe on your journey."

She clapped her hands and slid into a seat next to his place. "Between us we shall contrive, milor'. To understand each other."

Russell, dismissed, turned away disappointed.

"You are to explain to me of this hunt," said the lady. "My brother is new come from some savage place in the Black Forest – he boasts much and tells me nothing." He took his seat beside her, aware of a strong odour of civet, and offered a dish of spiced pears in wine.

"I am not the one to enlighten you, my lady. The mountains in England are not like these." She gave a toss of her head that set all the little ornaments dancing.

"Then you shall tell me how you hunt there." She talked and laughed and flirted until the last course of fruit and nuts, marchpane and sweet wines, was brought to the table and the guests began to move about and ease themselves.

It was the common practice to piss behind a screen in the corner, and Nick took himself off to the stables to talk to his horses and beg their permission to use their straw. He was not enjoying the company and was glad to be out in the quiet night. Coming out, lacing himself up, he paused before going back into the hot and reeking hall to take in the tranquil beauty of the country. The night was clear and cool, a three-quarter moon hung high over the mountains that floated their snowcaps bright above the belt of fir, boding well for the hunt tomorrow. Bats flew in and around the towers and a hunting owl swooped low, a rabbit screamed and a lone hound crossing the courtyard paused, paw raised, to listen. Among the night-sounds, Nick made out a low murmur of voices. Walking soft, he eased round the base of the tower in the shadows and there were de Longhi and Bullivant in close conversation. The Frenchman's body was taut with anger and he spoke too rapidly and low for Nick to catch his meaning. Bullivant's face was dark and swollen with temper. "I tell you there was nothing! Nothing in his cabin and m'wife searched his wallet when she helped nurse him – he has passed it."

"*A qui?*"

"To that damned arrogant Rokesby, I warrant you. It was through him the ambush failed."

"*Non*. Rokesby is Ambassador – unlikely he is concerned. You say Challoner had much to do with the other, the thin one. He has a hungry look to him. He is our man." It was enough and Nick prepared to slide quietly away to impart this gem to Toby. A murmur of skirts and that strange civet smell stopped him and he lingered. There was a brief grumbling exchange and Bullivant stamped inside. There was a long silence and presently Nick risked a glance round the corner. De Longhi and his sister were locked in a close embrace, broken by a growl from the man.

"You are over-zealous, *chérie*. Leave this to me."

"I wish to help you, André. It means nothing, you jealous creature."

"I do not like it."

"My dear, you brought me to—"

"We were dealing with an old man. I do not like this Rokesby."

"Because he is young and comely. You are a fool, my sweet. Come, we must not fail in this."

Nicholas waited until after they had gone inside and eased away to make his way back to the hall. Tobias did not dance – he claimed his old wound had lamed him – and Nicholas went to stand beside him against the wall.

"The baton is passed," he murmured. "De Longhi is our man. Tell you later." Across the room, Diane de Longhi was fanning herself and talking to their hostess. The musicians were attempting the longeurs of a pavane and he crossed to speak to her.

"Is this as it is played in Paris, my lady?"

"No, my lord, nor as it is danced neither."

"Will you permit me to show you the English fashion, lady?"

She furled her fan, narrowed her eyes and took his hand. "Whatever the fashion, milor', I assure myself you will show me with style."

Tobias smiled as he watched their stately progress and the delicate flirtation. "Never a time waster, Nicholas," he said to himself. "Go to it." He watched for a while then took himself outside with his pipe and presently Nick joined him. He told Tobias what he had heard.

"If she's his sister, I'm a pond full of ducks. You are top of the list, I'm afraid, Toby – watch yourself."

"While you bed the woman, I suppose. If we were the Borgia, now, we would sprinkle our belongings with a little poison and selah!"

"I want information not corpses. I think it is time we tackled John Challoner."

The old man was still awake when the two men looked in on him. He saw the gleeful look on their faces.

"A council of war, gentlemen?"

Tobias straddled his legs before the fire and Nicholas drew up a stool by the bed.

"They are flushed out," he said. "No more surprises. What remains is to know what is behind all this. With your permission, sir, if you are not too tired, I would ask you some questions."

Poor Challoner nodded. "Ask away."

"Who gave you this letter? And where?"

"We have a branch in Edinburgh, Nicholas. To serve the Scottish Court. A lady-in-waiting gave it me."

"Had you seen her before?"

"No. But the letter bore the Queen Ann's seal. I thought…"

"How did my Lord Cecil come to know of it?"

"I sent to tell him. Orders were delivered to me at Dover, before you came. You were expected."

"How did you know they were from Cecil?" Challoner drew himself up on his pillows.

"I have been privileged, *(Privileged!* thought Nick.) privileged to carry messages for his lordship before. My instructions were, if any unusual commissions came my way to let him know. The orders bore his signature…"

Both ends against the middle as usual, thought Nick. He went on, merciless.

"How were you proposing to deliver this letter, sir? You must be aware that our governors do not allow English travellers near Rome, let alone into the Papal City."

"I have a colleague, a Jewish merchant—"

"The Jews are being run out of Rome as we speak."

"Oh…"

"Does this not make you think, sir? This is a trap, Master Challoner, set for James's queen. The letter is meant to be found and published abroad – you are the catspaw to take the fall and be broken on the wheel. Tell me again how you came by it."

"In a parcel of stones to be reset…" his voice faltered. "Oh, dear God, I see. What an old fool you must think me, Nicholas."

Nick shook his head. "No, sir. Over-trusting, perhaps. But, with respect, this is a young man's game. You need to be broken to it early."

"So, what do you…"

"As we said before, sir, a scandal of this nature would destroy James where three assassination attempts have failed."

Challoner lay back, trembling. "What will you do?"

Nick had been thinking. He drew out the letter with its impressive seals and examined it.

"Who makes the royal seals, do you know?"

"We do, in our workshop."

Nick sighed. He caught Toby's eye, who shook his head slightly. No more questions. He made the decision and drew his dagger. He held the point in the candle-flame, and slid it hot under the seal. Challoner started up and fell back with a moan of pain.

"What are you about…"

"Seals can be copied, sir. I'll wager Toby's new boots our Stuart queen did not write this. She may be a foolish expensive woman, sir, but she is not such a fool as this. She knows which side her bread is buttered. She would never be queen of England and Scotland if such a thing came to light."

The letter was in plain Latin and it was dynamite. He passed it to Toby, who said, "Tsk,tsk," and rolled his eyes. Nick showed it to Challoner, then leaned forward and put the corner to the candle. He held it until it scorched his fingers and dropped it into a plate and stirred the ashes with his finger. He looked into Challoner's horrified face.

"I shall make report to Lord Cecil of your brave part in this, sir. Sergeant O'Dowd will see you safe home. And if I may presume to advise, if any more 'unusual commissions' come your way, refuse them. Robert Cecil is friend to no-one."

The old man had his hand to his mouth. "But he was concerned—"

"His lordship is concerned with whoever is behind this….which I am some way to finding out. It is out of your hands, sir. Look at it this way. You may look on your 'accident' as a mistake which may cost them the game."

"Do not 'sir' me, Nicholas. You are right. I am too old for this. What will you do, lad? If you will trust me."

Nick looked at Toby, who said with a grin, "If I read him right, sir, he will bait a trap of his own and see what rats come for the cheese."

Nicholas sat on an upturned bucket in the stable yard mending Oberon's bridle and thinking. He was concerned with the sheer ineptitude of these attacks. The previous attempts on the King's life had been overt and well conceived, had almost succeeded. This effort aimed at discrediting him was a horse of a different colour, the men chosen to bring it about amateur and inadequate. To Nick, it hinted of someone keeping behind the scenes, using whatever tool came to hand. It was a good scheme, nothing would hinder James' claim to the English throne more than the accusation of bringing back a Catholic regime. Russell was exonerated now that Bullivant had been discovered. Now de Longhi. The French connection. He put down the bridle and picked up a stirrup leather, his fingers working automatically.

The failed attempt in Scotland had been masterminded by Francis Bothwell from his exile in France. He was doubtless there now. Bothwell himself had no claim, was set on by someone else, someone with a strong claim to the throne. Nicholas called to mind the list of succession Cecil had shown him and a name sprang out. Lennox. *I need more information,* he thought. He finished his task, cleaned his gear, spoke to his horses and went to write his encrypted report.

Cow's calf aborted. Expect no visit from bull. J C is to be commended for his part, he is injured and the matter is dealt with. We may look to the French court for root and branch of this attempt on the succession, respectfully suggest enquiry re Douglas/Lennox would bear fruit. Marquis de Longhi and connections should be watched.

He sealed it with his thumb, O'Dowd would be entrusted with its safe delivery.

Soon after dawn next day, the hunting party mounted up to ride into the mountains to hunt the chamois.

The idea was to ride into the foothills as far as possible, when the grooms would take the horses back and meet them again next day. They would spend the night in a shepherds' hut built for the purpose on the mountain.

This kind of hunting was not to Nick's taste. He preferred to hunt on the flat with a good horse between his legs, throw his heart over a hedge and feel the lift of his willing beast under him, with the belling of hounds and the horns of huntsmen, the thunder of hooves and the rush of the wind in his ears. Up here, the air was thin and cold, the cliffs and ledges dizzying and the weight of crossbow and pack and a bundle of spears made balance difficult as they climbed. Toby climbed spider-like ahead, pick dangling from his belt, his long narrow limbs agile and easy in spite of his wound. The loud voices and shouted jokes died as the climb became harder, some of the party dropped behind, harried on by the mountain men who were guiding them.

Nick made an effort and caught up with Toby, and they rested with the guide for a moment for the others to catch up. The pine forest stretched out far below, beyond it the city and the wide river had shrunk to a miniature landscape in a painting, the mock castle a child's plaything. Tobias looked sideways at his friend. He knew why Nick had come. Nick's fear of heights was a constant burden to him and he was forever trying to conquer it.

De Longhi, who had obviously done this many times before, swung past them with a smile, unslinging his crossbow. The guide spurted after him, protesting. Tobias passed Nicholas his flask and tactfully led the way along a wider ledge rounding the crag. To his annoyance, ahead of them the ledge suddenly narrowed, blocked by a lumpy outcrop. Toby looked around for a more negotiable way and Nick, catching his breath, said lightly, "Strange shape, that rock. D'you see, it looks exactly like a—" The rock rose grumbling, stretched, and dropped on all fours to lumber away along the path. Tobias sat down abruptly. "Sweet Jesus—" Next moment he was flat on his face with Nick on top of him. A large boulder hit where he had been sitting and bounced off to rumble down the mountainside.

"'Ware rock!" came a belated cry from above and they looked up to see de Longhi and the frightened guide.

"'Ware bear!" shouted back Tobias and de Longhi scrambled to his feet, bringing up his crossbow.

"Give me a battlefield any day," grumbled Toby. "Get off me. Incidentally, my thanks."

Nicholas got cautiously to his feet. "Thought you were enjoying this," he said.

"Didn't reckon on bears."

A fine chamois had got up and with a great hallooing and blowing of horns the chase was on. The graceful creature leapt from crag to crag, daring them ever higher, and the mountain men, nimble as their quarry, went in hot pursuit. They were using their picks now, and Nick drove his deep into a fissure and paused to admire the beautiful animal. Tobias turned back, thinking he needed help, and at that moment, de Longhi, above, appeared to lose his footing and slithered down on them. Misjudging, he went over the edge, taking Tobias with him. Toby's pick caught and held on the path as Nick grabbed his belt and he hung there bent in half with all de Longhi's weight on his legs. Nick braced his knee against the haft of his pick and lay down, shrugging his rope off his shoulder. He had firm hold of Toby and with his free hand he looped the rope twice round the pick handle and let it fall past de Longhi's shoulder. The man made no effort to loose a hand to take it and clung on with one arm round Toby's legs, his pick dangling useless in the other. Toby was fighting to breathe and his hands were beginning to slip. Nick would not be able to hold them both, he peered over and saw what the man was about. He pulled out his dagger and looked into de Longhi's face. "Help yourself, fool, or by God I'll help you down."

The man saw he meant it, drove in his pick at knee level, stood on it, took the rope and swung onto it. Nicholas was ready for him and had tight hold of the other end, praying his pick would hold. Toby, freed, got a knee on the ledge, Nick heaved and he was up, rolling on his back and dragging in air. Presently, first a hand then de Longhi's head appeared and Nick backed away to give him plenty of room.

A guide came helter-skelter down, aghast at such an accident happening to the esteemed and competent Marquis de Longhi. Nick and Tobias were inclined to agree. To the unharmed marquis' disgust all three were shepherded back down the mountainside, and the guide went off at a jog-trot to fetch horses.

De Longhi elected to follow him. He turned with a stiff bow. "My thanks, my lord. For my life."

Nick shrugged and sat down, "I think you were in little danger, Monsieur le Marquis."

Tobias watched the Frenchman swagger off down the path.

"Amateur," he grunted.

With the rest of the party at the hunt, supper was a quiet affair, taken by Nick and Tobias with Challoner in his chamber and, with Toby in considerable pain, Nicholas took his turn to lie on guard across the door. He himself had a pulled hamstring to show for the episode and hobbled down in the morning in time for the tail end of a fine row. Bullivant's corpulent habit had kept him from the hunt and he was standing in the hall exchanging angry words with de Longhi. The marquis shrugged and stalked off, leaving Bullivant to quarrel violently with his wife. Shortly afterwards, the Bullivant family left – maidservant and children in tears and Mistress Bullivant with a nicely developing black eye.

"Thieves falling out, I see," muttered Tobias, still slightly bent over and hurting.

"Narrows the field," said Nick.

"Someone searched my room. Try the woman."

"My idea exactly."

Later on, the triumphant hunting party rolled in, boasting of their cuts and bruises and amazing feats of valour. No one had been killed, and they were in fine fettle for the feast that night. It began early and went on late: Nick's injury kept him from dancing and he spent the time in profitable dalliance with Diane de Longhi. She professed the deepest sympathy for his hurt and gratitude for her brother's safe return and, as the party grew boisterous, withdrew with many meaningful sighs and much pressing of palms.

Nicholas looked in on Challoner, who was deep asleep, and took up the empty cup of laudanum beside his bed. He winked at Toby, who raised an eyebrow, and left him to drag his truckle bed across the door. Up in his own chamber, he placed the cup with its aromatic dregs on a stool by his bed, undressed and turned in without bolting the door.

Time passed. He struggled to stay awake, and was beginning to think he had misjudged when the latch lifted softly and he smelt her.

A hunter's moon was enough to light the room. He had left all the hangings drawn back and watched through his lashes as she came closer, naked but for an open robe, her breasts a delicate pear-shape, the nipples pointing the thin lawn. Nick fought a silent battle with himself. She stretched out a hand to shake him gently, then saw the cup. She sniffed it, and sighed – with regret or relief, he could not say. She did shake him then, quite roughly, and he rolled over and began to snore. She wasted no more time, and set about a thorough search, his pillows and person first, which caused him some difficulty, and then his belongings. She did not trouble to hide her body and Nick began to think about waking up. But no, the point was proven and he did not want her round his neck for the rest of the journey. And he did not care for her smell.

She was very thorough and as there was nothing to find save Kate's last letter, she found nothing. She came to stand by the bed, hand to mouth, uncertain. He snored on and with a shrug she turned away.

Nick fell asleep.

He slept late and limped down next morning to find Toby foraging among the remains of breakfast. No sign of the ladies. He sat down and pulled a planchet of bread towards him.

"She came and went," he said. "You know the way. Empty-handed on both counts, I might add. He'll either give up, or turn his attention back to you, Toby."

"Excellent," said Toby, grumpily rubbing his sore stomach. "Why not just cut his throat and have done?"

"I have a better idea."

The young daughter of the house was at her sewing in the best light she could find, under the main window in the solar. She made a pretty picture and she played right into his hands. Of course she would be delighted to show him the splendours of the hall and the tapestries, and joined in regretting the passing of chivalric pursuits. She clapped her hands at his description of the royal tourney and swallowed the bait whole.

"But we have knights among us! A contest – I shall speak to my father at once…"

His object achieved, Nick played the part of a modest participant and agreed to make the arrangements. When told, Tobias raised an eyebrow.

"And how do you intend to kill him?"

"With a bated sword? I shall take my chance. What I would like you to do, friend, is search their belongings while I keep him occupied. If I can disable him as well, so much the better."

Count Barger was delighted with this opportunity for display and sent for all his friends. The thing burgeoned into a full-scale event of wrestling, fencing and shooting at a target; prizes would be given. The castle was like an overturned anthill, servants scurried about, a small mountain of food was prepared and weapons found. The banqueting table was put to one side, the floor was sanded, and targets were set up in the courtyard outside. A lady – the count's daughter – was chosen as Queen of the Revels and the stage was set. Nick had enlisted the help of one of Barger's guests, Baron Suchet. It was a wonder such a man was there; he was a nobleman of the old school, a stickler for honour and correct procedure, an old duelling scar across his cheek and a cleft near the hairline from a more serious encounter. He would be master of the fencing. Nick declined to put his sore leg to the strains of wrestling, choosing instead to watch Tobias trying not to win the archery contest. Covered in glory and carrying his prize, he accompanied Nick to check the weapons. The bouts were to be fought with rapier and dagger, all safely buttoned. Lots were drawn, and play commenced.

Inevitably, as the only two real swordsmen present, the final bout was between Nicholas and de Longhi. They seemed evenly matched; if there was an advantage it was to de Longhi, who was uninjured. The punctilious Suchet pointed this out and de Longhi shrugged.

"I will allow him a hit."

Suchet frowned at his tone and Nick shook his head. "I fancy I can win at the odds."

De Longhi laughed and strolled across to take up an elegant pose at the mark. Nicholas gave his sword to O'Dowd to hold and took his time choosing a rapier of the right length and heft from those laid ready on the table.

He drew his dagger and walked to stand straight-backed and relaxed, waiting. Tobias slipped away.

The baron approached for the ceremonial bow and salute, knocked up their blades and retired precipitately. Nothing happened. De Longhi's point stirred, tracing a lazy circle. Nick watched him. The man smiled and exploded into a flurry of attacking moves, sword and dagger flashing a dizzying pattern, black against the light. Nick moved to the side, and again, to get the light at his back. De Longhi came on, a dazzling display of thrust and counter thrust.

"My brother is said to be a master swordsman," murmured Diane, perfectly audible in the silent room.

Stamp and lunge, retire and traverse, circle and advance, de Longhi tried in vain, over and over, to pierce the barrier of steel that blocked his every move.

"Fight, damn you!" he shouted. Nicholas dropped his guard, inviting the lunge, his blade hissed along his opponent's and neatly popped off a button.

"A hit!" called the baron, coming forward. De Longhi lost his temper. Seething, he flung down the rapier.

"Playfighting is for boys," he snarled and ran to the table for his own unbated weapon.

"As you wish, m'sieur." Nick turned and O'Dowd threw him his sword.

115

"My lords, gentlemen…" The shocked Suchet started forward to knock up their swords and stop them, but too late, the fight had started.

De Longhi was indeed an excellent swordsman and duellist, trained at the French court in the elegant Italian style. Nick's rapier was an extension of his finger, his weight beautifully balanced. His style polished by the best swordsman in Venice, he still fenced like a fighter, cool and instinctive.

Point circling point, daggers weaving figures of eight, the first moves were slow and exploring, the first swift lunge and riposte rang out to draw a gasp from the watching crowd. De Longhi struck like a snake, his point was turned aside and Nick's dagger flashed across to lock between them. They thrust apart, then en garde and thrust and parry, forward and back, sparks flying from the flashing blades. Locked together again, Nick disengaged with a shout and a swift passado, running past his opponent to take him by surprise, slashing his laces as he went. Before de Longhi could turn, Nick's point had pierced the padding of his breeches and pricked his backside.

"A hit!"

De Longhi howled with fury and, pushing the horrified baron out of the way, hurled himself, hose slipping, at his elusive opponent. Odds were now even: de Longhi was hampered and had lost the last rags of control. This had never been the gentlemanly exhibition of skill the baron intended, and now it developed into a real brawl, the combatants reeling round the room, scattering the spectators in their wake. Lunge and engage, they were breast to breast for a second, and with a twist of Nick's blade, de Longhi's dagger flew across the floor. A convulsive heave from de Longhi and Nick's foot slipped, his hurt leg gave under him and he fell at the feet of the stuffed bear. To a groan from the crowd, de Longhi's sword swept down to cleave his enemy's neck, to meet a cruciform of steel held by sinews of iron. His sword almost jarred out of his hand, he backed away, and Nick got to his feet, drove his dagger into the bear's chest and went on the attack. Rapiers only now.

Tobias slid back into the hall in time to see a furious de Longhi being driven back into the circle of watchers and desperately countering a flashing onslaught. De Longhi dodged behind his sister, his point reached over her shoulder and opened a slash across Nick's cheekbone. The room held its breath. To a moan of anguish from Baron Suchet, Nicholas stepped back.

"Touché. My thanks, m'sieur. The obligatory scar."

It was the turning point, for Nick as well as the contest: all the pangs of frustrated love and the clinging webs of intrigue dropped away, his eyes were sparkling as he handed Diane out of the way and hounded de Longhi back into the centre. This he could do.

The only sound was the rasp and ring of the blades, the stamp and slither of feet and de Longhi's ragged breathing. Beside Tobias, old Baron Suchet drew a breath.

"Upon my soul, the boy's a swordsman!"

Enjoying himself now, Nick forced his opponent steadily backwards, de Longhi parried just in time, their hilts locked and he gave ground, backing into the leaking bear. He snatched out Nick's dagger and brought it round in a vicious sweep. Nick seized his wrist and closed with him; they reeled across under the gallery. A squeeze and a twist and the dagger dropped, Nick leapt and thrust and his point went through de Longhi's shoulder. The man fell back into the steely embrace of the suit of armour, the antlered head on the wall leaned out and fell. Something snapped and de

Longhi screamed. Nicholas stood back, wiping his point on his sleeve. He bowed an apology to the excited Baron Suchet as Diane flew across to kneel by her lover and Tobias sauntered through the wreck of the room to offer his kerchief.

"Better let me see to that," he said. "Welcome back, Nick."

In his bed-chamber, Tobias stitched the cheek as delicately as a woman hemming a petticoat, to the accompaniment of Challoner and O'Dowd re-living the fight blow by blow.

"What did you find?" asked Nick.

"Be still. Like I said, a pair of amateurs: their instructions – unsigned, I'm sorry to say – hidden where anyone could find them. Proof at least. There. Don't smile for a bit."

Nick gave him a lop-sided grin. "Just when there's something to smile about," he said.

Chapter Six

O'Dowd left with a trumpet-call and a gay rataplan on the drum, bound for Geneva and home, taking with him John Challoner, Jocelyn Russell, the bankers and their families and the original escort. It was a reduced company that was to cross the St Gotthard: three merchants bound for Milan, Venice and Naples, an envoy to Venice and points east, a young man and his bear-leader and an artist on his way to Vicenza. All able-bodied men: only two of the Rokesby escort, brothers, accompanied them.

His foot in the stirrup, Toby observed,

"It's a swine of a crossing, this. We should try to reach the hospice before nightfall." The groom loading the cart looked up.

"As to that, sir, did the master not tell you? It's gone, sir – not that they aren't rebuilding of it, but it's not what you might be expecting."

"Gone?"

"Aye, sir. Over-run by a pack of German mercenaries this winter past. Only a few monks left, they say."

After a long silence, Tobias said, "We seem to have chosen a bad time. They're half-way through building a new bridge, stands to reason they won't have spared much time for the old one."

"Bridge?" said Nick.

"The Devil's Bridge, they call it. I doubt we'll get the cart across it. Come on, we shall contrive." So saying he vaulted into the saddle and clattered off.

The first part of the journey skirted the shore of a great lake ("Lucern," said Toby,) and followed the river beyond, ("the Suhr," said Toby,) and then through a steep-sided valley to a little town called Bellinzona. Here they exchanged the cart for a baggage mule and Toby thanked his maker there were no women requiring litters and the help of the local peasants. The ascent of the ridge was vertiginous, and to Nicholas one long nightmare. Some parts of the track were horribly narrow, chopped out of the living rock; there were gaps spanned by suspended bridges, and although the views and waterfalls were spectacular he had no eyes for them. After a final steep climb between the peaks of Camoghe and Tamara, they came in sight of the ruined hospice. Toby groaned.

"I had hoped the tale was false," he said. As they drew near, they could see that work was indeed going on, about to be abandoned for the night. One of the monks, a working robe of sackcloth over his habit, came to welcome them. There was only plain fare, he told them, and one shared dormitory, the rest had been laid waste. "But the men were fleeing from the war," said the eldest of the monks, "they were starving, beyond reason."

Shaking his head, Tobias took some of their party to help with food and blankets, Nick called the two brothers, Peter and Paul Taylor, to bed down the animals. In spite of, or perhaps because of, the spartan conditions, they enjoyed the simple meal, eaten in the open round a roaring fire. Mead was passed round. The monks might have lost their hospice, but not their vocation; it was rare hospitality. It was cold, the air thin and clear. There was no moon at first to dim the brightness of the stars, and the two friends strolled away from the light of the fire to name them. As the moon slowly rose Nick was able to marvel at the majesty of the country through which they had passed, peak beyond peak tipped with snow, white waterfalls and dark defiles, at the top of their world, the highest he had ever been.

The descent the next day was a little easier but no less terrifying. The gradients were still steep and the paths narrow, and Nicholas dreaded at every turn to see the notorious Devil's Bridge. A hairpin turn and there it was, a wooden span with no handrail flung across a deep gorge, its river a thread at the bottom. A puddle of cold sweat gathered at the base of Nick's spine, and he was conscious of his heart pounding his chest.

Men were working on the new stone bridge, the arches growing from the riverbed and the sides of the gorge, and Toby waved. Three hundred feet down, a row of tiny faces gazed up and someone waved his cap, bright red in the sunshine. Nick swallowed. The party dismounted and one of the merchants fell to his knees.

Tobias had made this crossing before and had come prepared, with a plan. He had brought rope and tying off one round a rock at waist height, he walked calmly across the planked bridge, hauled it tight and fastened it. He made the return journey in the same way with a second rope and lo, however illusory, the drop had lost some of its terror; there was something to hold onto. One by one, helped by Peter and Paul, the travellers led their horses across, each man anchored to the rope-rail with a running loop, Tobias going first, the muleteer with the baggage and Nicholas bringing up the rear. The artist carried a long thin wood panel, on which was depicted yet another "Last Supper" or "Wedding at Cana", or a "Feast of Fools"; Nick had not been able to make out which. The man had this slung across his back, and at the last moment he decided not to burden himself with it and thrust it among the packages borne by the mule. Inevitably, halfway across it slid out of its sacking and planed over the edge, lazily twirling down, graceful as a sycamore seed.

"My painting!" yelled the painter, the startled mule balked and the rest of its load tilted. "My ducats!" shouted the bankers.

"Quiet," said Tobias, and came back to where the frightened animal stood trembling, back on its haunches, front feet stiffly planted, immovable.

He went to the animal's head, speaking quietly to it, and sidling round behind, began to unload the baggage. The Taylor brothers went to help him, and once free of its load, the mule consented to stand up. And there it stayed, stubborn and trembling. Nick could hardly breathe, surely the bridge was not constructed to bear so much weight concentrated in one spot. Tobias evidently thought so too, for he ordered the brothers to start ferrying the bags and boxes, himself staying with the mule. The muleteer dropped the lead-rope, picked up the last pack and made for safety. The baggage safe, alone with the mule, Toby came to its head and slowly coaxed it leg by obstinate leg on across the divide. Nick followed close behind, admiring, and a cheer went up from the bridge-builders below. Nick clapped his friend on the shoulder.

"A feat to remember, Tobias."

"We're all afraid of something," muttered Toby. "Just don't put me near any snakes."

After that, the journey seemed easy; the gradients were kinder, the paths wider. All manner of wild flowers bloomed among the rocks, flame-blue gentian, edelweiss, rock roses and a tiny star-shaped yellow flower. Toby picked one and stuck it in his cap. After some five hours, with rests, skirting the lakes of Lugano and

Como, they gradually descended from the firs of the mountains through woods of silver birch and whitebeam to the slopes above the plain of Lombardy. From one viewing point, it spread out below them: a tranquil landscape of laced rivers and striped fields, spiked with cypress and poplar, the fortified walls and castle turret of Milan a fretted silhouette in the distance against the lowering sun.

Tobias would stay vigilant until his party reached Naples, but his shoulders relaxed a little as he turned to grin at Nick.

"Thus far, by the grace of God," he said.

"And some meticulous forward planning. Take some credit, man."

Chapter Seven

The envoy to the Turkish court would go on to Milan with the party and ride post to Venice. Nicholas took his leave of Toby and peeled off eastward to take a more direct road to Verona and Kit Marlowe. Once alone, all his troubles came flying back, buzzing and pricking like the flies that plagued him as he rode across the plain in the muggy warmth, and like the flies he tried to swat them away. On the second day, as he rode through the fields, he came upon a young labourer with his family. He watched the joy on the man's face as his little boy came to him in a stumbling run, to be caught up and tossed in the air with squeals of delight. Nick's whole self ached for the feel of Jack's sturdy body in his hands, fat little fingers patting his face. He came to a decision. Again. When his tasks were done, he was going home. For the moment, his first concern was Kit Marlowe.

He arrived at the charming little house he had taken for Marlowe when they first fled from London to find it shuttered, dark and empty, evidently no longer lived in. Alarmed, he tried first their favourite tavern, and then others, finding Kit at last in the worst of them, slumped over a pile of papers in the heat and din and stink, gloomily stabbing his quill into the ribbed tabletop. He seemed to be in the throes of a difficult composition and he showed no surprise at seeing Nick. Hiding his dismay, Nick wasted no time in telling him of his decision to go home when his stint in Venice was done, throwing off his cloak and sitting down opposite him, his back to a group of mercenaries celebrating having money in their pockets. Marlowe was his usual intransigent self, laughing at Nick's proposal, intent on keeping him close. Deeply into a new work, which seemed to involve some dilatory prince and a wicked uncle, he sat there in his stained and shabby doublet, ignoring the noise and press of bodies, feverish words tumbling over one another in his eagerness. He looked older, febrile and unwell, no longer the nattily dressed, sophisticated scholar of the Mermaid tavern; his elite circle of friends would hardly have recognised him. Nick was worried, and when the inevitable fight broke out behind him, hauled him back to the squalid lodging over a papermaker's shop, where he apparently now lived. Marlowe was still in the grip of this new idea; seemingly Nick's arrival had inspired him, and he seized quill and paper to begin scribbling furiously.

Nick sighed. He had come to see Marlowe fully determined to finish this task he had been set and go home as soon as possible, but the state he found Marlowe in deterred him yet again. His own plans must wait, as always coming second to this great poet's needs. Marlowe must be cared for, fed, made to change his clothes and sleep, and Nick prepared to see it out, trimming the wicks in the lamps and making up the fire before settling himself to rest on the floor in front of it. Worn out, body and spirit, he fell asleep.

Hours or minutes later he was startled awake by a cry of fury. Marlowe was up and striding around, swearing and crumpling sheets of scrip.

"Curse you, you miserable tripehound! The thread is broken!

Why must you come with this talk of home, of England, where I may not go! Why do you come, only to talk of leaving – when I see you I know I am truly lonely…"

"I am here, Kit. As long as you need me." Something in the exhausted voice and tired eyes stopped Marlowe in his tracks.

"I am a selfish bitch," he said quietly. "Something has happened, sweeting." He came to kneel at Nick's side and take his hand. It was too much for Nicholas: the dam broke and the story tumbled out, he was back riding over the hill to see Rokesby burning…

The shutters banged in the shop below as the papermaker arrived to start the day's work, and in the quiet room above the hoarse voice ceased at last. Marlowe had Nick in close embrace, tears streaming down his face.

"Oh, my Niccolo…and I have treated you like a child, here to do my bidding, mocked at you. Forgive me. And this, here on your face." He stroked a gentle finger beside the healing cut. "Who did this? Here, a glass of wine and we will talk – what would you have me do?"

Nick managed a smile. "Nothing, Kit. Finish your new play for me to take back for Will Shakespeare, when my duty here is done. I can only do what is laid down for me – time will show the rest. I'm done with trying to make decisions." The familiar blank look came into Marlowe's eyes, he turned abruptly and went back to his table. He stood for a moment looking down at his manuscript, then seized a quill and sat down to begin writing. Nicholas waited for a few minutes, watching him. Kit was scribbling furiously, showering blots, lost, and presently Nick, equally lost, shrugged and left him to it.

He found Tom Walsingham's letter and left it where Marlowe would see it and went to attend to his horses. Leaving them with a full hayrack, he made his way across the winding river and up the sugar-loaf hill on the other side. Here he sat elbows on knees watching the little town come to life, carts lumbering in with produce for the market, workers making their way into the fields; a soldier in half-armour clattered down the road from the castle that circled the top of the hill and tipped him a greeting. Spirals of mist rose from the river as the day warmed up. Larks sang.

Telling his tale seemed to have brought an answer. He had been wrong to leave as he had and in time he would go back. For the present, he had work to do, a promise to keep. Marlowe and his words could do more than petty politics. 'For those with ears to hear,' said a small voice.

"If not now, then it will come," he said aloud.

Later, a little rested and more settled in mind, he went to find Julia, the comely young widow who had looked after them before, and had welcomed him into her bed. If he was hoping for similar favours on this occasion, he was to be disappointed. He met Julia on his way, a heavy basket on her arm, coming from market. No longer in widow's garb, she was in country clothes, her apron bulging over an obvious pregnancy. She was married again, she told him, and her new husband had forbidden her to have anything to do with Marlowe and his questionable friends. Nick drew her into the shadow of the round-arched church.

"I suppose I am tarred with the same brush," he said. "I'm glad to see you so happy, *cara*." He felt in his pouch. "Something for the babe—"

She was looking anxiously over her shoulder.

"No, no, Mario will want to know…"

"Yes. I see. At least tell me what happened. When I left—"

"There was no holding him, Niccolo," she said. "I tried, I knew you would wish it, but he grew wilder and wilder – and the parties…There was a quarrel. That young man - you remember – left and took all he had. Since then there have been others – I could not…"

The poor girl was blushing and Nick took her hand and kissed it. "Of course not. I should have been here. He seemed settled when I went, but it is very hard for him, Julia. He has to make a new life for himself. It is hard. And I must leave him again, I'm already late. But he is working now, in the grip of it…"

"He is a man possessed," said Julia, crossing herself. "Not an evil spirit, Niccolo, I know that, but he frightens me."

"He can only harm himself by neglect. We will be rewarded, I promise you. Not with money, but with what he will bring forth. He is a great man."

"I may not help you, Niccolo, there has been talk enough. But you love him, and so I will keep watch. Leave me some token I can send if you are needed."

It was hardly fair, he realised, to burden Julia with such a task and he shook his head.

"I shall contrive. Go with your God, little one, and be happy." He bent to kiss her cheek and watched her make her way up the cobbled street, kilted skirts swinging, to be met at her door by a burly young man with a scowl on his face. He sighed and turned away.

"All this matrimony is a sad mistake," he grumbled to himself. "Much ado about very little. Can't see Tobias as a married man, either." He was spitting into the wind, and he knew it.

He sought out the landlord of the little house in the courtyard that had seen the birth of Romeo and his Juliet. The man was obliging enough to agree to find servants – for a fee, of course – and Nick took himself off to find the man he remembered from the night-long discussions in the garden, setting the world to rights.

A vigorous man in his fifties, Professore Paulo Montano was eking a meagre living giving lessons in Greek and mathematics, and he jumped at Nick's offer of free bed and board in exchange for congenial companionship. He spoke no English and Nick did not ask why he no longer taught at the University of Padua. No doubt Kit would know. And the manuscript would be safe from prying eyes.

The servants arrived, a man and his wife to cook and clean, and over the next few days they set about resettling the abstracted poet.

Marlowe left his writing only when it was forcibly taken away from him, following it to the desk set for him by the window into the garden, sitting down at once to dip his quill in the ink. He ate what was put under his nose, slept when he could no longer see the page. At one point he seemed to be stuck, sitting gazing unseeing at the wall. Nick seized the chance and took him down to the river for exercise, the professor holding the poet's other arm. They spoke over Marlowe's head, trying to draw him in and, finally running out of polite conversation, Nick tried to make an amusing tale of the gothick castle and the duel with de Longhi. Marlowe's head came up and he stood still. "Tell me again," he said. But before Nick had finished, he had turned on his heel and was hurrying back up the hill, muttering. Nick shrugged and let him go.

He had given up his sleeping quarters to Montano, and at last, with Kit relaxed and working at a less frenetic speed, felt free to make ready to leave for Venice. All this domestic detail had become increasingly irksome, and he found himself actually looking forward to his stint as her Majesty's ambassador.

Dressed and packed, he went to bid farewell to his possessed poet. In the grip of his daemon, Marlowe looked up with blind eyes and waved him away. Nick bent and lifted back a lock of hair to kiss the white forehead. For a moment, Kit was back, dropping the quill to seize Nick's hand in both his.

"I owe you this, Nick. This is for you – come back soon, sweeting, I shall miss you."

No you won't, thought Nick. *As soon as my back's turned, you'll be back in your gloomy palace with your mad prince for company.*

"You will be looked after," he said. "I'll be back as soon as I can. I'll write." But Marlowe had already turned back to his work.

Nick went to saddle Oberon.

Chapter Eight

Nicholas Talbot's first entry into the palatial villa where Henry, Lord Stanley entertained and housed his considerable entourage was a quiet one. No fanfares and no display. Nick trod up the imposing flight of shallow steps alone, no royal deerhound to keep him company this time. Indeed, "Where is your hound?" were the first words to greet him as he entered the sunlit room. Nick had surmised – and very much hoped – that owing to the many delays on his journey the ambassador would already have had news of his recall. And so it proved.

Lord Stanley beckoned him irritably forward. He was lying on a daybed, a leg swollen with gout propped on a cushioned stool. The tall open windows looked out on a formal garden where fountains played and countless birds whistled and sang to their caged counterparts dotted about the room.

"I shall miss all this," said Stanley, waving his arm. "M'birds and so on. You'll look after them for me?" More likely to set them free, Nicholas bowed politely. "Tell you what I shan't miss, young Talbot – all the goddam letter-writing." He nodded at the table in the corner, fully six feet square, at which laboured two secretaries, half submerged in a sea of unrolling scrolls. Nick's sensitive nose caught the whiff of an ageing unwashed body, the smell apparent in spite of the open window, and he noticed a bed set against the wall, covered with gold-laced velvet, a close-stool beside it. The previous busy world of statesmanship, balls and elaborate dinners seemed to have shrunk to the compass of this one room.

"I had no notion you were sick, my lord. I am sorry to have been delayed so long, you must be anxious to be at home."

"At home! That would be a fine thing. If you think you can slide quietly in and take over you are very much in the wrong of it, young man." He reached for the handsome pitcher at his side and splashed wine into a generous goblet. "Hah! Tell him, Martin. Five more secretaries in the next room dealing with all the arrangements, never mind the painters and carpenters and chefs and masque makers for the entertainments, hey, Martin?" One of the men at the table raised a pouched and gloomy face, gave a shake of the head and returned to his work. "Not to mention the blasted transport."

"My post is only temporary, my lord—"

"Yes, and the whole damn-fool charade will have to be gone through again. Still, that will be your concern, not mine. My fault. Made a point of telling Vanni who found their proofs for them last year – you won't be allowed to pass unnoticed, Talbot."

"That's a pity."

"Yes, well. Spilt milk, water under the new bridge, hey? Sit down, sit down, find yourself something to drink out of— Oh, by the way, you'll find a fairly tangible reward waiting for you in your rooms. Gifted by the Council. Don't spend it all at once."

"My grateful thanks, my lord." Nick took a goblet from the gilded and inlaid sideboard, polished it with the square of linen he kept on him and poured himself wine. It was a fine, full-bodied sherris-sack. He wandered to the window and stood looking out.

"What are all these arrangements?"

"Someone'll tell you. And there's this business with the Pope."

"My lord?"

"Call me Henry, for God's sake. The Vatican's decided to be busy chasing all the Jews out of Rome and wants Venice to do the same. Imagine! If the Doge closed down the Business Quarter, what would happen to trade, hey? Venice might as well shut up shop and slide into the sea. Not content with that, Clement wants to forbid printing the Talmud. Half our presses would be out of work! They're threatened by the damn French as it is. Pah! Damn this leg. Martin, my medicine. No, my lad, there's trouble brewing, so drink and be merry while you can. Grimani likes things lavish, remember."

Nick did remember. An unforgettable banquet given by the Doge to celebrate his wife's birthday came to mind. It had lasted three days. Even by Venetian standards it had been lavish indeed.

The door opened and a page ushered in a doctor and his assistant, carrying a bag, a cupping-bowl and a covered basin apparently holding leeches. One was escaping down the side. Stanley groaned and Nick swallowed the rest of his wine and bowed his way out, running down the stairs into the fresh air of the courtyard. Breathing deep, he leaned against the wall for a moment and thought. Presently, he called for his horse to ride out to Callisto and visit his fencing master, Pietro Cavalli. He went for no other reason but a desire for freedom and exercise and contact with Cavalli's astringent personality.

Cavalli professed himself delighted to see Nicholas Talbot again, made no remark about the missing hound and commented only on the red line across his cheek.

"A little careless, *signore*?" He obliged with two hours of exhausting practice and left Nick with a jug of water and a cloth to mop himself, going into the quiet house to return with a folded note.

"This was left some weeks ago, my lord Rokesby. In case you should come." He waved away Nick's offer of payment.

"There is little more I can teach you, *signore*. I enjoyed our little bout. Come again." He paused. "Our mutual friend sent word also. Let me think. It was one word only…Galicia, that was it. The name of a ship, perhaps?"

Gallio, turned pirate, thought Nick. "Perhaps. Or more likely a woman, don't you think?"

Cavalli laughed. "No doubt. He has as many lives as a cat, that one, and a woman for every one. Come again, *signore*, when you can escape your duties."

Riding slowly back, Nick unfolded the note. It contained simply an address and a crudely drawn sign of the zodiac. Gemini. So, the Antolini twins were still in Venice. He had been waiting for these two to show themselves. If they had not wanted to be found, it was no use looking for them. Now they had come to him. He sighed, tore up the scrap of paper and let it flutter away on the breeze. He had the kind of memory that stored information without effort. It had proved useful in his days as a player and soaked up languages as visual images. He visualised the twins now, as he had last seen them, each a mirror image of the other, hangdog and anxious, huddled behind a table in the worst tavern in town. He would have to seek them out later, but not yet.

Back at the villa on the Brenta canal, he found the place in uproar, looking for him. Apparently he had to be fitted for clothes and thoroughly briefed in the procedures of the next few days. His plans for the evening, which had included a visit to La

Bellissima, Gallio's erstwhile mistress, being thwarted, Nick allowed things to take their course. Like the Antolini, she would have to wait.

The next two weeks were a madness of extravagance. For a day or two there was a constant refrain of "my lord Stanley always…" and "when my lord Stanley was inducted…" until it was understood that my lord Rokesby had ideas of his own. He had been here before, after all, as Envoy, and although he knew the ropes to a certain extent, he had no mind to set an impossible standard for his successor. Nevertheless what he did must be worthy of his position and of his craft as an actor. He was astonished and delighted therefore, when Christopher Marlowe, all dark sophistication, sauntered through the door. He was exquisite. Doublet and breeches of indigo satin, with the merest hint of silver embroidery, were tailored to perfection and showed an excellent silken leg. His beard was a witty outline to his mouth and his hair fell clean and curled over his shoulder. He smelled exotic.

Nick jumped up as the playwright swept off his feathered cap with a flourish.

"Your one and only jigmaker, my lord, *masquer extraordinaire*, at your service."

Nick shut the door in the footman's face and turned, to be swept into a vast hug and kissed on both cheeks. Marlowe clapped his hands on Nick's shoulders and held him at arm's length. They gazed at each other. Nick saw again that his beloved poet had aged, silver showed in the black elflocks, his lustrous sloe-black eyes shone deeper in his head. His elegant clothes were, on closer view, a little worn, but over all still hung the power of the man. For his part, Marlowe now saw clearly for the first time, a tall young man coming to his full strength, with the wide brow of a thinker, the mouth and muscle of a fighter. His eyes sparkled.

"So my young cub has grown into a lion! An English lion to roar in St Mark's Square. Let them beware."

"You come openly, Kit…"

"M'sieur Parolles, if you recall, my dear. Much in demand for my masques and entertainments. French, Greek, Latin, what you will – pouf!" He flicked his fingers and handed Nick a parcel of scrip. "Here you are. Commissioned a month ago, the Ambassador's masque for the Doge. And I have just the man to set it on. A comely young Englishman, here to study. Quite charming – a coming man, I assure you. I even like his accent."

"Have you thought more of what I told you?"

"Yes indeed. All most unfortunate and I feel for you, sweeting. But as they say, it's the dog on the spot that gets the biscuit." He laughed at the look on Nick's face. "Sorry, my dear, sorry. Unkind and uncalled for. My current writings must be coarsening me. We will speak of all these things again in proper terms and in the proper place. Not here and not now. Here you are the Ambassador, not my friend. Will you see Master Jones? I'll have no other, I warn you." A servant entered with a tray and Nick gathered his wits.

"Of course. Leave this with me and ask Master Jones to make an appointment. Your health, M'sieur Parolles. One has heard of your skill in these matters. I look forward to reading it." Marlowe smiled a mischievous smile over the rim of his goblet.

"I shall send my young genius to wait on you, my lord. Time is of the essence if we are to do her Majesty's representative credit." He stood up and stretched. "Incidentally – the Antolini…I'm sure they will have been in touch. It occurs to me that I have never seen that charming pair apart. They seem joined like those I saw

136

at the Bartlemas Fair. What an opportunity for befuddlement they miss – for comedy if not for intrigue." His eyes were vague, unfocussed. "Mmm. More to be mined from that vein, I feel…"

The outraged footman was standing in the doorway. Marlowe set down his cup, adjusted his cap at a jaunty angle, bowed low and, with a wink, was gone.

Slightly breathless, Nick waved away the servant and sat down to pick up the roll of scrip.

"La Serenissima rising from the waves." He began to read. The piece was an allegory, the two figures of Logic and Reason personified, supporting a beautiful woman, La Serenissima, fighting to free her from a horde of greedy elements striving to drag her down. She rose triumphant, as Venice had risen from the sands and misty swamps of the Lagoon. Figures representing the Doge and Council came to cluster at her knees like children. The language was powerful, the imagery resonant, Marlowe had gone back to his mighty line. This made Nick think Marlowe had his tongue in his cheek for most of the piece, added to a deal of wishful thinking. This triumph of reason was what he would like to see at home in England. *Don't give up, Kit,* thought Nick. *Things are changing.*

There were attached several pages of delightfully accomplished drawings, showing the great Venetian buildings rising slowly behind the players. Clear diagrams indicated how this would be done. Excited, quite forgetting his other problems, Nick read it again. It was far better – and shorter – than the other offerings on his desk. He would make it the climax of the ceremony rather than a mere accompaniment to the banquet, and he would not stint in its making. There were some compensations for this posting after all.

An address was scribbled on the back of the drawings and Nick sent for the talented Master Jones forthwith.

Inigo Jones arrived as Nick was dressing for a ball given in his honour at Lord Stanley's official residence on the della Beccari. Two new suits of clothes had been delivered and Nick, anticipating a long hot night, opted for the sleeveless doublet and Venetians of almond-green satin embroidered with silver and buttoned with peridots. All this finery went with the job, he supposed. He had got as far as breeches and fine-pleated linen shirt, the full sleeves embroidered with green, when a knock came on the door. Expecting his valet, Nick called him in and turned, holding out a ribboned cuff. A young man his own age stood there, twisting his cap in ink-ingrained fingers. He had a roll of paper under his arm.

"You sent for me, my lord. Inigo Jones." He spoke with the lilt of the Welsh mountains overlaid with a London twang, and Nick was suddenly back at home listening to the shepherd who minded the Rokesby flocks.

"I gather you have something to show me," he said. The young man hesitated, looking round for a table, and seeing none, stepped forward impatiently to spread the papers on the bed. The valet hissed, and Nick leaned over to hold down one side. His eyes widened. The figures were beautifully drawn in soft sepia ink, the buildings and ingenious mechanical devices sharply defined in pencil, with notes in tiny writing. Nick looked up.

"You are an engineer?"

"An artist, my lord."

"I can see that. But these devices?"

"I was apprenticed…"

"I need time to study these." The valet was fussing now with ribbons and cuffs. "Come tomorrow…" He looked at the man's hungry eyes. He knew something of the ways of patrons, "…at noon. We will talk and eat, Master Jones."

A footman stood at the door. Jones jumped up hastily and with an awkward bow was gone. Nicholas tore himself reluctantly away from the enticing drawings to attend yet another overlong revel.

Marlowe's young genius was punctual, food was brought, Nick sent his man for wine and settled down with Jones to talk shop. The wine in the flagon on the table went steadily down as the two young men sat and talked and found much in common. Born among the crowded houses of Billingsgate to a cloth maker from the hills of North Wales, Inigo Jones was driven by ambition and a prodigious talent. He was here in the household of William Herbert, and this commission was the first of its kind. He seized on it hungrily, and Nick watched him as figures and buildings and devices came to life under his eager fingers, smudged in with charcoal and ink and fine-pointed lead wrapped with string. His long protuberant nose grew steadily blacker as he talked and drew and rubbed at it. All the lines of his face sloped down, the outer eyelids and the corners of his mouth, giving him a look of permanent enquiry. At that moment, his eyes were intense and brooding, his work absorbing all his energy, talking, talking.

Nicholas interrupted him with a glass of wine. "An interesting name, Inigo. Easy to remember."

"I shall be remembered for more than my name, my lord." The touch of arrogance amused Nick and he warmed to the man. Time was passing and he had another appointment with the officials organising his formal entry.

"Very well. The commission is yours. We will talk again."

The scanty rehearsals for the masque took place in the inner courtyard of the leading lady's imposing rented villa. The Princess Angelica d'Alighieri, voted the most beautiful of all the Patrician ladies at the Doge's court, was to portray the Spirit of Venice. Her husband Alonso was in his dotage, the ridiculously rich lord of a microscopic principality further up the Adriatic, where nobody went except traders in alum, that most valuable commodity for makers of dyestuffs. The lady was wealthy in her own right, coming from a richly forested area in Northern Italy, providing timber for ships, buildings and export. She was also related to the Medici, which was no bad thing for anyone in these times, with a foot in the courts of both Florence and Paris. She herself made nothing of this, showing a childlike interest in everything to do with the masque.

To be the most beautiful in a city of beautiful women, she must be outstanding indeed, thought Nick. His first sight of her took his breath away. A moon-goddess to La Bellissima's sun, she was fair and white-skinned, with a nose as straight and classical as one of Inigo's columns. Her eyes were the colour of the Aegean, her voice cultured and soft. There was an air of innocence about her, in spite of being dressed as became a Venetian woman of fashion, her perfect breasts much on display, veiled only in the lightest of gauze. Master Jones primmed his lips and looked everywhere but at her; Marlowe watched Nicholas.

One quiet evening, the workmen gone and the last rehearsal finished, Nick played truant from his duties and sat with Jones and Marlowe and the lady herself in the loggia to go over final points. She had provided excellent food, and wine had been taken

– enough for her to encourage Nick to entertain her with stories of his adventures, some tall tales, some true.

"'…Longnose Wattie wins the papingay every year,' and someone hit me on the head with a hammer. Or so it felt." The gravelly actor's voice ceased, and the princess leaned forward, laughing.

"One day, my lord, someone will marry you for these tales."

Jones gave a surprisingly coarse laugh. "He'd rather be married for his—"

Marlowe kicked him and he subsided, scarlet. Then, "Why do you say that, lady?" asked Marlowe, intent.

"Oh, the way he tells it perhaps. His voice – the dangers he has passed, the creatures he has seen. I would like to see a llama."

"The dangers he has passed…" murmured the playwright. "Yes. Yes, it is possible. The most unlikely match could come about…"

"All greatly exaggerated for your amusement, my lady."

"I think not, my lord."

Marlowe upended the last bottle. "Let us drink to the power of the spoken word – to enslave, to cozen and persuade, to lead on to glory…" he raised his glass to the woman, the glow of the sunset in her face, "or to love."

Flushing, Nick drank to Angelica, declaiming at the top of his voice, "'And gentlemen in England now abed, shall curse the day they were not here, upon Saint Crispin's Day!' Rousing stuff, Kit. But…" he hesitated. "What of the subtle poisons dripped daily into men's ears? Politics…"

"Cicero was a great orator…" began the lady.

"What of the constant repetition of the catechism?" Marlowe interrupted. "What I say three times is true—"

Jones was frowning and their hostess raised a hand.

"Gentlemen, we stray on to dangerous ground. Let us leave philosophy for another day. M'sieur Parolles, a poem, if you please." Marlowe turned over his pages of scribbled notes and handed Nick a crumpled scrap of paper, one of Inigo's discarded drawings, he noticed. It was a sonnet.

He began to read.

"Let me not to the marriage of true minds admit impediment, love is not love that alters when it alteration finds…" he faltered, and looked up to see Marlowe's eye fixed on him. His colour rising, he read it aloud to the end, folded the paper and stowed it in his sleeve.

"When all this fuss is over, we will talk, Niccolo."

"Words, words, words!" cried Inigo. "A pen is for drawing – see!" He had been busy during all the talk and now cast his work on the floor for them to admire the clever caricatures of themselves. In one Nicholas had the body of a hawk and Angelica a dove, in another the roles were reversed. Marlowe he had shown sprawled Roman-fashion on a couch, pen in hand, watching. Himself he had drawn striding among pygmy buildings, a city in each hand.

"Who has betrayed himself most, I wonder," said Marlowe quietly.

Chapter Nine

The handing over of authority from Henry, Lord Stanley, Her Majesty's Ambassador in Venice, to Nicholas Talbot, Lord Rokesby, his temporary replacement, was an elaborate affair. Venice was in the grip of summer and the moist heat was oppressive. On the day of the induction, all the English in the city, together with the English students from the University of Padua, waited on the quay with the Ambassador and his suite to be rowed across the Lagoon to the island of San Spirito. The significance of this part of the traditional ceremony escaped Nicholas and he would have dispensed with it if he could.

Laced and buttoned into malachite-green taffeta, he stood beside Lord Stanley's litter concerned with its safety as it was lowered into the gondola. The black velvet trappings were getting in the way, and he made himself stand still as the litter tilted dangerously. Stanley was already sweating in his heavy robe of office and lay back on the cushions, fanning his purple face. Nick feared for him, it was still only eight o'clock and it would be a long day. Once on the island, they were received in the gardens of the monastery by the black-robed monks of St Augustine, and waited while a delegation of sixty Venetian noblemen were rowed across in gondolas also decorated with black velvet. Lord Stanley greeted them and the whole assembly was then rowed back to the city by the fleet of gondolas, where by now every street and bridge was crowded with people. "Pointless," thought Nick. To the sound of drums and trumpets and flutes and organised cheering, the procession, headed by the red and black of the Council, paced into the Piazzetta, cleared for the day of its stalls and booths and entertainers. Here the Ambassador's party was presented with the traditional silver baskets of candles, wax, sugar and sweets, and two pages rolled up a butt of malmsey. Nicholas stepped forward, with a herald in the Rokesby black and gold livery, to present the senior member of the Council with the only gifts the Doge was allowed to accept: rosewater, sweet herbs and flowers, and a casket of balsam. This ceremony achieved, everyone bowed, the trumpeters excelled themselves and the gathering broke up, the English contingent to another endless banquet and the Council to whatever deliberations they were concerned with at the moment. In the late afternoon there was a regatta, highly popular, and all Venice turned out to watch. Gondolas assembled like shoals of sprats, be-ribboned and garlanded, their gondoliers arrayed in clothes most unsuited to falling in the canal, to race in teams and singly up the Grande Canale and between the islands. Betting was fierce and the din ferocious as the crowds screamed and shouted their teams to victory and fished the many casualties out of the water. Nicholas retired early.

So ended the first day, the day of the *entrata*. The next day, the day of the *audienza*, promised to be an even greater ordeal for poor Henry Stanley. It began warm, and grew steadily warmer as he was crammed into his official velvet gown, trimmed with lace and lined with fur. Nick feared the unfortunate man would have an apoplexy. He did not look forward to wearing the gown himself.

Coolly expensive in finely pleated black silk, and clean-shaven, he walked beside Stanley's litter along the arcaded frontage of the Doge's Palace to be received by a delegation of senators, in the name of the Republic. More drums and trumpets and they were escorted round to the Gothic gate leading into the building, passing on their way three crosses hung with the upside-down corpses of recently executed traitors. They bore the marks of their torture, and Nick, abruptly reminded of his own sojourn in the Tower in the hands of Topcliffe, straightened his back and looked ahead. Through the gate they came to the Giant Stair and the procession halted for Stanley to be lifted and carried by the linked hands of two enormous Turkish slaves. Up the two long flights of steps to the platform where the Doges were traditionally crowned, and the English entourage fanned out and stayed behind while Stanley was transferred to an equally gigantic pair of guards in elaborate scarlet livery. The next obstacle was Sansorini's magnificent staircase with its gilded ceiling and colossal statues of Neptune and Mars. Stanley was no light weight, but the guards made nothing of the three flights of stairs to the ambassadors' waiting room. They wheeled smartly right through the carved and gilded doors and deposited the out-going Ambassador in the waiting chair. Here there was more evidence of the pervading hand of Palladio in the rich ceiling frescoed by that other grand master, Tintoretto. There was a slight flurry as some of the more elderly councillors and clergy made use of the pots behind a screen in the corner and the trumpets and flutes played gamely on. Nick made sure Stanley was comfortable and the procession rearranged itself. As they entered the great hall he caught a whiff of turpentine among the perfumes and other odours in the room and noticed an unfinished corner of a great painting by the same master who had decorated the anteroom. A forbidding portrayal of the Battle of Lepanto hung over the Doge's chair at the far end of the room, almost the length of a tilting yard away, and Nick looked away from it and up at the ceiling. Another hand had been at work here and Nick resolved to ask someone who had painted it. He had been told with some pride that all the paintings in these rooms had been commissioned and completed in the last twenty or so years and the brilliant colours were fresh and immediate, in some cases still unfinished. Nick had only penetrated to the anteroom on his last visit and now in the pause while Stanley was seated and everyone settled themselves he was able to look about him, incurring a distinct feeling of visual indigestion. Every inch of wall and ceiling carried its bright and gilded paean of praise to Venice and her doges with their God and the Virgin Mary, most by the master Tintoretto and, no doubt, his students. The plain black and crimson of the councillor's robes showed to imposing advantage against this riot of colour and activity, only the sumptuous jewelled robe and horned cap of the doge giving it any competition.

Marino Grimani, the present Doge, sat with his Council under the Battle of Lepanto, and Nick walked calmly the length of the room to stand beside his fellow countryman, set down in his litter facing them, and sent a brief vote of thanks in the direction of the players, who had taught him how to do this.

A brief silence fell.

Everyone clearly heard the sobbing wail from outside in the Room of Cords, abruptly cut off as a man-at-arms swiftly closed the half-open door beside the Doge's throne. Grimani cleared his throat.

Stanley and Nicholas bowed three times, Stanley awkward in

his chair. The Doge and Councillors rose; Nicholas bowed twice more and advanced to the Doge to kiss his hand. Grimani embraced him, Nick presented his credentials, Grimani accepted them, and they all sat down. Nicholas was shown to a seat at the right hand of the Doge, next to Alessandro Vanni, the power behind the Council, whom he had met before. Stanley was relieved of his robe of office and carried to a seat on the other side, his aide took the robe and stood with it behind Nick's chair. 'So far so good,' thought Nick. It was time for his speech; he'd put the wretched thing on later.

He rose. His beautiful actor's voice carried clearly through the room and those who had been preparing to doze sat up. He delivered his speech as if he were onstage at the Rose and began by thanking the Doge and Council and praising the work done by Lord Stanley in promoting the friendly relations and trade between their two countries. He went on, "Venice has been governed for some twelve hundred years in the same fashion, with an unfailing display of the highest qualities. True, from time to time she has been shaken, as the storms lash up the Lagoon, but she has always recovered, renewed her youth, regained her *serenita*." He took a deep, disciplined breath. "Each time I think of her orderly government, her sound institutions, her magnanimity in trade, the encouragement of her youth in the service of her country and her tolerance, I am forced to believe that, come what may, she will survive until the final dissolution of the elements themselves." Another breath and he ended, "I shall do my best to continue my lord Stanley's work as her glorious Majesty would desire me. I wish him a speedy recovery and a fair wind for home." He then repeated his words in the Venetian form of Italian and sat down to a gratified murmur.

Grimani leaned over. "Well spoken, my lord Rokesby. You must come to my next party."

An aide approached quietly and passed Vanni a slip of paper. He held it close to his short-sighted eyes and smiled. Under cover of the next speeches, compliment and counter-compliment, he turned to Nick and murmured in his ear.

"You will be pleased to hear, my lord – congratulations on your elevation, by the way – that the villain who escaped you last year has been caught. He turned pirate and was a little over-ambitious."

"You mean Count Gallio?"

"The same. It seems he could not leave his whore alone. Such a strong energetic young man, is he not – a waste of a fine body to have it tortured and hanged. He is for the galleys. He can make himself useful and we shall avoid possible unpleasantness with Portugal."

His face impassive, Nick replied, "La Bellissima betrayed him?"

"Of course. You had some traffic with her yourself, messire, through her you obtained for us our proofs. Venice has regained her *serenita* and you are rewarded."

"Had he nothing useful to say?"

"All he could say of the attempt to take the city, we already knew. Thanks to your excellent work. I look forward to our further association, my lord." He sat back and Nicholas breathed out. Count Gaspare Gallio was a buccaneering mountebank after Nick's own heart: he did not care for the idea of him as a galley slave.

Speeches and ceremony over, it was time for Nick's entertainments. Inspired by Master Jones' ideas, he was determined to make his mark as ambassador after all, his successor would just have to keep up.

Outside in the Piazza, a platform spread with blue had been erected for the masque, and the Doge's men-at-arms cleared a way through the crowd for the great ones to take their seats. Angelica d'Alighieri rose from the moving waves in gauzy draperies as La Serenissima, flanked by Logic and Reason. Her voice might be pleasing but it did not carry among the trained actors, so it was as well Marlowe had given this embodiment of Venice nothing to say. Jones had dressed her in thin muslins and a mock breastplate that pushed up exposed breasts and painted nipples. Not an uncommon sight in Venice, certainly, but startling enough in a Patrician woman. A breeze off the lagoon flattened the gauze against her body and lifted the artful tresses that fell to her waist, and, looking round, Nick was reminded of James, King of Scotland, forever with fingers fiddling in his codpiece. The man did himself no favours.

"As well her husband is not here to see her flaunting herself before all Venice," said a carping voice behind Nick. "A dutiful wife would have accompanied him to Aleppo, poor old man." This occasioned much laughter among the other ladies.

"Do pots and kettles come to mind? How is your dear Piero faring in Modon? And your music lessons?"

"That marriage is a travesty. She was married off far too young. They say she is still a virgin. I wouldn't blame her for going her own way—"

The rest of this fascinating insight was lost as masked actors spoke Marlowe's words, minstrels sang and Master Jones' buildings rose smoothly splendid behind them with only a little creaking. A small masterpiece of engineering, everything went without a hitch or a wobble or an untimely squeak and Nick, who had been holding his breath, went forward to take La Serenissima by the

149

hand and present her to Grimani. Her fingernail scratched his palm and she squeezed his hand before making her courtesy and graciously accepting her gift from the Doge's own hand. A fanfare, and a man with a wheelbarrow containing a small boy scattering flowers and comfits walked the high wire slung between the Basilica and the new library, acrobats and clowns swarmed over Inigo Jones' handsome set, music played and the assembly dispersed for a brief respite and a change of clothes, to meet again for the masked ball.

"Well done m'boy," wheezed Henry Stanley as he was carried away. "Couldn't have done better m'self."

The ball was to be held at the Palazzo da Mosto on the Grand Canal, and Nicholas, arrayed now in brocade the colours of autumn leaves, a gilded mask with the face of the Green Man in his hand, took to the water with his party in gondolas festooned with ribbons and balloons. He spared a thought for Tobias making his way back from Naples and was rather glad he was not present to mock all this ostentation.

The Palazzo was a strange mixture of storehouse and marketplace on the ground floor with an external staircase to the luxuriously appointed apartments on the *piano nobile* above, with its Byzantine windows and balconies. The Embassy commissariat had sweated blood over the banquet, and trapeze artists swung and juggled over tables laden with elaborate food. A huge fish, aspicked to death, lay beside an ice sculpture of Neptune hand in hand with La Serenissima, melting gently in the heat. A roast swan with cardboard feathers swam towards dishes of glazed pigs' trotters, pink shoals of shrimp, barons of beef and ham, and a towering confection of spun sugar representing the Doge's Palace.

Silver dishes of fruit, crystal glasses and gold candelabra threw back the light of a hundred candles and a small orchestra sweated away in a corner. The heat and noise and mixture of perfumes was stupefying, but Nick had got his second wind by now and worked the room, eating little and drinking less. He had made himself responsible for the cabaret and brought in some of the Scots members of the Rokesby escort for a display of dancing and wrestling. The sophisticated Venetian audience was highly diverted by the brawny Scots twirling and leaping on nimble feet and suitably impressed by the no-holds-barred wrestling that followed.

Nick had remembered meeting Signore Catalini at one of Kit's parties in Verona and had invited the famous castrato from Milan to be the highlight of the evening. In the blessed interlude of attention given to the soaring voice, he found himself beside the Princess d'Alighieri, taking advantage of the slight breeze by one of the windows.

They moved out onto the balcony, where other smaller rooms opened off.

"All over now, *madonna*. You played your part well. You will be the toast of Venice."

"As did you, my lord. But must it be all over between us? I would have you come to a small gathering of like minds at my home – not here in Venice – in the Veneto. The Villa d'Alighieri."

"I am honoured, *Principessa*."

"Six of the clock. But before then…" She seemed to make up her mind. "Before then…perhaps we should know each other better." She drew him after her into the small darkened room and put up her mouth for a kiss. Nicholas hesitated, his hand on the shutter. He had found Venetian women over-free with their favours and had kept his distance. Now, his own desires urged him

151

on, polite manners demanded a response, but this was not a willing wench to be tumbled. Angelica laughed, put her hand over his and pulled the shutter closed. She dropped the latch and stood close, her fingers busy with his buttons. Was this how she thought it was done? Moved, he took her face between his hands and looked into her eyes. A little flown with wine and excitement perhaps, but not so much that she did not know what she was doing. All the same...

She smiled up at him. "From what I am told, with a Venetian the business would be over and done by now. This English reserve is formidable. I'm told you are a man of impregnable virtue. Would you refuse me too?"

The noise of a successful party roared on next door, bars of rippled light fell across her upturned face. Her lips were parted and she was trembling. For all the bold approach, she was no wanton, he thought. The perfume of her body reached him and he bent his head to kiss her. The kiss prolonged itself and he freed himself with reluctance.

"Not here and not now, lady. With you it should not be over and done in a few minutes. Nor for me. If you are of the same mind tomorrow, send and I will come. Swift as an arrow and discreetly."

"Discreetly, of course – my lord Ambassador." She turned away. "I may not send."

" I shall be the loser." She stared at him, puzzled.

"I think I am a little frightened of you, Niccolo."

"This is no light thing. In straight speech, I would talk with you, know you better. I do not care to use or be used, my lady."

She had regained her poise. "They tell me you spoke well today."

He shrugged. "An actor's trick."

"Of course. You are a man of the theatre."

"No longer – or at least, not at present. See, we are talking."

"And we will talk more. I return home in the morning, my lord, and you shall wait on me there. You shall have wine and conversation." Nick caught her eye and started to laugh.

"Mistress, I do not mean to exchange the one for the other. I can make love and talk at the same time."

"An enviable faculty, sir. But you shall see. Wednesday, six of the clock."

A drunken voice yelled from the balcony outside.

"Boat ho! Boat, you rascals…"

"You will be missed," said Angelica. "Time to go back to your other guests."

"I am dismissed?"

"You have surprised me, my lord. I had not— We shall meet again."

He bent over her hand, and took his leave to mingle with the crowd coming out onto the balconies to watch the fireworks, his heart beating fast.

The banquet was over at last. He stood at the head of the steps to bid his guests good night and give them presents, and if he was flushed and heavy-eyed, he was no different from many of those leaving. Wine, ales and spirits had flowed freely that evening and many had to be carted bodily down into the waiting gondolas. The princess was one of the first to leave, eyes sparkling behind her mask, and a note was slipped into his sleeve. *"Six of the clock. A man will come."*

Grateful for the day's respite, Nicholas rode out into the Veneto with the princess' groom to keep this command appointment, wondering where all this might be leading. He was not worried about his turnout, he and Nero were both groomed and polished to within an inch of their lives, but he felt this might be a testing experience. He seemed to be entering a different world. His first sight of the princess' home was not reassuring.

The Villa d'Alighieri was a small mansion built in the new Palladian style so beloved of Inigo, set on a rise and surrounded by formal gardens and fountains. Pastureland and groves of trees stretched away on all sides, vines lay in disciplined rows, heavy with fruit. He rode up the wide gravelled path and handed the reins to the waiting groom, glad of his new double-velvet doublet, forest-green slashed with silver, well tailored and without ostentation. As he trod up the wide steps, he could hear music stealing from windows opening onto the terrace, and voices raised in civilised dispute from a room across the octagonal marble hall. Statues stood in alcoves between sets of double doors leading off in all directions, light came from an eight-sided lantern in the domed roof.

A door opened and Angelica d'Alighieri came to meet him. She led him into a light-filled room that seemed crowded with his elders and betters. Nick sent up a prayer of thanks to his old tutor, who had grounded him well in study of the classics, and prepared to fight his corner. Most of the party had a grasp of English and he was called upon to draw on his store of poetry and the writings of such men as Bacon and Ralegh. He felt he did not quite disgrace himself in this company.

The French ambassador to Venice had been standing in an alcove, exquisite in quilted yellow satin, a bird of paradise among all the sober gowns of the wise ones, idly turning the pages of an

154

illuminated manuscript. Seeing Nicholas released at last from the interrogation of the learned doctor from Padua, he approached with a smile. The neatly carved beard bracketing his mouth recalled the delightful de Longhi.

"You had good sport on your journey here, *M'sieur l'Ambassadeur*. André de Longhi retired hurt, I hear."

"*M'sieur le Marquis* preferred to fight with naked poniard, milor."

"The flower of our court cut down. Tch. Tch."

"Cut down? Merely inconvenienced, I believe."

"You are right. He will return to plague us, like the gilded fly he is."

Nicholas raised an eyebrow.

"Not a member of the King's faction, as I'm sure you know, milor."

"Henri le bon has no enemies, surely," said Nick.

"Name me a monarch who has no enemies, milor Rokesby." He selected a sugared plum from the plate offered and looked at it. "Why are you here?"

"To fill a gap, *M'sieur l'Ambassadeur*."

"My name is Ann de Montmorency. The gap is filled to overflowing. A superb debut."

"If you refer to the masque, who could fail with such an abundance of beauty and talent?"

"With your permission, I shall wait on you, milor. We may be able to assist each other." He popped the sugarplum in his mouth, dusted his fingers with a flourish of silk, bowed and strolled away to take his leave.

"He only came to take your measure, Niccolo," said Angelica at his elbow. "A man of influence – when he is not cuckolding men of higher rank. Which is why *he* is here and not in Paris."

"I must strive to impress him, I see."

"In your usual style, I imagine. The English sang-froid…Our dinner is ready. Your arm if you please."

The other guests had gone and she had detained him. He stood watching her where she stood at the window looking out, playing with the thick bullion tassel of the curtain. There was a sad droop to her mouth that he found himself wanting to kiss away. She was older than he had thought. He had seen her in her proper setting now, at ease with these men of letters and seasoned diplomats, listened to her play and sing, watched her moving among her guests. Thanks to early teaching by Oliver Knowles, good schoolmastering later and what he had learned from talking and listening to Kit Marlowe, he had just managed to keep afloat in this erudite sea. Interest and admiration now seasoned desire for her beauty and he waited for her to speak.

"We shall not be disturbed. My servants have all the discretion you could wish, my lord Ambassador. The house belongs to me alone."

"A fine and private place to entertain a lover."

"You will be the first to come here. If a lover is what you are."

"I came at your bidding, *principessa*. I could have pleaded a headache." He grinned at her and she started to laugh. "Let us be brave, lady, and grasp the nettle. You have nothing to fear from me."

She was not a virgin after all, but perhaps had not chosen her few lovers wisely: she was as ignorant of sexual mores as Nick was of the mating habits of the dodo. He did his best to show her some of the subtler pleasures of the affair, fighting for restraint after his long abstinence, and she followed him eagerly. He discovered in her a warmth and tenderness he had not expected, returning his care for her. An interesting, testing time, and they paused, laughing, for breath. He stroked a finger down her breast and gently kissed her shoulder.

"Why, *bellissima*?"

"Do I need a reason other than liking? I liked your voice and the stories. You have an air about you, a little sadness perhaps, things you do not speak of. I was lonely, Nicco. It may be you are lonely too, so far from home."

"I have no home, only a concept. For now, home is where I find loving kindness such as this. You cannot know, Angelica, how much you have comforted me… I have found a friend in Venice."

"You have taught me much, Nicco. You have not wasted extravagant breath on my beauty – you have shown me what it is for."

Nicholas Talbot, Lord Rokesby and Angelica, Princess d'Alighieri had indeed much to learn from each other. A Florentine, and related to the Medici, she was able to tell him a great deal about the French court. She had met her husband there, in the train of Henri's first wife. She could match Nick's travel tales with one of her own, a fearsome journey to Holy Russia. An educated, erudite woman, all the civilised arts at her fingertips, Angelica seemed to relish Nick's straightforward view of the world. She took to the arts of love as ardently as to her books and music and they moved freely from the one to the other. Marlowe had been right, she was as easily seduced by Nick's tales of adventure as by the strength of his body, she would keep him waiting for her favours until the end of a story, and then keep him busy 'til dawn. She taught him how to listen to music and look at a painting and sat patiently while he drew her and spoke of plays and sailing and the logic of mathematics. Nicholas thought of all the books in the library at Rokesby, now destroyed by fire, and began to look about him to replace them. He was having to dredge the remnants of an excellent grounding to keep pace with Angelica and her circle, and he set himself to learn, making a quiet time in the day to study. This uncluttered relationship suited them both, and so they left it, a delicate toy that amused and satisfied, and for Nicholas, a necessary counterbalance to his other tasks. His delicately poised and dangerous plans were never far from his mind.

A brief interval of leisure while he waited for news led him to fall in with Inigo Jones' desire to visit the theatre in Vicenza. With Jones lagging behind on his hired horse, they rode north across the Veneto, passing Angelica's fine mansion among many others by the hand of the same master and making their way through vineyards with their crouching vines now harvested and pruned for the winter and fields furrowed and empty. Nick had caught some of Inigo's passion for the works of Palladio and begun to visualise how such a building might look in the folds of the Warwickshire hills. He began to think of money and a setting for Kate. He broke into the flow of talk to broach the matter of a new manor at Rokesby. The idea stopped Jones in his tracks and he sat with his eyes gleaming and his body pointing like a gundog.

"You shall have the finest house in the shire, my lord, drawings you shall have, plans—"

"Nothing grand, Inigo. Go and visit the site and we will see." He spurred ahead, tired of talking and listening, looking for himself.

Coming in sight of Isola and the river, Jones caught up and spurred ahead, galvanised by the Palladian glory of the Palazzo

Chiericati rising behind the old prison in the distance. They crossed the bridge over the Bacchiglione and clattered through paved streets past many buildings showing the hand of the master, Inigo's head swivelling to take it all in.

The Teatro Olympico was a gem embedded within the high walls of what had once been a castle, then a prison. They were coming in the back way, under the arch of the Bruti gateway into what had been a military compound, now softened with flowers and nymphs and pink marble. Above them rose the Observatory Tower, and Nick would have lingered to examine the fascinating marriage of old and new, but Jones was pushing open the stage door in a great hurry. Along a short corridor obviously hastily adapted from the prison buildings, through an elegant odd-shaped space with a high ceiling, and they were there. The familiar smell of glue and plaster and sawdust took Nick straight back to the Rose on Bankside, but there the resemblance ended.

The auditorium was dim, steeply banked tiers of seats rose in a shadowy crescent to ornately painted stalls, a gallery and a walkway, an elaborate gilded and coffered ceiling drew the eye, but the actor and the designer stood transfixed by the stage. For a start it had a flat proscenium arch, brightly lit by oil-lamps, separated from the rows of benches by a narrow pit. No apron jutting into the audience, a long, shallow acting area was backed by a painted scene. And what a scene! Buildings so real you could walk into them lined streets leading deep into the distance, and as they watched, the lights changed to reveal another perspective through the three solid arches. Used to words painting the setting, Nick could not believe his eyes. A rehearsal was going on, with much shouting and argument, women among them – another strange thing.

Jones strode forward. "We are men of the theatre," he announced in a loud voice. "Connoisseurs of the drama, come to see your *scena*."

Nick cringed inwardly as the person in charge turned to stare.

"Inigo Jones, masque maker, at your service, *signore*," went on Inigo. "And…er…"

"Nicholas Talbot, of the Rose in London," said Nick. "We interrupt you…"

"Five minutes," said the man to his performers. The two women promptly sat down in a billow of skirts, dangling their legs, and the men abandoned bladders and wooden swords to get out pipes and tobacco. "Outside with those – how many times…" He beckoned over a little man with bowed legs and an anxious expression, clutching a tattered sheaf of paper.

"You are welcome, messires. We are busy as you see, our lead for tonight has a throat and we must make do. Alfredo here will show you round. The Rose, you say."

"You know of it, *signore*?"

"We have heard of a new playwright, setting the Thames on fire."

Theatre people are the same the world over, thought Nick, *in a universe of their own.*

"William Shakespeare, *signore*." he said. "I have played in some of his pieces."

"We will talk. Look around – amuse yourselves. "Alfredo…" He clapped his hands, the cast reassembled and the rehearsal went on.

Backstage the puzzle of the perspective was resolved. Like the Commedia in Paris, but infinitely more sophisticated, the depth of the scene was the measure of a small room only, built of wood and plaster cunningly shaped and painted into perspective – a new concept. Oil lamps were placed to add to the deception, the changing light and shade would give an extra dimension. Nick was not sure whether Kit Marlowe's creations would benefit or lose in this artificial scene. He resolved to visit the play and see how it worked. They came out blinking into the sunlight and Nick left Inigo with his sketchbook and went to find lodging.

He was to be disappointed with the performance. In spite of the repressive rulings of Venice, the play substituted for Pace's *Eugenio* was an opera buffo, for which he was not in the mood, and its excesses made Inigo draw in his chin and avert his eyes. They left before the harlequinade and parted, Nick to his lodging and the contrary Jones to find himself a whore. He hurried in when Nick was saddling up to leave and announced he would be staying on.

"I have opportunity to speak with the scene designer, no less than Scamozzi himself! And the Rondo is so near," he said. "I will make my own way back."

"Very well," said Nick. "Have you money?"

Jones avoided his eye. "There have been unlooked-for expenses—"

"Inigo, we have a business arrangement regarding Rokesby." He fished in his pouch. "An advance."

"I am most grateful."

"You will build me a fine house."

Chapter Ten

Lord Stanley had long gone home. Established now in his new role, which he regarded rather as an actor approaching a new part, Nicholas accepted the regime of the Embassy and applied himself. He took over Stanley's rented villa, a four-square well-appointed building on the Brenta, an elegant canal leading into the Grande Canale, with charming grounds, not far from the Botanical Gardens. When not returning like a homing tom-cat from Angelica's bed, he formed a pleasant habit of rising at dawn before the mosquitoes started biting to take a skiff up the Brenta, followed by his daily sword practice at Callisto before beginning the day's work.

On this particular morning, Toby returned from his long travels to find Nicholas washed, shaved and in his shirtsleeves, established behind an imposing desk, its gilt and intaglio entirely obscured by disciplined piles of paper. He was writing orders, signing letters and initialling lists, the paperwork moving in a steady stream from right to left. He glanced up to see Toby in the doorway, crossed his eyes and flung out his arms in a luxurious stretch.

"Never so pleased to see you, friend," he said. "But don't stop me now – I've just found my rhythm."

"Thought I'd find you at the bull-running," said Toby. "Nearly got trampled to death on my way here."

"Bull-running? Dear me, no. Far too dangerous. I've put away childish things."

Tobias came forward with a derisive snort and laid down a bundle of dispatches.

"I see they've left you in charge. Where are all your secretaries?"

"*'Oh, I am the cook and the captain too, And the mate of the 'Nancy' brig…'*" sang Nicholas. "Head cook and bottle-washer. They've all gone to the bull-running. Don't put those there – on that pile, if you please. Well, since you will interrupt me, let's drink on it. Glad to see you safe, Toby."

Tobias was wandering round the room, fingering the piles of books.

"Are you turned scholar, Nick? And do you expect me to cart that lot home?"

"I begin to see where the great ones find their ideas. Nothing new under the sun—"

He broke off and poured wine for them, picked up a sheaf of papers and the two men with mutual accord went out across the terrace to sit in the shade of a great cedar. Nick began without preamble.

"The two men I have been looking for have surfaced. First, I want to know who's paying them apart from Cecil, and second, they could be useful. A man I know is in the Arsenale sentenced to the galleys. I want to get him out."

"You want to get him out? He must be valuable."

"I'd rather have him for me than against me. The galleys won't hold him. And I want his help. Look at these." He handed some papers to Toby. They were copies of reports from the Spanish and Venetian ambassadors to their respective employers, each complaining bitterly of the depredations of a certain set of English

163

privateers. The Venetian Ambassador in Constantinople, Agostino Nani, had written:

> *I enclose letters describing the plunder of Signor Zuane de Mosto by the English. The case is desperate. <u>Care must be taken that the English and Turkish buccaneers do not establish themselves at Modon and Coron, to dispose of their booty.</u>*

This last was underlined twice. The first report was from de Mosto himself.

> *I left Alexandria on the 29th of November on board the Venetia, Master: Dandolo of Milo. On the 14th December we were off Cape Malea with a light head wind. We were attacked and captured by an English berton with a crew of about eighty men, of whom fifty were armed with muskets. They took all our weapons, and about thirty of them boarded us and kept us there for four days. We were in doubt as to our fate, for the majority wanted to kill us so as to hide all traces of their guilt. They finally resolved to take our ship and put us aboard theirs. To do this at their ease they took us into the Channel of Sapienza. On the 19th they took us into Modon and cast anchor, giving us leave to go. We were in serious risk of being made slaves by the Turks. On the 21st we reached Zante, where I reported all to the illustrious signor Nani, who had arrived the same day. The captain of the English is a certain William Piers of Plymouth, England, and most of his crew hail from there as well.*

Toby set aside this artless document with the observation, "This de Mosto seems a bit...er..."

"He's an old man, retiring consul in Alexandria. He has relatives on the Council."

"Ah." Toby read on. There was a further note from de Mosto stating that the English pirates had taken a whole house in Modon to store their booty.

"Nani didn't have much success, then," he said.

"Imphm."

The next dispatch confirmed the tale of the unfortunate de Mosto.

17th January. Maffio Michiel, Venetian Ambassador in Zante

The very day I reached this port, that was the tenth of this month, the luckless crew of the Venetia also arrived. She was plundered by the English, as your Serenity has already been informed. These men had been to Modon to try to recover their ship; in this they failed, and on their way home were again attacked by another English ship and robbed of what little property remained to them, and of their vessel as well; two of their number were also carried off and they were left with one little boat in very bad condition. She made so much water that they could not sail her, and were forced to sell her in Coron to a certain Patinoti for a hundred sequins. With this money the hapless fellows paid their passage to Zante, as your Serenity will more fully understand from the depositions enclosed.

"Writes a good report," said Toby, getting out his pipe. "I suppose there is some point to all this."

"We'll come to it."

Toby got his pipe to draw to his satisfaction and picked up a further short note from Michiel.

These occurrences have thrown into the greatest anxiety all those who trade in these parts: for if they escape the light boats that swarm in these waters, they are caught and plundered by the bertoni, and so they do not know what course to take. I will say no more on this point, which is quite worthy of your Serenity's attention.

The next dispatch was an extract and very much to the point.

January 15th. Piero Bondumier, Venetian Governor in Zante.

When it suits them these villainous English spare neither friend nor foe. More than thirty a year pass the Straits of Gibraltar. They trade in cloth, and instead of landing it here as they were used to do, they take it into Turkish ports, to the damage of Venetian customs dues. They have homes (trans. cassefermes) in all those ports. They bring broadcloth, cables, tallow, iron, arms, sausages etc, and take away silk, cotton, linen, indigo, gall-nuts, carpets, camelots. They are made very welcome by the Turk and are thoroughly acquainted with those waters of the Levant, so much so that even passengers do not think their lives safe except aboard an English vessel, although the fares are double.

"We don't seem very popular," said Toby.

Nick handed him another document and a letter.

Minutes of the College, Venice. January 9th

Secretary Scaramelli is going to England on public service; no officer or judge in this city shall allow him to be cited or named to his damage during the whole time of his absence.

166

The letter was to the Queen of England.

> *Much merchandise belonging to our subjects has been seized by*
> *the English on the open sea; we are sending our right trusty and*
> *circumspect Secretary of the Senate, Giovanni Carlo Scaramelli,*
> *to ensure its restitution at the hands of your Majesty's singular*
> *justice, and through the excellent disposition we are persuaded*
> *you hold towards us. We therefore beg your Majesty to lend him*
> *the same credence as you would to us ourselves, &c. Grimani.*

Toby's white-blond hair was standing on end by now as he raked
his fingers through it.

"Well? What next? Dare I ask. Never mind how you got hold of
these."

Nick grinned at him. "All part of the job. They can ask for
restitution 'til they're blue in the face – I've a letter here from the
Queen's officer at home. Piers of Plymouth and Sir William
Turnbull," he held up another sheaf of papers, "– many *many*
complaints about him – can prey on foreign shipping as much as
they like, provided a goodly portion finds its way into her Majesty's
coffers. Especially Spanish gold."

Toby had got his pipe going again and leaned back against the
wide bole of the tree.

"Aren't we supposed to be trying to make peace with Spain? The
treaty—"

"The Spanish are sending troops into Ireland to help with the
rebellion."

"Ah." He blew smoke rings. "And that would mean taking more
of our troops out of France. I see. What has all this to do with your
friend in the Arsenale?"

"Where there are troopships there's money to pay them. And money for the Irish rebels. Pirates could be useful as long as they're not thought English pirates. Mustn't upset the treaty. Gallio is a Portuguese pirate. These days. With a number of eager friends. Ergo…"

Toby considered him from beneath his fair lashes. All this zeal and activity, he thought. Was it to keep from thoughts of home and family or had Nick taken another step forward. *Hard to tell.*

"How much of this is in your orders, Nick? Or is this your own idea?" Nick shrugged.

"Part of my task here is to keep our trade with Venice and the East open and flourishing. Turnbull and his like probably don't need help or protection, but I don't see why they shouldn't have it. Not openly, you understand. They certainly need directing away from here. Spanish gold on its way to Ireland may attract them. On the other hand, we don't want all the gold disappearing into their pockets. I need Gallio. And I need him to owe me another favour. He is condemned to the galleys."

"The Arsenale is a big place. Do we know where he is? I had not thought it was a prison."

"It is not. But I remind you the galleys are manned by freemen and slaves, and the slaves are kept in a building at one side. I'm told they are put to work in the tar and rope-making sheds when not at sea." He smiled. "Gallio won't be liking that."

Toby was blowing more smoke rings. "I don't much fancy wandering around the Arsenale looking for him on this paltry amount of information."

"I have a meeting tonight with a couple of Cecil's intelligencers, the men I told you about. Fits in nicely with something else I'm supposed to do. I think they'll amuse you, Toby, you've arrived at just the right time... Look, you need not come, but I'd be glad of you at my back. They're an infamous pair."

"Try and keep me away."

"Just don't turn your back on them."

In a dark suit of clothes, a black woollen cap covering his bright hair, Nick was stuffing a stiletto into his boot when Tobias returned late that evening. He looked up and nodded.

"I doubt if we'll see action tonight," he said. "Depends what the Antolini have to say."

"You're dressed for it, I see."

"I like to be prepared."

"I know."

The two friends grinned at each other. Toby was dressed in dark leather tunic and breeches, a workmanlike dagger at his belt.

"My staff watch me like cats at a mouse hole," said Nick. "But one of my predecessors seems to have been a man of *affaires*. He had a bolt-hole. Come." He twitched aside the heavy red velvet at the head of his bed and unbolted a small door in the panelling. Narrow spiral stairs led down to a recess behind a clump of oleander overhanging the water, where a two-handed skiff was moored in the shadows.

"Hmm," thought Toby, admiring the practised way Nick ran down the awkward stair. The villa stood on a tiny tributary to the main waterway and the two young men rowed quietly down the Brenta towards the Grand Canal. Nick had arranged to meet the brothers at the scene of their first encounter – the place held no fears for him now. After a couple of false casts he found the little opening off the main canal and they tied the skiff to the ring in the dripping wall, and felt their way along to the low door Nick remembered. A rasp of tinder and a candle suddenly bloomed, revealing the two men who had been waiting for them in the dark. Nick heard the hiss of Toby's breath and smiled grimly to himself. They were a fearsome sight indeed, the darkness their natural milieu. The candlelight sent tall black shadows skittering up the wall and carved deep pits and channels in their faces, their eyes a-glint in cavernous identical sockets.

"Who is this?" said one of them in his gutteral Italian. Tobias closed up behind Nick.

"A friend. Where is Gallio?" said Nick. The other twin closed the door and lit another candle. There was wine on the table and the brothers sat behind the makeshift board to pour it. Toby stayed by the door and Nick took a seat opposite them, addressing the right-handed one.

"I've no time to waste, Francisco." The man looked surprised for a moment, then pushed across a mug.

"In the Arsenale," growled his brother. "They're refitting the *Doria* and he goes out with her."

"And?"

"We either contact those of his crew who escaped and fit out a boat big enough to take on the *Doria* or we break him out."

Toby leaned his shoulders against the door and crossed one boot over the other. "Quite as likely to kill him as not, in a seafight," he observed quietly.

Pushing aside the wine, Nick said, "I suggest we do both. We'll need a ship to take him off and I have plans for our gallant friend." He unbuckled the pouch at his side and slid a clinking bag across the table. "Money for the ship. Is the gatekeeper bribeable?"

"I know a way in," said Tonio and "I know the man on night duty," said Francisco. "He likes a gamble."

"And when he gambles, he drinks," said his brother.

"Do we take it then, that you deal with the man and I go in?" said Nick, who had never seen the two men apart.

"'Cisco softens him up and I take you in," said Tonio. "After that…" he shrugged and doodled with his knife point on the board.

"The Arsenale's a big place. Can you get your man to tell us where Gallio is?"

"If not then, later," said Tonio with a vicious gouge at the table.

"Is it so important?" asked his twin.

"This meeting wouldn't be taking place if it was not."

"That wasn't why we left you a message."

"No?"

"*Nenne*. But that can wait." He was looking in the bag of money. "Hey, Tonio? First things first, hey?" Tonio added a flourish to his carving and grunted.

Nick was thinking. "How long to find a ship and crew?"

"Day or two."

"I shall be watching the jugglers in the Piazza at noon on Friday. Just time and place will serve."

"How many will be coming to the Arsenale?"

"Just we two," said Tobias. Nick gave his short nod and got up. Toby moved away from the door and opened it. The Antolini sat side by side and silent, their elbows on the table, and watched them go.

Back in the skiff, Toby shipped his oar and passed his sleeve across his forehead.

"I can think of a pair of jackals I'd rather do business with," he said. Nick pushed the boat off into the stream.

"I have a feeling their usefulness is coming to an end," he said. "Perhaps I can contrive to have them arrested."

"Not just we two, then."

"No."

Chapter Eleven

Nicholas pored over the many dispatches until he was reasonably sure where to find the pirates' storehouse in Modon. There was a Devon man in the Rokesby escort, a likely lad and a distant connection of Richard Grenville. He offered him the task of carrying a message.

"Simply leave it at this house. Do not wait for an answer or get into to any argument. This is dangerous enough. I shall think no less of you if you refuse."

The young man's eyes were alight with mischief.

"William Piers, my lord? My aunty knows his cousin. I'll go with pleasure."

"I mean what I say, Trelawney. No skylarking."

"Oh no, my lord."

With some misgiving, Nick handed him the letter. It was a bow at a venture, but Spanish troopships and Spanish gold were a powerful lure. Unless Gallio had crossed Piers, in which case it was back to the second plan. Nick was beginning to enjoy this ambassador caper, of which he took a broad view. Inside knowledge was – well, inside knowledge. He was starting to see the fascination of all this intrigue for Robert Cecil. He cleared his desk and went to put on his new ribbed silk doublet for Angelica's supper party.

Their pillow talk that night veered away from the delicious indelicacies of Ovid to Nick's developing passion for the sea and his intention of commissioning a galley for the courier service. She sat up, combing back her hair with her fingers, suddenly the businesswoman.

"Do not allow them to cozen you into one of their ready-built keels in the Arsenale, Nicco. I can show you a man to build you a fine ship – but, oh…" She hesitated, finger to lip. "Must you? These marauders make our seas the most dangerous places on earth. Not one of our ships goes out without falling prey to them." A thought struck her and she nestled down to stroke his chest and tease the flat brown nipple. "They are your countrymen for the most part, Nicco. You are the Ambassador, can you do nothing?"

"Nothing, *cara mia*. My writ does not run outside Venice. Arm your ships."

"Then they could carry less cargo."

"A difficult choice."

"You laugh at me." She got out of bed and pulled on her robe.

"Never in the world, Angelica. I merely point out that both sides wish to make a living and turn a profit. Balance your losses. Arm your ships."

She poured a cup of wine and stood nursing it, looking at him lying with his hands behind his head and ankles crossed, a long dark shape in the welter of linen.

"It occurs to me you are something of a buccaneer yourself, my lord. They tell me you are a notable swordsman."

"A sword is not a cutlass, my dear. No. My point is, so many complaints cross my desk that I wonder these merchants do not stop squeaking and put up a fight. Or band together. Skilled seamen and a few cannon would soon make a difference. Money spent on adequate escort—"

"Is that what you would do?"

"It's what the Spanish do with their fat argosies from the New World. For myself, for a safe courier vessel, yes. Word would get round. The Rokesby escort meets little trouble these days."

"On land, Nicco. A ship is not an efficient body of horsemen. Come with me to the Arsenale and see them a-building. You would see for yourself if your notion holds water." She giggled. "The play on words was not intended. I am serious, Nicholas, your English privateers know what they are about."

"They know they will encounter little opposition. The game is rigged in their favour. So to speak." She was laughing and he held out his arms. "Come back to bed."

"It is near dawn, and you should go."

"The lark and not the nightingale…"

"The nightingale?"

"No matter. To the Arsenale, then. You shall educate me in this as in so much else."

And so it was. He went straight to Callisto and sword practice and then returned to his villa to catch an hour or two's sleep. He took his midday meal at his desk and boarded a gondola to meet her at the Great Gate in all the ambassadorial glory of indigo velvet and starched ruff. His boatman approached the massive twin towers on either side of the canal and Nicholas stepped onto the paving to be met by a bevy of officials all in their best clothes. No beggars, thieves or courtesans here, instead artisans and traders thronged the wide square and a cacophony of sound rose from behind the crenellated walls, banging, shouting, hammering and the whine of saws. It was Deptford to the power of ten.

Angelica arrived to much bowing and exchange of compliments and they were conducted with all ceremony towards the triumphal arch of the Great Gateway. Nicholas was disappointed. He had hoped to turn this visit into a quiet survey and had his notebook accordingly. He gave Angelica his arm and they proceeded into the vast entrance.

"They claim they can build a boat from keel to launch in the time it takes for a state feast," she murmured in his ear. "You will see it is no idle boast."

The place was like several cathedrals joined together, each with six large windows, the vaulted ceilings magnifying the din. Pitching his voice against it, he asked how many galleys they launched in a week.

"None for the past month, my lord, trade is sadly fallen off. The pirates…but we are prepared for when things pick up. See."

Nicholas saw. The whole place was as busy as a beehive, many hundreds of workers and craftsmen too busy to pay them any heed. The first great warehouse they came to was the Corderie, the smell and dust of hemp and rope tickling Nick's nose and making him sneeze. They passed through quickly into another vast space where the air was full of sawdust from the oars.

"Please, *principessa*," implored Nicholas, "May we not come to the tarring, to clear the rheum." She laughed and lent him her handkerchief, walking ahead on the arm of the proud factor. The heat and sharp tang of the tarring sheds did indeed clear his head and the linen mopping his eyes allowed him to scan the rows of workmen and slaves stirring the huge vats. Gallio was there, half-naked, his hands wrapped in rags and his athlete's body marked with burns from the boiling tar: his expression would have been comical anywhere else.

On they went, past the bakeries with their tantalising smell, towards the Arsenale lagoon, where the finished product was launched. Nick saw now how the whole vast complex of warehouses was arranged so that one assembly could follow another at the greatest possible speed. Against the high walls were racked, one above the other, rows of waiting keels. Further along was sheathing, decking, masts, sails and oars, all that was needed to put a boat into the water in twenty-four hours, ending at the huge gates that opened onto the lagoon.

Carried away by the beauty and economy of it all, before they left he opened negotiations for a custom-built galley. It would be rowed by free men and would have just space enough for passengers to make it viable. He came back to the villa carrying rolls of drawings and a sheaf of costings to float the idea to his partner. He also had his notebook full of helpful little drawings of the layout of the Arsenale. He showed these to Tobias first.

"Thought it would be useful if anything should go wrong."

"Did you see him?"

"From afar, toiling in the tarring sheds. Still trying to save his hands, I noticed."

"And the Antolini?"

"Have two masters already. I make a third. I haven't eyes in the back of my head, which is why I need you, Toby. I have devised a plan. It waits on young Master Trelawney."

"A promising lad. And the next?"

Nicholas produced his sheaf of costings and, pressed for time before an ambassadorial dinner, went to change his clothes while

Toby looked at them. He came back to find his business associate smiling and shaking his head.

"You are bewitched, Nick. Either by the blue eyes of your timber-rich mistress, or Venice is eating your brains as the pox eats the noses of her citizens."

Still buttoning his emerald buttons, Nick faced him. "And what is so impossible, pray?"

"Any number of things. You are going to be late – and I have something to show you. We'll talk in the morning – if you do not drown yourself in malmsey tonight."

A footman came to tell Nick his barge was waiting and he had to content himself with, "Sour grapes, friend."

Nick confronted Tobias with a remarkably clear head next day, prepared to do battle for his galley. The spirited argument lasted through breakfast – fresh langoustine served with ginger and polenta, which gave them pause for a moment – and on well into the morning, Toby's cold logic finally persuading Nicholas that the speed, manoeuvrability and firepower – for defence, pleaded the out-gunned Nick – of a galley were not the prime attributes for a vessel intended for passengers and cargo.

"Nothing to stop you indulging in a private galley of your own if your pockets are grown so damnable deep," said Toby. "Have you sailed in one…? I thought not. You'll see. But I take your point. Our enterprise would command the journey from start to finish – good idea. Bad idea – to sink, hah!, sink our capital in a cramped and sinkable galley, when we can lease a roundship." He was jotting down figures and adding two columns at once. "I admit to you, friend, since seeing a phrase or two in those dispatches – you remember – 'an English ship, even though it cost double?' – I've been thinking." He put away his reckonings and got up. "Come down to the harbour, there's something I want you to see."

Warped up to the wooden pier jutting into the lagoon was a shark among minnows. A three-masted roundship of some two hundred tons lay alongside a galley in for repair, sloops and skiffs and a galliasse taking on stores, all rocking in the wake of a merchantman heading out to sea. Shabby in her paintwork, still she showed elegant lines and a capacious body, her prow and beak adorned with the peeling figure of a woman in the act of turning into a swan. And she carried cannon.

"I even like her name," said Toby. "Which is a mercy, since these superstitious sailor men say it's bad luck to change it. Mind you if it was *Turtledove* or *Bluebell*," he minced a few steps with a flirty turn of the wrist, "we might have had to risk it."

She was in fact named the *Swan of Avon*, for the Bristol shipyard that built her. Nick smiled to himself. *A good omen.*

"We get her on favourable terms," went on Toby. "The current owner was badly bitten by the slump in sugar. Coat of paint and repairs thrown in."

"I wonder she is not named *Leda*," said Nick.

"These Bristol builders have no truck with your Greek myths. What do you reckon?"

"Brilliant work, Toby. I'm impressed. Captain and crew?"

"Ready when we are. You'll like Morris."

The next bag from home brought a further barrage of instructions, mostly things already dealt with and a bundle of letters and drawings from Jack, together with a note from Mistress Melville with a concise account of the child's well-being. Nothing from

Kate. He supposed he should make the first move to mend their quarrel, but could not bring his mind to it. Instead, he wrote to Mistress Melville thanking her and sent the usual drawings and gifts to be shared out. He felt it was the best he could do at present.

Chapter Twelve

Tim Trelawney returned smelling of booze and sweat and leather and horse, clearly bursting with news. He had taken the letter as instructed to the house in Modon and handed it to one of the seamen guarding it. He had then hung about, watching. He had spotted a young fellow much his own age he had thought he recognised, and followed him to a ramshackle tavern by the shore.

"He lived in the next village at home, my lord, one of those I wasn't allowed to play with." Boon companion after a few pitchers of ale with brandy chasers, the man had become careless. "We were talking, my lord, you know, women and such, begging your pardon," said young Trelawney. "Seems he had this peach of a lay – beg pardon, my lord…"

"Get on. You got him drunk and then?"

"Well, my lord, he was that horny to get back to her. And talk! They're careening, my lord, in an inlet across the bay. If there's someone you're wishing to talk to, I reckon that's where he is. Stuck."

"There are many inlets across the bay."

"Yes, sir. What I could work out of him sir, it's here, just north of Pula." He produced a grimy scrap of canvas with a drunken outline scrawled on it. "He was all for taking me over for her sister. Sir."

"This is first-rate work, Trelawney, for all that you disobeyed orders. I suppose I should be thankful you didn't take him up on his offer."

"I wasn't that drunk, sir," said Trelawney, with a flash of excellent teeth.

"Commendable. Report to Master Fletcher, and get yourself some decent clothes. I shall want you again." A clinking bag changed hands and Nick sat back, well satisfied. A considerable corner had been cut.

That same night he set off with Tobias in a hired dhow. It was a clear moonless night ideal for their purpose, with a soft westerly breeze, the stars hanging low and bright in an indigo sky. They rowed out far enough to catch what wind there was, hoist the lateen sail and set course across the bay to Istia. The stars were paling and the eastern sky beginning to show pink when they sighted the dark line of the coast and Tobias spotted the twin buttresses of rock marked on the scrappy map, standing out into the sea, disguising the cleft in the low cliffs. They took to the oars again and, watchful for reefs and snags, slid in to drop anchor in the shelter of the bigger rock. Nicholas pulled off his boots and wrapped them with his sword in a strip of canvas. He slung it on his back and went over the side.

"Give me an hour," he said. "Unless you hear trouble." The water was pleasant, what tide there was, with the wind veering round behind it, was making, and the swim was easy.

The pirate ship was beached on legs and rollers on the near side of the inlet. A bonfire was blazing on the shore; there seemed to be some sort of party going on. *They must have near finished,* thought Nick as he crawled out of the water. He pulled on his boots, belted on his sword, and made his way up the beach in the

181

lee of the ship. Hull and rudder were clean and free of barnacle and weed; even with bottom exposed and vulnerable she was a beauty and he marvelled at her sleek lines as he crept along, counting her gun-ports. A makeshift hut had been built next to a heavy-duty hoist trailing cables to the ship. A lantern shone through the half-open door, men were talking softly. Nick straightened up, pulled down his dripping tunic and knocked.

The murmur of voices stopped, the door was flung wide and a cutlass point was at his throat. His hands well away from his weapons, Nick said politely, "Captain William Piers? Nicholas Talbot would like a word."

The sharp point did not move. A face appeared over the man's shoulder, scrutinising. "Take his sword." Nick unbuckled it and held it out. "Bring him to the light."

In the light of the lantern, William Piers of Plymouth was so much the archetypal pirate as to be laughable, until you encountered the single sky-blue eye and took note of the knotted muscle of the thick body. He had an eyepatch, a crimson head wrap and for the moment, a crutch, due to a ball that had carried away three toes. His furrowed face was haggard in the moving light. In his late thirties, he had the high colour and fair hair of many of his countrymen, but the black patch and a number of missing teeth did not add to his looks. His voice appeared to be dragged up from his boots.

"How came you here?"

"A rumour, a lucky guess?"

"That idiot, Pawsey. He needs his tongue cut out for this."

"A good turn, perhaps, captain. Letters are all very well. But time is pressing. What I have in mind will not wait on messages."

"What is so urgent, my young Daniel, that you stick your neck into a den of lions?"

"English lions. Spanish troopships and Spanish gold. And a friend in trouble." Piers gestured to the other men to leave. As the door slammed behind them, he leaned forward.

"What friend is worth your skin?"

"A rival, I fear, captain. Gaspare Gallio, enslaved to the galleys."

"The Portuguese. An amateur. He does not trouble me."

"He will have a good crew and a fast ship. I have a golden prize."

"Tell me."

How good a patriot is he, wondered Nick. He spoke only of the target and his reasons for intercepting the aid to Ireland, no mention of time or place. "Pickings must be lean this time of year," he concluded. "And I should warn you the next cargo ships will go in convoy with an escort of war galleys."

This was not strictly true, but he was working on it. The pirate was sitting with his elbows on the table, picking his teeth with his eating knife. Nick sat down opposite him.

"Dispatches cross my desk urging the Queen to repay losses and take steps against you," he said. "This enterprise, once won, would be dear to her."

"The old woman would want her share."

"Equal shares, equal glory." Nick stood up. "If it is not to your fancy, Henry Turnbull—"

"Turnbull will come in."

Nicholas breathed out. "Better still," he said. "A meeting? When Gallio is free."

"And when will that be? I don't ask how you propose to do it."

"It is in hand."

Piers grunted. "Many a slip… I don't know you, Talbot. Send

183

word when it is accomplished. For me, Gallio is expendable. I like it not that your enterprise waits on him. I could get from you now what you have not told me, but you speak of desks and dispatches. I doubt it would serve my turn to do you harm, young whippersnapper, whoever you are."

"Her Majesty's Ambassador to Venice, captain."

"Hah! Just so. Send to the 'Golden Horde' in Modon. Leave Turnbull to me."

"In three days."

"Done." He spat on his palm, English fashion, and held it out. Nick shook it. He picked up his sword and buckled it on.

"A pleasure to do business with you, sir."

"We shall see."

No let-up for those three days. Even Tobias, used to Nick's ways, gasped a little at the pace as men and documents passed smoothly through Nick's private office at the villa. Nicholas visited his acquaintance at the Medici bank and spent a wearing two hours raising the money for the Rokesby enterprise and another morning with Tobias and a notary dealing with figures and signing papers. He was guaranteeing the loan himself, planning to recoup on the *Swan*'s first cargo.

"Never took you for a gambler," muttered Toby.

"Needs must," said his partner and went off to visit warehouses. A cargo of silk, spices and sugar – going at a record low price – opium and hemp, alum, costly cut-velvets, ivory, carpets and works of art went aboard the *Swan*. No passengers on this trip. Rope and canvas and wood, powder and shot, casks of salt beef and pork, flour and biscuit and barrels of grog, a half-ton of water, and crates of live chickens went into her hold; similar stores were packed into barges to be ferried out to the ship anchored outside the lagoon, a galliasse found by the Antolini. Some of the *Swan's* old crew were still hanging about the harbour, the essential carpenter and sailmaker among them, and they knew of others. Tobias had found her master drinking in solitary gloom in a run-down alehouse near the Arsenale. With his usual caution, Toby had asked about the man and learned that he was a ferocious drinker ashore but never known to touch anything but lime juice and watered wine at sea. His seamanship was not in question. He was an Edinburgh Scot, Morris by name, sandy-haired and middle-aged, who had started his career as powder monkey with Drake. He had lost a hand in the battle of the Armada and sported a fearsome hook. Tobias had felt they could not do better.

Nicholas dealt with licences and taxes and tolls, everything kept scrupulously aboveboard. He saw no sense in inviting unwanted inspections. The Antolini had kept their word regarding the escape vessel, although it had gone against the grain for them to lease her in proper legal fashion, and the *Hawk* was a shapely two-masted galliasse with a double bank of oars, twin brass cannon fore and aft and a formidable row of iron bombards lining her sides. Nick declined their choice of crew and Tobias went to find men, taking Trelawney with him. As he expected, the young man knew the houses haunted by seamen without a ship, and they were fortunate that a galley had come in to be broken up. They enlisted a timonier and free oarsmen, and a crew of experienced seamen, among them a grizzled Portuguese who could take the *Hawk* out with Gallio if Piers failed them. Timothy Trelawney proved surprisingly knowledgeable on maritime matters. It seemed that he had joined the courier service to avoid being pressed into the army. Nicholas sent for him.

185

"I would quite have liked to go to sea, sir," the young man told him. "But my mother – well, you know what mothers are."

"Imphm," said the motherless Nick.

"I crewed aboard my uncle's ship," offered Trelawney. The lad was positively salivating at the idea of a Rokesby roundship. "I can learn, sir."

"Very well. You can join the crew of the *Swan* if the master approves you. In the meantime, I have another task for you. I take it you can row?"

"Oh yes, sir."

"I will send. Hold yourself ready."

With everything in train, Nicholas sent a message to William Piers with time and rendezvous. The night before the attempt on the Arsenale there was a heavy storm sweeping the lagoon and Nick feared for their enterprise, but it passed and word came that the vessels had come to little harm – a lost spar or two. The game was afoot and it was time.

Her Majesty's Ambassador to Venice and Tim Trelawney of Plymouth crept out in the dark of the moon to break into the Arsenale. In dark tunics and breeches, caps pulled down, they rowed a stout dinghy to the end of the narrow street leading down past the rope-sheds. Nicholas shipped oars and stepped out. Trelawney would take the dinghy round to the lagoon of the Arsenale and wait.

Nicholas slipped down the cobbled alley hugging the wall and turned the corner. Halfway along the fortress-like wall was a low archway. One of the twins stepped out, muffling the clink of a pair of enormous keys. Nick did not ask. He followed the man into the building, into territory not covered by the guided tour with Angelica. He knew roughly where he was, however, and was not surprised when the other brother materialised out of the dark and fell in behind. Their way led steadily downwards, lit here and there by torches burning low, no word was spoken. Ahead a glow showed where the passage opened onto a small chamber. Francesco, or it might have been Tonio, crept forward dagger in hand. There was a brief flurry and a cry and a man crashed at Nick's feet, unconscious or dead. One of the two tossed his brother the keys from the man's belt and stooped to cut away his purse. He was right-handed. Francisco, thought Nick, remembering. He did not wait to see what else Francisco did; he followed after Antonio into a reeking passage, its green-stained stones dripping with sea-water. Clumps of weed and barnacles humped here and there, the roof was so low that Nick was stooped almost double. They passed several silent barred openings and Nick tugged Antonio's sleeve.

"What about these?"

Tonio shrugged. "Extra high water last night from the storm," he said and loped on. They came to black-slimed steps leading up into a wider passage where the cells had low arched doors each with a tiny barred grille. Bony knuckles appeared at one, and a bearded face. Evidently the tide had not come this high. Tonio bent to unlock the door.

"The West Gate, Boffo," he said. Four ragged figures fought to get out and a fifth followed, moaning and barely able to stand. He fell. Tonio stepped behind him, helped him up and quietly slit his throat. He looked over his shoulder at Nick and jerked his chin at the disappearing backs.

"We like to help our friends," he said. Nick looked down at the still-twitching body and the spray of blood.

187

"Yes," he said. "After you."

Antonio went along the passage unlocking doors. The last they came to held the slaves destined for the galleys; it was larger and had an opening high up facing the lagoon. Gallio stumbled out into Nick's arms. His hair was long and wild, his beard unkempt and he was naked save for a twist of cloth round his hips. "Nicco—"

"That way," said Tonio with another jerk of the head. Nick hustled Gallio down more steps to where a narrow chute slanted into the lagoon, greasy with unthinkable slime. He hardly liked to think what it was used for. He steadied Gallio.

"Down you go."

"I can't swim…"

Nick toed off his boots, stuffed them in his tunic and pushed Gallio hard. He slid after. He came to the surface and looked about: no Gallio. He dived once, twice and the third time grabbed hair waving like seaweed. He got a hand under the man's chin and struck out for where Trelawney should be waiting. The boy had seen and was pulling fast towards him. Between them they hauled Gallio into the boat, coughing and spluttering, Nick heaved himself in and took up oars. Trelawney had taken the tiller and after a moment Gallio unshipped the second pair of oars and began feebly to row.

"Pull, man," said Nick. "Don't tell me you haven't been practising."

"Hah. They don't even give time for the scar to heal. Disfigured for life – like you, my friend. Pleased to know someone can get under your guard."

"Row, damn you."

Nick was smiling to himself. Gallio seemed to have stood up

to imprisonment pretty well. He watched the wiry back in front of him with its weals and half-healed brand. It had lost none of its muscle and from the sound of him the man had lost none of his swagger. Out where the *Hawk* lay waiting, a ladder tumbled down the side and Gallio swarmed up nimble as a monkey. Trelawney tied off a line and followed Nick up on deck.

The *Hawk's* second-in-command stood waiting with a tidy line of seamen and regardless of Gallio's half-naked state, they stood straight and saluted with all due ceremony. Piers had sent a fellow countryman, ex-Navy and overlooked for promotion. Well aware that his investment depended on the dubious honesty of these men, Nick eyed him warily. The man pulled off his cap and bowed.

"Welcome aboard, sir," he said, in the soft accents of Devon. "Nathaniel Wells. I believe you will find clothes in your cabin, captain. Should I signal?"

"Signal? Signal who?" said Gallio.

Further out to sea, Nick could make out the dark shapes of two galleons hove to beyond the bar.

"A little closer, if you please, Master Wells. Then signal 'All well,' at your discretion," he said. "Come, friend, we'll put you to rights and I'll tell you the tale."

In the cabin, Gallio ignored the suit of clothes laid out for him and fell upon the food. As he wolfed down the bread and meat, he listened to Nick, his eyes sparkling. "So, my young friend, it was not for my bright eyes that you rescued me. You need my ship."

"She is not your ship until you pay me," said Nick. "I need someone I can trust to make up the numbers."

"And I owe you a debt of honour. Two lives, in fact. I see." Nicholas grinned at him.

"And I don't see you as a galley-slave, Gaspare."

Gallio stood up and kissed him on both cheeks with his mouth full. "Yours to command, Nicco."

"You stink. Get yourself cleaned up and come and meet the professionals."

A signal flashed from the *Hawk*, and boats were lowered away from the galleons to row swiftly alongside her. Turnbull, and Piers without his crutch, ran up the ladder. There was a distant rumble as guns ran out on their waiting ships.

"Ready to blow me out of the water, I see," said Gallio. "Welcome aboard, gentlemen." He turned his back and led the way to the main cabin on the poop, managing to achieve a certain elegance in spite of his still half-naked state. Food had been higher in his priorities than the mere matter of clothes. At least he no longer smelt.

Once in the cabin on the poopdeck, Piers and Turnbull waited in uneasy alliance. From Trelawney's point of view this was the experience of a lifetime. Crouched unregarded in a corner, he watched the men gathered round the table, the lantern swaying in its gimbals to light each face in turn. The cadaverous face of William Piers was alarming in the swinging light and dark, Turnbull, by contrast, full fleshed and choleric, would have looked more at home with a horse and a coursing hound. Gallio stood hands on hips surveying them, the marks of privation plain on his reckless face, his head cocked and grinning.

"So, gentlemen, we are to be allies. I understand my friend here has a plan."

Nicholas drew up a chair for him and poured from the flagon on the table.

"Be seated, gentlemen. I have new intelligence." He looked

190

round at the unlikely brotherhood and kept his face schooled and confident, Henry Five at Agincourt.

"Philip of Spain is dying. The Irish question waits on his order. The ships we want are still in Lisboa – we have time." He drew up a chair and unrolled an unnecessary chart – Piers and Turnbull knew these waters as well as their own warts, Gallio did not. The wine sank in the flagon and Nick called for another as they thrashed out the strategy. Nick took little part in this, other than suggesting that Gallio should sail for Oporto at once. The two professional pirates decided that Piers would wait in Modon for the signal to make rendezvous with Turnbull at his favourite base in the Azores. They made what contingency plans they could in a season not always a happy one for seamen. At last, Nick rose.

"We are agreed. I've a mind to let Trelawney sail with you to Oporto, Gallio. He needs to learn the ropes – a Plymouth man like yourself, Captain Piers."

"So I see."

"Someone to keep an eye on me, Nicco? What if I decide to cut his throat?"

"You are answerable to me for his life, Count. If he is willing to go."

Trelawney jumped up. "Oh yes, sir. I would be honoured."

"Very well. Watch yourself. Word will go to Modon and I will join you in Oporto. Understood?"

"Yessir." Trelawney sank down again hugging himself. A Devon man, the sea was in his blood, and he was to sail with Gallio. A pirate. What his mother would say did not bear thinking of. But he would walk over hot coals for Nicholas Rokesby.

Chapter Thirteen

The wind was blowing off the land, well for the ships gliding out to sea but against Nicholas pulling for the shore of the lagoon. The water was black and warm, setting up little ripples of phosphorescence as he rowed steadily towards the point where he confidently expected Tobias to be waiting. The fishermen were out with their lamps and spears and paid no heed to him as he passed between them. It took longer rowing single-handed and he slid between the gondolas lined up like piglets to their sow, blowing hard. He shipped oars and lay over them a moment and when a helping hand reached down to pull him up onto the quay he took it gladly. A knife pricked the side of his throat.

"Quiet," said Francisco. Nick stood perfectly still. Tonio pulled his arms behind him and expertly tied his wrists and hobbled his ankles. The point of the knife was transferred to the small of his back and the brothers urged him towards a narrow dark alleyway. He turned his head to see the *Hawk* gliding silently out of the lagoon towards the open sea.

The Antolini scurried through their natural habitat, hustling Nick through a rat-run of down at heel buildings and turned into a noisome lean-to against the wall of the Arsenale. Back where they had started. It was black as the underside of hell and Nick heard one of them fumble for a tinderbox. It sparked and Tonio held up a stub of candle. The tiny flame was a miniature sun after the dark and Nick closed his eyes for a moment. There was a board with a hole in it raised on bricks over a culvert and Francisco pushed him down onto it.

"Where is the Queen's letter?"

"I sent it on," said Nick. The knife pricked under his eye.

"Which would you rather lose, your eye or your balls?"

"How much are you being paid? I'll double it and forget this – charade."

They laughed, leaning together and stamping their feet. "There's those would pay a king's ransom to have you out of the way, milord Rokesby. It can be slow or quick, as you please."

Tonio was still giggling and his brother's voice was suddenly iron. Nick shrank back, allowing a look of naked fear to cross his face. Tonio stopped giggling and watched avidly. Francisco moved closer to take a grip of Nick's hair, and Nick swung both feet together to take him hard and accurate between the legs. He screamed and doubled up, Nick twisted sideways to topple the board and fell into the stinking culvert. It was deep and narrow, a turgid stream running through it, and in no time he had wriggled along, jack-knifing his body, under the wall of the lean-to. He felt for the little knife that nestled in the small of his back, wheedled it out and, trying not to breathe the foul air, curled himself to thread his legs between his arms. The knife was bitter sharp but still it took a moment to cut the twine that bit into his wrists and by then Antonio was waiting for him. Nick could hear the other twin still sobbing in agony and risked sliding back up the culvert to the other side of the hut. He cut his feet free and scrambled out as quietly as he could, sliding in the muck, and circled the hut to come silently up behind Tonio, who was still hesitating to step down. The stink should have warned

193

the man, but Nick's arm was round his throat before he could turn and the knife inch deep beneath his ribs.

"Will you live or die?" Tonio gurgled and went rigid. "Who is paying you?" No reply and the knife slid deeper. "I will only ask once more. The Council can get it out of your brother." The man gasped and told him. Nick was unsurprised; his guess at the involvement of the Lennox faction was confirmed.

"Your usefulness here is done, Tonio. Get your sorry arses back where they belong." Nick drew out the knife, reversed it and hit him hard behind the ear. He let the man slide into the culvert and turned to find Toby standing silent behind him, two of the Rokesby escort at his side. They took a step back from the smell and Nick said, "The other one's in the hut," before starting to tear off his foul clothes, bloodied now as well. If his memory served, there was a well somewhere near and he set off in oozing boots and hose to find it. Tobias could be trusted to finish clearing up.

A pot-bellied moon had risen and was peering behind the campanile when Toby found him. He was lying naked in a fountain surrounded by marble nymphs, his feet dangling over the edge. Toby began to laugh.

"You can laugh, damn you. Where were you?"

"The sly creatures doubled back through the prison, would you believe, letting out all manner of carrion to trouble the city. It's been one gaudy night."

Nick kicked water over him. "Don't stand there like a grinning ape – find me some clothes. Or give me some of yours."

Toby handed him a motley collection of garments contributed by the amused escort. "No boots, I'm afraid." He picked up the sodden hose between thumb and forefinger. "These can go on the bonfire with the rest," he said. "The English Ambassador was never here."

Hardly surprising after this little adventure, Nicholas fell ill with violent stomach pains and sickness and fever. Tobias had gone on a brief and lucrative escort to Milan and Florence – "Someone has to mind the shop…" – and Nick dismissed the physician with his bowl of leeches and dosed himself with a decoction of figs and cinchona. This left him exhausted and shaken, but better, and he had the sense to keep to his bed for a day or two. Angelica called and was denied entrance. She left some books she had been speaking of, and Nick asked for a chair to be set in the little lemon grove where the fruit might keep away the worst of the midges. He still had a continual thirst and a headache, and once comfortably settled with a jug of honey-water and a book on his knee, he took thought for the future. He would be relieved of his post soon, his tasks for Cecil were done, and apart from his own urgent and private business with the Spanish troopships, he would be free to leave. There was still no place for him at home. He'd had half a mind to take Gallio up on his offer – the rakehell life of a corsair had its appeal. What was the alternative? A subservient life at court, dancing attendance on a peevish, ailing queen, trying to survive the infighting that went on behind the scenes. These were the only scenes he was likely to see; it was very doubtful if he would be allowed back into the Actors' Company. Nick had no ambition for a state position, jockeying for favour, constantly watching his back. He did not like this sense of being still in the power of others. He needed a position of strength. He needed to make something happen. Like capturing troopships.

He dozed off.

He was startled awake by a panting manservant. "M'sieur de Parolles, my lord." The man was pushed aside by Marlowe, on a tide of euphoria.

"Your favourite wordsmith, my dear! But what is this? Not up and doing? God's breath, you are not ill…?"

"No, no, I thank you. Better. I pray you, don't shout."

"I must shout! I am delivered, my Niccolo, at last, of my masterpiece. My dear, the gestation of an elephant! So long… But it is done, I am free of it, light as air and already conceived of the next! It is true," he was unpacking his satchel, "true, that old wives' tale that birth-pangs are forgotten 'til the next time. But wait, Nick, until you see how this play will be received. It will be acclaimed; it is my best!" He dumped a pile of manuscript in Nick's lap. "Read. Read it! I have things to do, Niccolo, I will return and you shall rejoice with me. Did you hear? It's finished!"

"Yes. Good."

"Good! It is magnificent! Read…" And he was gone.

Nick picked up the first page and Marlowe's difficult writing blurred before his eyes. Groaning, he placed the script on the grass and went to hold his head under the fountain. An idle breeze scattered the pages across and under the trees, and cursing and chasing and bending, he gathered them up and anchored them with his book. By the time he had done this, he was fit for nothing but the cool dark of his bedchamber.

He slept 'til late the next morning and woke feeling much better. He managed a decent breakfast of bread and honey and eggs, allowed his valet to shave him and, dressed and more in command of himself, passed on into the salon, to find the wretched manuscript in the middle of the table with a note in Marlowe's scrawl. "You careless creature. If this is all you think of my greatest work, piss yourself back to London. I have done with you. Read, naughty ingrate, and grovel."

"Tuh!" said Nick and screwed it up. He stuffed the pages into a wallet and sent for his horse. To the dismay of the servants, he took a flask of wine, a hunk of bread and some cheese and set off, refusing to say where he was going. He made his way up the side of the Brenta, to the botanical gardens planted along the bank, where he found a shady spot with space for Oberon to graze and dismounted to sit on the grass. He sat for a while gazing out across the plain dotted with vineyards and cypress, badged in the distance with miniature houses showing the hand of Palladio. A house like these would rise at Rokesby, built for his son and his son's sons. He himself would very likely not see it finished. Presently he took out the manuscript and began to read.

Two hours later he came to himself to find tears drying on his cheeks and Oberon blowing warm breath down his neck. He gathered the manuscript reverently together and stowed it carefully inside his shirt. He got up to rub the patient Oberon between the ears and gathered the reins to mount. About to put his foot in the stirrup, he paused. There must be no more quarrelling. Marlowe had taken a huge step forward; the story was nothing – there had been Hamlets before – but the working of it, the language, the characters: sublime! He realised he was casting it in his mind. Perhaps the two great actors could be persuaded to work together. What a thing their new young boy player would make of Gertrude – perhaps he himself could play Laertes. He could hardly wait to see this play take wing onstage.

Hold on, he thought. *This means I'm going back to London.* It seemed the decision was made for him. As usual. Fuming quietly to himself he swung into the saddle to go and find Angelica. He needed comforting company.

Chapter Fourteen

News came at last, in a coded dispatch to his opposite number in the Spanish embassy. Cecil had spies there as a matter of course, and Nicholas was almost the first to hear that King Philip had rallied and was anxious as ever to pursue his plans to hinder Elizabeth in France. A successful rebellion in Ireland would draw off troops and money. A message went to Modon.

Relieved now of his post by Sir Henry Wotton, a competent, spade-bearded man in his late forties, the inductions performed with all due ceremony, his leave taken from the Doge and Alessandro Vanni and handsomely rewarded, Nick prepared to leave for his rendezvous with Gallio. There was still the question of Marlowe's manuscript. He could not risk the only copy of the precious play on the sea voyage and found a scribe to copy the text on the thinnest paper he could find in a miniscule script, and it would go in an oiled-silk wallet with his own papers inside his doublet. Tobias Fletcher would take command of the Rokesby escort back to London, with the diplomatic bag and the other copy of the play in a sealed packet. Michael would take it to Tom Walsingham at Scadbury.

An encrypted report to Cecil would go with Toby. *Twin piglets deformed and disposed of.*

He decided against any mention of pirates and Spanish gold

until after the event; he was acting on his own initiative, and simply added *All serene.* If he waited for orders and advice, to and fro from London, it would be too late to act. What had Kit written? "There is a tide in the affairs of men, which, taken at the flood…" Well, this was his flood and he was taking it. He sat for a while going over his various dispositions to make sure nothing had been forgotten.

Toby would take both Nick's horses and his own with the next escort over the Alps and see all arrived safely. Inigo Jones had opted to travel back with him and go straight to Rokesby. The roundship had left for Oporto with her cargo and would take young Trelawney off the *Hawk* and back to England. Gallio would keep his word. *Probably.*

There was a difficult task still confronting him that he should put off no longer. A letter to Kate. He made several failed attempts and finally gave up and went to wish his friend Godspeed.

"There may be another letter," he told Toby. "If so, I will be sure to catch you before you leave."

"No message for Kate?"

"Not yet. If I send no letter for her, remember me to her. And Tobias…if by chance I don't return – see her safe for me. And Jack…"

Toby cocked an eye at him and took him for a riotous evening at the Turk's Head.

Next day he packed his bags for Verona, a necessary digression. Marlowe had disappeared as capriciously as he had come, saying only, "Come and see me, youngling, I have words for you. And we will talk. I am still at the little house you found for me – a reformed character, I promise you."

Nicholas planned to ride post to Verona and on to Ligorno, to board a fast galley for Oporto, and make a further detour on the way to the Villa d'Alighieri to bid Angelica farewell. It was a parting made easy by her gift for gentle formality and sense of occasion. They exchanged keepsakes: Nicholas had found a hat brooch of emeralds and rubies in the shape of a sprig of rosemary and a book she had wanted. "For remembrance," he said. She had commissioned a pair of fine doeskin gloves, embroidered with falcon and dove and tasselled with silver. They stood hand in hand at the top of the steps.

"Godspeed, Niccolo," she said. "Think of me when you build your ships." Bowing, he kissed her fingers and then her lips, and turned to run down the steps and mount the hired horse. She watched him gallop away until he turned to stand in his stirrups and wave his hat with a flourish. She lifted her hand and watched until the rising ground hid him from sight, sighed and went slowly into the house.

Nick had made an early start and good speed, and by evening was walking down the familiar street, almost more familiar than Rokesby by now, past the church to the little house with the balcony, remembering Marlowe's last visit and curious about the "words". About Hamlet, he supposed.

Leaning on the little balcony of the house, Kit Marlowe watched him walk through the tiny passage into the cobbled courtyard. He saw the stiff spine and the look on the exaggerated actor's face, and thought, *Trouble, my dear, trouble. Like my prince, you need a catalyst. Action is your forte, my Niccolo. We must see if we can find you some.* He skipped down the stair and flung open the door to embrace the unyielding form that stooped under the lintel.

Well-paid for his masque and much in demand for more, Kit Marlowe was resplendent in a new suit of violet brocade, barbered and perfumed and glossy. Nicholas had to smile as his maestro flaunted before him into the little parlour. This had been refurbished also. The old maltreated furniture was replaced by a few handsome country-made pieces, bright tapestries on newly lime-washed walls. The room was full of the late autumn sunshine, filtered through blowing gauzes to keep out any remaining mosquitoes. An iron-bound chest, carved from the entire trunk of a tree, the strokes of the shaver plain to see, stood in one corner, with a pile of paper weighed down with a jewelled dagger. Nick unbuckled his saddlebag and laid Marlowe's manuscript down on the table.

"No, no, that is for later," cried Marlowe. "First your news." He fell into a melancholy pose, head on one side, eyes sparkling with mischief. "Poor Kit, alas, has none. No gossip, no new love. A poor soul sitting sighing by the old willow tree, alas and alack, or however the old song goes. But come, I give you a toast, my friend. To *Hamlet, Prince of Denmark*! And I have another waiting for you. The timing is poor for the piece I am working on, it will not be ready for Twelfth Night. Perhaps next year." He cocked his head at the scrip on the chest: "*Twelfth Night, or What you Will*– I told you I would find a use for those twins."

Bemused, Nick lifted his goblet and drank the toast. There was no question of taking another pile of paper with him, he would have to contrive another way.

Much later, he sat in the soft night, feasted and a little drunk, by the baby fountain in the tiny garden, the perfume of late roses blowing about him, the new manuscript on his knee. Friends of the *professore*, still in residence, had called, and he could hear someone playing a lute and singing softly. No raucous laughter or wild partying – the *professore* was earning his keep. Kit seemed to have entered a new phase.

A nightingale burst into song to emulate the lute and the lonely passionate soul in the garden felt like bursting into tears. Nick wiped his treacherous nose on his sleeve, set the manuscript aside and got up to walk about.

Come on, you fool. It's the drink taken and that damned bird. But Kate would love it here - wouldn't she? It was no setting for the aristocratic Angelica, fond as he had grown of her. She belonged in the gorgeous courts of the world, Venice, Florence, Paris, where he had no desire to be. Kate, in her new dignity and learning, would surely be at home anywhere. He thought of her, contriving and making a home for their child in what was left of Rokesby, or perhaps moved to the Gothic pile nearby at Lower Rookham. He pictured her here, sitting by the fountain, trailing her fingers in the water, grey eyes shining, her hair loose about her shoulders. Presently, he painted in their little one, splashing in the water, chuckling. He ground his teeth and thought about climbing the wall and going to find himself a woman, but in that place, with the pictures so clear in his imagination, it seemed the worst kind of treachery. He bent to pick up this new work and went to find solace with words and wine.

Later that night, with the *professore* finally persuaded to bed, Nick faced Marlowe across the table.

"What can I say, maestro. Your *Hamlet* is a wondrous piece of work. I am humbled."

"Nonsense. It would take more than my paltry words to humble you, sweeting. But if that is an apology, I accept. Good, isn't it? You will take it and we can continue. Yes?"

Nick gave his short nod. "Of course."

"Excellent. And now to your affairs. I owe you an apology, my dear. I have neglected you and I go on using you shamelessly. You come and go in my life like the stars in their courses, an inspiration, a breath of fresh air, and still I make use of you. You favour me with your confidence and I ignore you. But I did listen, and I have you always in my mind." He got up and came to sit at Nick's side.

"Heed me, and do not be angry. For you this happening at home was a disaster. But it is no tragedy, Niccolo – it is farce – a comedy of errors. Why make so much ado? No, listen. No one has died – except your hound, for which I'm sorry. You have a fine son and the wench wants you. Listen to me, infirm of purpose. You speak of honour. Was it honourable to bow to your own inclining and leave your Kate with a sick man, two children and an estate to run? Don't you see – she cannot move in this. She waits for you to overcome your knightly scruples – and hers. Yes, you will suffer – I suffer, daily, gladly, suffering is what makes or mars us." He went to rummage among his piles of scrip. "You remember Falstaff, my fat fool of a knight? He has the right of it. What use is honour when we are gone – if you wish to be well thought of, Niccolo, to stand well in your own eyes and those of other men, find another virtue. Try constancy – you are as fickle as the inconstant moon."

Nick fired up at that. "What do you expect me to do? I am no wandering minstrel singing barren songs of courtly love – I am flesh and blood—"

"And the flesh must be satisfied. Who am I to disagree? And what of Kate? Has she not desires? You expect her to stay faithful—"

"I expect nothing. I can ask nothing."

"So you go on your merry way…"

"What do you know of the love of man for woman," burst out Nicholas, and he stopped, horrified.

"I learn from you, Niccolo," said Marlowe with a wry smile. "But I tell you this. There is no love of any kind without pain – given or received."

Nick could only shake his head.

"What is it you want, Niccolo?"

"I don't know… Someone to talk to as I talk to you, someone to hold me when I wake in the night with fears of death, someone to greet me with pleasure and speed me with hope…I don't know."

"I think you do. And I think you have yet to find it. I know you well, my dear. You are a romantic young fool, about to grow out of your foolishness."

He picked up the neglected lute and began singing to himself.

"*In delay there lies no plenty, then go and kiss her, sweet and twenty, youth's a stuff will not endure…*' I surrender you to her gladly if it will ease you. '*What is love? 'Tis not hereafter, Present mirth hath present laughter, What's to come is still unsure…*' And what of your boy? You swam in and out of his ken like a comet, he will be a man grown before you know."

His pleasant voice ceased, and Nick, now in the grip of an exquisite melancholy, sat gazing at him. The man smiled at him. "Yes, go home, you young fool, I do well enough. You have given me inspiration enough for twenty plays, and my hesitant prince waits eagerly for his audience. And don't forget, this continent was my washpot when you were in petticoats. I can find safe passage for my work – Tom will see to it. I cannot have you wearying out your life and your horses fetching and carrying for me. Unless, of course, you do it for love of me. In which case, stay."

Nick flushed, remembering those secret words on the script.

"You know me, Kit. I would if I could."

"I know you well enough. Be honest with yourself, my dear one."

"Lord Cecil—"

"Hang him. If he is to be your excuse, so be it, but don't use me."

"I need no excuse. My duties are plain enough…"

"Only you can know what is important."

"You have confused me."

"I hold a mirror up for you to see yourself – a playwright's habit, I fear. I feel for you, Niccolo. And I know you are true to those you love. In your way. Enough. Life is for living, sweet lad, we make plans and the winds of chance blow us where they will. Remember your own motto, 'The readiness is all.'"

"You are turned philosopher, Kit."

"A sea-change. My England is forbidden me – and I am glad. I am free of the city of fools. I have no time for Cecil and his demands. Tell him I am sick and like to die – anything. I am done with all that. I know now what I am on earth to do."

"I envy you."

"You have brought it about. Take heart, my dear. My dilatory prince was cut off before he could realise his promise. If you love me, make sure that does not happen to you."

Next morning Nick fetched his penner and some paper and sat at the table. He could not think how to begin and he sat gazing out of the window for a while. Presently he drew the paper towards him, found and sharpened a fresh quill and began in his best handwriting, and without stopping to think.

Oct. 3rd English Embassy in Venice.

My beloved Kate

Can you forgive me for leaving so, without a word of farewell and harsh words still between us? The truth is, Kate, to be near you and not claim you was more than I could bear. I am only a man, and a weak one too, I blamed you for denying me the right to hold my firstborn in my arms. The fault was mine, and you have made me know it. I am so proud of you both. Rest assured that our son shall not lack a father. I miss you both more than I thought possible.

He paused. This should not be too much of a love letter. There must be nothing she could not set aside if she wished. No unforgettable words burning the page. As long as she understood his mind was not altered. He dipped the pen in the ink.

Someone will be coming to see you – a Master Inigo Jones. He is an architect and I think has a great future. With your goodwill, I have entrusted to him the task of rebuilding Rokesby. The Hall that is gone holds mixed memories for me, Kate, and I have a mind to set my new home – perchance it may be ours one day – on the site of the manor above Lower Rookham. The foundations and stones may be used and I believe the new style of building will show to better advantage on the rising ground. I have no doubt Hugh will already have set about bringing those neglected lands into order. I am writing to him.

I would have news from you Kate. Of our boy and your doings. I am learning, and I know now where my place should be – at your side with our son, however often I may be ta'en away. My heart lies in your keeping. My appointment here is done, and I return by fast galley. I hope to be back for Christmas, and this time there shall be no secrets between us. If you can only love me still...

He crossed this last out.

If the fates allow, perhaps this time it will come about. Write to me at Crosstrees in Deptford, where I shall come soonest. Nick

He sanded it and sealed it with his ring and went to find a messenger to take it to Tobias. Next step, his appointment with Gallio, and then if luck held, home.

Chapter Fifteen

Nick had sailed on galleons and roundships that were used as troopcarriers with his father, and on the merchantmen and bertoni that plied the Narrow Sea. He had seen and heard and smelt the galleys that traversed the Adriatic and the Mediterranean, admired the skill of manoeuvre and the speed as they fled across the water sleek as greyhounds. But he had never before set foot on one. The reality of what Gallio had faced struck him like a blow in the face.

The rows of scarred and branded backs, five to a bench, the fettered legs, the inexorable beat and chant of the drum keeping stroke was sickening. The rowers sat in their own filth, the top row better placed than the tier below, sluiced down once a day. The stink and noise was memorable. As they drew out into the main channel, their muscled backs and arms slammed to and fro, feet braced on the rests, the fifty-foot lengths of beechwood rose and fell in unison and the grunt of their breathing kept time to the beat: the slave master walked with his whip up and down the gangway between the banks of oars. *La Sorcière* was a fast two-tiered, twin-masted vessel, gay with gilding and bunting and vermilion paint, carrying little ordnance and a small valuable cargo, and once clear of the harbour with a favourable wind, the sails were hoist and the sweating rowers rested, slumped under a white sun over the oars.

Graceful as birds from a distance, up close the galleys were hell. Nick could only admire the seamanship and the endurance and go to his cabin under the poop praying to the god of sailors for calm seas and no pirates. None that he did not know, at least.

There were other passengers on board, two merchants and a priest. Nick gathered the ship was carrying a rich cargo of ivory, amber, emeralds and gold from Africa, great in value and necessarily small in volume. The priest was Spanish and returning from a Mission. Nick did not seek out their company and, hating the close confines of his narrow cabin, spent most of his time on the high-bridged poopdeck, squinting over the minute writing of his copy of Marlowe's play, writing up his journal and drawing. He shut his ears to the cacophony of shouts and cries and whistles, the beat of the incessant drum, the screaming of the gulls that wheeled overhead; he had soon ceased to notice the smell.

Days passed and Nick began to understand more about the workings of the vessel. Tobias had been right: a galley allowed insufficient room for passengers and cargo, they were primarily warships, fast and manoeuvrable. Even the larger biremes like this one, and the triremes, were still too full of rowers and ordnance to carry much else in the way of cargo. In the light of what he had seen of the privateers' ships, he began to adjust his ideas for expanding the courier service. He would not give up on it, his stint as an ambassador had sparked an interest in trade and the new routes being pushed out into the unknown, the notion of exploration excited him, and he found the tricks of the merchants amusing. If he wanted a position of strength, this might be the way.

This trip was unusual, in that it would brave the Western Sea as far as Oporto, hugging the coast. As they beat up the coast of

Italy and into the sea of Liguria there were long periods of calm and most mornings a gentle wind would get up at about eleven, sails were hoist and the oarsmen rested as their meal came round. There were free men among the rowers, skilled oarsmen, which accounted for the sweet handling of the ship. He remembered being told that a fighting galley could turn in her own length and began to speculate again on the possibility of acquiring such a vessel as guard and escort. He came to distinguish between the oarsmen and one slave in particular caught his eye. A huge negro, as skilful as the freemen, sat at the first bench on the starboard side, next to the gangway. He face was impassive as his powerful body swung to and fro, and Nick noticed him helping the man next to him when the food came round.

The passengers dined with the skipper, a swarthy man from Modon, by the name of Manolo. Nick recalled some of the dispatches and asked idly if he had heard of the safe house kept by the English pirates. Manolo shook his head vigorously, loudly disclaiming all knowledge of such things, assuring the merchants they were in no danger.

"Be easy, messires. We keep to shallow waters where the wicked English cannot come. All will be safe, believe me."

With a mental shrug, Nick changed the subject. October blurred into November and days and nights grew colder. Another birthday came and went and Nick wondered if Kate remembered it. He took to practising his swordplay on the poopdeck, regarded with amusement by the other passengers. He noticed the bow oar watching him beadily.

They were fortunate in a series of following winds across the sea of Liguria, and from Barcelona they hugged the coast of Spain as near as they dared: no English pirates so close in. They were making excellent time and Nick began to think he might be home for Christmas after all. The weather seemed set fair and they skimmed under the Pillars of Hercules in fine style, sails furled, an easy fifteen strokes a minute, well out of range of the guns of Ceuta. A pretty easterly breeze sprang up and Manolo, the ship's master, shipped oars and hoist full sail. The cook's mate brought up the bowls and the cauldron and passed between the banks of oars with the rowers' meal. They rounded the south-western cape at a good six knots and sailed out into the Atlantic and up towards Lisboa.

To Nick's disappointment, far from entering the great port, they sailed on past. Her harbours were crammed with shipping: men-of-war, merchant ships and huge ocean-going galleons, most flying Spanish flags. Nick spotted troopships among them, still riding high on the water. Delayed by unfavourable winds? Uncertain policies? Nick would have liked to put in, with a chance of gathering intelligence, but Manolo seemed intent on sailing up the coast while the weather was on their side.

Before long, however, heading north, things were different. The Atlantic was running a huge oily swell, the wind changed, and a navy-blue bank of cloud was coming from the north to cover the sun. The temperature dropped and a mighty squall hit the spread sails with a bang like cannon shot. Taken aback, the sails flapped and tore, the ship heeled over and the lower bank of oarsmen to starboard shrieked as they were pinned under splintering wood. The heavy cauldron slid across and toppled the shipmaster into the hold with a yell, the tall rudder swung wildly and the helmsman lost his grip and was swept into the sea. Nicholas picked himself up from where he had been thrown, seized one of the heavy axes from its bracket, thrust it at the negro at bow oar and ran skidding down the length of the gangway. He fought his way aft, shouting to the seamen to bring down the ragged sails. He had watched and learned enough on his travels to know the ship must be brought head into the wind and with half the rowers out of action and Manolo still scrambling out of the hold, the crew was without a leader. He grabbed a man to help him with the great sweep that formed the rudder, unmanned and swinging wildly. The timonier was blowing his whistle and shouting orders to the portside rowers and slowly the vessel righted herself and began to turn, wallowing, into the howling gale. It took all Nick's strength and the man beside him to get control of the sweep and gain steerway. With hands slipping and burning they hung on, beaten with drenching spray and a freezing rain, until at last the *Sorcière* was riding head-on to the waves.

Manolo and his crew were replacing oars and oarsmen, the master screaming orders and laying about him. The rowers reversed stroke and the *Sorcière* ran before the wind, stern foremost, seeking shelter. Or so Nick supposed, hanging on for dear life trying to keep the rudder answering, praying it would not snap. The timonier slid across the heaving deck to relieve him and nodded wordlessly at the seamen struggling with the mound of useless canvas that slithered across the deck threatening to engulf the battling oarsmen. Nick tumbled down the ladder and fetched up with a crash against the mainmast. Struggling against the screaming wind, his skull beaten and eyes stung with icy water, he fought with the others to subdue the unwieldy jumble of wet canvas. It was obstinate and weighed like a ton of pig iron, impossible to get a grip on, and by the time it was wrestled into place and lashed down he had torn most of his fingernails and lost all the skin of his palms.

The eye of the storm gave a little respite and they made some progress with fitting spare oars before it all began again. The ship had taken on water and was beginning to wallow; some of the freed slaves began to panic and lose what rhythm they had found. The other passengers were huddled under the forepeak, on their knees with the priest. Lending a hand where it was needed, buffeted and deafened and half-blinded by the sheets of flying water, Nick spared a thought for his plan. It would go on without him. Jack was provided for... He heard a new note in the wind, it was dropping, from a shriek to a moan. The waves flinging themselves down the deck were losing some of their force; the worst of it had passed. Slowly, gradually, things on board began to calm down. His flayed hands in his armpits, Nick straightened up to take stock, straddling the rail of the afterdeck. The injured men had been dragged out of the way, the oarsmen were keeping better stroke and presently jiggers of the Venetian equivalent of navy rum were passed round. It was a rough brandy and Nick took his gratefully, thanking his stars that his beloved horses were safe on land. Blown well off course, the helmsman now turned the vessel in its own length and steered for a steep-sided inlet with a little cluster of houses on top of the cliff. Night was coming on and he performed a small miracle in bringing the *Sorcière* to a safe harbour, a man calling the depths in the bows. The storm had passed as quickly as it had come, an eternity while it lasted. They dropped anchor and the rattle of the chain was the only loud noise as the quiet night sounds crept in, the hushing of waves on shingle, sleepy birds among the leaves, the rustle of falling water. It was like suddenly going deaf.

Slowly the other passengers crept whey-faced from their place under the poopdeck. The priest moved forward among the injured, doing what he could. Nick emptied the sea water out of

213

his boots, shrugged out of his ruined doublet and hung it over the rail. It was useless looking for dry clothes, everything in his cabin was soaking wet, and he brought out his fighting jack and weapons to clean and dry them. His papers and journal he carried always in an oiled-silk wallet inside his shirt.

The galley swung quietly at anchor, oars couched, as the last storm clouds blew away leaving a sky of luminous purple. It grew darker and Nick sat outside his cabin in his shirtsleeves binding up his hands and watching the stars wink out one by one. First Venus, then Pegasus and the Great Bear. There would be no moon tonight.

At the top of the cliff, a watchfire flamed into life. Uneasy, Nick stood up, listening. All he could hear was the moans of the injured men and a sudden cry of fury from below. The water casks had been broached. He had his night sight now and he looked out to sea. Nothing. He gazed round and the rustle of water resolved itself into a thin silver thread catching the starlight, falling down the cliff into a fine mist at the bottom. 'A well-found harbour indeed,' he thought. They were breaking out the skiff to go ashore for the water and he made a sudden decision. His points were tight-knotted with wet and his fingers too sore to deal with them. Instead, he pulled on his damp doublet, strapped on his money belt, thrust himself into his jack, belted on sword and dagger, and picked up his pistol and powder horn in their waxed packet. Thus armed to the teeth, he stamped into his boots, found his cap and cloak and went to join the shore party. If Manolo attached no significance to the watchfire, so be it.

Keeping a wary eye out, he helped with the filling of the casks and opted to sleep ashore. "Perhaps find me a fat coney or two," he said, lifting the pistol. Tapping their heads at the follies of mad

Englishmen, the seamen loaded the casks and rowed back to the galley. She was showing all her lights as the business of repair went on, and Nick crunched as quietly as he could up the narrow beach to the cliff. The waterfall had carved out a handy way up, but Nick had still not conquered his dislike of heights and elected instead to follow the cliffs inland to the source of the inlet. There was an easy shallow clamber along the stream at the far end, and he made his way up and back along the top of the cliff, screened by the thorny scrub that grew along the edge. He lay down where he could see the galley, wishing he had some food, and settled himself to watch. Presently, the lights were dowsed and all was quiet. No one replenished the watchfire. He checked pistol and powder. Both had been well wrapped in the waxed cloth and were dry. His clothes were clammy with salt and sea water and he stripped down to his shirt, his sore fingers clumsy with the buckles, and belted his cloak round him under the jack. He laid the doublet aside to dry and lay down to watch and wait. He dozed and woke and dozed again.

Finally woken in the pre-dawn light by the chirp of an early bird, he roused up and looked out to sea. And there was the thing he had dreaded. A three-masted galliasse flying a black flag, sails reefed, cannon run out, was gliding silently out of the mist to take up station across the mouth of the creek. Boats were swung out and a swarm of dark figures shinned down into them.

Nicholas stood up, checked his powder and cocked his pistol. He fired into the air. The echoes ricocheted round the cliffs, a cloud of birds, white, grey and black, erupted screaming into the air. Surely Manolo had set a watch. He reloaded and fired again, then dropped flat, half an eye on the white-walled cottages behind him. Someone had lit that watchfire with intent.

The boats rowed swiftly towards the galley where she floated idly, a painted ship reflected crimson in the still water. She exploded into life. Nick could hear the shouted orders as the crew strove to bring her round for the guns to bear, but it was too little too late. In no time, she was boarded and taken. The shouts turned to screams, men were flung into the water to sink or swim as they might, and the boats began a purposeful plying to and fro with cargo and those men worth a ransom.

Nick stayed where he was, hidden, straining his eyes, wishing ardently for the spyglass left in his cabin. A man in the last pirate boat stood and lobbed a dark object that sparkled and left a trail of smoke into the waist of the *Sorcière*, where it exploded with a flash of fire and a soft crump. Flames spread rapidly and Nick saw and heard an extraordinary thing: with a high-pitched squeaking, the gay scarlet paint turned to a pullulating black as the rats poured out of her ports. A dark tide of bobbing heads fanned out over the water and Nick heard the screams and yells of the surviving crew as they jumped ship and swam or waded ashore. The rats swarmed up the beach and disappeared and he found he had been holding his breath. A whiskered snout and beady eyes looked into his face and several rats ran over his body as he lay there. He ducked his head in his arms and when he looked again the spars of the pirate ship were disappearing back into the mist and in minutes she had slipped away as silently as she had come, leaving only the despairing cries of the men in the water to disturb the gulls.

"Slick," thought Nick. The whole operation had taken less than fifty minutes. One black head was ploughing a swift arrow through the water, towing a sodden bundle of trailing robes. Evidently the priest was not valued very highly. The rest of the survivors were galley slaves and a few seamen. The pirates had taken everyone of value or use together with the chests of gold and emeralds.

Nick watched as the flames rose higher, and *La Sorcière*, a spectacular bonfire, burned to the waterline and sank, her keel resting on the shallow bottom. The bulky tusks of ivory were going down with the ship. Salvage and payment for whoever set the watchfire? Perhaps. *Economical and efficient*, thought Nick. *Looks as if I'll miss Gallio after all.* He needed a friendly port and another ship. He needed to know where he was.

He sat cross-legged on the short turf, considering his options. An educated guess told him he was stranded roughly a third of the way up the coast between Lisboa and Oporto. He could go south to Lisboa in the hope of avoiding the Spaniards and picking up another ship, or set off on foot, heading north.

"My kingdom for a horse!" he said aloud. If I go back, the miles are to do again and no guarantee of a ship. North it is. His stargazing the evening before had not been solely for the beauty of the night. On the long voyages undertaken for Robert Cecil he had watched and listened and learned. His insatiable curiosity had given him some knowledge of how to find his way about the world, and now he eased his fingers inside his shirt for his wallet of papers. The watch made by M'sieur Corner of Paris was there safe and dry. He found a stick to set upright in the pale morning light and dredged through his hard-won knowledge for all he could recall of method and maps. The stub of lead wrapped round with string and a page torn from his journal aided his careful calculations, and he presently felt reasonably confident of their landfall, on the southernmost coast of Portugal, blown back just north of Lisboa, and he was sure of his direction. The night sky would tell him more. *So far, so good.* He stowed away watch and journal and looked again at the beach. Manolo, his senior officers and the merchants had all been taken for ransom, those left were able-bodied men and they had a Spanish priest with them; they should do well enough.

The mist rolled landward; only the growing light indicated the time of the morning. The sun would not show itself today. Nick became aware of hunger and thirst. "A fat coney" would be an excellent idea if he had time and means to snare one. A pistol shot would sound for miles and he was an indifferent marksman with a handgun in any case. He slaked his thirst at the stream and took a last look at *La Sorcière*. She was canted over, a few blackened spars above the water and the group on the shore was watching her dolefully. About to crawl back and stand up, he paused and glanced over the cliff. The marooned party was sitting and lying on the sand, the priest was arguing with one of the seamen, pointing up to the village. Shutters banged, a dog barked and a pump began clanking. Someone shouted at the dog and Nick heard children's voices. "Time I went," he said. He wriggled back and stepped down into the stream bed and, bent double, made his way along it.

Once out of sight and sound of the cottages, he straightened up and took a good look round. At this time of year, the flat tableland was covered with coarse dry grass, fissured with cracks and tiny streams, little cover anywhere. After a while the stream he was following bent away from the direction he wanted to go and he stopped to drink again before striking off due north. Rabbits had come out to feed. Nick crept as close as he could and tried his luck with his throwing knife. The movement was enough to scatter the coneys and he retrieved his knife, thinking, *I shall go hungry at this rate. A sling, that's what I need.*

Chapter Sixteen

At first he was stumbling across arid stony fields: his boots had dried hard from their soaking in sea water and grew increasingly painful. More and more little streams appeared and the now sloping land seemed more cultivated, small olive groves on the slopes, cork trees and rows of twisted vines cut back for the winter, stone-walled fields furrowed and harvested. He passed a flock of goats tended by a small boy playing a pipe, straight out of one of those paintings by that madman in Naples. Presently he came across a path and followed it, quickening up as he came to a huddle of adobe cottages, thinking, *Even a donkey would do...*

Gifted with a capacious memory and a love of words, Nick picked up languages as a dog does fleas, and he summoned up what he had gleaned from talking to Gallio. The first person he met was a toothless old woman, sitting on her step plucking a chicken. She looked up at him with milky eyes and a vacant gummy smile and shook her head. He heard the clang of hammer on iron and brightened. Where there was a smith there would be horses. Perhaps. He had begun to doubt the existence of such things in an area so far from any town. But a smith would have food, and grease for his boots. At the end of the tiny village he came to a building larger than the rest with a lean-to shed at the side, smoke issuing from a hole in the roof. He followed the sound of hammering and found a bent and wiry man with brawny blacksmith's arms working on a hinge for a gate. The man thrust the glowing iron back into the fire and straightened, hammer in hand. Nick kept his hands well away from his weapons and tried a greeting. The man's dialect bore little resemblance to Gallio's speech, but after a deal of mutual misunderstanding and gesture, he understood that Nick was enquiring for a horse. He burst out laughing. Nick felt in his purse for a silver coin. Mopping his eyes and thumping his chest to stop the coughing, the smith was understood to say Pedro up the hill had one, might sell, might not. The smith's wife had come out by now, with a young girl of about fifteen. Nick could not follow the rapid talk, but the girl was shooed back into the house, and the woman dropped a curtsey. He gathered he was being offered shelter. It was very tempting, he was tired and hungry and his feet hurt. He refused as politely as he could, and left them staring after him as he climbed the hill to find the man with the amusing horse.

Shown the colour of Nick's money, Pedro, a short, black-browed man with horrible red-stained teeth, from his speech obviously not from these parts, admitted to the ownership of a fine horse, the apple of his eye, he did not know how he could part with it. Nick had met his sort before in the army, and turned away with a shrug, tossing some coins in the air before stowing them away. Pedro followed him. He had another, the *senhor* should see him. Nick had no time or patience for haggling, anything with four legs would serve in the present situation and the bargain was struck, sight unseen. Pedro led him round the corner of the house to see what he had bought.

It stood in the lee of a barn, a lop-eared herring-gutted individual of about fifteen hands, dismal of eye and dull of coat, hanging her head. Furious at being taken for a fool, Nick rounded on the grinning owner, forgetting any attempt at Portuguese.

"What do you take me for, clop-head! This poor creature would not carry me fifty yards – nor would I ask it. If you treat your beasts no better than this you deserve to be run back where you belong on a rail – this animal's feet are a disgrace. I'll none of you."

The man caught the drift, the big stranger was angry, and not to be easily gulled. "But the other, sir, the other. More expensive, but what would you? And unbroken..."

"Tuh!" said Nick. "Show me." The man pointed. At the far end of a stony field, in the sparse shelter of a leafless tree, stood a large white shape. If Nick had a preference, it was for greys. He clicked his fingers.

"A halter. Oats." Pedro stopped grinning and fetched a frayed length of rope. He nodded towards a half barrel of grain.

"Entire?"

"A gelding, *senhor*." Thank the lord for that, thought Nick. He was in no case to deal with an unbroken stallion. A neglected gelding could be tricksy enough. He filled his cap with barley and advanced across the field.

At his approach, the animal flung up its head with a shrill neigh and cantered off. Nick stood still, whistling softly and shaking his cap. The creature stood about 17 hands, shaggy in his winter coat, but he had the proud neck and sturdy legs of an Andalusian. *Good blood there somewhere,* thought Nick, with a growing suspicion that these animals had been stolen from a cavalry troop. *Carries his head well –possibly not unbroken...with any luck.*

"Coo-op," he said, clicking his tongue. He waited patiently. Horses may frighten easily but they are inquisitive. If the villain had not taught this one to fear men, Nick had hopes. He liked the look of him. The horse circled, eyeing him warily. Nick stretched out the hand with the grain, scattering some on the ground. Presently the animal approached, snuffing and blowing, curious. Nick stood still. The horse snorted, jinked and darted away. The slow dance began.

Pedro sat down on the ground, chewing a betel leaf, waiting for the entertainment to start. He was to be disappointed. To Nick, breaking a horse meant winning its trust – quicker in the end. He got the halter on at last and gentled him, talking quietly, thinking of a name. "Corsair," he said. "How like you that? A dashing name – do you think you can live up to it?" The horse tossed his head and blew. Nick turned his back and walked away and the animal followed him. *This horse has been trained and then left,* he thought. He led him round the field, then slowly took off his jack and laid it across the animal's back. Leading him to a stone wall, he unbuckled his sword and climbed up to lie across him. After a while he slid a leg over and sat up. Corsair careered across the field trying to shake him off. Nick stayed put for a while, then jumped. The whole thing began again. Pedro fell asleep.

He woke to find Nick standing over him, the grey looking over his shoulder. "Saddle?"

The man scrambled to his feet. In the corner of the barn was a dusty jumble of equipment, and Nick walked over to stir it with his toe. It was beginning to look as if there might have been a recent clash of arms in these parts, there were arms, pieces of horse-armour, canteens and helmets and a pitiful heap of clothes. He looked over his shoulder at Pedro cringing by the door. One of the many vultures that preyed on a battlefield. Asking forgiveness of the fallen, Nick picked through the sad heap and found a high-backed saddle that would fit Corsair, and a stained woollen blanket. A bridle that had all its ornament removed, a pair of canteens and a helmet were the only other necessaries he could bring himself to take.

He tacked Corsair up in silence, tied the rest in the blanket and went back to the run-down creature standing with her turned-up toes in the yard. He put the rope halter over her head and mounted Corsair with the bundle in front of him. Pedro started forward and stopped as Nick loosened his sword.

"I am done here." He fingered out a silver coin and threw it. "Blood money. Take it and pray for those you robbed."

Nicholas rode slowly back down the hill to the little forge, hoping the smith shoed horses as well as he made hinges. The man flung up his arms at sight of him and hurried forward with a broad grin. Nick did not question where the shoes had come from, only thankful that the man knew his job. He held the horse for a while but the grey had settled into familiar territory by now and stood docilely enough. Nick applied himself to the bellows and presently the goatherd with the pipe came through the gate with his flock. He tugged his hair and nodded, disappearing round the back of the lean-to, and before long the black-eyed girl came with a shy smile to offer Nick a bowl of warm milk. He drank it gratefully and went back to his pumping with a will.

Presently the boy came and relieved him and he begged water and a brush to do what he could with the mare. Fed and watered, her feet attended to, she seemed brighter, and he left bothering her with brushing for later. "You shall be nameless, poor creature," said Nick. "Until I can see you properly."

The entire family – there were two more children, Nick discovered – entered into the spirit of this adventure in their lives.

This tall stranger obviously meant them no harm, he had money and, what was even more delightful, had got the better of the rascal up the hill. Food was brought out, and Nick ate with the smallest child on his knee, allowing the older boy to examine the chasing on his sword. The smith was eyeing it enviously, and after a while brought out something of his own. It was a bronze cup, a lovely piece, simply made with a border of vine leaves chased into the lip. His wife laughed, shaking her head and gesturing widely. Nick gathered that her husband was given to wasting his time with such things.

"Will you sell it?"

"No," said the smith.

"Fifty pesos," said his wife. Nick handed it back.

"It is a fine piece of work," he said. "If you would part with it, I will pay you its worth and more, if you can spare me some food for the journey." The smith held it in his huge black hands and stroked a calloused thumb over the vine leaves. His wife broke into an excited babble of speech Nick could not follow. He wished he had not made the offer.

At last, "I must speak truth," said the smith. "I did not make this thing. I could not. It is yours, *senhor*, for a fair price."

Nick put down the child and stood up. He felt in his pouch for a gold coin.

"For the shoeing and the children," he said. "The food and the cup I will take with thanks."

He rode off, with the mare making a better pace, thinking. *Horses, saddle, shoes and an officer's drinking cup. Spoils of war. So be it.*

Chapter Seventeen

It was soon full dark, the moon a thin paring low in the eastern sky. A low thicket of thorn trees grew in a dip, a carpet of leaves would make a snug bed, Nick thought. He hobbled the horses and, not daring to pull off his boots, he rolled himself in the blanket and tried to sleep. It was a fitful sleep: foxes barked, away in the hills something howled, night creatures rustled through the bushes and it was very cold. Nicholas had become accustomed to life in a crowded city, his childhood days in army camps seemed far away and even then there was shelter and bustle and human activity. "We've a long way to go," he said to Corsair, who stood asleep, a marble statue in the starlight. "I'll have to do better than this."

A freezing shower of rain woke him in the early dawn, and he climbed stiffly to his feet and stared round, taking stock. Barren scrubby hillsides stretched as far as he could see, dotted with thorn and bent acacia. Low cloud threatened more rain later. He led the animals to the nearest stream and cupped his hands to drink himself. At least there was no shortage of water. He made a breakfast of some of the bread and goat's cheese from the smith, saddled up and set off. He saw no sign of habitation that day, nor the next.

In recent years, much of his time had been spent in noisy smoke- and stench-filled cities. Even at sea there was a constant barrage of sound. The wind in the rigging could rise to a scream, the sails banged and cracked, wood groaned and the sea itself set up an unceasing orchestra of sound. All day long on the crowded galley, men had shouted, drums and trumpets sounded, bare feet pounded the decks.

Out here, alone, the silence and space dismayed him. Not even a chorus of insects and birds at this time of year.

Silence. His ears slowly tuned to small sounds, movements of grass and leaf, a snake or a lizard rustling over rock, the far-off cry of a gull. The air was clean and very cold, like a knife between the eyes.

He walked and rode, rested, rode and walked. Sparing though he was with his food, on the fifth day it ran out. This was not like campaigning with his father's troop, with a body of men well equipped and properly provisioned. He had only the clothes he stood up in, and one rideable horse. He had no tent to share with warm bodies and work up a comfortable fug, just his cloak and one thin blanket. No equipment save what he could contrive for himself. And he faced a journey of some fifty leagues, alone. As he swallowed the last crumb of cheese, and kicked ashes over his fire, he tried to calm his fears. One day at a time. He mounted up and rode on.

In the late afternoon, he came upon what was surely the site of the skirmish he had been expecting. Here was the churned-up turf, the stony mounds, the blown scraps Pedro and his like had not thought worth stooping for.

Nicholas dismounted, pulled off his cap and stood for a while, remembering his father and the good friends from his childhood with the army, men who had dandled him on their knee and talked of home and wives, men who taught him to hold a sword and draw a bow, all lost. These might have been different soldiers fighting for a different cause, but it came to the same in the end.

Remembering those days, other things came to mind and some of his boyhood skills began to come back to him, skills learned playing truant from his tutor to run off with the country-bred corporal who had been pressed into the army. Nat had taught him to fish and use a sling, snare rabbits and guddle trout, which nuts and fruit were good to eat.

Coarse grass had pushed through the stony mounds and Nick estimated several months since the fight. He turned aside with a nod of thanks to comrades of the past, and went on down the hill to a promising stream. Here he hobbled the horses and left them to graze and set about making a fire. He sat beside it to fashion a hook and snares from the gold wire of his sword-hilt, and a sling from strips of blanket and leather cut from Corsair's bridle. He should have thought of this before, at the smithy. That night he set snares for rabbits and caught a fish for his supper. He wrapped it in leaves and baked it on a flat stone in his fire. While it cooked, he found comfrey and nettles to make tea in the helmet and he drank it from his bronze cup. A feast. In the morning there might be a rabbit.

Chapter Eighteen

So began the pattern of many days and nights to come, a routine of survival. The nights were the worst. The days were cold, the low sun making little difference, and with its going down the temperature plummeted. He huddled over his fire in what shelter he could find, wrapped in cloak and blanket, trying to warm his fingers to keep his journal, afraid of losing count of time. His hands had healed quickly enough, it was his feet that were the problem. His boots were stiffened and cracked from sea water; no amount of grease would soften them, they were past hope. Ankles and heels were blistered and raw, his shirt tails went to wrap them, and where there was turf to walk on he went barefoot. Until he saw the snake sliding away through the grass…. He was sparing Corsair by walking part of each day, the animal was in poor condition. The nameless one was trotting along quite happily, her head up now and her ears pricked.

A forced march of thirty miles a day had been commonplace in his father's army, he had ridden in the carts with the women following behind. Nick, however, did not expect to make more than twenty, and was pacing himself as best he could.

He was following the coastline as much as possible and on the twelfth day he came upon a fishing village, the first habitation he had seen. Cold and weary, hoping to buy corn and bread to go with the coney he had snared the night before, he rode between the low-browed cottages in a thin rain, to find all the shutters and doors barred and bolted and no one in sight. The recent battles had left their mark. Troubled, he rode on, easing his sword in its scabbard, watching out for the menfolk, if any. Nothing stirred.

Beyond the village a dark shadow climbed the hill, a forest of pine trees. Grateful for the promise of shelter, he squeezed into a canter, ducking below the branches of the outlying scrub. Astonished, he pulled up. There was no sound, a cathedral-like calm lay on the place; aisles of tall trees pillared the way, shafts of dusty light fell on a deep carpet of pine needles. He slid down, pulling off his cap. There was a strangely spiritual feeling in the quiet of this forest, so suddenly come upon, and he took a deep breath of the resinous air. There was a trodden path, and he walked on, for the moment relaxed and at peace, going where it might lead him.

He walked until the light began to fade and the path sloped upward. Through the trees he glimpsed pale stone and smelt woodsmoke and he made his way forward into a clearing where a man in a brown habit was gathering pine cones in his skirts. The stone he had seen was a small shrine beside a low round building covered in bright tiles. The man straightened and turned.

"Welcome, *senhor*." Nick made a bow and came on, curious. The man bent his head and walked to the open door, lifting a hand. Nick dropped the reins and followed. Inside, smoke rose through a hole in the ceiling from a central brazier; there was no furnishing save a rough table, a bench and a low pallet against the wall. An altar stood opposite, with a breviary and a candle. Nick stood in the doorway waiting, while the man emptied his pine cones into a rush basket and turned to beckon. Without speaking the man began to set out bowls and spoons, setting a pot of water to heat, gesturing Nick to the bench.

"My name is Rokesby, Father, travelling to the Douro," offered Nicholas, his voice sounding strange in his ears.

"Tomasso." He said no more, busy with herbs and roots. Nick went back outside to hobble the horses on the sparse patch of grass and brought his coney to add to the pot. The man smiled, took it from him, muttered something over it and handed it back. Nick took it outside again to skin and gut it, not quite knowing if it had been rejected or prayed over. The meat was accepted with a bob of the head and added to the stew bubbling on the fire. Nick was silently invited to sit by it and given a steaming cup of aromatic wine. His host bowed and went to kneel at the altar. The silence was comfortable, and Nicholas sat peacefully sipping and wondering and occasionally stirring the pot. Presently, the hermit, or so Nick supposed him, rose and fetched a flat loaf of bread. He broke it, offered it up at the altar, and gave some to his guest with a dish of salt. Nick thanked him politely and so the time went on: the rabbit stew was eaten and cleared away, hardly a word spoken. Nick told him something of his journey and the man listened, his brown eyes, milky with cataract, fixed on distance. He offered Nicholas his bed and, the offer refused, knelt by it in prayer before lying down to sleep. Nick watched him for a while, and presently went out to check on his animals before rolling himself in his cloak by the fire. The air of the forest and a full belly, combined with the utter peace of the place, gave him the first real sleep he had enjoyed for many nights.

He started awake in the cold dawn, with a hand on his dagger. The mare was skittering about, snorting and Corsair was tugging frantically at his rope. He ran out to see beyond them a small wild pig rooting round the trees. He hesitated, the pig might belong to Father Tomasso. He put his throwing knife away and calmed the horses, found a bucket to give them water, and took some back inside. He had been wondering how to repay the hermit's hospitality, money seemed out of place. He went out and found an axe and attacked the pile of uncut firewood behind the hut. He left money anyway, beneath the shrine. A silent breakfast of bread and wild honey, and he was on his way, somehow encouraged by this strange encounter. As he cantered along the rides between the trees, hooves muffled by the pine needles underfoot, it began to seem like a dream. He found later that this was the Pinhal de Leiria, planted for timber two hundred years ago, and thought a holy wood. Holy or not, he felt the better for it.

The many streams that laced the low hills beyond the forest had joined together at one point to wear out a shallow defile, and he made his way along it. Presently, a pallid sun made an appearance soon obscured by heavy clouds. It began to rain again. A solid downpour developed and, seeing a clump of bushes growing out of the rocks ahead, Nick called a halt. He huddled there, sheltered by the overhang and the horses in front of him and, sitting with his hands laced round his knees, Nick wondered how much further he had to go. He had never been particularly gregarious, but this long solitude was beginning to tell. He talked to Corsair and the nameless one, reciting long speeches from plays to break the silence and to hear a human voice. After a little, the rain eased and he forged on, steeply uphill now, until he came to a level plain of fissured limestone, dry and empty of life save the few plants growing in the crevices, roots deep in the porous rock. Nick began to worry about water. Wary of the deep cracks and holes, when dark fell he hobbled the horses and resigned himself to a cold uncomfortable night in the open. The waxing moon rose and a wolf howled, answered by another, and some other creature made a strange coughing growl. Nick gave up any notion of sleep and he managed to light a small fire of dry brushwood, and watched, gritty-eyed, until dawn. A sip or two of water broke his fast, the rest held in the helmet for the horses, and he walked on, picking his way and praying now for rain. The grey clouds did not oblige and a cold wind blew. Nicholas was more and more conscious of hunger and his blistered feet, but the cold was the worst, penetrating his damp clothes and chilling his body in spite of his blanket. He tramped on, leading Corsair and the nameless mare, wary of cracks and feeling very exposed on this open ground. He was listening hard, tantalised by the maddening trickle of water deep in the narrow fissures, and speeded up. He could see wooded hillside far in the distance, this plain must come to an end soon.

When it did, it was hardly what he wanted. A steep cliff dropped sheer to a fertile valley far below, a river running through it, a dark belt of cork trees rising beyond. His head swimming, Nick cast about for a way down. He did not like what he saw. A narrow goat's path zigzagged across the face of the drop, crumbling limestone either side. The cliff stretched away unbroken to right and left as far as he could see. He moved back from the edge, weighing the options. Where a goat could go, a man could go, but with the horses? They could go along the cliff hoping for an easier way, but dusk came early and another freezing night in the open was not a sensible idea. He was reluctant to abandon the animals in this inhospitable place, he didn't fancy their chances with the wolves, but the idea of coaxing them down the face of the rock made his knees tremble.

He looked at the nameless one. She at least had her head up at last and was looking round. God, she was an odd-looking creature, still mud-coloured and filthy, but with kind treatment, her ears were now pricked and her eye brighter. Exceptionally large eyes, he noticed. He brought himself reluctantly back to the matter in hand. No point in delay, the choice would get no better; it was the goat path or nothing.

"I fear we must climb down," he said. Corsair snorted. Nick made a bundle of saddle and pack and anything else that would snag and hurled it over the cliff. He did not hear it hit bottom.

As always, the first step was the worst. The goats had carved a cleft in the rock, and, insides quaking, he took a deep breath and stepped off. Lead-rein in his left hand and feeling for the rock-face with the other, he went on, his gaze firmly fixed on the inside edge of the path. The horse hesitated and Nick made a dry-mouthed cluck. There was a bad moment as Corsair resisted the pull, then suddenly made up his mind and came with a rush, barging into him. The world steadied slowly, and getting his breath, Nick began to make his way down. Either the horse was more confident than he or he trusted his new owner, but he stayed dangerously close. In a cold sweat, Nick tried to transmit calm. He could hear sounds from above, but had to concentrate hard on changing hands to negotiate the first zigzag. *Only three more,* he told himself. *Get on.*

Halfway down, Corsair lost his footing and a back leg went over. Nick held on grimly and with a convulsive heave and scramble Corsair was back up, taking a slice out of the path. He had frightened himself and now stood stock-still and trembling. Cursing inwardly, Nick made soothing noises and slowly coaxed the trembling animal to move his feet, remembering Toby and the pack animal. "That makes two of us," he said aloud, and encouraged, the animal came on. The slow descent went on, the last bend was passed and they were down. Nick made much of Corsair, and tied the lead rein to a scrubby bush where a little rill of blessed water welled out. It tasted wonderful. He looked up. No sign of the nameless one.

It took all Nick's resolve to go back up that cliff. He took a deep draught of the water and started back.

Going up was not as bad as coming down and he made good progress until he got to the gap Corsair had made in the path. Vertigo suddenly seized him and he had to turn in to the cliff face and cling on, frozen, until it eased a little and he could shuffle forward, his back to the drop and his fingers digging into the rock. He fell on his knees the other side of the gap and crawled for a while until his nerve came back and he scrambled to his feet to go on and up. Once in reach of the top he threw himself forward and lay flat for a moment before lifting his head to look around for the horse.

She had her forefeet firmly planted on the rock in front of her, rolling her eyes. Stealthily he reached for the lead rope and she twitched her head away, backing. She led him a merry dance but she was not sweating up and he suspected she was not as frightened as she appeared. He stood still and spoke to her and presently she dropped her head to pull at a clump of plants seeded in a crack. He turned his back and went to sit cross-legged not too near the edge. He could give her a short while to settle, but it would be dusk soon and before then he would have to leave her; he would never manage the descent in the dark. Patiently he sat on, talking to her and whistling to keep his spirits up.

She wandered over to stand behind him, chomping, green stalks hanging out of her mouth. Corsair called to her from below, and the wretched animal whinnied back and calmly stepped onto the path and walked daintily down, a good imitation of a mountain goat.

When he got his breath back, seething, Nick got to his feet and followed her. "Horses!" he muttered. "Bloody minded, obstinate, chancy, capricious, fickle…" he ran out of adjectives and took to cursing instead, stepped across Corsair's gap and jumped the last few feet in a fine temper. Corsair and the nameless one were sharing a tamarisk bush by the stream, calm as you please, and presently the hard-pressed Nicholas saw the funny side.

"I'll be shinning up the ratlines with the best of them at this rate," he said to Corsair. Wiping away tears of laughter, he looked about him. The laughter died. Ahead lay a wide valley, laced with streams welling out of the cliff and dotted with stands of oak and lime, no doubt beautiful in summer when it was blowing with grass and meadow flowers, sheep and goats grazing, leaves on the trees. Now it stretched brown and barren, rising to a steep hill wooded with cork trees. The wind was bitter cold and strengthening, bringing a few flakes of snow. A frisson of fear touched him. Suddenly he was exhausted, his sweaty clothes freezing against his body, the scar on his cheek was hurting. He looked again, desperate for shelter, any shelter. Food could wait. At the confluence of two streams grew a welter of bramble and broom surrounding a group of limes. It would be better than nothing. He could make a fire…

Too tired to walk, he found his bundle, climbed up on Corsair and rode slowly downhill huddled in his blanket. The nameless one lifted her head, sniffing the air. She whinnied and broke into a trot. The mound of brambles resolved itself into a low hut, made for a shepherd at lambing time. Nick slid down and stooped to lift aside the woven branches that made a door. Inside it was dry, there was straw piled in a corner, a couple of sacks and a leather bucket. The sacks were empty save for a few handfuls of barley. Nick saw the animals settled in the shelter of the trees near the stream, and fetched water for himself. He built a small fire to make polenta with the barley. He did all these things with a mindless gratitude. He had ceased to worry about reaching Oporto on time: he needed to survive the journey. Feeling a little better, he went out to cover Corsair and the nameless one with his cloak and blanket, lay down in the straw – with the sacks and his head on Corsair's saddle – to recover himself and plan the next move. He shut his eyes to envisage the charts he had seen on a voyage south, and fell fast asleep.

There was a hard frost in the night and he woke to a world of white. Stiff and cold, he checked on the horses and warmed himself rubbing them down. He broke the ice on the bucket, made a new fire and gathered nettles for tea to wash down the polenta he had saved. The sun rose and began to melt the frost and he seriously considered resting there for the day: there would be fish in the stream and there were runs made by small animals. Not enough grazing for the horses, he thought; they were wandering further away. That decided the matter and he forced his aching body to pack up and leave the place as he found it, with a silver coin for the shepherd. He saddled up and rode north, over the stream, across the valley, up the hill and through the cork wood. The sun had gone in and it was trying to snow again.

He halted on the ridge, unwilling to leave the shelter of the trees. Through the brief flurries of snow he could make out another stretch of lowland, this time with a mosaic of low stone walls, enclosing what looked like vines.

"Where are vines, there are people," he said to Corsair. The nameless one had her head up and her ears were flickering. "Well, O wise one," he said to her, "let us go and find them. If they slit my throat, so be it." They passed a ruined farmhouse and an abandoned cottage, the snow stopped and the keen wind got up to blow in his face. He pulled up the blanket to ease the pain in his cheekbone and rode on.

He came to a paved road coming from where he knew the coast to be and followed it. He topped a rise, and before his watering eyes was not a farmhouse or a village, but a small township. There was a church tower and some tall buildings, and the wind brought cooking smells, the reek of wine and the warm odour of a smithy.

"We're in the Douro!" he said to Corsair, his throat closing up. "Well done, both of you." He mastered himself, took thought for a moment and dismounted in the shelter of a tumbledown hut to rummage in his bundle. Fifteen minutes later, he swung into the saddle, beard trimmed and hair tied back, most of the grime cleaned off face and hands, his jewelled sword bright at his side. No doubt he stank, but that couldn't be helped, any more than the state of his clothes.

"Bath first or food first?" he asked Corsair. "Food and a warm stable for you, I think. I wonder what day it is. Please God it's not a Sunday." He rode into the busy marketplace as if he owned it (it was not a Sunday) and in short order had a man following him to the inn with a basket of bread and wine and a serviceable suit of clothes. More gold bought him stabling with sweet straw and full mangers, with a promise of shoeing, a hot tub and a meal he could not finish, and a room with a fire.

"How far to Oporto?" he asked the landlord, barely able to keep his eyes open.

237

"A matter of five leagues, *senhor*, to the barrelling." Nicholas started to laugh and found he could not stop. He took himself, shaking, to bed. The walls closed in on him but he was too weary to care, even the fleas could not keep him awake.

Chapter Nineteen

He slept as if poleaxed and woke to set about some serious grooming. He strolled down for some breakfast, hair and body clean and deloused, his beard trimmed to a neat point, enjoying the feel of the rough clean linen next his skin. He found a saddler and asked for his leather jack to be cleaned and repaired, and bought boots of soft Spanish leather. In great good humour he visited his horses, to make much of Corsair who had served him so well, and the mare – the only one to have put on weight on the journey.

It was a crisp, cold, sunny morning, and he whistled as he led her out into the yard. He bought currycomb and brushes, stripped off his new doublet, rolled up his sleeves and set to work, sneezing as the dust rolled out of her coat. He changed his mind and fetched a bucket and washed her instead. He was surprised to find her mane coming up a deep russet, much the same colour as his own. As he worked and her coat dried she arched her neck and flourished her high-set tail.

Presently he stood back to look at her and his jaw dropped. Her curving tail dropped waving and tapering to her hocks, a long mane outlined a high crest behind her pointed ears. Her forelock fell between large lustrous eyes, her face was dished and her muzzle dark and velvety. The rest of her shone like dark bronze, short-coupled and slender-legged. With her sloping shoulder and rounded quarters she looked built for speed. The smith had come up to stand at Nick's shoulder. The nameless one reared up and sketched a graceful flourish in the air with her neat hooves, shook herself and looked round at Nick with a coquettish toss of the head.

"Fancies herself now, don't she," said the smith.

Nick remembered now where he had seen conformation like this: the palfrey on the voyage from Amsterdam. But that had been a more delicate creature, bred for a lady's ride.

"Arabian," said the smith. "See quite a few in these parts. The Moors brought em in. Can't beat 'em for speed and stamina, they say. From the desert. Is she broke?"

"I don't know. Very like. Her head looks small – I like her eye."

"Ah, you'll be used to a bigger sort. She'll carry your weight, senhor, never fear."

"She is beautiful." Nick untied the lead-rope and asked the smith to show her paces. At the trot, her knees came up in a high-stepping flourish, neck arched and head high. Nick stopped him there and took her along to the saddler. The only saddle to fit her was a high-backed affair of crimson Cordoban leather, circled and studded with silver, the bucket stirrups studded and chased. There was a matching bridle with bells on.

"It belonged to a great lady, *senhor*," said the man apologetically. "She died and so has no more need of it."

Nick sighed. "Take off the bells and change the stirrups and I might think about it." The haggling began and at the end of it, with a Spanish saddlecloth of striped and tasselled wool thrown in, a bargain was struck and Nick led away the nameless one in her new finery to try her paces in private.

Accustomed to the long steady paces of Corsair and the Friesian, Nero, he had to adjust to her shorter stride, but she answered him sweetly, her mouth soft as silk. He found a long straight stretch by the river, took off her saddle and vaulted onto her back.

"Go, lady. Show me."

It was like riding the wind. Neck stretched, nostrils flaring bloodred, she hardly seemed to touch the ground. Slowing to a halt at last, Nick slid off and flung his arms round her neck.

"I have a name for you," he whispered. "Shadow of the Wind. How like you that?"

The high-stepping Arab and the stately Andalusian were a sight to catch the eye as they entered the busy streets of Oporto. Nick had directions to the Quinta Gallio, and, with ample warning, Gallio was there at the head of the steps as he rode through the gates.

"*Por Dios*, Nicco, how did you come by this beast? How much do you want for her, hey? I had given you up for lost, man, and you ride in here like the Prince of Darkness himself, back from the dead!

"You – take the horses. Treat them better than your children…" He embraced Nicholas, kissed him on both cheeks and haled him through an arcaded colonnade surrounding a courtyard paved with mosaic, a fountain with a cracked basin in the middle. The whole ancient building was in a state of imminent decay, grass growing between the paving, houseleeks and lichen on roofs and walls. They passed between cracked pillars, Gallio talking nineteen to the dozen, into what had once been a splendid room, the painted ceiling with its gilded putti peeling and blotched with mildew. Smouldering braziers were dotted around and a log on glowing ash in the marble fireplace did its best to mitigate the chill. Gallio clapped his hands and shouted and an old woman and a boy appeared with trays. Nick wrapped his frozen fingers gratefully round a steaming cup. A woman had followed them in, tall and stately, glossy black hair skewered on top of her head, disdaining fashion. Tiered skirts swung above bare braceleted ankles and she topped Gallio by several inches. She nodded to Nick and poured herself wine, sitting down with knees apart and a tinkle of bangles.

"Carlotta, my love, this is the man I told you of. Spirited me out of slavery to be enslaved by you as slick as you please. Don't ask me why."

"For his own reasons," she said. Her voice, velvet-deep, matched her looks. "I can think of no other."

Nick bowed. "Enchanted, *senhora*."

She gave him a long unsmiling look and pushed a plate towards him. Gallio kicked a stool across.

"You look half-starved, man. Sit and eat. What took you so long – we heard of the *Sorcière* going down. Nothing to do with me, I assure you."

"I did wonder. It was beautifully done. You'd have liked it. In, out and away with a king's ransom. I walked."

"From Lisboa! Carlotta, I told you he was a madman."

"No ships leaving Lisboa but Spanish and war galleys. Troopships still there. What's going on?"

Gallio sobered. "You have been out of the world, my friend, and will not know. Philip of Spain died not two months since. They say he suffered greatly." He shrugged. "May he get what he deserves in the next world. We are in for bad times, Nicco. His

242

son is hot-blooded and ambitious. His writ is running now in Portugal. The good news is the troopships have been commissioned and there may be more than two. We should be ready."

"When you are."

Gallio laughed. "You are in good time. Eat and rest – get out of those horrible clothes. I cannot be seen with you looking like that. Where is my sleek silken ambassador, hey? You're a scarecrow, man, your horses fared better than you."

"It shall be looked to," said Carlotta. She rose in one movement. "Come, my lord Rokesby, I will show you your bed. Gallio is a mountebank and would keep you talking all night."

"Just show him, my dear. He was always willing to wear my nightcap."

"I have not walked from Lisboa to fall out with you, friend. Where is Trelawney?"

"One cannot tear him from the ship. And when he is not there he is besieging the fortress of a pretty girl in the Avenida di Castro. A thankless vigil: that fruit will not drop for less than a title or a fortune. But it keeps him out of the stews."

Too tired suddenly to enquire why the lad had not gone with the *Swan,* Nick shook his head and followed the swaying skirts of his hostess.

After the first deep sleep, Nicholas woke hot and uncomfortable and thereafter tossed and turned on the soft yielding mattress until, groaning, he rolled out of bed to wrap himself in the coverlet on the floor by the tiled stove. A pale winter sun was high in the sky when he woke a second time. A fine suit of clothes and clean linen had been laid out for him on the bed and beside it a tray of bread and meat, fruit and water. A tub of water steamed on the floor. When he walked into the salon, much restored, he found Tim Trelawney waiting for him, making lists. The young man jumped up, his eyes shining.

"I knew you would come, sir. Thrice welcome, sir."

"What are you doing here? You should be halfway to England by now."

Trelawney flushed. "I took it on myself, sir, to wait with the *Swan* awhile. In case of a change of plan – after we heard of the *Sorcière*. And the delay of the Spanish. *Swan*'s new cargo is loaded, sir, she wants only the word."

"Imphm. Glad to see you show initiative, Tim." He smiled and Trelawney relaxed, a broad grin spreading over his face.

"That's a fine horse you brought with you, sir. How did you do it?"

Nick had been thinking. He did not want to part with Shadow, nor risk her on board ship in a sea battle. Nor was he prepared to face Trelawney's mother if harm came to her boy. A useful solution presented itself.

"Never mind that now. It's a tale for a warm fireside. You have done well. Come down to the harbour and show me."

Gallio's vessel had been named simply the *Hawk,* but in conversation he persisted in referring to her as the *Golden Hawk,* which Nick took to be a deliberate parody of Drake's great ship, now laid up in Gravesend. He refused to rise to the bait and after a while, the *Hawk* she remained. She was a galliasse of some eighty tons, with a double bank of oars and twin masts. Newlypainted azure blue and scarlet, with a mermaid gilt as to hair and nipples at her prow, her lines were pure as a diving bird. Cannon were now mounted fore and aft and Nick saw leather-shrouded gunports at her sides. Her crew under the master sent by Piers had been welded into a disciplined fighting unit, raring to go. They were to rendezvous with Piers and Turnbull as soon as the troopships left Lisboa. Beside her lay the *Swan of Avon,* riding low in the water, half her cargo sold and exchanged for the dark wines of the Douro.

Nicholas and the lad combed the crowded taverns of the wharf to find Captain Morris, who would be drinking away his hours ashore. They found him in his usual state between drunk and sober, never the one nor the other except at sea, his fist round a leather bottle of his favoured drink, a black brew of porter and brandy. He staggered up at sight of Nick, waving his bottle in the air.

"Knew they couldn't sink you, lad – hey, drink for my friend! We'll be off now, then, hey? About time—"

Nick's two horses were swung aboard in slings followed by a bitterly disappointed Trelawney, denied his share in the fighting but entrusted with dispatches and letters and the care of Shadow of the Wind. He stood on the sterncastle waving his scarlet cap and Nicholas watched him go, dwindling as the *Swan* spread her sails and curtseyed to the waves, bound first for Bruges with her dyes and alum and pearls, and then London.

Nick sighed. If he were not committed, he would be with her and home in a matter of weeks, the god of ships and storms permitting. He returned to the *quinta* in melancholy mood, to be greeted by Gallio at his most ebullient.

"Word has come! The troopships have left – no more dallying here, Nicco, we leave with the tide."

Chapter Twenty

They flew up the coast of Portugal with all sail spread before a friendly wind from the west, and provided none of the storms that so beset the Western Sea at this time of year struck them, Gallio confidently expected to catch the Spanish convoy. The larger galleons of Turnbull and Piers, the *Circe* and the *Dolly May*, kept station to the west, their greater breadth of canvas half-reefed to keep the *Hawk* in sight.

The *Hawk* was well found, Gallio was not a man to stint, and dinners were convivial, well cooked and served with fine Spanish wines. Off watch, the crew played strange music and danced, strong contrast to the daily gun practice and disciplined handling of the ship. Nicholas was unsurprised; what Gallio did, he did well, and if he did it with dash and laughter so much the better. The flamboyant Portuguese left the finer arts of seamanship to Wells, the ship's master, and concentrated on gunnery. Gallio was in a fine state of excitement, constantly shinning up the rigging for a sight of the quarry. Nicholas stayed on deck, writing up his journal.

A momentary drop in the wind had them becalmed for a day. Rather than take to the oars and draw away from the others, Gallio seized the opportunity and after some signalling, had the longboat swung out to visit. He and Nicholas, in their best velvet and brocade, were rowed ceremoniously over to the *Circe* for dinner.

It was an occasion not to be forgotten. Piers with his black eyepatch, cadaverous in the swinging lamplight, the jolly farmer's face of Turnbull in his gold-laced doublet, a fine ring on each finger, arguing over battles fought and prizes taken, the devil-may-care Gallio, toasting his current mistress. And Nicholas, watching. *All four dangerous men, in their way.*

Turnbull ran his ship on lines that would become navy tradition, and they sat down to a fine dinner of four courses served on silver. The table was scarred but polished, like everything else in sight, and the swaying lanterns struck pools of red through the wineglasses. While eating, the talk was wide-ranging like that on the *Northern Star*, until the board was cleared and they got down to it, planning strategy with the silver salts and nuts and oranges. Piers' end of the table was soon littered with nutshells and he took his wine in a silver-gilt tankard with someone else's crest on the sides. Presently he began to sing in a tuneful bass, and he banged on the deck above to bring down a seaman with a Jew's harp. Slapping broad hands on the table, he launched into a fast, lewd round; with the four of them singing their turn the meaning was almost lost. Bells rang, midnight came and went, one song led to another and the party looked like going on 'til dawn when a brief rattle in the shrouds and a dip of the keel brought Piers and Gallio to their feet. Men were crying orders, the boats were swung out, the *Circe* was like a kicked ant's nest, the crew running aloft to catch the moving airs.

Nick and Gallio were rowed back to the *Hawk* with dispatch and they swung inboard to find Wells already making sail, the hands swarming in the rigging. The fitful breeze dropped to a universal groan, then came again, a zephyr, then a pygmy, then a giant, a hell of a much of a wind, the sails ballooned and the bowsprit dipped her mermaid breasts in the waves; white water hissed along the sides. Nick gave a hand to stow the boat and got out of the way. All three vessels were crowding on canvas and the *Hawk*, lightest and fleetest, was soon making a good ten knots.

She was the apex of a triangle now and was the first to sight the lumbering troopships ahead. A yell from the masthead had Gallio shortening sail to drop back to the others. The plan was for Turnbull and Piers with the heavier guns to sail between the three ships as they sailed in parallel, and for the yare *Hawk* to harass on all sides, with the main idea to dismast and capture, not sink the enemy with all her gold.

Gallio left the handling of the galliasse to the talented Wells and concentrated on the guns, Nick stood by with the boarding party and the grappling irons.

The Spanish ships crammed on sail in the hope of outrunning their attackers, but they were old and unwieldy; evidently the new King had not chosen to send his best ships and crew to Ireland.

The seamen of the *Circe* and the *Dolly* knew the next manoeuvre backwards. Both ships fired a warning shot from their bow-chasers, rapidly overhauling the Spanish. The reply from the stern cannon of the three ships was over-hasty and wide and Turnbull and Pierce flew straight for the open sea between them. The larboard vessel veered abruptly toward her sister ship, in an attempt to thwart Turnbull's intended double broadside, but it was clear Turnbull was quite prepared to ram her and the Spanish skipper lost his nerve and changed his mind, bringing her round on a tack that lost her air across her sails. She lost way and wallowed a moment and the double broadside is what they got as the *Circe* slid triumphantly through the gap, firing all guns. William Piers and the *Dolly* were on exactly the same game and the unfortunate ship in the middle lost topmast and mainsail and most of her rigging in a fog of red-hearted smoke and flame. The din and noise was deafening: the roar of the guns and the squealing recoil tearing up the decks, the scream and bang of sails and rigging, the groan of tortured wood and the shrieks of the wounded mingled with the cries of the battened-down troops. The middle troopship was invisible in a thick shroud of smoke, lit from within by the scarlet flashes of cannon, and as they passed the outer vessel, Nick could see men scrambling to free the tumbled mast and rigging. Deafened by the noise in unaccustomed ears, he did not hear the orders yelled at him and was picked up bodily and slammed against the tiller where both timonier and helmsman lay in a groaning heap. He gathered his senses and followed signals as Wells took in sail and ordered out the double-banked oars. The *Hawk* flew over the sea to the fast chant in battle order: the bow, the larboard, then the stern bombards fired as they passed. They rounded *Circe* and *Dolly* tacking for a return run and fled down the other side of the convoy. For convoy it was. Nick yelled at the same time as the lookout – two ships were coming up fast to larboard.

Only one of the troopships remained to give any trouble and her captain had already shown his lack of seamanship. The *Hawk* turned in her own length and readied herself for this new threat. Turnbull was already on a new tack that would take him between the approaching ships. They were small men-of-war, the same size as the privateers' two galleons, and Nick spared a glance to see what *Dolly* was doing. Threatened by *Dolly's* guns the remaining troopship had struck her colours, and a boarding party was swarming over the side. It would take time for Piers to change his strategy, and Nick saw Wells' intention. *Hawk's* boarding party had downed irons and was lending a hand with the guns, Gallio shouting orders from the poop.

The speed of the galliasse would take her past the leeward frigate out of the range of her guns, she would be hard put to turn into the wind to bring them to bear as the *Hawk* circled across her stern. *Hawk*'s guns poured a withering cannonade along her decks and turned to come again. Turnbull had seen what they were at and did what he was best at, engaging the other vessel at close range, exchanging shot for shot, his guns trained low. *Circe* took some punishment: she lost a topsail and most of her taffrail, a sign of the inaccurate shooting of the Spanish gun crews, and she wore away to give *Hawk* some sea-room. As she did so, a red tulip of flame bloomed in the waist of the Spanish ship and her magazine blew up. Debris rained onto the sea all around, some falling on the *Hawk*, wood and flaming canvas, limbs and bloody scraps and burning rope. A gun carriage flailed across her poopdeck, narrowly missing *Hawk*'s gun crew and disappeared over the side taking most of her rail with it. Wells was intent on keeping his prey afloat and re-passed the Spaniard's stern rowing at battle speed, firing along her deck from stern to stem. Her mainmast went with a crash and lay over her side trailing shrouds and canvas, her crew leaving the guns to seize axes to clear it. Turnbull had gone about and now appeared close-hauled to larboard, grappling irons and boarding crew ready.

"Damn him!" yelled Gallio, beside himself. "He would steal my prize—"

The rowers backed oars and Nick steered to come alongside; he passed the tiller to a seaman, the oars went up, the boarding crew threw the grappling irons and they swarmed aboard. There was a short flurry of hand-to-hand fighting and Nicholas found himself facing a man in an elaborate uniform all embroidered with bullion. The Spaniard fought bravely but to little purpose and in short order was pinned to his own mast with Nick's point at his throat. After that, little fight was left in the beleaguered Spanish, she struck her colours and her bloodied captain stood offering his sword. Gallio and Turnbull faced each other across him, Turnbull still in the grip of battle fever. Gallio bowed gracefully.

"The wind is backing, captain, I do believe we should disengage. The prize is ours." He took the man's sword and offered it back. "Gallantly fought, sir."

Turnbull bowed in his turn and bellowed for his shipmates to come and take command of the prize.

Gallio climbed down into *Hawk* among the rows of sweating oarsmen collapsed over their oars, with words of praise and a slap on the back for his men. The seamen were shouting and cheering and the physician Nick had insisted on bringing was at his work. To his surprise, Nicholas found he was bleeding in several places from flying splinters, none fortunately as large as the foot-long piece sticking out of the helmsman's shoulder.

The clearing up went on into the night, and a watery dawn found a new convoy composed of the three marauders and the Spanish man-of-war with her prize crew, escorting two sparsely-manned and empty troopships. The third disabled vessel – robbed of its gold, cannon and armoury, and now carrying all the troops intended for Ireland – they left to fend for herself. The officers of the captured ships were imprisoned on the man-of-war, bound for England and ransom. Piers had been all for sinking the crippled ship, troops and all, but Turnbull, watching Nick's face, had shrugged his massive shoulders.

"Poor devils – pressed, like as not. Let 'em save themselves if they can. This little foray has turned into an exploit, man. We can afford a smidgeon of mercy."

"Maybe you should find another trade."

"Fighting is one thing – close on nine hundred helpless souls on the wrong side of my ledger I can do without."

Seaman first, pirate second, this surprising Englishman went on to read the service over the sheeted dead as they shot, weighted feet first, into the sea, the froth from the white-capped waves showering his book. Waiting his turn with the physician, Nicholas stood bare headed on the heaving deck and listened to words he had not heard before.

"We therefore commit their bodies to the deep," said Captain Turnbull, his roaring voice brought to a rumble, "to be turned into corruption, looking for the resurrection of the body when the sea shall give up her dead, and the life of the world to come…"

Looking round at the solemn faces of men who only hours before had dealt out death and mayhem, Nick thought of the words inside the wallet next his skin. *That bourne from which no traveller returns…* he thought. *Who has the right of it? And when we finally know, what then?* He shook himself. "Come," he said aloud, alone in his quiet corner. "These are fine disembowelling thoughts for the middle of the Western Sea with a freshening wind and the Bay of Biscay still to come. Give thanks and get on with it." Favourite lines from some unknown, like him far from home, crept into his mind. *"Western wind, when will you blow, that the small rain down shall rain? Christ, that my love were in my arms and I in my bed again."*

"A familiar melancholy," said Gallio in his ear. "The battle waged, the battle won, and any man who can call himself a man takes thought. If he is not too far gone in mischief. Take heart, my friend, we are for England."

Chapter Twenty-One

London. November 1598

Tobias and the Rokesby escort made safe landfall at Deptford docks. Their sponsors had word of their coming, and Toby disembarked to find John Challoner waiting. The goldsmith had been first to hear of the loss of *La Sorcière* and her valuable cargo.

"Our friend was aboard her," said Challoner. "Did you not know?"

White-faced, Toby shook his head.

"Come, I know where we can find news."

Lloyd's was abuzz. *La Sorcière* was not the only vessel to have fallen foul of the pirates infesting the coasts of Spain. The good news was that they seemed to have fallen out among themselves, and rumour had it that Spanish troopships bound for Ireland and the rebellion had been intercepted and ransacked. The surviving troops, taken by surprise, had been abandoned to fend for themselves, at which point three English galliasses flying black and gold pennants had sailed in on the wind, engaged with the marauders, and had landed at Portsmouth with prisoners for ransom, Spanish gold and two empty troopships. A man-of-war had been sunk and another dismasted, for the survivors to take if they could. John Turnbull, Piers of Plymouth and the captain of the third vessel had taken their share and departed. The Queen was quoted as saying she "deplored such a masterstroke against our friends in Spain."

"So Gallio kept his word," thought Tobias. "You choose your friends well, Nick."

Challoner buttonholed a fellow-trader and asked for news of *La Sorcière*.

"They say she burned. Two merchants held to ransom. Genoese. The cargo is gone. Valuable, I hear. Was any of it yours? I hope you were covered, my friend."

"What of the others?"

"There were others?" He tutted and shook his head. "A sad business. Bad for trade." He bustled off leaving Tobias gazing after him in horror. Challoner was beside himself.

"Little weasel," he said, grinding his teeth. "Covered indeed! Bad for trade! The likes of him take no chances, I can tell you."

"What did he mean?"

"They lay wagers whether or no a ship will come safe to harbour. Five for one. No matter if a crew be lost, they are safeguarded on the turn of a coin. Pah!" He spat. "These poor Genoese – I will try for news of them."

"Are you sure Nick was aboard her?"

"So I heard. But so much is uncertain, Tobias – all may be well. Leave it to me. I will seek what news I can and come to you."

Toby found Inigo Jones sitting patiently on the dockside with the horses and dunnage. Lucius O'Dowd had come to take charge of the escort, still waiting to be paid and dismissed. He rolled up red-faced and beaming.

"A dilly of a trip! Where's Nick? We made a mint on that— What's the matter?"

"It looks as if he was on that galley that was taken. You may have to find a ransom out of your mint…I hope so."

Days later there was still no news. O'Dowd haunted the shipping offices and Tobias delivered Nick's reports, wondering if he'd mentioned the Spanish gold. Back at Crosstrees, he sorted through the pile of letters waiting on the table. Most looked official, one bearing the Queen's seal, and at the bottom, one from Kate. Toby recognised the writing and weighed it thoughtfully in his hand. Should he open it? He had sent Inigo on ahead with Nick's letter and his commission; he could not accept the idea that his friend might be lost. This letter was torn and travel-stained, much overwritten with addresses. The earliest mark he could make out was six months ago. *Best be prepared,* he thought. *If I have to go and tell her…*

The letter was short and to the point.

Nicholas, Hugh is sick and like to die. He would speak with you. Come.

Nick would have a word for all these troubles, Toby thought.

He just missed Tim Trelawney sailing in with the Swan on the next tide.

Chapter Twenty-Two

Plymouth. December 1598

The idler on the dockside, leaning hands in pockets and chewing on the stem of an unlit pipe, straightened and grabbed out his spyglass as three ships flying black flags rounded Penlee Point and tacked up the Sound. Behind them limped two broad-beamed vessels of Spanish build, low in the water, masts and sides splintered, flying a white ensign. A man-of-war with a spliced and braced mainmast came after.

The two pirate galleons carried 48 guns apiece and the galliasse a workmanlike arrangement of cannon fore and aft on poopdeck and stern chaser. Beneath the black flags he could make out the ensigns of William Piers of Plymouth and the black bull on silver of Sir Henry Turnbull. The third ensign he could not place, black hawk on gold. Their guns ran out and fired a salute, navy fashion. There was an appreciable pause as the guns of the shore battery, wrong-footed, took time to unload ball and shot and reply in kind.

The sounds echoed round the harbour and men and women poured out of inn and warehouse to line the dock cheering. William Piers was one of their own and there was not a customs man nor an officer-at-law who would dare arrest him, quite apart from the fact that he and Turnbull carried Letters of Marque – a pirate's licence.

The ships stood off in the main channel, and boats were lowered. Men swarmed down, heavy-laden, to man the boats and stow chests and begin to row ashore. After them came the captured ship with its load of prisoners, and the empty troopships with their skeleton crew to drop anchor near the Hard. The galliasse flying the black and gold pennant had reefed sail and now shot up the channel à l'outrance, oars flashing, drums pounding. She feather-stitched between two roundships lumbering to the sea, and with a shout and a trumpet and a change of beat, glided graceful as a swan to stay, her oars gently moving, out in the strand.

Swiftly she lowered boats and handed down boxes and bundles. In the first sat a sailor with his feet on one of several large chests and in the second a man with russet hair blowing in the wind.

The idler waited only to make sure of the identity of the russet-haired man before hurrying to find someone with a fast horse to carry the news to London of Nicholas, Lord Rokesby's return.

Timothy Trelawney, come to Plymouth with Shadow and Corsair after delivering Nick's dispatches, had haunted the quayside and the headland for sight of a familiar sail. When it was too dark to see, he repaired to the stables to commune with Shadow of the Wind and groom her to satin perfection. Corsair had his share of attention, nodding his head as Tim told him his master would be home soon.

Morris steadily refused to put to sea to look for him.

"Are you out of your muttonhead mind? A thousand square miles to miss 'em in. If you've nothing better to do, look to that gun-housing."

On this day, Tim's vigil was rewarded. He had taken Corsair for a pipe opener up on the headland and had seen the first glimpse of *Circe*'s sail through his spyglass. Galloping back through the town, he was the first to greet Nicholas as he stepped out into a foot of water, hair and beard curling wildly, his clothes a wreck.

"You did it!" Tim shouted. "By all that's wonderful, you did it – your horses are well, sir – come, come with me, my mother has had all ready this two weeks…"

Nicholas reached out and hugged the young man to him, the shingle beach heaving under his feet.

"Presently," he said, his voice rough and uncertain. "There will be much to do – find me a cart. Fetch me my horse. Oh God, Tim, I'm home…" and he turned with a whoop, planted his feet and waved, both arms above his head. The gold and black flag dipped and rose, a cannon roared and the galliasse reversed stroke to row swiftly, with whistle and drum, out past the galleons and back to the open sea.

"There he goes, the merry bastard," said Nick. "I doubt you'll see his like again." He dropped his arms and stood watching as the *Hawk* grew smaller and boxes and bundles piled up round his feet.

"But – her boats…"

"He'll anchor well out in the Sound and wait. Here, he gave me this for you…"

Nick dug inside his torn tunic and handed Tim a small object on a leather thong. It was a large gold coin, pierced through to take the cord. A Spanish piece of eight.

"Plenty more where that came from," he said. "The thing is done." He stooped for a handful of pebbles, chose one, tossed it and put it in his pocket.

"A talisman, to remind me to think twice next time."

Chapter Twenty-Three

Rokesby. December 1598

Tobias, back from hauling in the Yule log, heard a challenging cry from the gatehouse. He walked out to see a lean weather-beaten figure with a curly beard and a mop of russet hair riding in on a fine Arab, her mane and tail gay with ribbons, and leading a grey laden with packages.

"Nick!" he yelled as his friend swung out of the saddle, and he broke into a run. He was forestalled. Jack tore past him straight into his father's outstretched arms. Nick looked over his head and smiled.

"I told you I'd be home for Christmas," he said. Toby went to embrace them both, his own eyes bright with tears. "You devil, where the hell have you been?"

"Here and there, here and there. Now I am here. Bring on the dancing girls. Where's Kate?"

She was standing on the steps of the keep, her face white and set. Their embrace, encumbered by the child and watched by the gathering crowd of Rokesby people, was necessarily decorous. Nicholas looked round.

"Where is Hugh?"

Kate drew back. "Of course, you could not know. Hugh died this six months gone. I wrote, but…"

Nick looked at her, his face clouded. After a long silence, "My love, I am sorry for that. He was a good man, and a good friend to me. To us."

"He made a good end, Nicholas. He was in such pain – he spoke of you. Of both of us."

"I would have had his blessing."

"He never wished you to leave."

Tobias was running into the house, calling for wine, and Mistress Melville, neat and precise as ever, came to stand smiling and watchful. Hal Shawcross, a tall slender youth of fourteen or so came out and stood grave faced in the doorway of the keep, Knowles' hand on his shoulder.

Nick stretched out a hand. "It is a sad loss, Hal." The boy shrugged and turned away. Knowles came forward.

"It is hard for him, Nicholas. Welcome home."

"And not before time, you would say."

Jack was gripping his father's jaw, trying to turn his face. "Look at me, look at me! You're all prickles – have I not grown? Did you miss me – I knew you were not dead like uncle Hugh…"

"No, I am not dead and you are grown very heavy. And big enough to help with these parcels. You may take that one. The others must wait for the Yuletide feast."

The rest of the household had come out now, many new faces among them. Little Nick Wapshott, thumb in mouth, gazed solemnly at his godfather from his mother's arms. Impromptu celebrations began and Nicholas moved among his people, Jack on his shoulders with his hands skewered in Nick's hair. Even Hal's silent presence could cast only a pale shadow. Presently, setting Jack down to run to his nurse and find his present, Nick drew Knowles aside.

"Noll, tell me. How has it been? The boy worries me."

"I won't say things have not been difficult. Whether you were here or no, it would have still been so. Harder with you here, perhaps, for Kate. Hugh never fully recovered after the fire. The boy misses him. As do we all, a fine man. Towards the end, he confused you with your father, Nicholas, loyal to you both. But he was clear in his mind about you and Kate. Why have you come back, Nicholas – are you as clear in yours?"

"I was wrong to leave as I did. I see that clearly at least. I am here to make amends – if she will still have me, take me as I am. Things are happening among the great ones, Noll, I am not my own master even yet."

"Hugh understood that and so will she. She would not believe this tale of a second death, she has been waiting for you."

"She has spent too long waiting."

"The choice was hers, Nicholas. There has been no shortage of…er…suitors."

"Is that so indeed? She may not choose, then, such a one as me, away as often as not, nor wish to be dragged at my boot heels over half the continent. I would not blame her."

"Ask her."

Nicholas stood for a moment, strangely troubled, watching Kate overseeing the broaching of a cask of ale.

"I must thank you, Noll, for all you have done here. And without Hugh – it has not been as I thought."

"There is much goodwill. We have gone on well enough. Your new-come friend took all in hand – another who believed and waited."

"I am indeed most fortunate."

"Do you not think we make our own fortune, Nicholas?"

261

"I have another friend who would agree with you."

Much later, the boys in bed and the feasting almost over, Tobias tactfully removed himself and Nick took Kate by the hand and led her upstairs.

"Kate? Where—"

She pushed open the door behind her and stood to one side. When he made to draw her in, she moved away.

"No, Nicholas. It is not as easy as that. I must know where I stand."

"Did you not read my letter?"

"One letter. We are tossed up and down like that toy you sent Jack. He has had more from you than I. We will talk. Tomorrow. Elsewhere."

"You do not trust me?"

"I don't know. Sleep well after your journey." Her damask skirts rustled as she walked away, leaving him to such rest as he could find between his disturbed thoughts and the cold comfort of an unaccustomed bed.

He did not see her alone until the next afternoon when Mistress Melville had taken Jack, protesting, off for his rest. She led him into the estate office and he held a chair for her. It was a fine studded leather chair, rescued from the fire, he noticed, and she rested her head against its back. He drew up a chair to sit by her and she kept her hands folded in her lap. Chilled, he began hesitantly. "You know why I have come back, Kate."

"You have come and gone before, my lord."

"You would have wed me the last time, if not for—" He started again. "I have not changed, I am fixed, Kate. You are and have always been my morning star and the star of the evening – in the darkest times you have come to me and kept me steadfast, I want no other and nothing more than to keep you safe."

"Fine words, my lord; they smack of the playhouse – a prepared speech."

"Perhaps I have been among courtiers too long. Very well, to be plain, Kate, I am heart-sick of travel and trials, of time passing without the joys other men know: home, a family; you have given me a son that I hardly know…" He got up to kneel at her side. "Listen to me, Kate. I am no longer the boy you think me, to be told to run away and play. You speak always of shackles and ties and letting me go free to 'make my way in the world.' My way is made, Kate, and the ties you speak of so fearfully are the ties that bind us to the only thing worth having, the thing that lays the ground for other things to grow." Desperate for her to understand him, he took both her hands in his. "You see only what is between the four walls of Rokesby, beloved. Reading and hearing is not the same as knowing, there is a world out there waiting for you to take your place, a world of new ideas, new lands, new invention. Let me show it to you. I shall have duties still, yes, and promises to keep—" he paused, struck. "Now I bethink me there is a project I have not broached with you…"

"You see, my lord, you will always be up and doing."

He laughed. "Presently. Now I am talking to you. Serious matters, Kate. I am not fooling now." He stood up. "I am asking you, again, to be my wife. In all this you should be with me, not languishing at home like – what did you write me once – Penelope, that's it, weaving her web and waiting. I am no Ulysses, Kate, more a hungry suitor with less than the normal amount of patience." He took a deep breath. "Will you come with me as my bride or no?"

"Such eloquence, my lord."

"Will you or no!" he shouted.

"I will."

He stared for a moment, then started to laugh.

"You have been teasing me. You shall pay for that, mistress. But wait – have I convinced you? I am in earnest, Kate."

"I am convinced you are grown into a man to be reckoned with, Nicholas. If I misjudged, I am sorry. Understand this. I have a child and he had to be thought of. And there is Hal—"

"We have two children. Their future is our concern. Hal's training should have begun last year. I will see to it." He bent to kiss her. "Anything else?"

"One thing."

"Yes?"

"Your beard, sir. I shall be scraped to tatters."

He laughed, relieved. "Consider it gone. You will have a piebald husband. Come then Kate, come and help me."

"It is not the time, Nicholas."

"Oh." He thought he understood the reason now, for her cool reception. "Then name the day and we shall be wed as soon as may be. I can wait 'til then."

The Yuletide feasting done, a notary was sent for from Stratford, the very man who had drawn up the papers for Will Shakespeare's purchase of Hall Place. He trotted in on a little dun pony and established himself, precise in his lappets and black bonnet, in the lower room of the keep. He settled his papers and uncapped his inkhorn.

"So, my lord, if I have this right, you wish, on your marriage, to settle on Mistress Shawcross one half of your fortune and the interest accruing from the rest, one quarter of your interest in your business and the entitlement of the lands and messuages of Little

Rookham: the house and demesnes of Rokesby to be held by her in trust for your son, Jack Talbot."

Called in to witness the signatures, Tobias hesitated and drew Nicholas aside.

"Nick, is this wise? You are stripping yourself of most of your money and lands and involving her in a business of which she knows nothing—"

"What are you saying? I owe it to her. She would hold it in fee for my son. If I die—"

"Appoint trustees, then. Your kinsman at Court would advise—"

"Who better than my wife? I don't understand you."

"She is a woman, Nick – an efficient one, I grant you, but in the worst case, she could marry again. You wish to be generous, but…" he paused and drew breath. "How well do you know each other now? It has been so long. I only ask you to think."

Nicholas stared at him, rolling the pen in his fingers. The notary shuffled his papers and coughed.

"The boy has your name and will inherit," said Toby desperately. "This gives her power over the estates. I beg you reconsider."

Nicholas got up and went to gaze out of the window. Mistress Melville was in the snowy courtyard helping Jack build a snowman. The little boy had on a big red woolly cap and mittens, patting the snow into place with great attention, his tongue sticking out. Hal was standing with his arms folded, watching. Jack looked up at that moment with his father's smile and flung a handful of snow at him. Hal suddenly smiled back and retaliated. Mistress Melville stood back to allow them to chase laughing round the lumpy snowman, presently joining in herself.

Tobias stood at Nick's shoulder.

"That woman is a gem. Captain Shawcross found her, did you know? She has had care of the boy since he was born."

"And his mother." Tobias did not answer and Nicholas turned. "Boys need their mothers."

"Children need one person they can always depend on. You had your father. Jack had Mistress Melville and now he has you. And his mother," he added.

Nick frowned. Marlowe's last words to him came into his mind. "What do you really know of this woman now, Niccolo, apart from boyhood dreams and lustful fantasies? More to marriage, they say, than four bare legs in a bed." Kate had refused him her bed until after the wedding. They had hardly spoken in private. She had not mentioned his scarred face.

"Very well," he said slowly. "I will reconsider."

"Very wise, your lordship," came the dry tones of the notary. "If you will allow, I will make another draft with the necessary safeguards, should your widow remarry and so on."

Nick shivered suddenly, pushed past Toby and ran out to join in the snow fight. The notary caught Toby's eye, nodded, and gathered up his papers.

"Very wise," he said, and left.

Chapter Twenty-Four

Rokesby. 1st January 1599.

Nicholas stood before the parson in the little church, Tobias at his side, trying to control the tremor in his hands. Holly and ivy, scarlet and black with berries decorated the pews and stout pillars; braziers failed to do more than take the chill off the old stone. In his best fur trimmed green velvet, Christmas roses brooched to his cap with emeralds and another jewel trembling in his ear, he was white with excitement and dread.

He had not set eyes on Kate since supper the night before.

"Don't fret, man, she is coming. Brace up," said Tobias, fresh as a bridegroom himself in blue the colour of his eyes. "I hear them—"

The choir of children burst into song, Oliver Knowles and Hal, the only witnesses, stood up and Kate appeared in the doorway, all in silver-grey brocade patterned with rose, with a crimson-cheeked Jack carrying flowers and bursting with importance. Nicholas went to meet her and take her hand; the parson picked up his book.

Over the children's voices came a growing thunder, coming nearer and resolving into a clatter of many hooves. Tobias pushed past Nicholas and out of the door, confronting a body of men-at-arms in royal livery. Their leader, a man in herald's tabard, rode forward with a scroll.

"Nicholas, Lord Rokesby, is commanded into the Queen's presence," he said, in a voice that carried into the church. The Reverend Quincy dropped the book and Nick leapt forward. Jack started to cry.

"You interrupt a wedding, sir," said Tobias.

"Lord Rokesby is commanded forthwith. Come, sir, no disobedience, if you please. We are to escort you to the Tower to wait her majesty's pleasure."

"The Tower—" cried Kate, and, "For what crime?" said Toby.

The herald shook his head. "My orders are to brook no delay. Come, my lord. Your horse?"

Nicholas stepped forward, a scarlet flush on his cheekbones. "This is beyond bearing. Your warrant?" The scroll was tossed at his feet and the men-at-arms closed round him. He read it and passed it to Toby. He turned to Kate and picked up the little boy to soothe him.

"There is some mistake. I am accused of no crime—"

"You will be if you don't go," said Tobias quietly. "Go, Nicholas, I will deal with things here and follow you."

"No, stay until I send. This is some quirk of Her Majesty's. Kate…"

"Go, my lord," she said, her face like marble. "It will be as always. Go."

A groom had brought up Oberon in his bridal array, his mane and tail plaited and dressed with ribbons, spotted with the light snow that had begun to fall. Tobias handed Nick his cloak and stood by with Jack in his arms as he swung into the saddle. Nicholas was shaking with rage as the troop ranged round him, two before and behind, one on each side, the rest a smart column at the rear.

The wedding party stood frozen and watched them go.

They rode through the night, and most of the next day, silent, stopping only for a brief rest and to bate the horses, the snow falling thicker. At Tower Gate, instead of to the Keeper, Nicholas was handed over to another party of men in armour. His fury had sustained him until now, but this turn had him thoroughly bewildered. The sky was leaden, but the snow had stopped as he was firmly escorted to the gates of Whitehall. The guard dispersed all but one and he waited to see Nicholas ride through. He was met by an usher, left Oberon in the charge of a guard and trod in a black rage after the man down the familiar passage to the office of Lord Robert Cecil.

Cecil was pacing to and fro, the curve of his crooked back pronounced under the fur of his robe. As Nick entered, he rounded on him with a snarl.

"At last! What in the name of all the devils in hell are you about? Ambassadors do not vanish into thin air and reappear with no word! Where have you been?"

"My report—"

"Report! Hah!" He snatched up the papers on his desk and brandished them. "You call this a report? Cows, bulls, pigs – am I a finagling farmer?" Cecil, usually so calm and equivocal, seemed beside himself. "Where is the detail? Oh, I understand you well enough, but how? Why? The detail, man! Facts! And no mention of troopships or gold – I must find out your part in that for myself. And was it not beyond the bounds of courtesy to tell me you survived the wreck? I require information!"

Planted foursquare and fuming, Nick surveyed him. He no longer feared this man. "You dared to interrupt my wedding, my lord."

"Wedding? What wedding – Her Majesty will hear of no wedding, I warrant you. Talk you to me of 'dare'? Bethink you, Rokesby. You are no moonstruck calf to be dangling after a childhood sweetheart. Use that brain of yours, man – unless you keep it in your britches these days. Will you or no, you have made a name for yourself – disappoint Her Majesty you may not! But you talk of weddings. I may have saved you from the Tower after all. The Queen has other plans for you. As have I—"

"I am promised,"

"You are promised to me!" He was almost shouting now. "You have sworn an oath to your Queen, *Sir* Nicholas. Christ's blood, one Ralegh and his perishing wife are enough in my lifetime. What is it with you? Scratch your itch how you like, young man, but in God's name get on with the job!"

"Marriage will not hinder—"

"You think not? How will a wife and mewling babes help you at the French court, hey? Tell me that."

"To send armed men with talk of the Tower to affright my bride is not seemly, my lord, and I dare to tell you so."

Cecil sat back and stared. "A misunderstanding. Her Majesty has sent for you, it is true. If I have been over-impatient…" He shrugged. "Listen to me. The Queen may be ailing, but she knows where the interests of her country lie. We know, you and I, who was behind that letter. The Queen would have that particular snake scotched. Ha, good, eh? 'Scotched'…James' claim to the throne is in constant danger, as you know to your cost. Would you throw away all you have done? That snake is a

Hydra, lop off one head and it grows another. Are you listening, you young fool?"

"I am well aware of the danger. Statecraft is your business, my lord, not mine, and short of murdering the—"

"Bring him to me, guilty, and I will deal with him. Or find some pretext and dispose of him yourself. A Borgia would not hesitate."

"We are not dealing with a man. Douglas is a tool for his wife."

"Ah, now we come to it. The Lennoxes. Again." Calmer now, he sat down and waved Nicholas to a chair. He poured them wine and sat musing, nursing his cup. Nicholas, still standing, set his aside, untouched.

"'Uneasy lies the head that wears a crown, Rokesby...'" He broke off. "Where did I hear that?"

"In the playhouse. *Henry Four, part two.*"

"What! Tchah! These are serious matters."

"It is a serious play."

"Leave the playhouse out of this, Rokesby, and attend."

"I hear you, sir, and I am steadfast. I will marry Kate Archer. She is of good family: if that is your theme, there can be no objection."

"We may not marry where we will, Rokesby. Has she fortune, will she further your career?"

"What career? I have no desire to be a Court fly. If I ever had an ambition at all, it was to be an actor, but—"

"An actor? Phoh! What sort of ambition is that for a man of your talents?"

"I was about to say, sir, now I would turn the page, build my house, raise my children. Do what is in my power to keep this flickering flame of new thought alive."

"Perilous talk, my lad."

"We are on the crest of a wave, my lord," Nick went on unheeding. "We should not slide into the trough of idle politics and self-seeking. No, listen. Look at the wider picture. You laugh at the playhouse, but these poets' words are important, they will outlast any petty dealings of ours." Cecil stirred and Nick held up his hand. "Very well. This last threat to James must be dealt with, I agree; anarchy and the old regime must at all costs be avoided. I will go to the French court as you wish and finish the task, if fate allows. And I shall return for my bride."

Cecil gazed at him with narrowed eyes, twiddling his thumbs over his rotund little belly. He recognised at last the strength and iron will in the man facing him: one of the few who dared challenge him. He flattered himself he had done something to bring this about and he did not want to lose him. He smiled, and Nicholas kept himself from flinching.

"Yes. Well, better to marry than burn, as the good book says. Something may be contrived." He picked up a paper. "So, to matters of moment. A name has been mentioned. More than once. And a new face. Alexandre d'Aubigny."

Nick's nose came up. "Esme Stuart? He was d'Aubigny."

He made the connection, recalling one of the audiences with James of Scotland, reading and talking. The king had passed him a paper, his hand lingering on Nick's. "A poem. Written for a dear friend. You see, here, I call him an 'exotic bird, unique in beauty.' I see a little of him in you, Master Talbot. Read it aloud for me." Nick had sat still, his eyes on the page as he read. Presently the hand was removed. "He was old enough to be your father – I was only thirteen. They made me send him away. Named him a traitor." The king's eyes had been full of tears. The moment of intimacy had not been repeated and soon after Nick had been allowed to leave. But not before making some discreet enquiries.

"A disastrous relationship," said some. "A pernicious influence, dangerous." "Esme Stuart?" said others. "A charming fellow. Better off back in Aubigny."

"He was very close to the king," Nick said now to Cecil, drawn in in spite of himself.

"No, no," said Cecil. "You are looming, man. Sit. No, they talk of a younger man."

"Related?"

"Aren't they all? Damned incestuous bunch. This monstrous tangle of Stuarts and Douglases and Lennoxes is like a ball of yarn given to a kitten to play with." This unwonted flight of fancy tickled Cecil into a chuckle that turned into a fit of coughing.

"Yes," he said, recovering. "Well, you may be right. If there is a relationship this fellow may consider himself a candidate for the accession. I can find no record of such a man. Wrong side of the royal blanket, perhaps. You speak of a woman."

"Arabella Stuart, granddaughter of the Countess of Lennox – she was a piece of work, I hear."

"What a clear head you have for these things, dear boy. We must see you keep it on your shoulders."

"Very like, the Lady Arabella knows nothing of this – is she not young still?"

"Twenty-three, and with a clear claim to the throne. I hear no rumblings yet from that direction – unless this affair of the letter is the first."

"Imphm," said Nick. "We need facts."

Cecil relaxed. His man was engaged with the enterprise.

"Which is why you are going to Paris. Flush me out this Douglas who is pushing d'Aubigny."

He turned to his table and began to write. "Take this, if you will, to Ned Faulds at the Cardinal's Hat. He will go too, not with you, but to be at your back in case of need. I do not underestimate the guile of those two. The old woman Lennox especially is dangerous – 'a piece of work', as you say. Take someone with you that you can trust, as go-between, a page or some such. Not Fletcher, he is too well known and would be watched."

Hal Shawcross, thought Nick, watching the pen glide smoothly over the buffed paper. *I wish Kit would lay out his money on paper like that. Hal is ready, I may get on better terms with him.* Carey had offered to take the lad under his wing to begin his training, but Nick did not see the wilds of the Border country as suitable grounding for his foster child. This was a chance to guide the boy himself. He had heard great things of the French court of Henry the Good. Something positive could come out of this for Hugh's son.

He gave his short nod and took the sealed letter. *I wonder what other orders he's given Ned Faulds*, he thought. *We shall see.*

"Now," said Cecil comfortably. "I have waited long enough. The detail, if you please. Her Majesty is pleased. You are to be rewarded, though I imagine you have already rewarded yourself. I do not wish to know. But how? And who? I am greedy for news, you wretched boy. Cold meat is better than none."

Nick had to laugh. "My apologies, my lord. There are things best not written even in cipher." It took over an hour before Cecil was satisfied he had wrung every ounce of information from the report, and nodded permission to leave. Nick was at the door when Cecil called him back.

"What did you do to my man Poley? He's a broken reed. I must say I thought you would dispose of him. He has dangerous secrets."

Nicholas smiled grimly. "Keep him close, my lord. Love him, cherish him. Find him useful employment."

Lord Cecil was still laughing as he quietly closed the door.

Nick went on his way to Bankside still angry but feeling he had not come out of it too badly. There were a number of things Cecil still did not know and there were signs his union with Kate might be looked on with complaisance. Worth the delay, perhaps. At least there was something he could tell her when he sent for Hal.

Nicholas bumped into Ned Faulds coming out of the Cardinal's Hat and passed him the message.

"I will meet with you before I leave," he said. "My fond duty to your cousin."

"She will be pleased to know the tales of your death were exaggerated, my lord," said Faulds with a sly grin. "In the pink and off to see the Queen. With Essex in Ireland and out of favour, if you play your cards right, who knows?"

"What news of his friend Mowbray?"

"Still in the Tower awaiting trial. And still in the best of health, unfortunately. We have scotched the snake, not killed it, my friend," he said, an unconscious echo of his master. "Watch your back in France."

"I thought that was your job."

"We shall not be moving in the same circles." He swept a mocking bow. "Your servant, my lord."

Nick shook his head and remounted. He would not visit his anger and frustration on Meg a second time. He had made himself a promise in Verona and he would keep it. He felt like a good fight. Perhaps he would go home to Crosstrees and get drunk. He pulled off his cap and dropped the dead flowers in the mud. "I will send."

Chapter Twenty-Five

Nick Talbot rode out of the alley and along Willow Street. A playbill caught his eye and a notice beneath it. He read the notice and tore it down, muttering to himself. A voice hailed from an upstairs window, and in a moment, Robin, sometime friend and fellow player, hurtled into the street. Nick sighed; he wanted to get to Crosstrees and send a message to Kate.

Robin would not take no for an answer and haled him along to the Rose to hear all the news. He found the players cock-a-hoop with news of trouble at Blackfriars.

"Their lease of the ground has run out," Robin told him gleefully. "And the elders won't renew it – they want the playhouse closed down, miserable killjoys. Still, more business for us, hey?"

Nick liked Richard Burbage; he had given him that first chance, and as an actor he was head and shoulders above any other. As soon as he could extricate himself from the crowd of excited actors and avoiding the anxious eyes of Will Shakespeare, he rode out to Blackfriars to see what was going on. He crossed the bridge, glad of his furs in the freezing wind, and was immediately transported back to the Low Country where he had met his temporary nemesis in the form of a Jesuit priest. The Thames was frozen deep. The scene was the same as in Antwerp: the river frozen solid, boats and ships immobilised, their masts fringed with long icicles. People were skating, children in bright caps playing with sledges and toboggans, their laughter mingling with the cries of the hucksters who had dragged their stalls onto the ice. He smelt roasted chestnuts and cheese, some enterprising soul had set up a hog roast on the bank, groups of musicians dangled their legs over the sides of the hamstrung boats. All London seemed to be partying. He asked a passerby with a scarlet-cheeked child on his back, "How far up is it frozen?"

"Up beyond Maidenhead, they say. Won't be no trade comin' in for a month o' Sundays they do reckon."

Nicholas urged Oberon on and up Threadneedle Street, past the frozen well and under Bishopsgate Arch, where icicles hung pendant from what was left of noses and chins and kneecaps left rotting there, an obscene ice sculpture. He was wondering, if the Theatre was really doomed, if those two great actor-managers, Burbage and Alleyn, could be brought together by a play of the magnitude of the one he carried in his satchel. All was silent in the Artillery fields and as he turned down Hog Lane he heard raised trained voices carrying on the still air. He dismounted and led Oberon behind him into Burbage's fine Theatre.

It was bedlam. The entire company seemed to be assembled, shouting. Burbage was up on the stage, arguing with a thin greybeard in black fustian waving a sheaf of papers. Nick hitched Oberon to a sturdy upright and pushed his way through the crowd as the greybeard shook his head and stamped off, leaving Burbage standing white faced, his massive shoulders slumped. Nick climbed up to stand at his elbow. Burbage did not recognise this tall young man with the scarred face and fine clothes for a moment, then a gleam lit his eye.

"Nick Talbot, by all that's wonderful! Made your fortune, I see."

"What's happening here?"

"The last fine tragedy I shall take part in. We're finished. Ground cut from under us."

"I don't understand. You've been closed down before—"

"The lease on the land is up on Lady Day and the buggers won't renew it. The law's on their side this time. We're done for."

"And the building? The Theatre – they own that too? I thought—"

"No, by God, my father built this theatre and all that's in it – damn their eyes, they shan't have that, I'll burn it down first." Nick had been looking round at the strong wooden structure where he had staged so many play-fights and learned his actor's craft. It had been built in the usual way, beams cut and dovetailed and pegged with wood. *Like a jigsaw,* he thought. Inigo's detailed drawings for the masque came to mind, everything numbered for position.

Burbage had jumped down and was now the centre of a dejected group of players. Walt, the chief carpenter, was sitting on the edge of the stage almost in tears. Nick sat down beside him.

"Does Burbage still have that parcel of land near the Rose?"

Walt shrugged. "Dunno. What's it matter, we can't afford to build a new playhouse on it…"

"Why not move this one?"

"Eh?"

"You put it up. Number the beams and take it down. It's your building, take it."

"*Take* it?"

"Why not? Enough men and a bit of expert knowledge, why not?"

Walt stared at him and sat for a while transfixed, his lips moving, his eyes fixed on a distant prospect. He began to grin, and jumping up, he yelled for quiet.

"We're going to steal our theatre," he shouted. White faces turned up to him and, hands sketching the air, words falling over each other, he told them. "Have to move fast," he ended, "afore they get wind of it."

"Where would we put it?" asked a practical soul.

"Store it!"

"Sell it!" They were all talking at once. "There's a warehouse by the docks…"

"Move it twice? No thanks," shouted Walt, carried away. "Take it where their writ don't run, the south bank…"

"How?"

"Over the bridge…"

"They'll soon guard the bridge," said Nick. "Try the river."

"The river's frozen…"

A long silence.

"So it is," said Burbage, slowly. "So it is."

A cheer went up. "Carts!"

"Wagons – horses…"

Nick was amused. Images of fierce discussions on board the *Northern Star,* flying north to Archangel had come to mind, his own talk of ways and means for the courier business had sparked it off – fertile minds finding ways to carry trade to the ice-bound heart of Russia. "No, no," he shouted above the din. "Sledges! Make the big beams sledges for the smaller, send men across with ropes and pulleys, make a fulcrum and it's done. Find an engineer."

It was like poking a wasp's nest with a stick… Carpenters went for tools, someone went to fetch a brother who worked in the shipyard, eager hands scrambled to begin the work of demolition. There was no time to waste, word would reach the city fathers soon enough. Nick could not resist. He suggested they set a guard, pulled off his fine fur-lined cloak, dropped it with sword and wallet and seized a mallet and chisel. The two lads playing female leads found crayons and got busy numbering the beams.

"Don't worry too much about that," said Walt. "I doubt she'll go up the same shape she comes down."

"Plenty of time to think about that," roared Burbage, crimson with excitement and exertion. "Get it done! Rope, Francis! Ladders!"

Carpenters, joiners, actors, scene painters all swarmed over the building. Thatch and tiles pitched into the street, roof trusses began to come down. Friends and relations arrived, with carts and wheelbarrows and baskets. Actors from other companies arrived to lend a hand and the noise grew. Nick sent a boy with a message to Ponsonby to send men to stand guard. Early in the afternoon the low sun began to go down in a fume of red, and the stars came out hard and bright in a darkening sky. Flares were lit to rival those on the river as the first sledges took shape.

"Horses," said Nick. "To get to the river." There was a barracks nearby, across the archery ground, and slipping and sliding, cramming on his doublet, he fetched Oberon and went. Back again with six horses and more willing helpers, he found the top of the building down, trusses roped to the half-ton beams, ready to glide on the slick cobbles, and a furious group of burghers with some of the Watch, shouting at Burbage. Ponsonby's men stood impassive between them and the work going on, and after a great deal of futile argument they departed, threatening all the might of the law.

"It'll cost me a lawsuit or three," said Burbage. "But what of that? I'm in the right of it. They won't get my Theatre."

281

Men were busy at the riverside by now, rigging block and tackle. They had chosen a spot where frozen debris narrowed the flow and the ice was thickest.

"We'll need draught horses the other side," said Nick. "I'll go. There'll be a guard on the bridge by now but they won't like to stop me." Hans Reuter, a Dutch engineer, had come with Francis' brother and he went with Nick to oversee the operation on the south bank. In his furred cloak and jewelled cap, Nick encountered no resistance from the guard set on the bridge. They called in at the Elephant where a few coins secured the help of four burly draymen and their horses, and cantered along Willow Street and through the silent Paris Gardens, a youth trundling a barrel of ale behind them. Excitement was running high and the barrel was greeted with a shout.

Men were skating and sliding across the river now, thin ropes snaking behind them tied to thicker ones that followed on, the structure of pulleys went up under Hans' direction and the big steal began in earnest.

"Not a steal," said Burbage. "This is *my* Theatre. My father built it," he repeated, "and by God I'm going to build it again."

"New place, new name?" said Nick. He had things to do and was preparing to leave. The sheer volume of men willing to cock a snook at authority meant the whole business was going amazingly fast; it was time to get to Crosstrees and see to his own pressing affairs. And perhaps get some sleep.

"The New Theatre?" said a voice.

"No, no." shouted Burbage, waving his arms about. "It's got to be *big*, something that means…it's got to show the world…"

"The Conquest," said someone. "The Universe…"

"Too long," panted Burbage. "Mind that rope there. One syllable…"

282

"The Star…The Globe!" said Nick. Burbage straightened up and took the mug held out to him.

"The Globe. The Globe… I like it. Universal – takes it all in. I like it."

"Got to build it first," muttered Walt.

"Come the spring, the foundations. Open by summer. We'll need a new play."

I have just the thing, thought Nick, pulling on his gloves. *Master Shakespeare shall have the new Hamlet after all.*

The exercise of moving the playhouse had cleared his mind and channelled his anger. Nick's letter to Kate went off that night, carried by Michael.

My dear Kate

It was all a monstrous mistake. I was sent for it is true, but for a task only - the hullabaloo was a nonsense. Do not worry. I am sent to France. You may not come with me as I hoped, but I would have you entrust young Hal to me as my friend and page. Thus he will have opportunity to begin his training for the place he will occupy in the world. It is high time. I will care for him as my own and shall allow him into no danger, I promise you. Nor should there be any, I go as emissary only. (A little disingenuous, Kate. I'm sorry.) He should come as soon as I send. I am to have the promised (not threatened,) audience with the Queen before I go, but the sooner gone the soonest back, sweet, and we shall finish what is begun, the rest of our lives together.

I am as much galled by this as you, Kate, but be patient as you have ever been and all will come right. I shall have much to amuse you, how a playhouse moved as if by magic, and how my

masters change their tune. Master Jones will return to you; he
knows what he is to do; I trust he will not prove a burden to you.
He is a great artist and craftsman; he will build us a home fit
for you to adorn. Bear with him. Kiss Jack for me and tell him
his will-o'-the-wisp father will soon be home.

Yours in duty and affection, N

This vital task done, he took himself to bed and slept.

Chapter Twenty-Six

The Palace at Whitehall

In the morning, he looked out suitable clothes to attend the Queen and presented himself at the obligatory palace breakfast in the indigo velvet he had worn to the Arsenale. Thinking of the warmth of Venice, he walked through the icy passages and chilly halls of the palace, greeted as he passed by a number of eager acquaintances and men who remembered him at the joust. He was met and conducted past the whispering knots of courtiers and supplicants, following the straight back of the Gentleman of the Bedchamber with his silver rod. A servant trod silently behind bearing the gift he had brought from the Spanish captain's cabin, a magnificent silver-gilt saltcellar by Cellini, probably stolen many times over. Crossing the Great Hall, he stopped so suddenly that the servant cannoned into him. Ignoring his horrified apologies, Nicholas stared across the room at the flaming red head of his cousin. Young Colin Melville, last seen as his raw and roaring squire at the tourney, at court to acquire polish and conduct, stood there, tall and brawny and perfectly still in an excellent suit of hop-green damask, his knee bent in negligent pose, one hand on his sword hilt – a perfect parody of Nick himself. Someone had taken the lad in hand – Robert Carey probably. Even his freckles seemed to have joined up. No: he caught sight of Nicholas and flushed, and they all jumped out again. He began to push through the crowd and the gentleman with the rod turned impatiently to urge Nick on. Nick waved to Colin – "later" – and moved forward, oddly happier.

The audience chamber was full as usual, men and women wearing the price of a troop of horse on their backs, all waiting Her Majesty's pleasure. There was no one here he knew, until Robert Cecil hurried through amidst a knot of black-robed councillors. A doctor arrived in his scarlet robe and cap, with his assistant carrying his box. The babble of conversation hushed until he returned smiling and the noise began again, heightened. The queen held no audience that day nor did she appear at dinner. About to leave, Nicholas was waylaid by a page and shown where he was to sleep. Mercifully he had the room to himself. Someone seemed to have stuck a knife in his lower back from the long standing – he had forgotten what it was like. A servant came to pull off his boots and deal with his buttons. He was asleep before the man left the room.

The next day was much the same, enlivened only by a flurry of messengers and a captain still in his muddy clothes and battered cuirass, come from Ireland. Cecil and the council arrived in a hurry and were closeted with the Queen until dinner. By the strange osmosis of the Court, word had got round and Nick was noticed and his attention sought. His goblet had been filled a number of times when a stalwart leg was flung over his bench and a gentleman who from his profile could only be a Talbot settled beside him. A well-set-up man of about fifty, he had the high colour and the white fans creasing the eyes of a man who had spent his life at sea. He pulled a dish of pears in crust towards him and got out his knife.

"So, Rokesby, how does my godson? A fine addition to the family – pity about his birth. A little hasty, there, my lord. I hear you've acknowledged him? Good. Going to marry the wench? Not that it matters, you have your heir."

Recovering from this broadside, Nick raised his cup. "My lord Admiral?" he said. "I'm obliged for your attention. Jack will be grateful."

"Your father was a stiff-necked bastard, Rokesby, I trust you have more sense. You seem to have made a good start, keep it up. You may want to reconsider the boy's future. I liked that nurse. Good style. Robert Melville's granddaughter, he who was Privy Seal. Shawcross chose well." He had finished his pears and started on a mess of brown meat. "This duck is too sweet... You're not eating."

"I've had my fill, my lord."

The Admiral cocked an eye at him and grinned and the family likeness sprang out.

"By God, you're like him. No offence, young man. All in the family. Look here, Rokesby, I've no sons of my own – five daughters, bless 'em. I'm taking an interest. You are away on the Queen's business and good luck to you. Want to keep an eye on the boy... "

"Believe me, Sir William, I am fully sensible of the honour—"

"But you don't know me. That can be remedied. We shall expect you for supper tomorrow. My lady wife wants to meet the man who brought in three Spanish ships."

He had finally achieved his object and made Nick laugh.

"Not all by myself, sir."

"That's better. Ten of the clock. Her Majesty may see you in the morning."

Young Colin caught up with Nicholas on his way out and beat him on the back.

" Do you know who you were talking to? Is he kin? That's the

287

man who followed Drake to beat the Armada! Don't often see the Admiral at court. What did he want?"

"Come outside, you cheeky infant. There's something I want to ask you."

It was afternoon before Lord Rokesby was summoned. He was ushered through the crowded anterooms straight into the Small Audience Chamber with its newly covered throne – brown again – and left alone to wait. It was a long wait, but she came at last, dressed all in white velvet, walking slowly on the arm of a gentleman-usher and attended by two ladies-in-waiting. Nicholas went on one knee. Once established on her dais, quilted skirts with their flashing emeralds arranged to her satisfaction, she flapped a hand for the attendants to leave.

"You may rise." She surveyed him beadily from head to toe and Nicholas looked sturdily back. He saw to his distress how much she had aged. Her head nodded a little within its stiffened frame, neck and hands were withered and spotted, under the white paint her mouth was puckered and her eyes deep-sunk and pouched. They had lost little of their brilliance, however, and she stared him down.

"Well, my lord Rokesby, how do you find your prince now? Are we changed? And before you open your mouth, we want from you what we have always had from you, honest answers if few. No pretty courtly speeches, if you please. I have my fill of those." She leaned forward as if to see him better. "Someone has marred that handsome face, I see. Not invincible, then. Now, young man, I have sent for you because it seems you will not clamour at my door – if I wish to see you I must send." She held up a jewelled hand. "Be still. I do not sue for your service, Nicholas Talbot, but it seems I have it without asking. I do not choose to be indebted. This last exploit –

I imagine you have ta'en your tithe already, like those other rascals. Although one can never have enough money." She sighed and fiddled with her loose rings. "So, what would you? An earldom? There has long been a place for you here at court which you seem loath to occupy."

She tilted her head in its crimson wig with a grotesque echo of past coquetry. An earring flashed green. "What can we offer you? You may speak."

Nick hesitated, then said boldly, "I seek permission to marry the woman of my choice, your Majesty, and to be allowed to play in your Majesty's company of players."

For a moment he thought he had gone too far, the boot-button eyes narrowed and the turtle mouth hardened. Her fingers drummed on the arm of her chair. A long silence. Her arms stiffened and she sat back with a grim smile.

"You do not fear to displease us, Rokesby. The second wish is easy to grant, provided the play is brought here to Whitehall to entertain us. As to the first, we have chosen a bride for you. A woman you know – have known already too well, if the tattle I hear is true. The Lady Rosalyne."

Nicholas had gone on his knees. "Your Majesty—"

"Do not dare to interrupt me, sir. The Lady Rosalyne is a wealthy woman, otherwise unlucky in her husbands. To lose two seems a little careless. She may be more fortunate in her third, as indeed she is. You are quite a catch, my lord."

"Your Majesty, I am betrothed—"

"Be silent. You are betrothed indeed. The wench is willing. When you are done in my service in France, I would have you here at Court to cheer my declining years…" She smiled a mirthless smile. "Of which I am often reminded."

For a moment, the beguiling charm of the young Elizabeth peeped from behind the painted mask. "Come, my sweet lord. Thus far you have been worthy of my trust. I will tell you something. Get off your knees and sit here by me."

Nick rose to sit on the step at her feet. She went on quietly. "Before I am dead, the carrion birds pick at my carcase. These Lennoxes are not the only ones to conspire for my throne... Essex. My dearest friend and boon companion, Essex. Before he left, he burst into my bedchamber– yes, my person in disarray and he in such a fury. I begin to fear him, Rokesby. I need an honest man to stand between us."

"My lord Cecil—"

"They correspond. Oh yes, my little elf is not the only commander of secrets."

To his dismay Nick saw a sparkle of tears in her eyes. "You may command me in anything, your Majesty, but I pray you not to ask me to betray a vow."

"Are you as loyal to me, my lord, or is your fealty only to my realm."

"They are one, my Queen. I tremble for you both."

She looked into his face long and hard.

"Well, we shall see. Weddings can be delayed, can they not? Work with me in this, my lord, and you shall have your reward. We are agreed? Now, tell me how you came by that scar and two empty troopships..."

Nick left the audience chamber shaking, dismayed by Elizabeth's ambiguities and vague promises. She might be an old woman, but she knew very well what she was about. She had given Essex power and it was turning against her. *These powerful men,* he thought. *They all do it. Give me the playhouse, where we poison only in jest.*

He spoke to no one on his way out, and those who spoke to him gazed after him, wondering what he had been promised. Tongues would wag busily that night.

He found Young Colin waiting for him in the stables, admiring Oberon. Nicholas could not spare time for more than a brief and buffeting exchange of news, and his confirmed offer of a trip to Paris met with an echoing yell of excitement.

"Steady," said Nick. "You'll burst your fine buttons. If you can get leave, come to Crosstrees in the morning." He eased out of a bear-hug and mounted up, eager to see if there was news.

By the time he turned into Deptford Strand, past the butchers' yards and the bloody reek of the slaughterhouses, he was racked with guilt over his interview with the Queen. What had he agreed to? Elizabeth had seemed to connive with him, implying this was some game, but he knew enough of her ways to mistrust her. "Agreement" was diplomatic talk.

"Coercion, more like," he said aloud. "My head in a noose." To be betrothed to the Lady Rosalyne, the woman he had taken in a young boy's frenzy – no. He would make for France with all speed, before the thing could be made reality. He prayed that no kind soul would leak the news to Rokesby.

The sight of the Rokesby roundship at her mooring crystallised a vague plan that had been forming in his mind. If he could present Elizabeth with a fait accompli, she might be merciful. *As she was to Ralegh and his Bess?* said a small voice. Nick shrugged. What better example?

He found Timothy Trelawney in his berth on board the *Swan*. Tim had been offered a choice of excellent lodging or a room at Crosstrees, indeed was well enough rewarded to set up for himself, but he preferred to stay on the ship, a member of the Rokesby company.

They sat in the master's cabin at the stern, Nick occupying the bench under the broad window, looking downriver through a tangle of shipping, a cup of wine turning in his fingers.

"So you see, Timothy," he concluded, "there is a difficulty. My lady and I could be wed by proxy– if she would agree. Tobias would stand for me. And I want young Hal brought safely here. I need a man I can trust. Will you go?"

Trelawney's freckled face was pink under his fair hair. "Like a shot, sir. But the Queen – would you defy her?"

"It is a risk I must take. But you need not."

"It is not that, sir, but – after all, you have only to wait…"

"My lady has waited long enough."

"Then of course I will go. And sir, if you please, I would go with you to France. It is not right you should take only a page."

"I thank you for the offer. We shall see. Now go. There is need for haste, but don't kill my horse."

Nicholas spent a convivial and reassuring evening with the Admiral and his wife. The two unmarried daughters were admired and flirted with, the sea battles re-enacted and the battle of the Armada fought with nuts and knives and oranges, taking him back to the cabin on the *Circe.* Lady Talbot retired and, far from raising domestic problems, Sir William spoke of Nick's father and the wide-ranging Talbots. He did not mention Jack until he was seeing Nick to the stables.

"This is a difficult time, Nicholas. Be easy. There are those who will watch over your boy."

Trelawney was back in five days, riding in as the last of her cargo was loading into the *Swan,* and bringing Shadow with him. He was red-eyed and tired, not only from the cold of the journey. Behind him rode Hal Shawcross, with a mutinous lip. The boy went straight to the stables with the horses, and Tim strode into the house throwing off his heavy cloak. He laid a thick packet on the table. Nick looked at him and pushed across a flagon. Taking up the packet, he cut the threads and the wax and opened it. A ring rolled out and spun on the table, the emerald flashing sparks in the firelight. Ignoring the flagon, Trelawney bowed and left the room. Lord Rokesby would need his privacy.

There were two letters: Nick opened the one in Kate's precise writing first.

> *My lord Rokesby.*
>
> *Consider yourself free. I release you from a betrothal that is proved inappropriate and a danger. I am to enter the household of her grace of Shrewsbury, as your kinsman arranged, where your son can be brought up as he thought fitting. Generously given your name, his begetting will be no shame to him. I pray you do not seek to change me in this. I shall be conscious always of what you have taught me – so much now, in so many ways. The patterns of your life are not mine, my lord and can never be.*
>
> *God keep you. Kate Archer*

Nicholas sat motionless for a while, his heart beating fast, the heels of his hands pressed into his eyes. Whatever he had expected, it was not this. Presently he took up Toby's letter. It was a scrawl, obviously written in some distress.

> *Nick, she is adamant – and angry. She set this in train as soon as you left. Shawcross arranged it when he knew he was dying and*

you not home. The connection is from a kinsman of yours at court, William Talbot. He stood godfather to your boy. I suppose there has been no time for you to learn of this.

Nick looked up for a moment. Despising nepotism, he had avoided meeting his kinsmen when at Court before, not wishing to be seen to curry favour. Now he had met William Talbot, he could only be grateful to Shawcross for his intervention. Toby's writing grew steadily more illegible.

My friend, I am sorry– argue as I might, she is afraid and will not entertain a proxy marriage. A letter came from Whitehall telling of your betrothal to the lady Rosalyne. It bore the royal seal, no gainsaying it. I could not believe it but Kate took it badly. In your interest, short of violence, nothing for it but to give them escort and see them safe – from one building site to another, a great mansion is a-building in Derbyshire. Bess of Hardwick is a tartar as everyone knows, but your boy will be safe and Kate protected. It is a learned household, my lady Shrewsbury has little time for courts and politics – except of course, her own. I have taken it on myself to stop all building work on the new manor until I know your mind – Jones is not pleased. I shall remain at Rokesby until a new steward can be found. Your lady would have kept Hal with her but he refused – on fire to go to France or join the army – either would do in his present frame of mind. I judge he is better with you, perhaps you could do something with him. Trelawney will help. If this is an unwelcome burden to you, let O'Dowd lick him into shape. You have my loyal friendship in this trial, Nicholas.

Yours to command, Tobias.

A cold draught blew through the room as the door opened and banged shut. Hal Shawcross stood there, the image of his father as a young captain, slim and straight, hazel eyes steady…although Nicholas had never seen Hugh with such a mulish expression.

"Well, do I go with you or no? It's all one to me. As soon as I am my own master I am for the army."

Mastering himself, Nick said quietly, "You could do no better than follow your father. In the meantime, a little polish at the French court will do you no harm. If you are willing to go as my page, I will see what can be done. There will be jousting and exercise yards—"

"Not as esquire?"

"I'm afraid Trelawney has seniority there. A page has status and responsibility, it is no menial post. There may be danger, which is why I hesitate. Perhaps you would be better training with Captain O'Dowd. Or you could be placed in the household of—"

"O'Dowd is an old man. I am not afraid of danger – and I will not be placed like a parcel in anyone's household."

The last word came with a fine scorn. Nicholas looked at him. "I will excuse you this once for your innocence of how the world works outside Rokesby. You will not find others lenient of impertinence. You will not interrupt me again. Or speak idly of your betters. How old are you now – fourteen?"

"Fifteen next month, if it's to any purpose."

"Fifteen next month, *my lord*. Yes. Yes, I will take you to Paris for our fathers' friendship. I owe you that. But answer me back one more time and you will be on the next transport back to Sergeant Ponsonby. You will wish you had chosen Captain O'Dowd. Can you shoot, fence, wrestle?"

"Of course."

"Of course…?"

"My lord," in a mumble.

"A little modesty in these matters is always preferable. Better to surprise with one's skill than otherwise."

"Just because you didn't get what you want—"

"*Yes?*"

A long silence. *At your age I had my first woman,* thought Nick. *Kate.* He began again, "Hal—"

"I prefer Henry."

"Very well. You have now used up your last chance. Like it or not, *Henry*, you are my foster son, and I wish to see you do well. What happens in my private life has nothing to do with what passes between you and me. You have been privy to your father's suffering and much else, for which I make allowance, but I will not be lied to or disgraced by ill behaviour. Understood? *Understood?*"

"Yes. My lord."

"You wish to come to France, then. Good. Now tell me the truth. Who taught you to shoot and so on?"

"No one. Myself. My lord."

"Sir will do, in private. My lord when on duty. For the look of the thing. I will arrange for proper training as soon as may be. Supper in an hour, go and wash. We sail on the morning tide. And Henry…"

"Sir?"

"I'm pleased you are coming."

Less than seven years older than the boy he was now committed to, Nicholas sat for some time in the draining light, his hands like ice, listening to the skirmishing going on above and trying not to think.

Chapter Twenty-Seven

London. February 1599

Young Colin joined them on the quayside with all his gear, grinning all over his face with excitement. Trelawney squared up to him and the two young men circled each other like a pair of dogs. Even in his present state of mind, Nicholas had to smile as they took each other's measure: they would have to shake down together as best they could. He would have no favourites.

As part-lessee of the *Swan* he had a small cabin to himself and kept to it. He used the time on the crossing to try and make sense of what had happened. Kate's last words to him had been as ambiguous as the Queen's. "It will be as always." He had taken her to mean she would wait for him but now the words jostled in his head, juggled with the tone of her voice and the look in her eyes. Perhaps as with Hal this had been his last chance. He had a constant burning pain behind his eyes that kept him from food and sleep. "It will be as always." In the end he wrote to Bess of Hardwick thanking her for offering hospitality to his son and his son's mother, with a polite request for news of them, and explaining what had happened. He wrote also to his kinsmen at Court. He wrote to Jack and he saved the usual drawings for a little book of folded paper in which he pictured a lumbering knight who made all manner of comic mistakes and a wise young page who gave advice. He made other drawings, of ships and battles, places he had seen, strange animals. He did not write to Kate; he was still too shaken by her refusal to find words. *Give her time*, he thought. *It was a shock – she is afraid, Toby said. No wonder, poor Kate.* He needed time himself to know what to say; hit hard, he hardly knew his own feelings.

He had hardly slept and had not shaved or changed his clothes since the letters from Rokesby, and as Calais appeared on the horizon, he realised that he must now set an example to Hal – no, *Henry*. He assembled himself with care and sustained Trelawney's anxious glance, feeling that to outward appearances he was the same. He was wrong. The eager young man who had left Plymouth in a blaze of happiness had gone. The cool reserved captain of the Rokesby enterprise was back, with tired eyes and a rasp to his voice.

The smart body of men in black and gold livery disembarked in the harbour of Calais, with a small train of mules and carts carrying their equipment, Nick's armour and weapons, gifts for the King and his consort and a formidable amount of clothes. Nicholas meant to make the right impression. To travel, he wore his comfortable leather jack over a plain doublet, and the long soft boots from Spain. All of them had durable heavy cloaks, which was as well. The journey was abominable.

By this time the exceptional winter had relaxed its iron grip and Flanders was a deep morass of mud. Melting snow had swollen the Somme and it flowed high under the arches of the bridges, leaving little room for boats to pass. It was raining: hard, driving rain that penetrated their clothes and found its way down the backs of their necks.

The roads were a quagmire. Once they were forced into the ditch by a galloping troop of horse and again by the following cannon. The cart carrying their gear stuck and they abandoned it, distributing the load among themselves, and struggled on, desperate for shelter. The inns suggested by Tobias would have been passable but for those same troops going before. Disinclined for speech, Nicholas forced himself to talk and joke and sing to keep the men in good heart, and found that away from Court, Young Colin was not so much changed, still apt to explode in boisterous laughter and rough games and dirty jokes. The men took to him and Trelawney relaxed, in spite of the God-awful weather.

Several times Nick caught Colin's eye on him. No doubt Tim had been talking. The two of them smoothed his way in small things; Henry rode with the men in sullen silence. As they drew near Paris, conditions underfoot improved slightly and Nicholas briefed his page and squires on what they might expect.

"We are emissaries for peace. We are not at war with France but we do not want her to join with the Netherlanders against Burgundy and Spain and add to her strength at this time, thus the present situation is uneasy. We are here to show goodwill; all I wish you to do is carry out your duties and keep your eyes and ears open. Without seeming to do so. On no account ask questions. The names Lennox, Bothwell and d'Aubigny are of special interest to me and to me alone. Understood?"

Tim Trelawney's fresh, fine-skinned face was patched red and white with cold, the blue eyes pink-rimmed and bright. He nodded and sleet slid off his cap.

"Henry?"

"Yes. Sir." The boy seemed to have perked up.

Young Colin swept a courtly bow and straightened up laughing. "When does the fighting start?"

They were twenty miles from Paris and it was late afternoon when the rain came on again, heavy and persistent. Nicholas looked round at his troop. The horses' hooves were sticking and slipping in the mud, the men weary, and he called a halt at the next inn they came to. He would not arrive in Paris with his men in this bedraggled state. The inn looked a miserable affair with a long sway-backed barn clinging to one side, but it would have to do until the weather cleared. Glad to be out of the downpour, men and horses crowded into the barn. Except for a spreading puddle at one end and a rusting harrow, it was empty; that troop of horse had already scoured through. Young Colin had proved himself on this journey: the blood of reivers in his veins, if food and fodder and drink was to be found he found it. The inn keeper, no fool, had another tidy little barn hidden behind trees. Young Colin came back from his foraging with news of clean hay and straw, followed by a protesting inn keeper. At the sight of gold coin, he stopped complaining and struck a bargain, hurrying off to chivvy his cook.

Nicholas always saw to his animals himself and had just finished bedding them down when a soaked and panting courier, plastered with mud, galloped in with a bundle of dispatches.

"I was told to catch you before you reached the city, my lord." Nicholas rewarded the man and told him to take his rest.

"There may be letters to take back. Tomorrow." Trelawney had brought Nicholas out a cup of hot, spiced wine, and he drank some of it gratefully as he took the packet to the light of the lantern. He set the wine on a ledge and stuffed the official letters into his shirt to look at later. He peered at the two others, one with a crest he did not recognise. He broke the florid seal and opened it, the expensive vellum crackled as he flattened it out against the wall. It was written in a vile hand and worse language, short and brutal and took him like a knife under the ribs.

Nicholas Talbot, Knight, Scottish Order of Merit, Lord of Rokesby and Rookham, and Thane of Strathyre

I do myself the honour, my lord, to inform you at my lady's behest, of my coming union with Mistress Shawcross, formerly Archer. She does me great honour. The one flaw in my happiness is the cuckoo in the nest. She of course says she wishes to keep the child, but as I tell her, there will be more to fill the cradle. At your leisure, my lord, I trust you will make suitable arrangements.

Your servant, John, Lord Westerbrook of Westerbrook and Darnley

Holding down nausea, he read it again, unbelieving. He felt frozen, the cold seemed to penetrate to his very soul. He reached for the wine and took two long swallows. It rose again sour at the back of his throat and he ran outside to vomit again and again into the pile of dirty straw.

"Are you ill, sir?" One of the troop had come across.

"No, no, not ill. Something…get yourself in out of the rain."

"Sir, let me—"

"Get in, I tell you!" Nicholas straightened up and wiped his face on his sleeve. "Just going to finish up here…" He went blindly back into the barn and stood leaning his head on Shadow's moist warm neck, his hands clenched in her mane. Sensing something of the black murderous rage that was building in Nick's head and fracturing his thoughts, she shifted uneasily and turned liquid eyes to see and nudge him.

Nicholas could not tell if it was the content of the letter or the sheer devastating arrogance that so enraged him. If the author of it had been there he would surely have killed him. The fury boiled up again at the idea of Jack anywhere near this man. "Cuckoo in the nest?" he shouted. *"My son!"* Startled, the other horses threw up their heads and jostled. He was upsetting them. He made a great effort to calm himself, the churning in his gut settled a little and he stooped to pick up his soaked tunic and struggle into it. His first instinct, to fling himself on his horse and ride full tilt for England, would not do. The letter was still clutched in his hand and he stared at it. "At my lady's behest…" Could she not have told him herself, given him some warning? "'Frailty, thy name is woman,'" he muttered. *Kit, did you foresee this? No, you couldn't have…frail, yes, but not frail, anything but fragile… 'God has given you one face and you make yourselves another.' Oh God…* He was shaking now and he slowly made his way across the inn's yard, oblivious to the still pouring rain. He went in through the kitchen to avoid questions and reached his room shivering like a wet puppy.

All the way here his squires had been concerned to give him his privacy, sensing his troubled mind. Everyone else shared but he could always be sure of a place to himself. The room was dark, its squalor only faintly revealed by the light of a brazier of hot coals by the bed. A bottle of aquavit stood with his drinking cup and a good wax candle on the rickety table, a stool drawn up to it. This thought for his comfort was almost too much for him and he went to lean his hot forehead against the streaming window pane. A mouse scuttled in the wall, rain drummed on the roof and flung itself against the bottle glass as if it were trying to get in.

A ribald shout from the room below broke in on him. He was cold, he crossed the room and dragged the brazier closer to the table, burning his hand, and fumbled to light the candle and send away the dark. Time, he needed time and there was none. He must "make suitable arrangements." He became aware of his state of body and dropped the letters on the table, dragged off his wet clothes and wrapped himself in one of the blankets from the bed. He sat on the stool, huddling near the brazier and pulled across the bottle. He splashed some brandy into the vine-leaved bronze goblet from Portugal. He could not remember why he had kept it with him, except perhaps it had become a talisman. He had not thought of his father since Portugal, and now he found himself wondering, not for the first time, what his mother had been like. Jack Talbot had never spoken of her. *I killed her,* thought Nicholas. He picked up his pouch and found her miniature. His father's wife. A beauty, with the Melville colouring, his colouring, Jack's. He had drawn a little picture of Jack and it lay on the other side of the locket with a curl of Kate's hair. The twist of auburn fell to the floor and he let it lie. Nicholas had had wet-nurses and corporals and tutors and sergeants. Mistress Melville had been the mainstay for his own son. He had been told so and he had seen it for himself. *More to fill the cradle, Westerbrook? I wish you joy.* He hardly knew which pain was worse. His hand hurt and he dragged out his square of linen to wrap it. He poured more wine, his hand shook and drops of red fell on the letter from Westerbrook. The thing had to be dealt with.

After a long while, he rose and fetched pen and paper. The first note was simple. He wrote to his kinsman William Talbot, giving the present whereabouts of his son – the very place, in fact, that the admiral had arranged for his safety – and enclosing the spotted letter from Westerbrook. He asked him to see Jack brought to London with his nurse. To Kate he wrote: *If this is your desire, I*

*wish you joy. I will take our son with love and sorrow and rear him
with pride. Nicholas*

That done, he curled his fingers round his bronze cup and sat
thinking, his thoughts turning again to his father. "I married for
love, Nicholas," he seemed to be saying. "At first sight. Now you
are grown, you will know it when you find it. Stop whining and
get on."

The second letter lay accusingly on the table. Numb, he picked
up his knife and broke the seal.

My Lord Rokesby, and my dear Nicholas.

*So we are to meet again. I have followed your rise with interest
and I am conscious that the Queen's wishes may not be yours.
My wishes are nothing to the purpose, but you should know that
I am willing, should you bring yourself to it, for the sake of what
passed between us. It was no idle whim, Nicholas, and you will
see that you were not betrayed. I will obey you in this, my lord.
What else is to be said must wait on your return.*

Rosalyne

Rosalyne. That had been a *coup de foudre*, a beauty on a white
horse, smiling at him, curling his fingers over her gift, inviting
him to her bed. He had thought of it often. Marriage to
Rosalyne, or the Tower? Not a hard choice. He had an abiding
horror of the Tower and his torture there. Honourbound to
Kate, he had been prepared to face it, but now? It came to him
that perhaps Kate acted as she did for his safety. He shook his
head. A nice thought, salve to the wound, but he had been taken
behind the scenes now. He would believe it, however, for the
sake of what they had shared.

It took him a long time, but in the end, this letter was as short as the others.

> *The Lady Rosalyne Sexton*
>
> *You are right. What has to be said must wait. I am honoured that you welcome the proposal and I pray you will understand that at present I cannot know my mind. Much has happened since what passed between us. I can only say that it was never forgotten. May I hope to call on you when my task here is done.*
>
> *Your servant, Nicholas Talbot*

He sealed the letters with his ring and put them aside for the morning. The rest of that wretched night he spent huddled in his blanket by the dying brazier, readying himself to show a cheerful face for the last leg of the journey.

Chapter Twenty-Eight

Paris. Early March 1599

Fortunately, the timing was right. The atrocious weather had delayed the French Court's spring migration downriver to the various palaces and hunting grounds favoured by the King, and a pleasant house had been made ready for them by the pleasure gardens.

Unfortunately, when Nick finally went to find his bed, grim faced and worn out, his baggage lay open and strewn over the floor, every garment in it slashed and ripped and bare of every sewn jewel and button. His armour was gone and everything reeked like a Venetian brothel of the expensive scent pressed on him by Gallio. He stood in the doorway and looked at the mess. Thankfully his personal jewels and money were carried in a strongbox under guard.

"So soon," he said aloud. *A warning? First strike to you, whoever you are. And foolish, to put me on my guard.* He sent for Trelawney, and after the horrified exclaiming, asked him to make discreet enquiries.

"Someone may have been seen. No fuss, and no official complaint, I think. Oh, and ask Young Colin to lend me a shirt. I've an audience with the King in the morning."

He only had what gear he stood up in and did what he could, made no excuse, and presented himself and his perfumed credentials with everything about him clean and polished and smelling of soap. His armour and weapons had been found in the shrubbery under his window, and his sword hung now at his side with its jewelled hilt catching the light, the chains of his Orders gleamed across the shoulders of his battered leather jack. Henri the Good was said to be a judge of horseflesh and Shadow of the Wind was proud and glossy in her silver-studded harness and ribbons, enough in herself to get him through the gates. His retinue in their livery of black and gold carrying the Rokesby crest were no disgrace.

Halfway across the gravel and paving he was accosted by Ann de Montmorency.

"My dear, is this the fashion obtaining in England? I must see my tailor. Or is it perhaps a statement? You scorn our idle preoccupation with matters of style? I had not thought so in Venice."

"That would hardly be thought good manners. A mishap, soon remedied. But not in time to mend my appearance, I've no wish to add lateness to my deficiencies."

He dismounted and Young Colin led his horse and the rest of the men towards the stables after a corporal in the uniform of the Scottish Archers.

De Montmorency accompanied him past the guards at the door, chatting amiably, and handed him over to a splendid gentleman loaded with many more gold chains than Nicholas, turning aside to give some quiet orders.

The King had been hunting and received him an hour later still in his own mud-splashed riding clothes. Nick appreciated the courtesy.

"We understand you were robbed in the house of our choosing. What was lost has been replaced. We regret such a happening to a guest at our Court and an envoy from our cousin, Elizabeth. Rise. You will take wine."

He waved Nicholas to a stool, and disposed his long horseman's legs on the window seat. The weak sunlight through the coloured glass lit the thin curving nose and the quizzical brows. The set of the mouth was firm and kindly.

"We shall not keep you long. You will convey our thanks to your queen for her gifts of men and arms at time of need. She has honoured us with her approval – the Edict. You know of it?"

"*L'Edict de Nantes*, sire?"

"As a good Protestant she must approve. But we fear we have angered her of late. The treaty with Spain – still not a fait accompli, you may tell her – and other matters. We would mend the friendship. Scotland of course was always our friend."

Nicholas decided to risk it.

"King James has many rivals. And enemies…" A long finger came out and lifted the chain of Nick's Order.

"From whom you saved him. There will be a meeting of my councillors. Come to breakfast."

Nicholas, in his scarred and polished leathers, was dismissed.

Lord Rokesby returned to his lodging to find the other half of the escort and his three young men standing about watching in amazement as servants unloaded a train of gold-fringed sumpter mules and made their way into the house with parcels and boxes and bales. Inside, a steward in a doublet badged with the fleur-de-lis was directing the unpacking. He bowed with a flourish.

"His Majesty is pleased to make reparation," he said in excellent

English. "We have enquired of your taste – you favour green, I believe." There was certainly a great deal of it. Cloaks and doublets and trunk hose, hats with feathers and hats without, velvet and silk and brocade… The shirts and small-clothes, mercifully white, were of finest linen and silk, the ruffs the small pie-crust frill favoured in France.

There were tapestries for the walls, carpets for the floors, crystal and silver plate and monstrous candelabra. Sheaves of good wax candles, some of them scented, bedlinen and silk coverlets made their way in on parti-coloured page boy legs. Finally, two pages struggled in with a silver-gilt epergne loaded with fruit, pineapple and figs, grapes and oranges. Seeing nowhere to place it, they put it on the floor. The nuts rolled off.

The major-domo waved a lordly arm.

"In token of His Majesty's friendship to your Queen." And as a further bale was carefully unwrapped, "For the banquet. A tailor will call." The doublet was of taffetas, the changing colour of a pigeon's breast, its embroidered roses centred with amethyst and the pale green of peridots. The short cloak was edged with silver fox. *France prospers*, thought Nick. Aloud he said, "How can I thank His Gracious Majesty for such gifts?"

"An insult was offered in his house. The culprit shall be found and punished."

"It is in hand. I beg the Court will not trouble itself further." He caught sight of Henry, standing behind Trelawney, his face greenish-white. He murmured to Young Colin in Scots, "if that boy is going to be sick, get him out of here."

The mules departed, the major-domo rode off on his palfrey, and the house servants took over. Tim picked up a tunic and held it against himself.

"Is all this for you?"

"Help yourself. The tailor will call…" Nick started to laugh and laughing still, left the room to find his bedchamber. It had been swept and garnished and he leaned against the closed door and wept.

Expecting to be placed at one of the lower tables, Nicholas was surprised to be placed near the top, next to Ann de Montmorency. The Frenchman kissed him on both cheeks.

"An improvement, my friend," he said. "Not that you are not charming in battle array. Do you see who is here?" Nicholas looked along the raised top table and saw, leaning to listen to the woman next the King, Angelica d'Alighieri in her own form of battle dress. He had not thought to see her again. She looked up and saw him: a soft flush began at her bodice and swept to her jewelled hairline.

"Fortunate, no?" murmured his neighbour. "Friends at Court?" The heat and noise grew steadily unbearable, the procession of dishes obscene. The King was entertaining embassies from Germany and Burgundy and the Low Countries, all noted trenchermen. Nicholas was worried about Henry standing so long behind his chair. He sent him away presently and Young Colin took his place, more accustomed to Court excesses. Long verses were spoken, someone sang to a lute, acrobats formed pyramids and juggled and the dancing began. The dances were formal and graceful, little of the leaping and lifting of the Tudor Court. He and Angelica passed and re-passed, he saw how her body moved inside the stiff bodice and remembered. He was not surprised when a note was pushed into his sleeve. As once before it was short. "Hôtel des Colombes. Tonight."

He went on foot, padding through the murmurous streets with one hand on his sword, down to an elegant little square by the river, Henri's new building programme well in evidence. The Hôtel des Colombes was a tall narrow house in a circle of gravel, steps leading up to a classic marble portico. He crunched as quietly as he could round to the side, past a dovecote shaped like a beehive for ten thousand bees and found a side door open. Soft light shone from a room at top of the curving stair. She was waiting for him.

Starved by his recent self-imposed restraint and still distressed, his only concern was that his long abstinence would overwhelm them both, but she knew him well enough now and did not keep him waiting, taking him in her arms and meeting his hunger with her own. Later, the first urgency spent, they sat with food and spiced wine and exchanged news. Her husband had died on a long journey from Russia.

"I advised him not to go, Niccolo. As I told you, I have made that journey – it was frightful – and at that time of year… But he was always a stubborn man. My Medici cousin invited me here – and I have business interests. Tell me, Niccolo, is it true what I hear, that you took two troopships and Spanish gold? I thought you were turning merchant, not pirate."

"Neither. I am set to work in my country's interest – to my wounding, it sometimes seems. Things have not gone well for me either, Angelica."

"I saw as much. Tell me."

"It is not one of those tall tales, my Scheherazade. It is too soon to speak of it. Tell me of your doings here."

"You are my dear friend, Niccolo, and I can admit to you that I wear black because it becomes me. I am my own mistress now and so I shall stay. No more husbands for me, to make use of my fortune and hinder my wishes. I am a rich woman and can do as I please. I am here to amuse myself."

You have no ageing Queen to pose a threat, thought Nicholas. *You don't know how lucky you are – Rosalyne is rich, yet she seems willing to take a husband...*

Angelica was saying, "Our witty friend keeps to himself these days. He has written a pleasing entertainment or two, but he prefers to stay in Verona – a shame, he is such good company."

"Not when he is working, my dear, he is like a wolf biting its own tail. I must go, it grows late – or early."

"Until tomorrow, then. I shall wheedle a tale out of you yet."

She knew nothing of Kate and his broken dream, and it was not until a few nights later that he could speak even a little of it. She propped herself up on the pillows and regarded him gravely.

"It is probably too soon to say so, Niccolo, but this may be for the best. A childhood romance does not always make a good marriage – and few of us can choose whom we marry." She stroked her fingers down his arm. "Only our lovers."

"You recommend a loveless match?"

"Need it be so? Does this Rosalyne disgust you?" He remembered with a jolt that last passionate encounter and his first sight of her.

"No..."

"Then obey your Queen and take her. And for the moment, you are here."

There was no shortage of amusement at the court of Henri le Bon. The weather cleared and the Court moved off. Great barges loaded with cooks and servants and their servants' servants, food, cook pots and stoves, plate and linen, beds and bed hangings, silver chamber pots and ewers and barrels of wine, followed the river south. Decorated barges with court ladies and their women, elder statesmen and children with their nurses came after and settled chattering into each new place like a flock of migrating birds. The men of the Court rode in a throng along the banks, a moving rainbow, talking, talking, talking, huntsmen and hounds of all kinds following with the troop of soldiers and the King's royal guard of Scottish Archers.

There was hare coursing along the way, and deer hunting and hunting the boar, hawking and races. At the chateaux and manoirs where the Court rested and then moved on, having stripped the place bare as a swarm of locusts, there was jousting and sword play, wrestling and archery. The knights jousted in full armour, favours flying, or in plain mail and fancy dress, bears fighting lions and ostriches attacking flamingoes in pink taffeta; a knight with a stuffed princess nodding behind him slew a dragon. Henri himself took part in the archery and swordplay, plainly dressed and competent. His supple armour fitted him like a glove.

At night the feasting went on into the small hours, with jugglers and acrobats, jesters and musicians. And conversation. Even at the Mermaid there was seldom so much conversation. Around the King gathered a smaller court of poets and philosophers and statesmen and soon Nicholas was admitted to this enclave, where, after Angelica and her gentle teaching, he had no difficulty holding his own. He found that in spite of the horseplay and extravagance and mind-numbing expense, there was little licence; Henri was a man of sense and sound policy, a good listener. Nicholas formed an impression of a court in good heart, admiring and respectful of their king. A long-avowed Protestant, there were those, certainly, who distrusted Henri's conversion to the Catholic faith as expedient. His offhand remark, "Paris is worth a Mass," had not helped. Under his rule, however, the country was prospering, the heavy debts had been repaid, and his expressed desire that every peasant should have a chicken in the pot looked set to be realised. Wherever he passed on this Progress, the people came out to see him and cheer.

On his last visit to Elizabeth's court, Nick had sensed an uneasy brilliance, a dying glare, a corpse-light of uncertainty. How could it be otherwise? The Queen was ailing, with no named successor; Essex was posing a threat, Europe in its usual state of turmoil. In the audiences granted him with the king of France, Nicholas was able to speak carefully of his hopes for his own country without fear of jeopardising his task. He asked if the King had any message for her. They were in the chamber hastily prepared for the King in the doll's-house chateau belonging to the Marquis de Conde, with its blue slates and pointy towers. Henri said, "Your queen is wise. Men reveal themselves in their struggle for power and so may be recognised."

He knows why I'm here, thought Nick.

"Tell your queen that when my time comes, I shall hope to leave a legacy such as hers." Nick felt this was altogether too like an epitaph. *An oral message can always be edited,* he thought. He certainly would not repeat the King's next remark.

"I could wish I had married her myself."

Nick smiled dutifully. Henri's first marriage had been a disaster.

"We are fortunate in having so many of your countrymen at court," said Henri, idly. He was stringing a lute. "William Boyd, for example, and my lord Bothwell. And they have made friends among us." The message was as clear as if he had shouted in Nick's ear. "Aubigny, and young de Longhi. A playful duel, I hear. You bear the mark. I doubt he will challenge you again. We are sending him to Cologne, to the Duke. He likes to hunt the chamois." His eyes were sparkling and his face quite straight. He obviously had a network quite as good as Cecil's.

"He is a skilful climber, your majesty."

The king laughed outright. "He would like to think so. Come, I see the lady d'Alighieri. We shall make music together."

Yes, thought Nick, following him. *Quite as good.*

Chapter Twenty-Nine

Paris. April 1599

At the beginning of April, the Court returned to Paris and settled down for the season.

Nicholas spared some time for his own affairs. He had not wasted his time in Venice and Florence and Oporto, or on the fruitful voyage home. And now he remembered the name of the Jewish widow he had brought safely over the Alps four years ago, and called at her discreet house by the river. Madame da Gama had not forgotten him either and they sat in her pretty garden eating early cherries and exchanging news. Presently she said, "You have come with a reason, my lord Rokesby. Your courier service prospers. Deservedly. All these young men galloping to and fro with messages is one thing, and very necessary, but to have safe escort for one's goods and oneself is most welcome. And in such comfort. You wish to expand? How may I help you?"

Madame da Gama was as good a businesswoman as Angelica and under her rule her late husband's business thrived. How could it not? She had relatives trading all over Europe and connections with Imperial Russia and the East.

"Letters of introduction, madame, if you would. I have a ship leased and another building. Safe ships, and the opportunity for one more. Passengers, yes, and cargo for myself this time. Would such a venture interest you?"

"As a partner, no, but an investment in your ships at the usual rate is something I would consider. Send me your proposal, my lord, and you shall have your introductions. You showed me tact and kindness. The house of my husband honours its debts."

"There is no debt, madame. This is a business proposition only."

"You have gained honours since we met, my lord. I am prepared to regard you as a sound investment."

Nicholas used her money to buy one of the captured troopships, the *San Domenico*, at a reasonable price – a quarter of which would revert to him in any case as his share of the prize money. He contacted the brokers for the Venetian Arsenale and commissioned a caravel, to be built of timber from Angelica's Tuscan forests.

He wrote to Modon. He wrote to Tobias. He wrote to Jack and separately to Mistress Melville where they stayed at the Admiral's house.

Letters and orders went to the merchants and traders he had met as Ambassador and he wrote to his successor asking him to recommend an agent. Venice was losing ground to Genoa, and he wanted someone on the spot.

The invaluable letters of introduction brought useful meetings with men of influence in Paris and Bruges, and things began to take shape. He wrote to Gallio.

For an annual fee, cargo and passengers on ships flying the Rokesby flag would be protected from pirates by the privateers. "Money for old rope," as William Piers put it. And of course, he added, young Rokesby had the ear of the Queen – Letters of

Marque could always be revoked. To do him justice, Nick had not thought of this.

The caravel and the refurbished troopship were ready and in the water in a month. Nathaniel Wells had abandoned Gallio at the first sniff of his homeland and the promise of legitimate employment, and took command of the *San Domenico*, now renamed the *Skua*. She left Plymouth carrying passengers, fine riding horses, woollen cloth and tin, her ballast iron ore. For her maiden voyage from Venice the caravel, *Snipe*, brought silks and spices from the Orient, nutmeg and pepper, olive oil in tulip-shaped jars, Cyprus sugar and wine, timber and alum and a harpsichord intended for the Queen.

Young Colin, exposed to the Rokesby experience for the first time, closed his mouth and applied himself. His first letters to his uncle in Edinburgh, who had sent him to the English Court as a maddeningly raw recruit, caused that gentleman to sit down with a thump and call for strong spirits.

Neither had Nicholas forgotten the lands in Scotland ceded to him by King James. He wrote first to his kinsman, with good report of his nephew, and then to Harry Munro with money and instructions. He found he was enjoying himself.

"Why, do you think, should that be?" he asked Angelica one night. He was peeling grapes and dropping them into her mouth. They were both deliciously sticky.

"Could it be that you are a free man, Niccolo?"

"Betrothed to Lady Rosalyne?"

"Free in yourself, I mean. The cord is cut. It was an unkind cut, but perhaps it was right, you are not suited to the life you planned. You are a born freebooter, Niccolo, it is a joy to watch you spread your sails. Ah, you made me forget. The man you told me of, who gave you that scar, de Longhi was it? He is coming to Court."

"Excellent. He may be just the loose end I'm looking for."

Poor Trelawney found that "keeping his ears open" was not much help. The French all spoke their baffling language too fast and so he kept what he had found out to himself and followed Henry. Who followed Nicholas. It was Young Colin, brought up with French at the Scottish court, who overheard de Longhi making arrangements to meet someone at a river boatmen's tavern near the bridge. In workman's clothes and with a woollen cap pulled over his red hair, he contrived to be at the next table, drinking and dicing with some new-bought friends when de Longhi's friend arrived. He almost ran back to find Nicholas with his news and did not notice the figure that came after him.

"It's Aubigny, Nick – my lord, I mean. You were right – they have men in Scotland ready to rise for him, the Lennox men and Boyd's. Bothwell is behind it. But they're not sure, Nick, the money isn't there and they don't trust Boyd – he's spent too long with the English."

Nick sat him down with a tankard.

"Slow down. How do you know all this?"

"Followed 'em, how do you think? I heard—"

"Were you seen?"

"No – listen. I know the Boyd. My great-uncle knew of Tom Boyd when he married the King's sister – second of the name that would be – and tried to get in that way. He ended up in England and she married again. They had sons though, Nick, don't know what happened to them – but the name fits."

Nick sighed. Henchmen who thought for themselves brought their own problems.

"You mention Lennox."

"Oh yes, that's the other thing. They plan to marry the lady Arabella Stuart to a William Seymour – does that mean anything? I mean, I know some of them at home would rather see her on the throne, being next in line and a Lennox, but my uncle was against it. Three queens in a row, you know…"

"Well done, Colin. You seem to have done my job for me. A little confirmation and we can go home."

He gave the praise due to Colin's enterprise, gave him wine and the best cuts of meat, and sat down to consider the note that had been brought while they were talking. It was in clear and he did not know Faulds' handwriting, but the message was plain enough. As brief as Angelica's notes, it summoned him to a meeting and bore Faulds' name. He knew Faulds had found himself a temporary job in the King's menagerie, but this was ridiculous.

The ostrich pen. Twelve of the clock. *Must take me for a green fool,* he thought. He sent for the captain of his escort and briefed him, told Young Colin he had earned his rest and to go to bed, dressed himself suitably and went to the zoo.

The menagerie at night was a strange place, full of the soft rustling of feathers and the shifting of heavy bodies on straw. He had been shown round it one afternoon by a grinning Faulds, and now in the moonlight he passed the sleeping elephant and the sad lion stretched on his straw and disturbed the wakeful hyena, which hurled itself at the bars and laughed its hateful laugh. No one came. Their duty done, the keepers had gone to their beds, noises in the night were to be expected. The monkeys chattered quietly among themselves and he passed the aviary with its puffs of sleeping birds. The Seraph was awake, its head with its ridiculous eyelashes reared above the roof of its cage, the square-patterned neck tiled in the light. The snake pit next, rustling, then the tiger, prowling sleeplessly to and fro, growling at the silent human. There was no logic in the arrangement of this assortment of animals: the ostrich pen was next to the tiger, its single unfortunate occupant huddled as far away from its neighbour as it could get.

A man stood, hands on hips, gazing up at the bird. It was not Faulds. The cage of jackals cackled and the attack Nick had been expecting materialised. They were many more than he had expected, and he was quickly driven back against the bars. He had only asked for three of the escort to accompany him, and they came with a shout and a rattle of sword and dagger, still outnumbered. The fighting was fierce, two were attacking Nick and the rest had turned on the Rokesby men. Out of the dark came a flying figure with sword upraised – Henry, closely followed by Tim Trelawney. The odds were instantly better, and Nick, anxious to avoid a bloodbath that would take some explaining, made the feint and retire and slid open the bolt of the tiger's cage. The maddened animal came out with a roar, everyone scattered and Nick threw himself at Henry and lay on top of him. As frightened as anybody, the tiger shook itself and loped off.

The whole zoo was awake now and, to a background of trumpeting, screeching and roaring, Nicholas picked himself up and took stock. Four down, three seriously hurt and one dead. The Rokesby contingent were all on their feet; Henry sat where he was, winded. The first on the scene was Faulds, and between them, they dragged the wounded men into the empty cage and shut the door. Carrying in the man Nick had killed, Faulds looked up at him.

"Aubigny," he said. "Or so the bastard called himself. That should be the end of it. Make yourselves scarce. I'm off." Nick helped up the white-faced Henry and they faded between the cages into the night, avoiding the angry keepers by a whisker.

The inquest at their lodging was rowdy with wine and laughter. Nick gave them their head, watching Henry revive and take his share. What he was doing there could come later; he and Trelawney had fought well and timely. The affair of the tiger would be told and retold, and gather in the telling, he knew. He got the boy, suddenly half-asleep, to bed at last, rewarded the men and collared Trelawney as he left.

"I'll see you in the morning," he said grimly.

"Yes, sir."

Chapter Thirty

Trelawney stood in the doorway of the room Nicholas used as an office, twisting his cap.

"Come in, Tim. This is the third time you have exceeded your orders. What have you got to say for yourself?"

"Well sir, I've been doing it myself, sir, I didn't want anyone else knowing…"

"I've no time for riddles, man. Doing what?"

"Watching the lad, Henry. I did what you said, sir, made enquiries about your baggage. I'm sorry, sir. There was only him and one of the servants went near your room, and the servant was sent by the King, sir, a good old man, I didn't reckon it would be him – and he wasn't in there long enough."

"Why didn't you tell me?"

"You weren't rightly yourself, sir – and since then you've been busy. I kept my eye on him, sir."

"I see. He was following me. Sit down." Nicholas poured him some of his breakfast ale. "I should have seen this coming. I must thank you, Tim. And you were welcome, I can't deny. You fought well." He went to sit on the window seat and sat nursing his knee. "You kept an eye on him, you say. What do you suppose is wrong? He was wild to get away from Rokesby."

"He's mad for the army, sir. I reckon that'd knock the sh— er, nonsense out of him. And put him where he can't do you no harm."

"*Any* harm," said Nick automatically. "Very well, you may be right. Leave it to me now. His sword master speaks well of him. My thanks, Tim, I'm going to miss you."

"You're turning me off, my lord?"

"On the contrary. Master Wells needs a second mate on the *Swan* and I thought you might like it."

Trelawney's expression said everything. The two young men sent for another breakfast and shared a bottle of wine, Tim going over the night's proceedings all over again. He went off at last to pack his bags in a feverish state of divided loyalty. Nicholas sent for the captain of the Scottish Archers.

Walter Erskine was a tall spare man of middle years, his clipped accent was pure Edinburgh.

"A pleasure to make your acquaintance, my lord Rokesby. What can I do for you? Is it the lad you'll be wishing to speak of?" Nicholas poured wine for them both.

"He acquitted himself well last night, Captain, he did you credit. There is a dilemma. I shall be leaving soon and thought to take him with me and find a place for him, but it seems to me he is well suited here. He is young yet. Would there be an opening for him with the Archers? I am willing to back him."

"I like the lad. He shapes well. Commissions cost money, my lord, and his keep while he's training. If that is your idea, I'm willing to take him. He's no' Scots, but I knew his father. The men like him. He tries."

"We are agreed, then, if he wishes it. Will you speak to him? Perhaps he should feel he has earned it."

"Aye, well, I'll do that... There's another wee matter, my lord." He sat turning his cup. "Ye're a Melville, I'm told."

324

"My mother."

"Aye. I say this to you, my lord, and speak free – you don't get an Order of Merit for nothing." He looked up. "A Scottish king of England would be fine thing, now."

"Not everyone would agree with you, captain."

"I know that fine. Well, now, I have a cousin in the Archers that guard the Lady Arabella – you know of the lady? Daughter to the Earl of Lennox?"

"I've heard talk."

"Aye, well. She's a fine lass, for all she's been brought up in England. It's this marriage with Billy Seymour we don't like. Gives her a strong claim, d'ye see, and there's those of us who'd like to see wee Jamie put an end to the fighting."

And a Scottish king of England, thought Nick.

Erskine was saying, "That little fracas last night, now. I'll not be poking my nose in, you understand, but with d'Aubigny dead it's left the way clear for the Lennox – through the lady."

"I'm going back to London, captain. It will be dealt with. My thanks for your help – it will be noted."

"Leave the boy to me, my lord. He will be looked to."

The boy stood straight-backed and muscular, and offered his hand.

"I am sorry, sir. I was wrong."

Nick took it and sat with him on the settle. "Your appointment to the Archers has come through. Are you sure that is what you want?"

"Yes, and I am to thank you."

"Can you tell me what it was all about, Henry?"

The boy unbuckled his pouch and emptied out all the jewels and buttons.

"I am sorry," he said again. "But – you went away and didn't come back and she made my father wretched with her lovers."

There was an icy silence, then, "Be careful, Henry. I am willing to hear why you did this, but—"

"He explained, he said he understood and didn't mind, but I minded. And then he died and you'd gone again, and Jack—"

Nicholas got up and stared unseeing out of the window. "Jack has had Mistress Melville and you had no one. I see. I am the one who is sorry. Henry…"

"They call me Hal in the mess, sir," he said with a shamefaced grin.

"Good. It sorts better with Shawcross. I don't offer you my name, Hal, you neither want it, nor need it, but you have two families now, mine and the Scottish Archers. You have my protection whenever you want it. Your father was a loyal friend to my father and to me. He would have been proud of you."

When the boy had gone, Nicholas sat for a long time unmoving. Presently he called for his horse and rode out towards the fields and woods and little streams of Fontainebleu. He followed a baby torrent to where it fed into a lake, dismounted and turned Shadow loose to graze. He had himself in hand by now and walked along the margin of the lake more in command of his thoughts. So, Kate had taken lovers in the time he had thought her chaste and waiting. "Penelope weaving her web," she had written. *Not so. But why should she not?* As he had been shown often enough, women had appetites as men had. Why should he feel betrayed?

"I was false," he said aloud. Shadow lifted her head and pricked her ears. "But I kept faith, in my way." Kate had offered herself to him at the time of the fire and he had kept faith with himself. Had she taken her revenge for that by denying him before their wedding?

326

With hindsight, he could see he had built a false image of her – as a young woman she had taken time and trouble to mould the boy he had been, teaching him the gentler arts of the body for the pleasure of them both. Small wonder that at fifteen he had tumbled into romantic love with her. *She was experienced even then,* he thought. He had a child born of that dream— a happy confident child, Mistress Melville had seen to that. She, no doubt, had seen this coming, living as she did behind the scenes.

"You were right, Kate," he said. "We are changed – we live in different worlds." He hated to admit it, but Robert Cecil had been right too.

"No regrets," he said to Shadow. "We have Jack and she showed me how to love. I do not think I harmed her." He remembered now small things that had disturbed and puzzled him, things Hugh had said and implied, things he had seen. How Mistress Melville had almost sole care of their child, for one thing. *Callow egotistical fool,* he thought. *I took too much for granted. We had so little time.* It had not been easy for her, and now Kate, pragmatic as always, had made her choice. As Marlowe had said, it was not a tragedy, no one had died, hurt feelings and hurt pride would mend and he would see that Jack did not suffer.

"Enough," he said and got up to call Shadow. "What an ass am I. Enough of this womanish soul-searching. It is done, and cannot be undone. Kate is safe and so is Hal. Me, I shall take my chances and safeguard my son and the future of the enterprise. And I shall put on Kit's *Hamlet* and play Laertes. The sighing lover was never the part for me."

Shadow had come to the lake to drink and now shook her head, showering him with water-drops. He laughed suddenly, feeling somehow lighter, a burden lifted. It felt like the beginning of something, not an end. *No more pangs of dispriz'd love. Marriage to Rosalyne? If I want to keep myself from the Tower and see James onto the throne, so be it. Can't throw it all away now. And where is the sacrifice – I fell in love with her once…* Memories of that night in her arms came to mind as so often in his dreams, and he laughed again. She had taken him by storm.

"I should be grateful. And if she turns shrew after all – I can tame her."

And with that tantalising thought he swung into the saddle and rode back to the city.

Once back at his lodging, he sent for food and wine and sat down to make his report on the d'Aubigny affair. He suggested that a watch should be set on the Lady Arabella Stuart and her correspondence with a certain Lord Seymour. The listening campaign had borne fruit. The instigator, d'Aubigny, was dead and, like Faulds, Nick hoped that was the end of it. He encrypted his letters, sanded them, burned the originals and went to bid farewell to Angelica, as much his friend as his lover.

They lay close, their entwined limbs lax and spangled. Nicholas was conscious of her breast heavy against him, her breath on his shoulder, her fingers stroking the length of his arm. She spoke suddenly, teasing. "This is the arm of a swordsman, Niccolo. You joust and you draw a longbow. Where did you learn all these pretty arts of the bedchamber?"

Startled, he said, "'It is extempore, lady, of my mother wit…'"

"No speeches from plays, if you please. Tell me." He lay silent a long while, thinking.

"I see now," he said slowly. "I think I had a hard task mistress as a boy. 'You must do this in such a way and so and so—'" He broke off with a half laugh. "She was flogging a willing horse. But there was pleasure and I learned – I thought I was in love." He hesitated. "But there is more, Angelica. Women to me are wondrous creatures, they bear us in pain, and die for us a little each day. The least of you, who has more hair than wit, has some wisdom and kindness. An infinite variety. And I pray you, mistress, do not infer from this that my tally of lovers is a long one. You may count it on the fingers of one hand – almost."

"And what is it you seek, Niccolo?"

"That divine spark – a meeting of mind and heart and body – I don't know. Unless it is a world where men – and women too – can speak their minds without fear. If it must be fought for, so be it. Ah, I speak a great deal of nonsense. I have a friend, a poet, he sees things clearly. His words are for all to hear. If they would listen."

"And you go back to your quest. Niccolo, we have loved and talked – go back and bring up your boy as you would see him grow, strong, with a mind of his own."

"That would be something. Come, *mia cara*, no tears. We met again as lovers, a delight I had not looked for, and now we must kiss and part."

"This is wise, Niccolo. The time has come for you to marry and you must make a wise choice. Your Queen may know better than you. You need a wife who will stand at your side and play her part. If you can find love, so much the better. Is she beautiful, this Rosalyne?"

"Night to your day, Angelica, dark and bewitching. I must count myself lucky."

"We make our own luck, Niccolo," said she, an echo of Kit Marlowe yet again.

Nicholas and his entourage left Paris three days later for Dieppe and London and the world of politics and intrigue.

Chapter Thirty-One

London. May 1599

Lord Rokesby's first meeting with the Lady Rosalyne took place at the Queen's command in the full glare of Her Majesty's Audience Chamber. Summoned as soon as he set foot on the dock Nicholas was given barely time to change his clothes before riding with an escort to Whitehall. He had left most of the verdant wardrobe supplied by Henri behind and nowadays presented himself always in costly black, velvets, brocades, fine-pleated silk. This evening the Orders across his shoulders were the only ornament to relieve the matt surface of tailored black damask, a single emerald in his ear.

Rosalyne was almost as he had last seen her, her body within the stiff azure silks a little more rounded, her coal-black eyes softer. She was unpainted except for her remembered lips, her white skin had the translucent sheen of health. She was standing near the Queen and when Elizabeth saw Nicholas enter, she dismissed the men she was talking to and sent across a page.

Nicholas knelt at her feet and she hissed. "Yes, yes, get up. And what did our cousin of France have to say? Without too much interpretation, if you please."

Nicholas gave her the edited version and intimated the rest might not be for the ears of the court.

"Very well. You are in fine fettle, Rokesby. Something in Paris agreed with you. Come for your cake, have you? You shall have your reward. Here is your lady." She beckoned them closer and joined their hands, to a murmur from the crowded room.

"There – you are hand-fast. May God give you many fine children to grace this Court. No dallying." And with that she turned aside with a grim smile at her swift fait accompli, to beckon Chester Herald.

"Richmond House comes with her as your bride-gift." A thick roll of parchment dangling with ribbons and seals was thrust into Nick's free hand. Rosalyne's hand was cold in his as he lifted it to kiss her palm. Her eyes were brilliant in her white face as he led her through the path that opened for them, between smiling faces and sour, hands clapping and still, through the outer chamber and the picture gallery out at last to the riverside.

It was dusk. The riding lights of the ships across the river began to show against the sky, rocking and chiming. The busy hum of the working city was changing its note to the evening sounds of going home. Rosalyne broke the silence between them.

"This was not my doing, my lord. I would have given you choice. But I do not regret it, unless you do."

"I regret nothing, my lady. Are we to condole with one another?"

"By all means. May we not be happy also? We each have a son." His smile flashed out.

"And are bidden to have many more. Holy Palmer's kiss will not suffice."

"Let us make friends, Nicholas. We had no time. There are things perhaps that you should know."

"Let me find them out for myself then, mistress. If we begin our confession, we shall be at our prayers for a week."

"To whom do you pray, my lord?"

"A leading question. What do they say? No atheists on a death bed."

"A sophistical answer. I see I must work to win your trust."

"I understand this much, lady. I am no longer the boy who fell in love with you that day. Now, at the Queen's pleasure, you and the children are hostages to fortune and to my enemies. It will be my care to keep you safe. The rest will come. If the Queen's policymakers will only lie quiet, we shall have time."

She lifted a hand to his cheek. "Walk with me then, and talk, tell me how you came by that scar."

Surprised, he made a comic tale of it, reducing her to tears of laughter. She stopped to get her breath. "Wretch. How dare you make me laugh so much…Oh, the bear…" Laughing himself, he handed her his square of linen and spoke without thinking.

"I prefer you laughing, mistress. You are like Beatrice in the play – when you were born, a star danced."

She stared at him. "You found me out that first night. You made me laugh then. And…"

"And?"

She shook her head. "Take me back. They will be talking."

"Clap hands and a bargain, then?"

"Sealed with a kiss, rather."

Next day came the expected interview with Cecil. The little spy master's manner was oddly formal.

"I join with Her Majesty in wishing you every happiness, my lord Rokesby. She is pleased, her mind is at rest. Those who helped you have been noted and will be rewarded. You will be glad to hear the other hole you spoke of has been stopped – the Lady

Arabella is restrained and under guard, as was the unhappy Queen of Scots. There will be no marriage with Seymour. Only one more thing – but no, it can wait. I have it in hand. Just a word. If my lord Essex should approach you, let me know." He had produced his best wine for the occasion (Nick recognised it) and he sat back balancing his goblet on his little potbelly. His robe already had wine stains down the front.

"Well, Rokesby, you are going back to your play-acting…"

"For this play only, my lord. You should see it. Such a keen disciple of Machiavelli – you would enjoy it, even perhaps learn from it. Power corrupts, my lord, as I am finding out."

His first sight of Rosalyne's son, named William for her husband, or as some unkind souls said, Master Shakespeare, rocked him to his boot heels. A little younger than Jack, he was a well-made child, tall for his age, with eyes a greenish hazel and auburn glints in his brown hair. But the smile and the emerging nose… Nick looked at Rosalyne.

"You were not here, Nicholas."

"I seem to have been absent on a number of auspicious occasions. No, forgive me. I do not make light of it."

"I did not betray you, my lord."

"I see that now. Though you had every right."

She shook her head. "You gave me what I wanted. I make no complaint."

He took her hands to kiss them. "Nor I, my lady."

Chapter Thirty-Two

London. June 1599

The wedding was very different from the one that had not taken place. It was early summer and the gardens around Whitehall were full of flowers. Nicholas had wanted a quiet ceremony at St. Nicholas' in Deptford, near where Marlowe was supposedly buried, and was overruled in favour of St. Benet's behind Burleigh House. Members of the Queen's household took over all the arrangements and when Nicholas saw the exclusive guest list, he gave a feast for all his friends among the players and escort and townspeople that had been left out. He held it in his big new house at Richmond, among ladders and paint pots and bowls of plaster. Some of the carpets were never the same again. Will Shakespeare did not come: a sudden attack of the ague. Nor did Tobias, he was in Milan setting up the new office, and he sent a friend and fellow archer Jock MacNab in his place, a mighty fellow who could draw a fighting longbow with as much apparent ease as a child pulling a slingshot. With his arrival came another, the chief of the clan Melville, Angus Menzies MacFarlane Melville, first of the Name, who had condescended to make the journey from Scotland, uninvited, to cast an eye over this young sprig of the name who had done so well for himself. The two boys gazed up in awe at these giants, taller even than their father, whose deep voices rumbled in a speech they could not understand. Angus Melville took Nick aside to catechise him and initiate him into the mysteries of kinship. It appeared that on his mother's side he was related by marriage to the clan Menzies, whose lands, by happy chance, ran beside his own on the Tay. From being an orphan, he now seemed to have a spreading family of Scots to add to his kinfolk among the Talbots. While all this had obvious advantages, he began to feel himself pinned down by gossamer threads in a network of tangled loyalties.

At the end of this trying interview the chieftain professed himself satisfied and announced that he would attend the wedding. Nicholas wondered what his bride would say.

At the wedding itself, King James of Scotland was represented by Nick's Melville kinsman at court, Sir Thomas, now Vice-Chancellor with a new title. The Queen was represented by a Gentleman of the Bedchamber, the guests mostly members of the Court. The Talbot contingent was there without Jack. Mistress Melville had ruled against it: she was at home in Richmond with the two boys. Apart from a raised eyebrow on being introduced to William, she had taken it all in her stride.

As the note-takers reported, the bride wore silver tissue embroidered with emeralds, carrying red roses symbolic of love, the groom a suitable foil in taffetas the changing colour of a pigeon's breast, with pearls, an exception to his new rule. The Lord Admiral, William Talbot, was in the congregation, alongside the lately-released Ralegh and his wife Betsy and Robert Carey's father, Lord Hunsdon. The Challoners had come en masse, bringing with them a proud and perspiring Sergeant O'Dowd. A glittering assembly, wrote the note taker.

Young Colin Melville stood beside Nicholas as groomsman, very poised and glossy these days: Rosalyne appeared to have few relatives of her own, and Nick's uncle, Charles Melville, also come from Scotland, brought the bride to church. Bracketed by Melvilles, their vows were made and they left the church to a blare of trumpets.

Angus Menzies MacFarlane Melville walked ahead of the bridal pair as they left the church to more fanfares, his plaid flung and folded over a decent suit of claret-coloured velvet that fought with his hair, carrying a huge two-handed sword, point upright in front of his face, walking with a curious slow strut. Nick found this exquisitely funny and kept his face straight and his gaze rigidly forward. Rosalyne's arm was trembling in his and he looked down, concerned. To his surprise and delight, she was fighting to control a fit of the giggles, her face pink and her eyes sparkling. He smiled down at her and squeezed her arm.

"Not long now, my lady. We shall have mirth tonight, I promise you."

A little snort escaped her. "My lord, that sword – does he not realise…"

"He could hardly carry it point down, lady – t'would give quite the wrong impression." She almost laughed at that, but immediately schooled her face into such an expression of demure and modest innocence that by the time he handed her into the carriage, he was half-suffocated with suppressed laughter.

The banquet and the wedding night would take place at Westminster Palace and they made the short journey through a cheering crowd. Word of the Spanish troopships had got round, coupled with his victory at the tournament, and remembered for his Mercutio and Benedick, Nick had become quite a popular figure. The sight of the chieftain riding alongside with his upright sword drew more cheers, and between one thing and another the bridal pair were thankful to withdraw into separate chambers to compose themselves before all the speeches started.

Lord Cecil, now Lord Burleigh, had come to the church but not to the following banquet; Thomas Walsingham and his wife were at both and Tom drew Nicholas aside.

"You have not abandoned our friend in Verona, Nicholas?"

"Are we not putting on his finest play? He will expect to hear of it."

Walsingham relaxed. "He has sent me another," he said. "Magnificent."

"This one will run, I know it. May I bring my wife to see you?"

"My lady will welcome you. Come soon. You will like the tale of evil jealousy and the Moor."

Nicholas laughed. "After Hamlet they will be clamouring for comedy – might have to suppress the evil jealousy for a while."

Chapter Thirty-Three

Epithalamion

A Bride before a good night could be said,
Should vanish from her cloathes into her bed,
As soules from bodies steale and are not spied.
But now she is laid; What though she be?
Yet there are more delays, for where is he?
He comes, and passes through Spheare after Spheare,
First her sheetes, then her armes, then anywhere.
Let not this day, then, but this night be thine,
Thy day was but the eve to this, O Valentine.
John Donne

After the banquet, Nicholas and his bride were escorted in traditional court style to separate chambers where they were undressed and put into their night robes. Nicholas was prepared to put up with this, but once taken to the bedroom door with a great deal of ribaldry and helpful advice, he drew the line. They were not royalty. Anticipating something like this he had some of his guard on hand and slid through the door and locked it.

He had been very young when he first met Rosalyne. He had fallen in love at first sight, with a young man's passion: flattered by her notice, he had snatched greedily – a gaudy night that had haunted his dreams and been denied. This second time, he was able to take time, please and be pleased, savour what he was given. Or so he thought. The true savouring would come later, now there was shared laughter and delight in equal measure, each of them eager to bring what arts and skills they had to this union, and by so doing, rediscover some of the rapture of their first encounter.

"'Busie old fool, unruly sun,'" murmured Nicholas. He could see his miniature reflection in her eyes. "Morning is come, sweet, and we must show ourselves satisfied. What do you think of your bargain now?"

"The poets say it all and leave nothing for me. 'I am two fools, I know, For loving and for saying so…'"

"There speaks a Beatrice. We should not be afraid. The wedding may have been contrived but the marriage is ours to make. I fell in love with you five years ago, my Rose, a fledgling thing, a boy's passion. Now it shall grow, perhaps, into a thing worth having."

"I shall nurture it, Nicholas." She was smiling

"As you have our child."

"Perhaps he showed me how." She eased herself from among the pillows. "You must be hungry, my lord, you ate little at the banquet. I will send for food." Nicholas grinned at her.

"I see the nurturing process is to begin at once. Very well, wife, a princely breakfast and then I shall take you to your new home."

By custom left largely to themselves for a few weeks, they rode out together, paid the promised visit to Tom Walsingham, walked and talked, pored over her plans for the house and his ideas for the business. Nicholas told her of the masque in Venice and the man Inigo Jones knew who designed gardens.

"Master Trelawney spoke of a journey in Portugal, Nicholas, in winter. Alone. I wonder you survived it."

"Come, I'll show you."

He took her down to the river, where the willows drooped their leaves into the water, with no attendants and only a sack over his shoulder. He emptied it out and spread it for her, took off his doublet and set about building a small fire. He showed her the snares and hooks and presently coaxed her to lie on her belly beside him with her sleeves rolled up to try and catch a fish. Her hair came down and she was laughing too much to be much help; he sent her to tend the fire and look for flat stones in the unlikely event that he might catch anything. He did manage a small unwary trout and he showed her how to gut it and cook it. He had stretched a point and brought bread and wine; they sat on the grass and ate it all with their fingers. Smiling, she watched him sprawled on the bank in his shirt sleeves, his eyes half-closed, chewing a stem of grass. The sun was warm through the leaves and woke glints of gold in his russet hair.

"What we miss. This is not how ladies of the Court behave, Nicco."

He looked up suddenly and reached for her. "Nor is this."

Chapter Thirty-Four

Rewarded with this fine house and lands in Richmond not far from the Queen's favourite palace, with a wife who amazed him daily, Nicholas began to build their future. There were the plays to plan for and he bought shares in the Globe theatre, now acquiring its last lick of paint. His other plans, clear-cut and ready, wanted only his partner's signature. His further ventures were his own concern.

Rosalyne occupied the west wing with a lady to serve her, and Mistress Melville, her helpers and Oliver Knowles had their apartments with the children on the opposite side of the terraced courtyard. Both confident children, the boys had been prepared to like each other and had settled the matter with a satisfying ruckus on the first day. That sorted out, they got on like any other brothers. Nicholas had his rooms next to Rosalyne and offices in the main building, behind the public rooms reserved for family and visitors.

The first of these was Tobias, come from Milan with a sack-load of paperwork and a serious face. Nick had written of his plans and Toby had come ready to dispute them. Rosalyne greeted him with servants and trays of lemonade and little cakes. She sat composedly down and poured lemonade and Tobias saw his friend's new wife for the first time. He took inventory.

She filled the eye. Tall and poised, square-tipped fingers and hands finely shaped. Hair like a blackbird's wing and eyes to match, Byzantine in a pale oval face. Reddened lips over a firm chin. A slightly retroussé nose contradicted the classic severity and added a hint of mischief. The white skin of her neck…

"You will know me again, sir," she said with a smile. "You are very welcome, Master Fletcher. My husband's dearest friend. And here is my son. Come and make your bow, William."

A sturdy child much the same age as Jack had come in with his nurse. Tobias stared. The boy's hair was a rich chestnut, curling and sparked with auburn, his eyes long and hazel. He turned his head to look up at her and Toby registered the shape of the skull and the ears.

The boy sketched a courtly bow and straightening, favoured him with a blinding smile. Tobias sat down suddenly.

"My husband will wish to talk business with you, Master Fletcher, if you are not too tired. Fatigue is a word he does not seem to recognise. There is more substantial fare in his rooms." Tobias realised she was offering him lemonade and took the proffered goblet. Finest Venetian glass, he noticed. He remembered Nicholas naked and laughing in the Arsenale fountain and, when they first met, standing smiling as he drew the llama. He was speechless. Nick had come into the room and the boy launched himself at him.

"Where is he?"

"Jack? Out in the garden. Have you met Master Fletcher?"

"Yes, thank you. Can I have a cake?"

"You *may* take two. One for Jack. We will excuse you." The boy scampered off, his cheeks bulging, evading the grasp of his nurse.

There was conversation Toby could not afterwards remember

and presently he found himself facing Nicholas across a crowded desk.

"That is—"

"I know," said Nicholas. "The boys are treated alike, there is no jealousy."

"No wonder Mowbray hates you. That was his woman."

"She *is* my wife." Nicholas pushed across a platter of soft white bread and choice meats, and picked up a list. "I recommend the wine. Tell me of Milan."

Warned off, Toby made a soldierly report and listened as Nicholas outlined his plans. He spoke for some time, his actor's voice calm and quiet, referring occasionally and, Toby saw, quite unnecessarily to his notes.

Come primed to argue, Tobias found all his objections answered. Nicholas seemed to have money and resources he had not expected. And was prepared to deploy them.

He sat back and folded his hands round a second cup of the recommended wine.

"You seem to know what you are doing, friend," he said. "Estates spilling out of your pockets these days."

"Rokesby seems an ill-fated place to me, I've a mind to install Sergeant Ponsonby and his family to use it as a training ground. O'Dowd seems happy as he is – on the move. Rookham is tenantless, Toby. It is yours to live in, to rebuild if you wish. Inigo's plans are drawn. Or perhaps your ladylove will have a preference."

"I do not think of marrying, Nicholas."

"My example deters you?"

Toby shrugged. "Let us say I prefer my freedom. No. Like you, in time I want to build, but not yet. Your sons – William is undoubtedly your son. You're a family man now, my friend, with no nativity or napkins. Good strategy."

"You were not wont to be so sour, Toby."

"If you are content so am I."

"I have all I need. And my freedom."

"Kate?"

"I have had news of Kate. She made her choice. And so have I. She is safe and well. When she is not, I am still her friend."

Toby read his friend's face and changed the subject. He suddenly felt very tired and was glad when Nicholas tapped his papers together and smiled at him.

"We dine early, I am due at rehearsal. Our house is yours."

Tobias, wakeful and worried, heard his friend come in late. There were voices and laughter, and presently there came a tap on his door. Nick came in and sat on his bed.

"I saw your light. Toby…that was a poor welcome. I owe you more than I can repay for your care of Jack – and all the rest. And if I have not consulted you, I am consulting you now. To offer you Rookham may have seemed a shabby thing, I'm sorry… I had thought to give you a choice. Estates can be stewarded. The company can be split. You may have plans of your own."

He was flushed and relaxed in his working gear for rehearsal, still elated from the work. Tobias shook his head.

"How long has it been? Nearly seven years. Worth any number of estates. Truth to tell, Nick, I enjoyed minding Rokesby for you. For a while. You go on making our fortune, friend, and I'll help you spend it. That is not what bothers me."

"I know what bothers you. There is no need. I have more than I ever looked to find – and Kate was well advised. It's over. The play's the thing, Toby, and Rose and I are suited. I tell you what I would like of all things – you with me at the head of the enterprise. Take tenancy of Rookham, freely given, install a steward and work here with me. There is much to do to keep what Cecil calls the ship of state on an even keel; I hear disturbing rumours of Essex. He has managed to delay Mowbray's trial a second time. I am concerned to keep all safe. Kate's husband has been warned, though she should stand in no danger now."

"Not just business, then."

"No, though I'm developing a taste for it. I'm letting others do the legwork these days – no more stravaiging up and down the Continent as Cecil's errand boy. Sleep on it, Toby, no hurry. Come to the playhouse tomorrow."

Chapter Thirty-Five

Over the next few days and weeks Tobias watched his friend make time for his children, and saw how he drew them together with games and stories and play-acting. Nicholas worked early and late, writing letters and setting his plans for the business in train; couriers came and went, he visited the shipyards where the new ships were building. The Challoners had seen a good return on their investment and were now also involved with that. The young Scot, Harry Munro, had fulfilled his promise, a much-travelled packet had thumped onto Nick's desk after sitting at Crosstrees for a month or more. "This is the most beautiful place I ever was at," he wrote. Nick could hear his voice with the soft Highland burr – "peautiful" – "the land is in good heart for sheep and cattle and is rumoured to be rich in minerals, though to my mind t'would be sin and shame to mine it. The buildings are in bad repair. There is much feuding activity, but so far our neighbours seem friendly enough. I am tending to the byres and making acquaintance with the tenants. Munro."

The second letter had been written on the day Nick had stepped ashore at Plymouth. Longer than the first, it bore marks of haste.

Sir, I am to thank you for my happiness . The women here are as

beautiful as the place and one most of all. My Margaret is lovely as
the dawn, and with your permission we will wed and take tenancy
of the empty steading on Schiehallion. That means Fairy Mountain.
I have not been neglectful of your affairs: I thought best first to
appease your tenants, who have been much neglected. There is much
still to be done with your dwelling-place therefore. I should tell you
that the factor here left soon after my coming with all the rents and
most of the siller. I regret I was not able at that time to find help to
catch him.

In pencil was added,

There may be trouble coming. There are those of us would band
together - it needs money, sir, if you trust me. Munro.

Nicholas mused over this for a while and presently sent for Jock
MacNab. He showed him the letters and told him how he had
met Munro.

"What do you think, Jock? This tale of the factor and now a
mysterious trouble?"

"You got him out of prison, my lord, he's your man now. It'll
be the MacGregors – it's the season." He sat down, ruminating.
"I've a mind to visit with my folk. My niece is to be wed. Just
north of the Tay, my lord, Weems. I could take a wee look. Mind
you," a calloused finger stabbed at the date, "I doubt it's all over
by now."

Nick remembered well the fierce raiding and skirmishing he
had encountered on the Border, Munro would need help. The
young man had gone far beyond his orders as scout. Nick's
contingency plan meant it must be looked into, and the time-lag

was worrying, but so soon married, he could not go himself, much as he wanted to.

"Take money and men, Jock, and stay out of trouble if you can." MacNab growled something and departed. Nicholas turned to the next matter demanding his attention. He found time to back Hotspur, Rowena's promising colt, and between all he was at the Globe, working on this new play. It was the Venetian embassy all over again.

The marriage was like no other Toby had ever seen. It showed best in company. Each a foil for the other, they never capped each other's stories, but rather led away from them to draw in their guests so that the dinner table sparkled with wit and laughter and good talk. There was music and dancing. They were a team. He noticed that Nicholas would always stop what he was doing when she entered the room and give her his undivided attention, while she allowed nothing to disturb the smooth running of her household and timed her appearances to perfection. A born organiser himself, he knew what that meant in terms of effort and gave her full marks. He watched them romping with the children, Rosalyne with her hair down and her skirts kilted up; and reserved and formal on state occasions, not even a sidelong glance to break the polite united façade. He had also seen them come home from such occasions, when Nick would seize off her cloak and chase her laughing up the stairs. He had caught Nicholas early one morning, still in his bed-gown of sapphire-blue velvet over nakedness, brilliant eyes and tousled hair. He had tipped a hand to Toby and passed on. Tobias still reserved judgement, wary for his friend, until he came upon her idle for once, sitting with an air of quiet contentment, her hands in her lap, watching out of the window for Nick's return. She turned and smiled, a radiant smile.

"He is here," she said and whisked out of the room to greet him. Tobias stopped worrying.

Tobias accepted Nick's offer of Rookham and passed Inigo's plans for the house. He agreed to the partnership in the expanding business, and then visited the playhouse, where he caught the players' complaint. The theatre entered his blood like a fever. Stage-struck but no actor, he was a natural contriver and involved himself in the making of machinery for effects. He could be found at all hours with a brush between his teeth or a tricky piece of metalwork in his hand, listening to the actors. With shares in the company and useful connections Nick had been welcomed back, and *Hamlet, Prince of Denmark* was coming together. He had no aspirations for a leading role; Burbage might be a little old for the part, but his name drew the crowds. Which was not to say Nick did not covet the role, he felt he knew the hard-pressed Hamlet intimately, but he was content with two or three smaller characters – Laertes, Rosencrantz or Guildenstern, and Bernardo – and managing the fight scene. Only one in this piece, and a struggle or two.

The Globe, smelling of new plaster and paint, had its last bundle of thatch tied in place to a drunken chorus of actors partying where the groundlings would stand – they had a new play rehearsing, a wonderful play whose depths still delighted and astounded them, and a new theatre where the laws of the City did not run. Alleyn admitted himself too old for the Prince and awarded himself a scene-stealing Claudius. Burbage had no such reservations, he grabbed the part with both hands and was surprising himself and everybody else. Nick, a straightforward

Laertes, felt he could hardly go wrong, given the material. Tobias, watching, thought his Rosencrantz held echoes of the Antolini. The balding Master Shakespeare, of whom the company was now a little in awe, was playing the Ghost.

No expense was spared on dress; they saved on scenery, the words were enough. Nick had a free hand with the duel. It seemed familiar – he remembered telling Marlowe about the Gothick castle in Basel, he didn't think the playwright had been listening. The man was a sponge, thought Nick, he absorbed information and squeezed it out transformed – a snapper up of unconsidered trifles. The new cannon arrived and was hoisted up over the musicians' gallery, Toby supervising.

Young Orlando came into his own, shedding the light touch he had brought to Rosalind and Beatrice, finding a new depth of feeling as Gertrude. The lad playing Ophelia had always been his foil, Nerissa to his Portia, Celia and Hero. The company cosseted this talented pair and watched anxiously for the first signs of puberty.

The pace of rehearsals hotted up and Tobias was amazed how Nicholas still found time for wife and children and correspondence: he wondered what would happen when this play was over. Nick had an understudy, an insurance policy that showed Toby that he still retained some awareness of the outside world. Dress rehearsal threw up all the usual problems and Gertrude became hoarse, frightening everyone to death. He gargled with a mixture of fortified wine and garlic and Hamlet and Claudius complained.

The day of the first performance, ostensibly a dress rehearsal before playing for the Queen, dawned fine and clear, and the new flag flew proudly from the tower. The audience started to arrive, many of Nick's friends at Court among them. Backstage was buzzing and Nick stood behind the curtain on the platform above the inner stage, swallowing and easing his armour; still nipping under the arms waiting for his cue. The noise of the crowd quietened as mist from the smoke machine rolled across the stage and a solitary drum rolled once. He was on, presenting his spear.

"Who's there?" cried Bernardo, in Nick's military voice.

"Nay, answer: Stand and unfold yourself," said Robin/Francisco. They were away, the audience drawn in at once. The play had them; they groaned and sighed and got all the jokes and were quiet as mice when Hamlet addressed them from the front of the apron. Burbage had allowed none of the usual clowning: Tarleton was only given his head in the gravediggers' scene, a welcome explosion of mirth before the denouement. A great gasp of horror went up as Nick leaped into Ophelia's grave to wrestle with Hamlet; the great actor's face was streaming with sweat and his eyes were Hamlet's eyes, his grief was tearing him to pieces. But when he came up to the mark for the duel he was cool and composed, smiling and confident. *The readiness is all.* thought Nick. *The wretch stole my motto.* He had a moment of déja vu as he picked up the unbated sword with its safety button and made his salute; he had to remind himself of his moves. He had spread himself on this one fight and it was dangerous.

He dropped his sword and clapped a hand to the poisoned slash in his arm, blood gushed between his fingers. He staggered, whispered his last few lines and lay dead at the front of the stage, his arm cunningly arranged so that he could watch the great beast that was the audience under it. Hamlet died and the beast shuddered. The trumpets sounded for Fortinbras and the soldiers shot. In that ineffable moment of silence when the audience was

351

still in the grip of it and before they drew breath for a shout, Nick blinked away the tears he shed every time and squinted through his lashes at the crowd. Looking for the red head of his kinsman, his eye passed over a greybeard among the groundlings and flashed quickly back.

Christopher Marlowe stood there beaming, tears streaming down his face, his hands clasped over his head with its old man's hat. Kit Marlowe – loved and reviled and not forgotten yet – *here*. By God, he was here. A kick reminded him to get up and take his bow for the yelling crowd, then, flouting all the rules about mixing with the audience in costume and paint, he leapt off the stage and forced his way to where Marlowe was caught in the crush. Pushed and shoved and slapped on the back, he reached him and flung his arms about him, crying: "Uncle, you came!" and manhandled him out to find a dark corner and pin him down.

"You damn fool, you will be killed! Why in the name of all the angels are you here?"

"I wanted to see it," said Marlowe simply.

"Did anyone see *you*?"

"Who would know me, Niccolo. A dead man walking."

"I knew you."

"Of course you did." He scratched at his long grey beard. "It's too long. Needs cutting…"

"Never mind your beard, what—"

"The play, fool, it's too long. Yet they stood through it," he said dreamily. Young Colin pushed through the chattering stream on its way out.

"They said you were out front…Nick, Mowbray is escaped. My lady sent, she is afraid—"

"Mowbray?" For a moment Nick could not think who

352

Mowbray was and then thought came with a rush. His contingency plan. Keeping firm hold on Marlowe, he said swiftly, "Tobias is here. Ask him to fetch them to the harbour. Is the *Snipe* in? Roust out her crew and get ready to sail. Quick as you can.

"Ever been to Scotland, Kit? I hope you have some warm clothes."

"But what of Mowbray, sir?"

"I shall be back to settle with him."

The English Succession

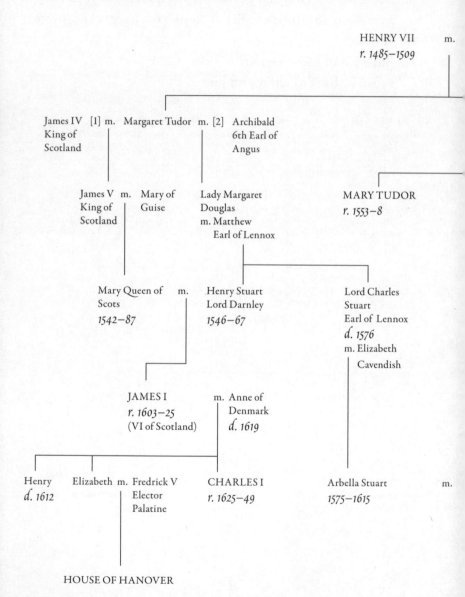

HENRY VII m.
r. 1485–1509

James IV [1] m. Margaret Tudor m. [2] Archibald
King of   6th Earl of
Scotland   Angus

James V m. Mary of   Lady Margaret   MARY TUDOR
King of   Guise   Douglas   r. 1553–8
Scotland   m. Matthew
                                  Earl of Lennox

Mary Queen of m. Henry Stuart   Lord Charles
Scots   Lord Darnley   Stuart
1542–87   1546–67   Earl of Lennox
                                          d. 1576
                                          m. Elizabeth
                                             Cavendish

JAMES I   m. Anne of
r. 1603–25   Denmark
(VI of Scotland)   d. 1619

Henry   Elizabeth m. Fredrick V   CHARLES I   Arbella Stuart   m.
d. 1612   Elector   r. 1625–49   1575–1615
                       Palatine

HOUSE OF HANOVER

Elizabeth of York

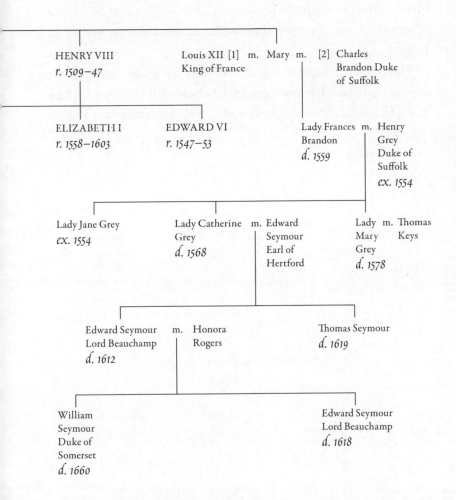

HENRY VIII
r. 1509–47

Louis XII [1] m. Mary m. [2] Charles
King of France   Brandon Duke
                                  of Suffolk

ELIZABETH I
r. 1558–1603

EDWARD VI
r. 1547–53

Lady Frances m. Henry
Brandon   Grey
d. 1559   Duke of
                 Suffolk
                 ex. 1554

Lady Jane Grey
ex. 1554

Lady Catherine m. Edward
Grey   Seymour
d. 1568   Earl of
                  Hertford

Lady m. Thomas
Mary   Keys
Grey
d. 1578

Edward Seymour m. Honora
Lord Beauchamp   Rogers
d. 1612

Thomas Seymour
d. 1619

William
Seymour
Duke of
Somerset
d. 1660

Edward Seymour
Lord Beauchamp
d. 1618

Author's note

I have taken the liberty of borrowing for Nick some of Sir Henry Wotton's speech on his induction as ambassador to Venice in 1604.

The verbatim dispatches and reports of the pirates are accurate in time and place, however, and make amusing if alarming reading in the Calendar of State papers relating to English affairs in Venice. Vol. 9.

MORE FROM HONNO

Short Stories, Classics, Autobiography, Fiction

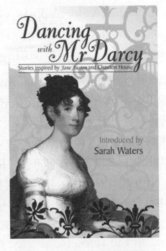
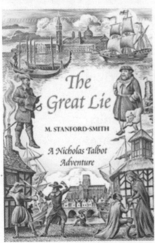

All Honno titles can be ordered online at www.honno.co.uk,
or by sending a cheque to Honno, with free postage
to all UK addresses.

ABOUT HONNO

Honno Welsh Women's Press was set up in 1986 by a group of women who felt strongly that women in Wales needed wider opportunities to see their writing in print and to become involved in the publishing process. Our aim is to develop the writing talents of women in Wales, give them new and exciting opportunities to see their work published and often to give them their first 'break' as a writer.

Honno is registered as a community co-operative. Any profit that Honno makes is invested in the publishing programme. Women from Wales and around the world have expressed their support for Honno by buying shares. Supporters' liability is limited to the amount invested and each supporter has a vote at the Annual General Meeting.

To buy shares or to receive further information about forthcoming publications, please write to Honno at the address below, or visit our website: www.honno.co.uk.

Honno
Unit 14, Creative Units
Aberystwyth Arts Centre
Penglais Campus
Aberystwyth
Ceredigion
SY23 3GL

All Honno titles can be ordered online at
www.honno.co.uk
or by sending a cheque to Honno.
Free p&p to all UK addresses